I looked over at the wall whose origins were lost in history. I looked at the thick vines that covered the wall, vines that were hundreds of years old. I thought about what Pham Van Tra had said, how if you looked closely at how each one climbed the rock wall it told a story. I wondered what past bloodshed the wall had witnessed. I wondered if it had seen Vietnamese beheading Chams, or if it had been a wall against which the French had stood Vietnamese before firing squads. I was afraid to look too closely. For I was afraid that the great snake might be looking back at me through the density of the leaves with its wicked, yellow eyes, its great hood ready to spring suddenly through the vivid green of the wall of flowers.

CHINA WIND

Dan Guenther

IVY BOOKS • NEW YORK

TABLE OF CONTENTS

AUTHOR'S NOTE

DURING THE PERIOD of the 1960s the Marine Corps had evolved into an elite, professional, amphibious corps. Disciplined, highly trained, and staffed with fine officers and NCOs, the Marines hit the beach north of Da Nang on March 8, 1965. What the Marine Corps found in addition to the elusive Viet Cong was political infighting among their South Vietnamese allies and no systematic way to identify and target the Viet Cong infrastructure (VCI).

It is self-evident that war is never rational or orderly. Moreover, no training program, however well-designed, can totally prepare one for extremes where traditional rules of engagement break down and the system has no constancy of purpose. The Marine Corps found itself in a war where goals and objectives were like the China winds that blew down from the north, things that changed with the season. High ranking officers grew increasingly tentative. Yet, a large number of individuals were able to demonstrate great flexibility and ingenuity in taking the war to that undefined enemy, the VCI.

Civilian pacification programs were implemented, and throughout South Vietnam individuals took various counterintelligence initiatives. Amphibian tractors, their mission normally ship-to-shore transport, were tasked to support some of these efforts out in the field; and it can be said that the period spanning mid-1967 to late 1969 saw a transition in the pacification effort: the Accelerated Pacification Campaign, proclaimed in 1968, emphasized development of local government, land reform, and the increased targeting of the Viet Cong infrastructure.

China Wind is about some of those initiatives and the story takes place during that time of transition. The Marine colonel who is the province senior adviser in this novel is a fictional character, and while province senior advisers were generally U.S. Army personnel, a number of Marine officers served on the CORDS staff and were involved with the Regional and Popular Forces as well as the Phoenix/Phung Hoang Program. In addition, a number of Marine officers served as province psychological warfare officers and as advisers to the paramilitary revolutionary development cadre. While the events of this novel are fictional, *China Wind* captures a point of view and tells a story that many will identify with.

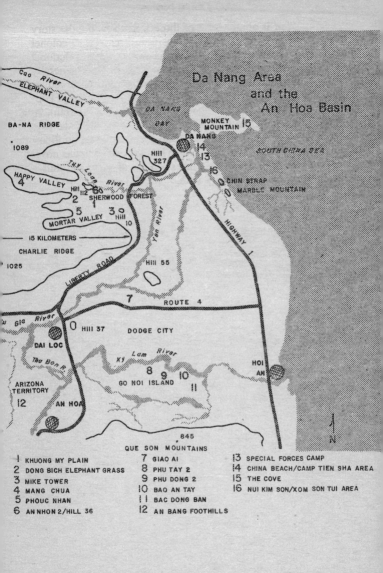

Da Nang Area
and the
An Hoa Basin

Cao River
ELEPHANT VALLEY

BA-NA RIDGE

DA NANG
BAY

MONKEY
MOUNTAIN 15
DA NANG

SOUTH CHINA SEA

1089

HILL
327

14
13

HAPPY VALLEY
4

Thu Loan River

16
CHIN STRAP
MARBLE MOUNTAIN

Hill 112

60
SHERWOOD FOREST

2

5
MORTAR VALLEY

3
Hill
10

15 KILOMETERS

Tra River

HIGHWAY 1

CHARLIE RIDGE

1025

LIBERTY ROAD

HILL 55

7
ROUTE 4

Vu Gia River

Hill 37

DODGE CITY

DAI LOC

Thu Bon R.

Ky Lam River

ARIZONA
TERRITORY

12

8   9   10
GO NOI ISLAND   11

HOI
AN

AN HOA

845

QUE SON MOUNTAINS

N

1 KHUONG MY PLAIN	7 GIAO AI	13 SPECIAL FORCES CAMP
2 DONG BICH ELEPHANT GRASS	8 PHU TAY 2	14 CHINA BEACH/CAMP TIEN SHA AREA
3 MIKE TOWER	9 PHU DONG 2	15 THE COVE
4 MANG CHUA	10 BAO AN TAY	16 NUI KIM SON/XOM SON TUI AREA
5 PHOUC NHAN	11 BAC DONG BAN	
6 AN NHON 2/HILL 36	12 AN BANG FOOTHILLS	

VIETNAM 1968

THE LUCK OF
ZERO DEUCE

May 24, 1968: 0800 hours

IN THE HEAT everything was slick with grease and sweat. Below, the Khuong My Plain was a glistening sheet of water from last night's rain. Stirred from their resting places in the tall grass, clouds of gnats hovered above our heads with a wild intensity. Ahead was the high ground of Hill 112, the rocky ridge line that marked the southern edge of the Sherwood Forest.

To the west, tall thunderheads were moving in to block the sun. More rain to bog the tracks. But also welcome relief from the heat. I yelled to the line of tracks to advance. The cloud-covered mountains to the west seemed to be listening like a group of dark, village kinsmen.

"Looking good, Gunny," I said to my gunnery sergeant.

"Most affirmative, Lieutenant. But there's a difference between looking good and being good," the Gunny said with a smile.

"Gunny, lately I don't know what to make of you anymore. You are actually smiling. What happened to that old pessimist that used to rag me all the time?" I asked.

"I'm too short to be a pessimist anymore, sir. Looks like I'm going to survive this tour. As short as I am, I'd say I've turned into an optimist. I'm just a guarded optimist," the Gunny re-

3

plied, still smiling, knowing that with only ten days left to go in the country, the odds were in his favor.

"Gunny, if I was as short as you were, I'd say the chances were in your favor. For sure!" I said, wiping my face with a towel.

"That they are, Lieutenant. And I don't think that it's bad luck to talk about it. I think that you make your own luck. By the way, I'm going to leave you a little of my luck when I leave. It will give you a big advantage," the Gunny said.

"What advantage is that?" I asked.

"I'm going to give you my .50-caliber machine gun, sir. Keep it on my old track, Zero Deuce. You will have the advantage if you ever get hit close up," the Gunny said, winking.

"Gunny, thank you! That old .50 might make a difference," I said.

"Got to always save a trick, Lieutenant," the Gunny said.

May 24, 1968: 0900 hours

We moved toward the base of Hill 112. I wondered what lay to our south and west. No one knew for sure. There were a few marine recon teams in the area. But for all I knew, under the mountains' canopy of umbrella trees, there could have been elephants.

May 24, 1968: 0930 hours

I looked back on the long curving line of amphibian tractors following Zero Deuce. Each was over twenty-four feet long with a beam greater than eight feet. Their thick silhouettes recalled some extinct saurian from the age of reptiles. When the LVTP6 amphibian tractor climbed out the water and onto the land, there was something lumbering and primordial about the vehicle. When you rode on top of that twenty-five tons, one couldn't help but feel the churning power.

I could see that power reflected in the eyes of some of the marines riding on top of the tracks. Some were excited, high on the action of moving out. The eyes of others reflected different

feelings. In some eyes I could sense fear and doubt. Some eyes
were just tired. Then there were those in whose eyes you could
read hate, even vengeance.

May 24, 1968: 0940 hours

"What do you think, Gunny?" I said, concerned about what
appeared to be firing to our west.

"We best hold up until battalion can give us the go-ahead.
No use in being used up, Lieutenant," the Gunny said, lighting
a cigarette.

"Fine with me," I said with a sense of relief.

"Sherwood Forest is nasty, Lieutenant. Hurrying in there
ain't going to get us diddly-squat. You listen to the Gunny, and
the Gunny will buy the beer when we get back to Hill 10," the
Gunny said, always with a smile.

No one that I ever met could tell me how Sherwood Forest
got its name. The brush and jungled-covered hills that made up
the forest spread over an area four kilometers long by one kilometer wide. The north border of the forest followed the Tuy
Loan River. A low-lying wet plain surrounded the rest of the
forest on three sides. Along the south edge of the forest a series
of steep hills rose out of the surrounding plains, culminating in
a kilometer-long precipitous ridge line called Hill 112. It was
just south of that Hill 112, in the Dong Bich elephant grass, that
the Gunny once had bad luck.

May 24, 1968: 0945 hours

We had started north from our base area, Hill 10, at 0600 hours.
Our mission was to proceed up to Mortar Valley in the northwest
corner of the Dai Loc map sheet. We were to pick up Lima
Company, Third Battalion, Seventh Marines. It was on the tail
end of an operation that had been running since March. Lima
Company had walked their way into Mortar Valley from the west
and south. The job of my platoon, First Platoon, Alpha Company, Third Amphibian Tractor Battalion, was simple. Pick up
Lima Company and give them a ride back to Hill 10.

"Gunny, we got the go ahead. No one really knows what the firing was all about. It wasn't any of our people. That's all that battalion knows," I said.

"Well, we best go ahead then, Lieutenant," the Gunny said, blinking.

"You okay, Gunny?" I asked, concerned about the Gunny's flushed appearance.

"I'll continue to march, Lieutenant. I'm feeling the heat a bit. Don't worry about the Gunny, I'll maintain," the Gunny said, sweat beginning to drip from his face.

The Gunny was in his late forties. He was overweight and had a bad habit of doing fifths of Jack Daniel's late into the night with the battalion sergeant major. I could tell that he was feeling hungover. But who was I to stand in judgment of this old gunnery sergeant, who had served in the Marine Corps before I was born. He had ridden tracks ashore on Iwo Jima and had walked out of the Chosin with Chesty Puller. I needed his technical know-how and his way of looking at the situation.

The plan had been to head west from Hill 10 across the Khuong My Plain to the east end of Mortar Valley. But during the night squalls had driven inland from the South China Sea bringing with them a heavy rain that had turned the Khuong My Plain into a bog. We would be forced to go north, around the plain, using the firmer ground along the base of Hill 112. Once on higher ground, we could drive south through the Dong Bich elephant grass until we reached the east edge of Mortar Valley.

There was a problem, however. My gunnery sergeant and some of the troops had doubts. No one had ever driven tracks across the Dong Bich. The Gunny had once lost two tracks to mines in one day at the edge of the Dong Bich. In spite of the doubts, we had headed out. To show my resolve, I had taken the lead with our best track, Zero Deuce.

May 24, 1968: 1000 hours

By May of 1968, the twenty-odd marines and ten tracks of First Platoon had run the length and breadth of the Dai Loc map sheet. Despite box mines, snipers, and night "reacts" in support of grunt patrols, First Platoon was a tight, cohesive group proud of their "can-do" attitude. These "track rats" had lived out in the "bush," supporting marine grunts in both the Dodge City area and the Arizona Territory. They knew that they had a combat role to play and could keep the twenty-five-ton tracks operating from the mud of Go Noi Island to the rocky foothills of the Sherwood Forest.

The Gunny had been the formative influence in holding the platoon together. A quick succession of lieutenants seemed to come and go. Two lieutenants were lost to illness. One lieutenant caught a sniper round just outside the gate at Hill 10. The lieutenant whose place I had taken had been lost to a box mine just at the edge of the Dong Bich. Through all this the Gunny had prevailed, keeping the men busy and handling conflicts among the troops as they arose. The Gunny seemed to hold it all together through his force of character. Not that he was a hard ass, he wasn't. Rather, he was always there, interacting with the men. He was there when tracks were stuck in the mud, which was often, and he was there when it came to playing cards and drinking beer down in the sanctuary of the tractor park, which was as often as the Gunny could make it. I wondered how I was going to replace him when he rotated home.

The Gunny and I got along well. I think it was because of the mutual respect that we had for each other. I had grunted for six months in the bush just south of the Marble Mountain area. I had spent another three months as platoon leader with the Headquarters track platoon at Third Amphibian Tractor Battalion. With many patrols and several successful ambushes to my credit, I wasn't cherry. One firefight in the village of Nui Kim Son had resulted in fourteen confirmed kills for my grunt platoon. The Gunny had been impressed.

"Lieutenant, battalion wants us to hold up at the Mike Tower until they can figure out who was firing what out at Hill 112," Crosby said.

Crosby, who was driving Zero Deuce, wore a red bandanna on his head. Crosby was one of the new men that had recently come down from up north. The Gunny had a problem with Crosby and some of the new men. They were too loose as he put it. The Gunny knew that they were also smoking dope.

The last two weeks had been complicated by a number of events in addition to the new men from the north. A new com-

manding officer by the name of Cheatum had taken over Third
Battalion, Seventh Marines. With the advent of the new commanding officer First Platoon's mode of operation had been
forced to change. First Platoon was doing more night reacts
running down Liberty Road in support of grunt patrols. Usually
we reacted to pick up wounded marines or to support firefights.
Twice in the last week my men and I had run down the road to
find ourselves "standing-by" as if Battalion were waiting for
things to develop. Crosby thought we were being used as bait
and held nothing back in telling both me and the Gunny what
he felt. He claimed that we were sitting ducks for VC and he
was right. The Gunny told him to keep his mouth shut. All of
this was unsettling to the men to say the least.

May 24, 1968: 1015 hours

Mike Tower was a small outpost surrounded by a six-foot-high
berm and a lot of barbwire. At the base of the tower several
communication technicians monitored the movement picked up
by special sensors that had been placed out in the hills. Based
upon the technician's reports, Division responded. Sometimes
Division sent out a recon team. Sometimes they sent out a grunt
battalion. If nothing else, Battalion would call in artillery.

The operation of Mike Tower was somewhat of a mystery to
all of us. None of us knew where it fit in the organizational
structure. The group that ran the technical side were communication jocks. The defense of the tower and what seemed to be
small unit patrols that departed from the tower from time to time
were controlled by a Captain O.D. Lowy. Lowy was a former
enlisted man and good friends with the Gunny. Lowy called his
group the Cold Steel Crowd much to the Gunny's amusement.
Yet, when I asked the Gunny what it was that Captain Lowy and
the Cold Steel Crowd did, the Gunny was evasive.

I had talked with Captain Lowy on several occasions. The captain was always upbeat and had a cold beer ready. Lowy seemed
to take an interest in both me and my men, having once received
support on a night react from the Gunny. Since Lowy knew both
the Gunny and the men of First Platoon, I felt comfortable in

discussing various leadership questions that I had about both the new men and the new commanding officer of 3/7.

That I had some leadership issues was clear. The new men from the north had come from up around Cua Viet. Although each of the new men carried a specialty in tracks, none had any operating experience. Up on the Cua Viet the new men had been used as grunts. For the most part they were cynical and lacked discipline when compared to the old hands of First Platoon who the Gunny had carefully trained and coached.

On the other hand, several of the men in First Platoon were very determined and committed to supporting the grunts. I had brought in a new sergeant E-5, a Sergeant Holstrom. Although too easy on his men, he thought that if the new commanding officer of 3/7 wanted to run us down Liberty Road, so be it! According to Holstrom we were there to support the grunts come hell or high water. The Gunny was more conservative, and he had reminded Holstrom on more than one occasion not to stretch his luck and the luck of Zero Deuce.

Zero Deuce was viewed as lucky. There were those that felt the luck of Zero Deuce lay in the vehicle's number. To others the luck lay in the vehicle's speed. Zero Deuce could hit thirty miles an hour on a straight road. Captain Lowy thought the Gunny was the source of luck for Zero Deuce.

No doubt Zero Deuce had power. No doubt the Gunny was a man of much know-how and experience. No doubt a deuce is often a wild card's number and can bring luck. But to me the force behind the track's good fortune lay in the vehicle's fire-power. For Zero Deuce had a .50-caliber machine gun mounted up front.

Ironically Zero Deuce really didn't belong to First Platoon. It belonged back in battalion. The vehicle had come to the Gunny as a replacement for one of those that he had lost to mines in the Dong Bich. Just having a replacement vehicle was something that I viewed as lucky.

"So what should I do with Crosby and these new men from Cua Viet, Captain?" I asked, having explained the situation to Captain Lowy.

"Well, all the technical know-how of the Gunny don't mean much in this situation. And I think the fact that you pride yourself as a 'doer' don't mean much to these men either. What you got to do somehow is make these men believers in spite of that jingle-butt Cheatum,'' Lowy said.

"Believers in what?" I asked.

"Oh, believers in their team, hanging tough together, everyone making a contribution. Believers in the fact that you aren't going to use them up. Believers in being track rats and taking pride in doing that. Let them paint faces or something on their tracks. Get them involved in making their tracks the best. There's a few ideas," Lowy said.

"Thanks, Captain. Some of that stuff the Gunny and I already discussed," I said.

"Another thing, Lieutenant. Always play to your strength. That Crosby has got some grit. Give him his head. I know the Gunny don't like him, but work with Crosby, listen to him. If he's an opinion leader, use him to our advantage. Find out what's important to him. Find out what he wants. Then give him some personal responsibility and put some accountability on him," Lowy said.

"You make it sound easy, sir. But, like what kind of responsibility are you talking about?" I asked, understanding but not quite believing.

"You got him driving the Gunny's track, Zero Deuce. Why don't you give him his own track. He's a corporal isn't he? Yeah, why don't you take him and give him his own track. You will also be taking the pressure off him. He probably don't want to drive the lead vehicle through the Dong Bich," Lowy said.

"Okay. That sounds good. But who's going to drive Zero Deuce? It's the leader because it's mounted with a .50-caliber machine gun," I said.

"Why don't you drive it, Lieutenant. You say you got leadership problems. Be a leader and drive that sucker through the Dong Bich!"

"Officers aren't supposed to drive tracks," I said.

"Who said? Battalion? You drive Zero Deuce and let the Gunny man the .50-caliber. Might help make believers out of Crosby and those new men," Lowy said, lighting up a cigar.

May 24, 1968: 1230 hours

So we headed into Sherwood Forest. By 1100 hours we had reached the base of Hill 112 without incident. We called back to our best communications man, Sergeant Holstrom, that we were about to head south. Holstrom had been disappointed that I left him at the Mike Tower, but I stressed both the importance of the job and the fact that I needed someone like him whom I could depend on to handle the communications link back to Hill 10.

About 1135, Holstrom called us to inform us that 3/7 had just received information that a marine recon team had seen movement in the area of the Dong Bich elephant grass. Hill 112 lay about two-and-a-half kilometers north of the mouth of Mortar Valley. The Dong Bich elephant grass lay halfway between us and the valley. The distance was not far, and of course, we had Zero Deuce.

May 24, 1968: 1300 hours

The run to Mortar Valley took us an hour from Hill 112. The elephant grass turned out to be no cause for concern. By 1300 hours Lima Company was loaded and we were headed out. Back through the elephant grass was fast going. All the grunt officers of Lima Company were amused that I was driving the lead track. Things were apparently going too good. One Nine, Crosby's track, struck the edge of a boulder and broke track.

I called Sergeant Holstrom to report One Nine's condition. Zero Deuce would stay with the disabled vehicle while the track was being put together. The Gunny would continue on with Lima Company and the rest of the tracks to Hill 10.

Sergeant Holstrom acknowledged the situation. He again alerted us to the fact that the recon team had seen movement in the area of the elephant grass. With that information I figured that we had better put out listening posts.

The grunts that were riding with us sent out two separate listening posts to the north and south. The listening post to the west was my responsibility. I had two men with grunt experience, Crosby and Tex, both men from Cua Viet. I asked them if they would set in a listening post to the west, appealing to the fact that I needed men with grunt experience. They agreed.

The elephant grass grew anywhere from five to ten feet high. Here and there the clumps were split by paths and little game trails. If one scouted these trails, he found swarms of little black bugs and booby traps.

May 24, 1968: 1355 hours

Crosby was about fifty meters out into the grass when he called in movement all around the listening posts. At that point the grass was about eight feet high and they couldn't see a thing. What they could hear was enough.

Sergeant Holstrom, back at Mike Tower, monitored Crosby's radio transmission. Crosby, understandably nervous, relayed what Holstrom assumed was a ''spot'' report. Everyone was confused. At that point I interrupted, negating the spot report, thinking that Holstrom had received my radio transmission. He had not.

A spot report means that you have a body, either a prisoner or a cold stiff. Without worrying further about that radio transmission, I cranked up Zero Deuce, locked and loaded the .50-cal, and churned twenty-five tons of track off into the elephant grass.

May 24, 1968: 1402 hours

We reached the listening post only to find a swarm of those little black bugs. Crosby and Tex boarded Zero Deuce and we headed further into the elephant grass. At that point the terrain took a downward slope. All of us could see clearly from our vantage point on the track.

Ahead of us the grass was waving back and forth from some movement beneath. Something or someone was running. I knew that this was as close to a free fire zone as one gets in I Corps. I also knew that the marine recon team was on top of Hill 112 more than a kilometer away. If it was friendly, why was it running? I opened up with the .50!

The .50 got off five rounds and jammed! Damn! I had timed

and spaced the gun myself. At the same time Crosby and Tex opened up with their M-16's. I tried to clear the .50. Nothing doing. So much for the luck of Zero Deuce.

There was no return fire. I cleared my head and yelled for everyone to cease firing. In the elephant grass about thirty meters to our front there was a tremendous thrashing.

"It's some critter, Lieutenant," Tex said.

"What makes you think that?" I asked.

"Saw part of him. Big hairy critter," Tex repeated.

"Bet it's a water bo," Crosby said, breathing heavily.

"Too hairy to be water buffalo," Tex said.

"Holstrom's on the radio, Lieutenant. All battalion wants to know what's going on," Crosby said, excitedly.

When I grabbed the radio handset, I found Lieutenant Colonel Albright Cheatum, the new commanding officer of 3/7 on the other end. Every time I would try to transmit, Holstrom seemed to interrupt. Finally, I cleared the air and informed Cheatum of the movement to our front.

By the time Cheatum had cleared us to proceed, the thrashing had ceased. Tex, Crosby, and I moved forward on foot. Then we heard a kind of grunt.

We were in a wet spot. All around us large, white trumpet-like flowers were growing, their vines woven into the clumps of elephant grass. The sweet smell of the flowers hung in the air. Hundreds of small dragonflies hovered about our heads, darting in and about the large, trumpetlike flowers.

Then his movement gave him away. Surprisingly, even though he was wounded in several places, he was still on his feet. Fully one third of the massive animal was head. Another third was thickly bristled shoulders. This was no feral pig run wild. This was the huge, and relatively rare, southern race of the Indo-Chinese wild boar.

The boar raised his head and made a kind of high-pitched, nasal whine. He began breathing in deep gasps. At a distance of five feet I emptied my .45 into his head.

May 24, 1968: 1415 hours

The boar had suffered injury before. There was a terrible scarring of the right front leg. The right foot was more of a club than a hoof. Later, when weighed at Mike Tower on a makeshift scale, we would guess his weight at better than three hundred pounds.

It was then that I made my second mistake of the day, depending on how one assesses some of the judgments that I had made. The first was without a doubt not clarifying to Holstrom that we had not called in a spot report. My second mistake was allowing Crosby to call in a confirmed "kill" to the Gunny and Captain Lowy. I didn't realize that Cheatum was still monitoring our radio frequency.

May 25, 1968: 0800 hours

It was 1600 hours when we got back to Mike Tower. Waiting for us was Lieutenant Colonel Cheatum, commanding officer of 3/7. Needless to say, there was no kill, only the dead boar.

If Cheatum was disappointed, the track rats were not. As far as they were concerned, the luck of Zero Deuce had held. In one day they had crossed the Sherwood Forest to the base of Hill 112 and traversed the hot tangle of the Dong Bich elephant grass. And they had returned! No mines. No ambushes. For a moment their fear was gone. Some of the doubt about those new guys from Cua Viet had been replaced by that trust that can only come from the experience of some shared hardship. More than that there came a special story, a story to which all the track rats gave great meaning relative to the luck of Zero Deuce and the time we killed the boar.

I watched Crosby; when he told that story you could see a light in his eyes. It wasn't a grunt story. It was a track rat story, the kind of thing that helps make believers and helps bind the team together, like belief in the luck of Zero Deuce.

First Platoon did eat that boar. First Platoon took all kinds of pictures of that boar. Tex sent a picture home to his father in Dallas where it was published on the front page of some Dallas paper.

Tex, Crosby, Captain Lowy, and the Gunny stayed up all night to roast that boar in a deep pit, painting the roasting flesh over and over with a mixture of vinegar, ketchup, and mustard sauce. I also stayed up all night. I was working on the luck of Zero Deuce. I was timing and spacing, cleaning and recleaning the vehicle's .50-caliber machine gun.

MOTHER AFRICA

May 27, 1968: 0900 hours

"YOU'RE GIVIN' THE men too much slack, Lieutenant," Staff Sergeant Mangles said, spitting on the ground.

"What are you talking about, Mangles?" I said, raising an eyebrow.

"You think all that they're doin' down by the river is washin' their vehicles? Come on, Lieutenant, they is takin' advantage of you and the situation!" Mangles said.

Staff Sergeant Mangles had been with the platoon for about five days. In that time he hardly said two words to either me or the men in my platoon. Now he had apparently drawn some conclusions and was making an observation, only the observation seemed more like a challenge to my personal style of leadership.

"Relax, Mangles. This isn't a marine barracks where we have to keep our boots polished and our brass shined. This is Hill 10, one of the more boring places in the Nam to pull your time. The men are bored. I'm bored. Even the whores down at the river are bored. Hell, it's a goddamn major event when they get a new skivvy girl down at the river for Christ's sake! For the last month it's all the men have had to look forward to," I said, a bit irritated with Mangles.

Mangles was some four years older than I was. But at twenty-

16

nine he had a head of gray hair. His face was furrowed and drawn. He had pulled two previous tours in the Nam and was a committed career marine.

"Lieutenant, I'm on my third tour in the Nam. You need to listen to me. Too much slack. Sergeant Holstrom is a clean-livin' kid, but he would have never made sergeant in the old corps. It's hard for me to believe he's a sergeant. He's too cherry to be a sergeant," Mangles said, spitting another load of tobacco juice.

Sergeant Holstrom had been acting platoon sergeant before Mangles had appeared on the scene. He was a clean-cut type, a tall, blond Swede from somewhere in the Midwest, the kind of guy you'd like your sister to go out with. His only problem was that he didn't push the rest of the troops. Yet, he was a smart marine who used common sense and good communication skills to get things done rather than the authority vested in the platoon sergeant's position. If he cut the troops a little slack, so what? Holstrom got the job done and seemed to keep harmony among the diverse elements of the platoon, even if he was newly promoted. That was enough for me.

"Holstrom's all right. He keeps the peace and gets the job done. That's all we need right now," I said, yawning.

"He's not tough-minded enough. The men have too much slack and they get sloppy. Shit, Lieutenant, half of them got the clap right now. Did you know that?" Mangles said.

The fact that half of the men had the clap was more than a source of concern to me. It was a real problem that I had been struggling with. I had put the word out to use condoms to no avail.

"Is it really half of them?" I asked.

"That's a big affirmative, Lieutenant. Damn! You got to do something before the word gets up to the commanding officer of 3/7. He'll call your company commander back at Third Tracks and have some of your ass, Lieutenant, with all due respect. Lieutenant, we got to get this herd under control!" Mangles said, spitting a third time.

First Platoon, Alpha Company, Third Amphibian Tractor Battalion, was, indeed, a herd. It seemed that I had every race and ethnic type in America represented in my platoon. I had conservative Jesus-freaks like Sergeant Holstrom, and I had laid-back hippie types like Corporal Crosby, who smoked a lot of

dope and affected a red bandanna. I had borderline black pan-
ther advocates like Corporal Atwood Potts from Chicago, whose
Afro annoyed Mangles. And I had rednecks like Mangles, whose
opinions and demands seemed to provoke all the rest, especially
at times when we had little to do. Sending them all to wash their
tracks down at the river seemed an appropriate diversion. Of
course, now half of them had the clap. I would have to make
the river, with its cute little whores, off-limits. That would certainly hurt morale. What I was more worried about was the fact
that Holstrom was going on seven days of R & R tomorrow.
Who was to be the buffer between Staff Sergeant Mangles and
my herd of track rats?

"Okay, you're right, Mangles. When the men get back from
the river, put the word out that there will be no more track
washing for a few weeks. Then let's get them all up to medical
and make sure everyone is being treated."

"Yes, sir!" Mangles said, a broad shit-eating grin on his face.

May 27, 1968: 1000 hours

Holstrom left on R & R just in time. The men were pissed with
my action. I called them all together and made the matter official. Stay away from the whores and no more washing tracks
down at the river. As the formation broke up there was grum-
bling. I ignored the grumblings.

"Lieutenant, I bet this is Mangles's idea, isn't it?" Corporal
Potts said, clearly upset.

Atwood Potts was tall and thin. He must have been six feet,
four inches because I'm six feet, three inches and he was at least
an inch taller than I was. Potts couldn't have weighed more than
a hundred and sixty pounds, ten pounds of which must have
been in his Afro "do." He had great hair. Another ten pounds
had to be in the mass of brass bracelets and in the shell casings
he hung around his neck. I had never seen anyone wear so much
shit.

"Potts. Half of the men, including you, have the damn clap.
What I should do is nail everyone who has the clap! But I'm not
going to do that because I'm not a chicken-shit son of a bitch.

But let me make it very clear to you, Potts, no more skivvy girls and no more clap! Is that clear?'' I said, somewhat pissed off.

"Yes, sir!'' Potts said, glaring at Mangles.

May 27, 1968: 1400 hours

We had got the word that we were to head south to Dodge City in order to be a blocking force in support of the First Marines. Finally we were going to do something. The men were fired up. Mangles was in his element, inspecting and directing the efforts, forming our tracks into a column.

"Lieutenant, I've got to show you something,'' Mangles said.

"What's that?'' I asked.

"Too much slack,'' he said, spitting on the ground.

We mounted the track called Zero Deuce. Mangles pointed to the way the .50-caliber machine gun was mounted in the sandbagged bunker on top of the track.

"This will never do. As soon as this gun is fired, it will kick loose. Who put this gun in this way?'' Mangles asked.

"I did,'' Potts said.

"Did you test fire it?'' Mangles asked.

"No, sir, I didn't,'' Potts replied to both Mangles and myself.

"Let's test it right now. I'll call battalion, let them know we're goin' to fire a .50 out over the wire,'' Mangles said.

The call to Battalion was made. Mangles fired some twenty rounds through the .50 and the gun began to break loose from the bunker.

"Too much slack,'' Mangles said, looking up at me.

May 27, 1968: 1800 hours

"Lieutenant, men and I been talkin'. We're sittin' ducks where they got us. We got to move our tracks back so that we're set lower in behind the rice paddy dikes,'' Potts said.

Potts was right. Whoever had decided to use us as a blocking force hadn't taken into account the high profile of our tractors. What Potts had failed to do was include Mangles in on his observation.

"Corporal Potts, haven't you ever heard of the chain of command?" Mangles yelled.

"Chain of command. Of course, sure I've heard of the chain of command," Potts replied, rattled.

"Well, then, why don't you observe the chain of command. I expect you to talk to me about these things before you go shooting your mouth off to the lieutenant," Mangles said, loud enough for the whole platoon to hear.

Potts looked at me. I looked away. Overhead incoming rounds were speeding toward some identified target. Potts muttered something under his breath that I couldn't hear and walked away.

"Too much slack," Mangles said to me.

May 28, 1968: 0200 hours

The rocket-propelled grenade passed over my head with a kind of swishing sound to explode to our immediate rear. Almost instantly the machine guns from the tracks began to slice through the thick elephant grass and bamboo hedge to our immediate front. A second rocket-propelled grenade came in from our left and hit Corporal Crosby's track, Cool Breeze. The projectile penetrated through the thin hull of the track and spun hot slag throughout the inside of the tractor. This time we were lucky. No one was inside the tractor.

"Damn. Damn! Damn! Damn!" I heard Corporal Potts say.

Then I ordered the tracks to back up some ten to fifteen meters, depending on their positions and fields of fire.

May 28, 1968: 1100 hours

Dodge City was flat terrain. At one time in the not too distant past, the whole area had been a grouping of small villages surrounded by rice paddies and borders of tall bamboo hedgerow. Those villages were gone. The rice paddies had been drained, and the once neat checkerboard, crisscrossed by little canals, was now overgrown with tall grass and scrub.

Deep within that scrub there was little breeze to bring relief from the heat. Tempers grew short and men who were normally buddies screamed and yelled at each other over the boom of the track engines. Exhaust fumes and dust hung in the air. It must have been better than one hundred and ten degrees.

May 28, 1968: 1200 hours

By noon we broke out of the Dodge City scrub and had reached Route 4. Route 4 was a dirt road noted for its box mines and frequent ambushes. North of Route 4 was patrolled by the U.S. Marines. South of Route 4 was patrolled by our allies, the Korean Marines Corps.

We pulled our tracks off to the side of Route 4. Several Korean Marines came up and started to swap rations with our men. Korean rations were much sought after. Usually the rate of trade was one case of Korean combat rations for two cases of our rations.

Corporal Potts and two other black marines were heavy into a swap that involved several *Playboy* magazines and about six cases of rations when Mangles came up to Potts and put a stop to the trade. Potts threw his *Playboy*s to the ground and started toward me.

"Where are you goin', Potts?" Mangles yelled, loud enough for everyone to hear.

"I goin' to talk to the lieutenant," Potts said.

"What are you goin' to talk to the lieutenant about?" Mangles yelled.

"That's my concern," Potts said.

At that point Mangles grabbed the skinny corporal by the front of his shirt and swung him around, slamming him against the side of a track.

"You want to talk to the lieutenant, you talk to me first, Corporal. I'm not like that cherry Sergeant Holstrom. I'm a staff sergeant in the United States Marine Corps who happens to be your platoon sergeant and who will command your respect! Do you hear me, Corporal?" Mangles yelled, eyes blazing.

"I hear ya!" Potts said, breaking loose and looking my way, his eyes pleading for me to intervene.

I turned away and headed to the front of the column.

May 28, 1968: 1800 hours

Corporal Potts and three of the black brothers were talking to the Koreans. We had set in for the night along Route 4. I had made a Vietnamese graveyard my headquarters. The walls around the graveyard seemed to me to afford some protection that we would otherwise not have had.

"Mangles, you were breaking pretty hard on Potts. What's the point?" I asked.

"The point is that once you give them too much slack, it's hard to take up the slack, sir," Mangles said with his shit-eating grin.

Mangles was right on that account. I just didn't want him to muscle the men. Mangles was physically very strong, with a lean, wiry kind of strength that he seemed to be always testing. All day long he squeezed a tennis ball, occasionally bouncing it off one of the men's heads, intimidating the younger, less experienced soldiers. No doubt Mangles was a bully who enjoyed exercising his authority. I wanted Mangles to be effective, but not at the expense of the good communication I had with my corporals. I wanted my corporals to feel free to come to me with any of their concerns. Mangles appeared to feel that everything needed to come through him. It was his way of maintaining control. Breaking hard on the men and making an example of Potts was Mangles's way of taking up the slack.

"You have a lot of diversity in this group, Mangles," I said, chewing on a blade of grass.

"Diversity?" Mangles asked.

"That's right, diversity. And that diversity demands a lot of tolerance. You know, different strokes for different folks!" I said, wondering if Mangles understood what I meant.

"As far as I'm concerned, they're all green to me, Lieutenant. I'm no bigot. There's just one kind of marine. He's green, squared away with a short haircut, and he don't smoke no shit! These other folks in this platoon, they're not marines, Lieutenant. Somewhere along the damn road, we lost them. I don't know if I can count on them in a tight," Mangles said, matter-of-factly.

"Mangles, neither you nor I will ever reconcile the differences of belief and values among these men," I said.

"That may be, sir. I don't know nothin' about that. I just know that when I got here, half of them had the clap and most of the machine guns hadn't been test-fired or inspected in weeks. That nigger hair-pile you call a corporal scares the livin' shit out of me. What if you or I got hurt real bad, could you depend upon that shitbird or that doper Crosby?" Mangles asked.

I was at a loss for words. I had seen people with Mangles's attitude before. I had also seen the effect on the troops of those attitudes and methods. What I wanted to avoid at all costs was that emotional contagion of fear.

"I've got faith in Potts," I said.

"With all due respect, sir, I think that that faith is misplaced," Mangles said.

"I think that he would come through in a tight," I said.

"I would hate to put that to a test, Lieutenant," Mangles said.

"Look Mangles, I've got a point I think I need to make. That point is that I don't want my men so caught up in their fear of you or fear of some imagined consequences that they won't come to talk to me with their problems. If people are afraid, they withhold information. If people are afraid, they won't take the initiative; they won't take risks," I said.

"Lieutenant, that hair-pile Potts won't risk his ass for any white man in this platoon," Mangles said.

"Mangles, up to this point we haven't had any racial issues in this platoon like they have had throughout the division. And I don't want you to start any," I said.

"With all due respect, Lieutenant, open your eyes. These men have had a cherry sergeant who hasn't maintained any discipline. I plan to take care of that problem most ricky-tick. I don't want no hair-pile messin' up my Marine Corps," Mangles said.

"Look at it this way, Mangles. I'm here to save lives. Part of that is keeping these men together as an effective team. I've been able to pull them together, and, as we often hear in the Marine Corps, link them together to make them effective. I'll be the first one to admit that there was too much slack when you got here, but I didn't have any racial problems, nor did I have anyone roll a frag grenade under my hooch. In this business there are a lot of trade-offs," I said, spitting out the blade of grass.

"When the machine guns don't work, Lieutenant, nobody's

goin' to be effective, no how. That's a big affirmative," Mangles said.

"That was one machine gun," I said, in defense of Potts.

"It was still a test, Lieutenant. Come nut-cuttin' time, it all boils down to the test. Either the gun fires right or it don't. Either hair-pile conducts himself like a marine or he don't. Because he's not my green, he's got to prove to me he's worthy," Mangles said.

"Being green isn't necessarily standing a test," I said.

"Is to me, Lieutenant. It's the test of whether or not Potts wants to be a part of my Marine Corps," Mangles said.

May 28, 1968: 1900 hours

I decided to take the initiative and talk to Potts. I didn't like the feeling that I had when I walked through the area. Everyone was sullen. No one was saying much of anything.

"Corporal Potts, got a minute?" I said.

Potts had on some rose-colored granny glasses. Mangles would really go for those I thought.

"Yes, sir," Potts said, running a long-tined comb through his Afro.

"I wanted to talk to you about what happened this afternoon . . ." I said, hesitating.

"I understand, sir. You couldn't butt in. Mangles is a staff NCO. Everyone knows the score," Potts said.

"They do?" I asked.

"It's all cool now, Lieutenant. Just one thing," Potts said.

"What's that?" I asked.

"If I want to talk to you without goin' through Mangles, can I still do that?" Potts asked.

"Yes. Yes you can," I said.

"I hope so, Lieutenant. Might have to put that to a test real soon," Potts said.

Morning brought a light fog hanging about the hedgerows south of Route 4. The fog drifted through the graveyard like a spirit, chilling me to the bone.

I drank my coffee with a little sugar. My stomach had been upset and the last few days my bowels had been loose. Normally I didn't use sugar. At this point I needed all the energy I could get.

I looked up to see Potts talking to several of the brothers. I couldn't hear the words, but from their actions I could tell that they were agitated. I had an uneasy feeling.

"I want to talk to the lieutenant," Potts said to Mangles.

"What do you want to talk to the lieutenant about?" Mangles asked.

"It's personal," Potts said.

"Listen hair-pile, you don't have no personal in this green machine called the United States Marine Corps."

I took a chance and intervened.

"What do you want, Potts?" I asked.

"I want to change my name," Potts said.

"Change your name? What do you want to change your name to?" I asked.

"Mother Africa," Potts replied.

Mangles and I were speechless. For a moment there was an awkward silence. Then Mangles got up and began to laugh, a slow laugh, looking at me with his I-told-you-so look.

"I'll tell you what, Potts. When we get back to battalion, we'll go up to the first sergeant and file the necessary paperwork. Until we file that paperwork to make it official, you'll still be Corporal Atwood Potts. When the papers come through, you'll be Corporal Africa," I said, trying not to sound patronizing.

"It will be Corporal Mother Africa, Lieutenant, and that's cool. That sounds fine to me," Potts said.

Potts turned and walked back to the brothers who were watching. Mangles turned to me and shook his head.

"Should have let me handle that hair-pile, Lieutenant. What do you think the first sergeant is going to say when he hears this shit?" Mangles asked.

"This is kind of like one of those tests you were talking about, Mangles," I said.

At that moment Potts returned with the other four black marines in the platoon. They stood directly in front of Mangles.

"We want to talk to the lieutenant," they said, in unison.

"What do you want to talk to the lieutenant about?" Mangles said.

"We all want to change our names," they said, again in unison.

"Why in the Sam Hill do you want to change your names?" Mangles asked.

"For some of us, it's a matter of black pride. For others, it's a protest against you and the way you do things," Potts replied.

Mangles turned pale. He sat back as if he had been struck. I intervened again, this time to save the speechless Mangles.

"I heard what you men said. I understand how you feel. Also, you know that I think a lot of how we have worked together in the past to get things done. We have had an effective team. Don't you think?" I asked.

"Yes, sir," they said, again in unison.

"Now, again, I understand what you want to do. Changing your name is your right. But there's one thing we need to talk about. What do you think the first sergeant's going to do when you all walk in and tell him that you want to change your names?" I asked.

"I don't know, sir," Potts said.

"Come on, Potts. Sure you do. The first sergeant will throw you all out of his office, that's what he'll do. You can bet on it," I said.

They nodded. Mangles looked up at me, the color returning to his face.

"What you men need to do is put this to a test," I said.

"What kind of test, Lieutenant?" Potts asked.

"Potts, what you need to do is go in to the first sergeant and tell him that you want to change your name. I'll even go with you. Since you're a corporal, I think that you have a good chance of making this happen. What I'm saying is that once Potts changes his name, you will have a precedent. Potts will be an example for those of you who may want to follow his lead later. Believe me, if you all drop in on the first sergeant, he'll throw you out. On the other hand, if you approach this thing carefully, like I know that you can, you can be effective," I said.

"Linking together for effectiveness," Potts said.

"That's a big affirmative," I said.

"Sounds like a plan to me, Lieutenant," Potts said, the other brothers nodding agreement.

Potts and the others returned to their work. The men were beginning to load their tracks in preparation for the day's activities. They were moving like men who had taken out the slack. Mangles rose and shook his head. He didn't know that within a week names would change.

"Well, I'll be damned," he said.

SITTING UNDER JESUS

June 18, 1968: 0600 hours

I SQUINTED THROUGH the haze of exhaust fumes and one-hundred-degree heat, checking the long line of amphibian tractors churning up the grade toward Hill 112. Even on this high ground our movement had slowed to a crawl, the long, twenty-five-ton tracks backfiring yard-long tongues of flame. In the wet gumbo at the base of Hill 112 our tracks just slipped and slid every way but forward. For every kilometer we gained, it seemed we stuck a track. Clearly this so-called mechanized thrust was turning into a joke.

"This is no way to use tracks, Lieutenant. No damn chicken-dick way to use tracks," Staff Sergeant Mangles said. Mangles had become my conscience as well as my technical adviser.

"You got that right. But like I said, Mangles, this Lieutenant Colonel Cheatum thinks he has all the answers. He wouldn't listen. He was sure that this ground would take the weight of the tracks," I said with a shrug of the shoulders.

Ba Na Ridge rose to the west, a green-humped mass of a mountain, part of the objective of this mechanized thrust. The overall idea had been to move Lima Company, Third Battalion, Seventh Marines, into a blocking force position near the base of Ba Na Ridge. My tracks were supposed to have moved Lima Company into position before first light. Only five kilometers over hard ground Lieutenant Colonel Cheatum had said. Cheatum had neglected to consider a seep that ran out of the base of Hill 112. The seep didn't show on the map, and two kilometers out, my tracks were mired in a black, gumbolike mud, my men wrestling thigh-deep with forty-pound hooks and tow cables trying to free our vehicles from the muck.

"I bet there's a hundred gooks sittin' up there on Ba Na Ridge just laughing their asses off at this mess," Sergeant Mangles said, spitting on the hot exhaust of our track.

"That's a big affirmative!" I said.

"Good thing our drivers got their shit together, Lieutenant. I'm beginning to wonder if this Cheatum knows his backside from a flashlight," Mangles said, spitting a second time onto the exhaust.

"Who knows, Mangles," I said.

"Our people know, Lieutenant. Sons of bitchin' track rats out in that mud know," Mangles said.

For some reason Cheatum tried to employ amphibian tractors whenever he could. In our brief conversations Cheatum had expressed his opinion that tracks were a resource that he intended to utilize. Be innovative and adapt, Cheatum had said. Even though the mission of the LVTP6 amphibian tractor was moving men and supplies from ship to shore, Lieutenant Colonel Cheatum was convinced that our tracks had a contribution to make. After all, he had said, tracks were part of the Marine Corps team and having an effective team was all a matter of how men and equipment were linked together. I was sure that at this point some of my men thought otherwise. I didn't know what to think. I just hoped that Cheatum's confidence in tracks was not misplaced.

"Actual, this is Jesus One, over."

The radio breaking in turned my attention back to the tracks.

"Jesus One, this is the Actual, go," I replied.

"Zero Deuce is stuck, Actual. Not bad. Got to hook up to pull Deuce free, over," Jesus One said.

"How long? Over," I asked.

"Maybe fifteen, over."

"Roger that last, Jesus One. Keep me informed. Out," I said, throwing the radio handset over to Mangles in frustration.

''Take over, Mangles. I'm going to walk down there and talk to the grunts,'' I said, jumping to the ground.

''Lieutenant. Check on that new driver from Cua Viet. Crosby or whatever his name is,'' Mangles said.

In the past two weeks several new men had come into the platoon from the northern part of I Corps. They were men who had been with First Amphibian Tracks up around the Cua Viet area near the border of North Vietnam. As experienced track rats, they had strong opinions about how our vehicles should or should not be used. Crosby in particular had voiced his opinions. Crosby and the others from Cua Viet had one other problem. They smoked a lot of dope. Mangles knew that they smoked and was constantly checking on them, checking on them to the point where they were less than enthusiastic about having Mangles around. It was apparent that in the last two weeks, the men from Cua Viet were having an impact in more ways than one.

''How do your people come up with these tractors' names?''

The question came from Captain Mike Milos, the commanding officer of Lima Company. He had a nice manner and was known to rarely lose his cool. Milos had already given up trying to get into position with his company. He appeared amused by the mechanized thrust. He called it Cheatum's fiasco.

''I let them paint anything they want on the tracks. I let them name them anything they want as long as it's not porn. Porn is out,'' I said.

The track known as Zero Deuce had a deuce of spades painted on its side. Deuce had a reputation as a lucky track. Therefore we usually ran it first or second in line. Jesus One had a profile of a bearded Jesus Christ with a crown outlined in white on the outside bulkhead just above the driver's side. Today Jesus One was running third in line behind my track, Dixie Peach. I had named Dixie for my last girlfriend back in the States, a flight attendant for Eastern Airlines who flew out of Atlanta. She hadn't written to me in six months so I was considering changing my track's name. That was considered bad luck. According to track rats, the only time it was appropriate to change a track's name was when the driver changed. Crosby had changed the name of his track to Cool Breeze and had painted the profile of a bearded, zonked-out hippie on the outside bulkhead. Crosby was running Cool Breeze fourth in line.

"How about that Jesus One? Isn't that a little blasphemous?" Milos asked, raising his thick eyebrows.

"That's Holstrom's track. Holstrom's an evangelist. Outright Jesus-freak. If you ask him about that, he will tell you that it's his way of sharing his faith with some of us who have spiritual hang-ups," I said with a smile.

"I see," Milos said, his eyebrows still raised.

"Holstrom hands out copies of the New Testament," I said.

"What does the battalion chaplain think of all this?" Milos asked.

"I asked the chaplain what he thought, and he said that since Holstrom's picture is meant to encourage the spiritual and not the carnal, it was okay. Kind of like a knight having a cross on his shield during the Crusades," I said, still smiling.

"Well, I suppose it's better than having the picture of a doper painted on the side of your track," Milos said, pointing to the profile of the hippie painted on the side of Cool Breeze.

"Yes, sir, I think that's what the chaplain would call carnal," I said.

We both laughed. Below us the tracks coughed and belched out flames and exhaust. Zero Deuce flung bits of mud and vegetation, breaking free of the mire.

"What do the troops think of Holstrom? Isn't he a sergeant?" Milos asked.

"Oh, I suppose that they think he's a little weird. The troops are not interested in taking up the cross and following Jesus," I said.

"Well, you never know. I've seen some hard-core grunts get religious out on the Laotian border," Milos said.

"Hey, Actual, we got a fire on Cool Breeze!" someone yelled.

By the time that I slipped and slid through the mud and brush to Cool Breeze, the fire was out. In the excitement all the grunts had jumped off the track and were milling around trying to get back on top of the track.

"What the hell is going on?" I yelled.

An impassive Crosby stared back at me, a red bandanna tied around his head, a cigarette sticking out from his droopy, black, handlebar mustache.

"No sweat, sir. Just an exhaust fire. Scared all the grunts,"

Crosby said, pulling off his skivvy shirt to reveal a powerful set of arms and shoulders.

Holstrom joined Crosby, carrying a fire extinguisher. The tall, thin Holstrom was a contrast to the thick, dark torso of Crosby. Sergeant Holstrom, always an optimist, just grinned and waved his slow wave, as if he had everything under control.

"Sergeant Holstrom, radio Mangles to move out as soon as we get all these grunts back on board," I yelled.

"Yes, sir," Holstrom said.

I started back up to Dixie Peach when Captain Milos stopped me.

"Maybe we ought to dismount all of my people. I think we would be better off on foot," Milos said.

"That's affirmative, sir, but I think that you had better check that one out with Cheatum," I said.

"Na. He wants to make Marine Corps history with all this mechanized thrust bullshit. It's all so that he can write some bullshit paper for the *Marine Corps Gazette*," Milos said, laughing.

I nodded, saying nothing. Up ahead Dixie Peach was moving out, the other tracks falling into proper interval as the line took form.

Then there was a boom that shook the ground. For a split second a small, umbrella-shaped cloud hung over Dixie Peach, the stunned men aboard Dixie Peach moving like sleepwalkers. There was a second boom as the gas tanks under Dixie Peach exploded.

"What happened?" Milos yelled.

"Box mine," I yelled back.

An intense fireball began to consume Dixie Peach. Several of the grunts managed to leap through the flames. The grunts lay on the ground, stunned from the explosion, their clothing still on fire, their hair singed into tight red kinks. One by one we dragged them clear of the burning track, shouting at each other above the growing roar of the fire.

Sergeant Holstrom drove Jesus One dangerously close to the fire. I saw Holstrom leap into the flames. Crosby followed Holstrom, pulling on his fire-retardant overalls on the run. Together they pulled Mangles to his feet and out of the flames. Two more marines from Jesus One leaped into the flames with fire extinguishers, but their efforts were to no avail. In spite of the fire-retardant suits, the growing intensity of the fire proved to be too much. Holstrom and his men were forced to abandon the track. In the process they were able to find and pull out the driver, who, although badly burned, was still alive.

"Praise the Lord," Holstrom yelled as he hit the ground.

June 19, 1968: 1800 hours

"So fourteen men are hurt. And the track is lost," Lieutenant Colonel Cheatum said, wiping his forehead with the green towel that he always carried.

"Fourteen all together, sir. Staff Sergeant Mangles, Keyworth, who was my driver, Corporal Crosby all were from tracks. Then there were some eleven grunts who were burned. We expect Crosby back," I said.

"How many critical?"

"Only Keyworth," I replied, looking off toward Hill 112.

A thirty-by-thirty half of a Southeast Asian–style hooch served Third Battalion, Seventh Marines, as the Hill 10 "Officers' Club." One end of the wall had been knocked out and a deck had been built under a large barringtonia tree. From the deck one could sit and view the wide panorama of low hills that rose gradually to the west. Behind those hills Ba Na Ridge loomed, a dark green malevolence. Behind Ba Na Ridge, distant mountains stretched away some thirty miles to the Laotian border.

"Loosing Mangles may be a serious problem. More than you can imagine at the moment. Anytime you loose a good staff NCO, you have a problem. In your case, Lieutenant, the problem is compounded by a number of factors," Cheatum said.

"Is that why you wanted to talk to me, sir?" I asked.

"Yes. Yes, it is," Cheatum replied, wiping his face with the towel.

Lieutenant Colonel Cheatum didn't fit my image of what a marine grunt battalion commander should look like. While he was tall, close to six feet, three inches, and seemingly in good shape, he was thin to the point of appearing frail, almost feminine. Cheatum was a contrast to the hard charging battalion commanders that I was used to. His age was hard to pin down, late forties or early fifties, and when he talked to you he stared directly into your eyes, the lean, dark, heavy-browed face impassive, his moist brown eyes distant, almost glazed. It seemed that Lieutenant Colonel Cheatum never blinked.

"Who will be Mangles's backup?" Cheatum asked, sipping his coffee, not taking his eyes off mine.

"Sergeant Holstrom. Just made E-5. He should be fine until my battalion comes up with an E-6 or E-7," I said.

"Have you talked to your company commander?" Cheatum asked.

"Yes, sir. Briefly," I said.

"We need at least an E-6. We need someone with experience leading men. We need someone with technical know-how," Cheatum said.

A sunbird landed on the lowest limb of the barringtonia tree, its green iridescence showing an interplay of rainbow colors in the sunlight.

"Sergeant Major Dillard is concerned about those new men who came down from Cua Viet. He's also concerned about Holstrom's abilities," Cheatum said, ignoring the bird.

"Concerned, sir?"

"He says that they smoke dope. He says that you got a Corporal Crosby who has painted a hippie on the side of his track," Cheatum said, now looking out toward the mountains.

For a moment I didn't know what to say. So I sipped my coffee, trying to think of a reply. I couldn't think of a thing to say, so I just nodded.

"Do you think your men are smoking dope?" Cheatum asked.

"Hard to say, sir," I said, my stomach suddenly upset.

"I've noticed that you spend your evenings up at the Officers' Club with the other lieutenants. There's nothing wrong with that. In fact, I like to encourage closeness among my lieutenants; however, one of the shortcomings that young lieutenants often have is that they tend to be a bit self-centered. They tend at times to need feedback when they get too far away from their primary duties," Cheatum said.

"Self-centered?" I asked, wondering what the hell was going on.

"You look upset, Lieutenant. I didn't ask you here to lecture you or to dwell upon any shortcomings. Rather, I asked you here because I had a sincere concern that I share with the sergeant major concerning your effectiveness," Cheatum said, looking me directly in the eye.

"What do you want me to do, sir?" I asked, my left knee shaking under the table.

"We'll talk about that in a minute. First tell me about Sergeant Holstrom," Cheatum asked.

"Oh, he's a Jesus-freak. Carries around a copy of the New Testament wherever he goes. He'll get out and proselytize from time to time. But that's no big deal. He doesn't smoke dope, that's for sure," I said.

The sunbird dropped down to the table next to ours and dipped its curved bill into what remained of a rum and Coke. The bird was barely two feet away. Cheatum blinked at that.

"Do you think that Holstrom has confidence in you?" Cheatum said, with just the hint of a smile.

I took another sip of coffee and again, for lack of knowing what to say, I nodded.

"How about the troops, especially those new men from Cua Viet, the ones that Mangles claims smoke all the dope, do they have confidence in you?"

I nodded a third time. I was still at a loss for words.

"Lieutenant, I'm taking the time to talk to you about these things because if I were in your position I would want someone like myself to do the same thing for me. You understand where I'm coming from?" Cheatum asked.

"Yes, sir," I replied.

"When you allow some doper to paint a hippie on the side of a Marine Corps vehicle it does not inspire the confidence of the officer corps. Moreover, I wonder what the men must think of an officer who would allow a corporal to do what Crosby did? By painting that doper on the side of his track, Crosby is showing contempt for both you and the Marine Corps in which we both serve!" Cheatum said, raising his voice.

Several of my fellow lieutenants were drinking beer at the far corner of the Officers' Club. When Cheatum raised his voice, they got up to leave. The sunbird, startled by Cheatum's voice, flitted back into the barringtonia tree.

"With all due respect, sir, I don't think Crosby meant any

harm. The troops down in tracks have always painted goofy things on their tracks," I said.

"That may be, Lieutenant. The point that I'm making here is twofold. Number one is that painting the tracks is unmilitary. Number two is that your allowing them to paint the tracks in the first place suggests to me you are giving them too much slack," Cheatum said.

"Slack?"

"That's right, slack. It's the little things that in the long run maintain effectiveness. I would suggest that you and Holstrom work with the sergeant major. He will give you some ideas on how you might tighten things up down in the track area," Cheatum said.

"Do you want me to paint over all the stuff painted on the tracks?" I asked.

"Actually, with the exception of the doper, no. Since Crosby's evacuated, I see no problem painting over the doper. However, if you suddenly impact all the others, it would hurt morale and it would tend to create hard feelings all around. No, don't paint over anything but the doper. But get rid of the doper as soon as possible," Cheatum said, wiping his face with his towel.

Cheatum was sweating freely. His towel amused me. It reminded me of that comic strip character in Snoopy. My leg had stopped shaking and I was under control for the time being. This whole thing pissed me off, but there was nothing I could do.

"I want you to keep your men real busy for the next few days. Find things, productive things, to keep them busy. Let's not give them time to dwell on the loss of Dixie Peach," Cheatum said, leaning forward, not taking his eyes off mine.

I wondered if Cheatum knew that I thought he was a pussy.

"Yes, sir," I replied, also leaning forward.

"Again, I will have the sergeant major stop by to make his presence felt," Cheatum added.

"Yes, sir. I'll work with him," I said.

The sunbird flitted back to the rum and Coke. The bird sat on the edge of the glass and dipped its slender, curved beak into what remained of the drink. I wondered if the sunbird was getting high.

"Lieutenant, keep in mind that my purpose here is to support

your growth as a leader. Leadership, to my mind, is best viewed
as a function within the organization. Accordingly, developing
leadership involves mutual support and linking together for effectiveness within our officer corps. You understand?'' Cheatum
said, his tone becoming more formal.

The sunbird wobbled at the edge of the glass. The sucker was
getting drunk. Son of a bitch, I thought.

''Lieutenant! Did you hear what I just said?'' Cheatum said,
raising his voice.

''Yes, sir,'' I said, not understanding fully all that had been
said.

What this all boiled down to in my terms was that the sergeant
major was going to come down on my area. Son of a bitch!

''One other thing. No! Excuse me. Two more things. One is
our common mission while we are at Hill 10. Two is the special
function that your tracks play in supporting that mission. To me
the role of tracks is very important, to say the least,'' Cheatum
said, gazing off into the distant foothills.

A second sunbird was now at the glass of rum and Coke. The
second sunbird also began to sip the drink. The first sunbird,
still wobbly, started to pick a fight with the second sunbird. Just
like a drunk I thought to myself.

''Our common mission?'' I asked, trying to appear like I gave
a shit.

''While you are attached to this battalion and since, to my
mind, your tracks serve a number of vital purposes, we need to
assure both ourselves and all concerned that grunts and track
rats know what their common mission is,'' Cheatum said, again
leaning forward.

My mind went back to yesterday's fiasco. I thought of the
muck and the heat. I thought of the screams, the smell of burning flesh, of the men, still burning, walking with their arms
outstretched, burnt skin hanging from their arms like wet tissue.
This mother was the one who had ordered us out on that wild
goose chase. Now I had to sit here and let him tell me what the
''common mission'' was.

''I see your tracks serving two primary purposes in support
of our common mission. One purpose is the perimeter security
of Hill 10 in the tractor park area. Secondly, I see your tracks'

ability to respond to support various night activities," Cheatum said.

There it is, I thought to myself. He wants us to run down the road in the middle of the night, sitting ducks for box mines and rocket propelled grenades. This guy is a half a bubble off center.

"Night activities, sir?"

"Yes. It may be to evacuate wounded. Maybe to drop off a squad-sized patrol. Perhaps to interdict some movement," Cheatum said.

The sunbirds were still squabbling. The second sunbird had now secured his position on the glass. The first sunbird appeared tired out, still wobbling from the effects of the rum.

"Interdict?" I asked.

"That happens to be the key word. Interdict. Interdiction is this battalion's mission. To interdict enemy movement between Da Nang and the foothills to our west!" Cheatum said, once again leaning forward for emphasis.

"I understand, sir," I said. I understood only too well. How was I going to break this to the troops?

"Again, keep your men busy. Don't give your men time to be preoccupied with the loss of Dixie," Cheatum said.

"Dixie Peach, sir," I said.

"Dixie Peach. Peach sherbet, whatever! Keep your men busy. Interact with them as much as possible to make your presence felt. And watch for dope. I don't want the word getting back to regiment that there's dope in our tractor park!" Cheatum said, sweat dripping from his nose.

"I'll take care of it, sir," I said, remaining calm.

"I know that you will. Now, in terms of your personal leadership, be the doer! Make sure that your men view you as someone with character, not someone who would let a shitbird like Crosby paint a doper on a Marine Corps vehicle! By character I mean someone who will stand for both the Marine Corps and our battalion's mission on Hill 10! Who has the integrity to keep it all together!" Cheatum said, his voice loud enough to scare the sunbirds back into their barringtonia tree.

"Yes, sir, I'll take care of it!" I said, trying to appear positive.

"Thank you. I'll see you later," Cheatum said, rising from the table and walking slowly toward the door.

"Keep me informed, Lieutenant," Cheatum called back.

For a time I just sat there, looking off at the mountains, wondering if I had been giving my men too much slack. No doubt I had just been squared away via the Cheatum method. In spite of what Cheatum had said, I felt I had been lectured to. I had been lectured to in the goddamn Officers' Club for Christ's sake. In front of my fellow lieutenants I had been, for all practical purposes, counseled. While the whole thing was humiliating, there were times when I felt that Cheatum wasn't really talking to me. It was as if Cheatum were talking to himself. I wondered if he practiced giving this speech before he laid it on me. I also wondered if he gave the same sort of speech to his company commanders. I would have to ask Milos if he did. Maybe I just got the watered-down version. At any rate, what I got was more than a pep talk. Lieutenant Colonel Cheatum was giving me his full attention. That made me very uncomfortable. I made up my mind that the first thing I was going to do when I got back to the tractor park was have Holstrom paint over that hippie-freak Crosby painted on the side of his track.

June 20, 1968: 0700 hours

The night patrols were coming back through the perimeter wire. Although the night had been quiet, the grunts looked beat. One of them waved.

"Painted over the doper, sir," Sergeant Holstrom said.

"Great. Now all we got to do is wait for the sergeant major to come down and mess with us," I said.

"Lieutenant, don't worry about the sergeant major. I can handle him," Holstrom said.

"How's that?" I asked.

"Just got to give him a sense of control. Or make it appear like he's got things under control," Holstrom said with a knowing smile.

"You mean kiss his ass like Mangles did," I said.

"No way, sir. Sergeant Major just got promoted. He's never been in the Nam. He don't want to make any waves. All he's going to do is make sure things don't get out of hand," Holstrom said.

"What are we going to do about Cool Breeze? Who's going to be the driver?" I asked.

"One of the new guys from Cua Viet," Holstrom said.

"Don't let him paint any hippie shit on the side of the track. If he wants to paint something, paint a dragon or a tiger or something on that order," I said.

"Yes, sir," Holstrom said.

One couldn't help but like Sergeant Holstrom. He was the kind of guy one hoped his sister would marry. I particularly liked his easygoing manner with the troops. Nothing seemed to shake him.

"Lieutenant, did you hear anything about when we might be going out again?" Holstrom asked.

"Cheatum said that the grunts would be using us for night reacts up and down Liberty Road," I said.

"Troops won't like that," Holstrom said, looking down at the ground.

"That's our job," I said.

"Think we ought to call the troops together and talk to them about it, sir?" Holstrom asked.

"You worried, Holstrom?" I said.

"No, sir, I'm not worried. But I think it would be a good idea to talk to the troops about what's going down," Holstrom said.

"Why? It will just get them all worked up. Those new guys from Cua Viet will bitch, smoke some more dope," I said, suddenly feeling very tired.

"Bitching marine is a happy marine, sir," Holstrom said, smiling.

"Is that right?" I replied.

"It wouldn't hurt for some of them to think more about what's going down. Some of them may take things more seriously when it comes time to smoke that funny weed. Some may even prepare personally for what's coming," Holstrom said.

"Prepare personally. What are you talking about?"

"Their personal evangelism, sir. I already got one who I think is going to be a spiritual fisherman," Holstrom said, beaming.

"Say what?" I said.

"Follow me, and I will make you fishers of men. Matthew. Fourth chapter. Nineteenth verse I believe," Holstrom said.

"You serious, Sergeant?" I asked.

"Sir, I got to place my faith in the Lord and His Son, Jesus. That's why I painted Christ on my track. You know that. Some paint their state flag. Some paint a fancy nickname, stuff like that. But when I go rolling down Liberty Road in the dark of the night, I'm sitting under Jesus. Jesus is painted there right beside me on the bulkhead of my track, and he's going to be with me all the way."

June 20, 1968: 0800 hours

The day was going to be clear and bright. There was a breeze blowing, just enough to keep the air moving. I thought about what Cheatum had said about keeping the men busy. He was right. The only problem was that there seemed to be only so much work to do. Once the tracks were maintained, the weapons cleaned and inspected, the troops fed and showered down, there was really nothing much to do except fight boredom.

Boredom. At times I wanted to mount out the tracks just for excitement. Yes, I was bored. The men were bored. We laid around in our hooches, jacked off, read paperbacks, listened to rock music, and some smoked dope. Bored. Cheatum was probably as bored as we were. Cheatum was probably bored when he thought up the Hill 112 fiasco.

"Look who's coming," I said.

"Who is it, Lieutenant?" Holstrom asked.

"None other then Sergeant Major Dillard," I replied.

"Good. I'm glad he found time to get down here," Holstrom said.

"What's the matter with you, Holstrom, the heat got to you?" I asked.

"No, sir, just waiting for my spiritual fisherman," Holstrom said, picking up a copy of the New Testament.

"What are you talking about?"

"Sergeant Major, sir. Chaplain says that he's into Bible study," Holstrom said.

"The only thing I've ever seen him into was a fifth of Jack Daniel's. That was the time he and Mangles got so shit-faced, Mangles couldn't find his way back to the tractor park," I said with a snort.

"Good morning, Sergeant Major. What can we do for you?" Holstrom said, all smiles as usual.

"Well, I came down for two reasons. One, to see the troops. Two, we got some bad news. Keyworth died last evening. His system just didn't respond to treatment. We probably should get a little memorial service together," the sergeant major said.

It took about a minute for me to respond. Finally Sergeant Holstrom responded for me. I got up and walked over to the troops and called them together. No one had anything to say. There was nothing to be said. Keyworth was nineteen. He had been burned, but when we evacuated him, he was conscious and able to crack a joke as we put him on the chopper. He didn't seem to be hurt that badly. The whole thing was so unexpected.

June 20, 1968: 1400 hours

Lieutenant Colonel Cheatum found time to come down and say a few words. I must admit that he was good, or, as Cheatum would have preferred it, effective. The chaplain, a little guy who was a Baptist from North Carolina, kept it short and to the point. I noticed that he and Sergeant Holstrom were tight. They spent a long time talking after the service. Cheatum's only words to me were to keep my men busy.

The word that I got from the battalion S-3, who ran all the operations in our area of responsibility, was that my tracks were to stand by as of 1600 hours. The mission was to be a simple one. Drop off two squads in the vicinity of La Chau 5, a village identified as having a high level of Vietcong activity within the last week.

June 20, 1968: 1500 hours

One could tell that Sergeant Major Dillard hit the bottle. He had those little red lines in his nose that boozers get when they drink too much hard whiskey. One night he barfed so hard he broke all the blood vessels under his eyes. Dillard looked like he had been in a fight and someone had given him two shiners. When I asked Mangles how the sergeant major got two black eyes,

Mangles laughed and said that he got tangled up with Jack Daniel's.

Dillard was tall and dark. He was thin, to the point of being bony, and had a haggard look about him as if he had suffered from some great hunger. The long, gaunt face was drawn, the eyes close together and separated by a thin, straight nose. It was an intelligent face, despite the tired look, and unlike Lieutenant Colonel Cheatum, Dillard made no pretense about where he stood relative to our so-called common mission. Dillard was a survivor, who had survived some twenty-odd years in the Marines Corps by keeping a low profile and keeping in the background. He chain-smoked, and although he spoke slowly and deliberately, it seemed that his long fingers were always trembling slightly.

Dillard was under pressure in a number of ways. He boozed too much, and Cheatum had told him to go on the wagon for a while. Cheatum also put pressure on Dillard to get out and around. Cheatum felt that the sergeant major had a special leadership role to play, and that as the most senior enlisted man in the battalion, Dillard should be out with the troops, modeling good behavior. That cracked me up.

"Well, Sergeant Major, what did you think of the memorial service?" I said.

"Brought tears to this old man's eyes, Lieutenant," Dillard said, lighting a cigarette.

"Yeah. Bad deal all around," I said.

"Speaking of bad deals, look what's coming down the road," Dillard said.

I looked up to see Crosby walking down from Hill 10. I could tell it was Crosby because of that cruddy old red bandanna he always wore tied around his head. The dark complexion I remembered had turned a reddish pink. The black handlebar mustache was gone. Without the mustache Crosby looked boyish. As soon as Crosby opened his mouth, all doubt was gone.

"Hey, brother rats, I'm back!" Crosby yelled.

"Get yourself a Marine Corps cover, raghead," the sergeant major said, laughing.

"Ah, lighten up, Sergeant Major. I just got me a Purple Heart, don't ya know. Say, Lieutenant, how's it going?" Crosby said, smart-ass grin on his face.

"You heard about Keyworth?" I asked.

"That's a stone shame, sir. They told me up in battalion that he bought the farm," Crosby said.

"You came close yourself," Sergeant Holstrom said, walking up from the tractor park.

"Sergeant Holstrom, how's your bad self? Still sitting under Jesus?"

"Careful Crosby. On the day of the Pentecost some mocked and some inquired," Holstrom said with a tone that I had not as yet heard from him.

"Where is that from, Sergeant?" Dillard asked.

"Acts Two, I believe," Holstrom added smiling.

"How's the burns doing, Crosby?" Dillard asked.

"Sergeant Major, I lucked out like a big dog. Man, I was wondering if I should call up Sergeant Holstrom here to get ready for the Sky Pilot." Crosby rolled his eyes.

"Sky Pilot?" Dillard asked.

"Yes, sir, Sky Pilot! You know, upstairs. The Lord," Crosby said, pointing to the sky.

"As he thinks in his heart, so *is* he," Holstrom said.

"Where is that from, Sergeant Holstrom?" Dillard asked.

"Proverbs. Twenty-third chapter, seventh verse, I believe," Holstrom said, almost smugly.

Something was going on here that I couldn't figure out. I had to get ready for the loading up of the grunts. For that matter we *all* had to get ready. It was clear to me that Holstrom and Dillard were playing kissy face. That was okay as long as Holstrom didn't start kissing Dillard's ass. What I needed was a sergeant I could trust, not a lackey. Mangles had been enough of a toad.

"How about your burns, Crosby? You fit to drive tonight?" I asked.

"That's a big affirmative, Lieutenant!"

"Great! Sergeant Holstrom, that takes care of the driver problem. All we need to do now is finish prechecking the tracks," I said.

"Yes, sir, I'll take care of that right away. Sergeant Major, if you come on down to the tractor park a minute, I would greatly appreciate it. I'd like your opinion on something," Sergeant Holstrom said.

I thought I would barf. But I had to admit that Holstrom had the sergeant major where we needed him, and that was on our side. If brownnosing that old fart was what was needed, so be it.

"Is Holstrom sweet on the sergeant major, Lieutenant? Or does Sergeant Holstrom want to become a lifer known as Staff Sergeant Holstrom?" Crosby said, mocking Holstrom's stiff, formal way of walking.

Any other time I would have laughed. But Keyworth was still heavy on my mind. I just couldn't believe that he died.

"Oh, man! Oh, man, that's cold!" Crosby suddenly yelled.

"What the hell's the matter with you?" I said.

Crosby fell to his knees. He pulled the bandanna off his head and threw it at the ground, throwing up a cloud of dust. For several seconds he beat his fists on the ground as if he were overcome with some terrible grief, in the process letting out a long, wailing moan.

"Holy shit! Holy, holy shit!" Crosby said, rising to his feet wild-eyed, with clenched fists.

"Crosby! Get control of yourself!" I yelled.

"Lieutenant, what the hell, over! What the hell did they do to Cool Breeze? Where's the zig-zag man? Do you know how long it took me to paint that beautiful zig-zag man?" Crosby was screaming.

"Control yourself, Crosby. Cheatum didn't want any hippie on the side of a Marine Corps vehicle."

"Cheatum! That big pussy! What's he know about anything! That big pussy almost got me killed! Shit!" Crosby yelled, stumbling down into the tractor park, past the dumbfounded sergeant major, who stood there with his mouth open.

"Lieutenant! Lieutenant! Do you mean to say someone can paint Jesus Christ on the side of a Marine Corps vehicle, yet I can't paint the zig-zag man on my vehicle! That ain't fair!" Crosby yelled from the tractor park.

"That's right, Crosby. When you make sergeant, maybe the Marine Corps will reconsider. In the meantime, keep it in mind that nothing in this damn war is fair." I turned my back and walked away.

I walked for some minutes, never looking back. I was almost to the top of Hill 10 when the sergeant major caught up with me.

"Just keep them headed down the middle, Lieutenant. Just keep them headed down the middle," Sergeant Major Dillard said, slapping me on the back.

June 20, 1968: 1600 hours

The word finally came and I headed out with five tracks and two squads to the village called La Chau 5. Our mission was to drop off the squads who were to patrol the area between La Chau 5 and what we called the blue line. The blue line was a river that also happened to be the border between two government districts. My tracks were to be part of a blocking force on the other side of La Chau 5. If the shit hit the fan, we were to react to the point of contact.

June 20, 1968: 1700 hours

We moved into a thick grove of bamboo and waited. The two grunt squads moved out without incident. It was steamy in the dense brush. The village was close enough to smell, the scent of burning joss mingling with the wood smoke of the cooking fires. From where I sat, I could see nothing. Sweat seeped and dripped until my skivvy shirt was soaked through. Gnats and other flying insects swarmed about our faces. We waited in silence for the order to move.

June 20, 1968: 1930 hours

We got the word to move to the rally point. Overhead the rippling, thumping sound of rotor blades told us that Lima Company was being choppered into position. It took us five minutes to reach our rally point. The VC were probably watching us all the way.

June 20, 1968: 2000 hours

The shit hit the fan. For ten minutes two marine squads exchanged fire from one end of La Chau 5 to the other. By the time fire discipline was restored, each squad had taken casualties. The squads had been shooting at each other.

June 20, 1968: 2200 hours

We loaded the bodies of the dead marines in almost total darkness. We had a bit of trouble loading one big one. The body must have weighed two hundred and fifty pounds. While I helped two grunts on the ground, Crosby grabbed the head of the dead man. Half the dead man's head was blown off and Crosby happened to grab what was left of the dead man's brains. Crosby vomited all the way back to Hill 10.

June 21, 1968: 1100 hours

Cheatum sent word down through the sergeant major to keep the men busy. Cheatum wanted every officer to get the word to keep the men's minds occupied with the tasks to be done. The problem was that by mid-morning we had run out of things to keep us busy.

"Lieutenant, me and the men was wondering if we could take the tracks down to the river," Sergeant Holstrom said.

"I suppose you're going to tell me that you're going to have the men wash the tracks."

"Well, yes, sir, that was part of it," Holstrom said.

"Who do you think I am, Holstrom, Charlie Tuna? You know the troops only have one good reason for going down to the river, and that's to get laid by some skivvy girl. Isn't that right?"

"No, sir! That ain't at all the reason I had in mind."

"Well, what did you have in mind?" I asked.

"To baptize Crosby, sir," Holstrom said.

"Are you kidding me, Holstrom?"

"No, sir. I've asked the sergeant major to go with us if you approve. Chaplain Smily is going to do the baptizing,'' Holstrom said.

"How come Crosby got religion all of a sudden?"

"Crosby has always been filled with the Holy Spirit, Lieutenant. It was just that he had to quit smoking that funny weed. This morning he, Chaplain Smily, and I had a talk. Crosby said he now has the courage to do what needs to be done if he is to be spiritually minded."

"Spiritually minded?"

"To be carnally minded *is* death, but to be spiritually minded *is* life and peace. Romans, I believe," Holstrom said, stone serious.

"And you say the sergeant major is going along, as is the chaplain, that right?"

"That's a big affirmative, sir," Holstrom said, now smiling.

"And what did you tell Crosby? What's in it for Crosby?" I was still suspicious.

"Crosby lays down the burden he's been carrying."

"Burden?"

"The burden of original sin."

I gave my approval. I had to admit that I had underestimated Holstrom. All in all it was a good thing from a number of viewpoints. The baptism would keep men occupied where otherwise I really had nothing for them to do. I might also get some brownie points with Cheatum since the sergeant major and Chaplain Smily were involved with my troops in what should be a spiritually uplifting experience. In the past, getting laid by one of those beautiful little skivvy girls down at the river would have been the usual way my troops achieved spiritual inspiration. That is, getting laid and then getting high. In the past I had just looked the other way. Maybe I was beginning to change. Keyworth's death haunted me. I needed to lift that burden.

June 21, 1968: 1800 hours

The baptism went without incident. When the men returned, I noticed that many of them seemed to have a new seriousness about them. Crosby wasn't wearing his red bandanna, and I had to admit that for once he looked squared away. Chaplain Smily was as happy as a hog in shit. I pumped the little guy up, telling him what a difference his ministry had made to my platoon. I told him I was going to pass that onto Cheatum. Smily beamed. Sergeant Major Dillard nodded approvingly and gave me a wink. Then we all shook hands. Later I went back to my hooch and had a shot of Jack Daniel's from the bottle Mangles left behind. Jack Daniel's helped take my mind off Keyworth.

June 21, 1968: 2300 hours

Out along the road to Hill 112 a squad of some fourteen marines had sprung an ambush on what they thought were four or five rice carriers. Within minutes it became apparent that the squad had bit off more than it could chew. Four or five rice carriers turned into almost a company of NVA regulars. The only thing saving the squad was a smart corporal and the thin neck of high ground upon which the corporal chose to make a stand.

By the time Cheatum called us out to react, most of the squad was wounded, including the gutsy little corporal. In less than five minutes we loaded a full platoon, went through the gate, and were on our way toward the firefight.

The terrain was mostly a dried-up rice paddy that had grown up in grass. The thin neck of high ground was capped by an old cemetery. Mortars or artillery were out of the question because the NVA were already into the cemetery and some of the fighting had been hand to hand.

The only obstacle I could see was a gully that ran to our front. The gully was about a hundred feet wide and full of tall elephant grass. On the map it showed up as a dry water course. I decided to take the chance that it was still dry. That was a mistake.

I took the lead. Sergeant Major Dillard was on my track, inspired at the last minute to join the react group. Sergeant Holstrom commanded the middle track in the column. Holstrom had the .50-caliber machine gun, and needed to be in a position to support my track and the three other tracks that were moving directly to my immediate right in an echelon formation. The four remaining tracks followed Holstrom, also in echelon formation in order to maximize firepower as needed toward the high ground to our immediate front.

As it turned out, the echelon formation saved us. For as soon as my track, the lead track, bogged down in the mud, I alerted the other tracks, who then broke hard right to drier ground. It was at that point that what must have been thirty NVA opened up at point-blank range.

Overhead, four-deuce mortar illumination dangled from little parachutes, making the night as bright as day. I peeked through the firing hole from my position on top of the track. Green tracers zipped through the elephant grass. The characteristic snapping fire of the AK-47 told me that we were flanked.

On top of each track we had built solid bunkers made of bridge lumber surrounded by two rows of sandbags. But direct fire at point-blank range was tearing the bunkers up. Since the volume of fire was from my immediate left, all the grunts that had been riding on top of my track slipped off the right side where the body of the track offered cover. I yelled at my driver to jump. Dillard and I were pinned down in the bunker. There was no way we could move without getting hit.

Holstrom tried to cover our immediate front with .50-caliber fire. The tracks beside him then swung in a wide arc to the right, flanking the NVA side of the cemetery. Cool Breeze, Crosby's track, was leading the assault.

About that time the first of the rocket-propelled grenades whistled over our heads. RPGs were the NVA equivalent of the World War II bazooka. The third one hit the right front corner of our bunker, knocking Dillard and me off the left side of the track and into deep elephant grass. I hit the ground and rolled. Groggy from the concussion, it took me several seconds to recover. I regained my senses only to find that I was laying on top of Sergeant Major Dillard. To my immediate front, only inches away, three NVA soldiers lay crouched, their AK-47s pointed at my chest.

June 21, 1968: 2330 hours

The firing had all but stopped. All around us, in the tall elephant grass, marine grunts probed carefully. Holstrom occasionally shouted my name or the sergeant major's. I guessed the NVA holding us to be no more than eighteen or nineteen. Each wore a full uniform and a pith helmet. I saw no rank, but from their fear and age my bet was that these boys hadn't been in South Vietnam for very long. The lack of wear on their field gear reinforced my feeling.

Neither the sergeant major nor I dared whisper a sound during the whole time we were held captive. It was as if we could read each other's minds.

Finally the tension proved to be too much for one of the NVA. He shouted *"Chieu Hoi"* at the top of his lungs, the equivalent of "I surrender." Almost immediately we were encircled by marine grunts.

June 22, 1968: 0700 hours

The tracks were on their way back to the river. The first five had already gone, taking the sergeant major and Sergeant Holstrom. Chaplain Smily was still trying to get me to go, believing all the more in his ministry since the sergeant major had asked to be baptized.

I had heard of men getting religion in combat, but I had never understood how dramatic a thing it could be once it gets started. Dillard simply said he couldn't sleep after the firefight, and that he had never come that close to death before.

I asked him if he had ever got religion before. He said that he had, but never quite under these circumstances. He said all the other times he had been worried about getting kicked out of the corps for drinking too much booze. Getting religion was a way of helping him through his problems. You ought to try it sometime, he said, giving me a wink.

I thought about sharing what the sergeant major said with Chaplain Smily. Then I changed my mind. Why bring the chaplain down with my cynicism? Who was I to deny the sincerity of people's motives and actions? After all, like Holstrom said, everyone in this battalion, even that sorry mother Cheatum, we're all sitting under Jesus.

ROCKET PISTOL

"HERE'S TO LYIN', stealin', drinkin', and cheatin'! When you lie, lie to save a friend; when you steal, steal a woman's heart; when you drink, drink with me; and when you cheat, cheat death." Major Crandle drained his beer can in one gulp.

A shout went up from the rest of the lieutenants. Seeking favor from his hero, Peeples, a prematurely balding supply officer from Atlantic, Iowa, thrust another beer into Crandle's hand. Crandle accepted the beer without acknowledging the tall, thin Peeples, turning his attention instead to Mingus, the big black lieutenant from New Jersey. Crandle and Mingus were grunts, officers with infantry as a specialty, and both had served much time in the bush. The party was for Mingus, who was rotating back to the States in two days. The party was being held in Major Crandle's hooch because Crandle had been banished from the Officers' Club. Technically speaking, we were all breaking battalion rules by drinking black market Jack Daniel's whiskey and imported Beck's beer. Beck's beer, probably the best beer in the world and unobtainable through U.S. sources, had been supplied by the motor transport officer, a Jew named Kaplan, who, like the rest of us, was an outcast.

"Mingus, I bet that big black pecker of yours gets semihard

52

just countin' the minutes down,'' Crandle said, slapping Mingus on the back.

Crandle then grappled the big, two-hundred-and-thirty-pound Mingus, who had played nose guard for Brown, and tried to wrestle him to the ground. Two months earlier such behavior would have had me on my feet, seeking to calm the wrestlers. After two months' exposure to the impulse-governed, I just sat back with the rest of the outcasts and watched, amused that a major in the Marine Corps, especially a little sucker like Turkey Dick Crandle, would presume, even in jest, to mess with a killer stud like Adolf Mingus.

Killer Stud, as Mingus was nicknamed, was indeed a killer. He had been nominated for his second Silver Star and had two Purple Hearts. By my own counting, Mingus should have had five Purple Hearts and been flown out of the country long ago. His stamina and pride prevented that, however, and on April 6, 1968, he accounted for seven kills in the vicious hand-to-hand combat on Hill 112, the night elements of a main force Vietcong battalion overran Mike Company, Third Battalion, Seventh Marines. I had watched all the action from about four kilometers away and was in the relief force the next day. I had seen and heard first hand all the details from those who survived.

''Major, with all due respect, you had better knock this shit off. You're setting a bad example for all us lieutenants,'' Kaplan said, with a smirk.

Major Dick Crandle was the battalion S-2—intelligence officer—for the Third Amphibian Tractor Battalion. He was short, rugged, had a reputation for hard drinking and brawling, and in general was given to all sorts of wretched excess. He also had two Purple Hearts and was limited to where he could go in Vietnam. While he would have much preferred an assignment out in the bush, with two Purple Hearts he was locked into a staff job.

''I'm goin' to get this big sucker to the ground if it kills me!'' Crandle said, clearly unable to budge the massive Mingus.

It was amazing to me that Mingus put up with Crandle's bullshit. No one else in the battalion did. Perhaps the tolerance we saw in Mingus was due to the fact Crandle was a brother grunt in a hostile and unforgiving environment. Perhaps it was the attention Crandle gave him. Perhaps Mingus took pity on the "boy-major" who was treated differently by his brother officers who held similar rank. For Major Dick Crandle was one of the untouchables. He had been passed over twice for promotion, and there were many forms of discrimination, some subtle and some not so subtle, in this green mother called the United States Marine Corps.

Peeples was an outcast because he was the supply officer. In the Marine Corps at the time, Supply was where you put guys like Peeples. It may come as some surprise, but there were marine officers, who, in the judgment of their peers, lacked leadership. When this judgment is made at the Basic School, they make you a supply officer. At the same time they make you an outcast from the mainstream of Marine Corps business, which is infantry, armor, or artillery.

Again, at that time in the summer of 1968, in Northern I Corps, the only thing worse than a supply officer in the Marine Corps officer hierarchy was a motor transport officer. To be a supply officer, one has to be smart. If, in the judgment of your peers at the Basic School, you were dumb, they made you a motor transport officer. But there is obviously a much higher survival rate if you serve as a motor transport officer, as opposed to a grunt. It didn't take Bennie Kaplan long to figure that out. Kaplan was a very smart man who had played dumb enough in the Basic School to become a motor transport officer in Vietnam. Although Kaplan was very smart, he was also very confused. He openly wondered why he had joined the Marine Corps in the first place. Not that I didn't wonder about why I joined. I wondered about that all the time. I just kept my mouth shut. Kaplan couldn't. He had a big mouth. He didn't buy into the program. He was an outcast.

"Major, if the noise wakes up the chaplain, he's sure to tell the Buzzard in the morning," I said.

The Buzzard was Lieutenant Colonel Harkness, already selected for full colonel. Our chaplain, a Baptist do-gooder named Bingham, kissed the Buzzard's ass, and was the primary reason why Crandle had been exiled from the Officers' Club.

"The chaplain can kiss my ass! Hear that, Chaplain! Kiss my ass!" Crandle said, breathless from his effort with the immobile Mingus.

"Calm down, Major. You got to calm down, sir, or they'll write our ass up," Mingus said, softly.

Crandle flopped to the ground and lay spread-eagled on the floor. With one hand he reached up and grabbed another Beck's beer from Peeples. He poured the beer over his face.

"I do believe Beck's is the best beer in the world," Crandle said, raising his head and blinking through what remained of the foam.

"Have another, sir," I said, tossing over an ice-cold Beck's.

"Life is short and death is certain," Crandle replied.

Crandle's S-2 job involved gathering intelligence about enemy operations in the area. I always thought that being an S-2 would be a great job. One had flexibility, and, in getting around the division area, one could make a lot of contacts and meet a lot of interesting people. Turkey Dick Crandle found the job boring with two exceptions. One exception he found to boredom was the navy and army nurses stationed in Da Nang. Accordingly, most of the intelligence he gathered had to do more with the whereabouts of certain nurses than it did with threats to the Third Amphibian Tractor Battalion. The other exception to the routine was Green Beret Major "Beau Brummell" Boden from C Company, Fifth Special Forces. C Company lay to our north and Boden was the Green Beret S-2 in charge of intelligence-related activities.

Like Crandle, Boden was bored. And, like Crandle, Boden used a lot of his time to find out where all the nurses were "hiding," as he put it. Boden looked more like a pro tackle than a decorated Green Beret major. In fact, Boden was the only overweight Green Beret that I ever recall seeing. Unlike Crandle, Boden was held in high esteem by his fellow officers. I heard that his compulsive eating and drinking problems stemmed from two previous tours in Vietnam and before Vietnam, Operation White Star, in Laos, where he had been severely ill. To Dick Crandle, Boden was fit company for a marine grunt officer, better company than all the "ass-kissin' " tractor rats back in Third Amphibian Tractor Battalion.

"Who wants to make the run tonight?" Crandle asked.

There was no immediate reply from the lieutenants. Making the run had once been a wonderful respite from the day-to-day boredom of Third Amphibian Tractor Battalion. Since the advent of the Buzzard, all that had changed. While the former battalion commander had looked the other way when his officers had made the night run to Da Nang, Harkness had a different attitude toward such frivolity. That conservative attitude extended to drinking in general and, in particular, the drinking behavior of Major Dick Crandle. So it came as no surprise to me that there were no immediate takers to the night run to Da Nang.

Prior to the Harkness era, Turkey Dick Crandle had been given to drinking late into the night at the Officers' Club. On occasion Crandle was given to bullying those officers he sensed were weak or vulnerable. You were weak or vulnerable in Crandle's terms if you hadn't seen combat. If you drank a lot and sucked up to Crandle as he told his war stories, he would tolerate you. As for the other officers, it wasn't that they were afraid of Crandle, it was just that they were serious about their careers in the Marine Corps. Punching out a rummy like Dick wasn't worth risking one's career. Crandle also carried a stiletto in his boot, and who knew what a crazy would do in the heat of a brawl.

"You mean you wimps are going to let me screw all that Vietnamese pussy myself?" Crandle said with a smirk on his face, pleased with his ability to shock such greenhorns as Peeples.

"Buzzard will have our ass if we get caught, Major," I said.

"We'll tell the asshole we had to go talk to Boden. What's he going to do, call me a liar?" Crandle said, draining his Beck's.

"He'd probably send us to the bush," Kaplan said.

"And that's exactly what I want that skinny sucker to do. I want to go to the field, Kaplan. I want to go to the field and get away from all the phony bullshit. I want to go back where you can trust that your commanding officer will take care of the business of killing gooks!" Crandle said, raising his voice.

"Major. Please keep it down. We'll all be in deep shit if we're not careful," Peeples said.

"Peeples. Do you want to kiss my ass?" Crandle said, moving to within inches of the supply officer's face.

"No, sir," Peeples said, visibly shaken.

"Then get the hell out of my face. Get the hell out of this hooch unless you want to go eat some Vietnamese pussy with me. You hear?" Crandle said, in his best bullying style.

"But, sir, this is my hooch. This is where I've got my bunk," Peeples replied meekly.

At that point Crandle picked up Peeples's cot and shoved it through the screen of the hooch. He then picked up Peeples's footlocker and threw it outside. "Go sleep in the grass, Peeples. Once I went six months in the field sleepin' on the damn ground. Either come and eat Vietnamese pussy with me or sleep on the damn ground," Crandle said, having totally cowed the entire group.

There were those among our fellow officers who felt Turkey Dick Crandle's contempt for track officers and his general belligerence were simply a defense mechanism. I wondered about that. It was clear that while Dick was a rough guy who had proven on several occasions both his guts and coolness under fire, Dick was a flop with women. While Dick may have had a kind of rugged, blond good looks, when it came to women, he was just stupid. With the navy nurses his reputation preceded him. To compensate, he got pushy. When his aggressiveness failed, he would drink. When he drank, he liked to talk dirty. He especially liked to talk dirty to navy nurses.

"Mingus, let's go shock the shit out of some navy nurses. What do you say?" Crandle said, looking for support.

"I don't know, Major. If we go, it would be better to wait until the perimeter patrol goes out in about an hour," Mingus said, shrugging his shoulders.

"Don't you want to gross out some nurses? Have some goddamn laughs, for Christ's sake," Crandle said, a disgusted look on his face.

The pattern was always the same. The next morning, after whatever scene had taken place, Dick would make the rounds and apologize, blaming his belligerence on the fact that he was from Texas and part Indian. The apologies got real old, real fast, and somehow the blond blue-eyed Crandle didn't seem convincing as a Native American.

At least the Buzzard wasn't convinced. He called Dick in on the carpet on several occasions to call Dick an immature, selfish, and self-centered ingrate. Dick repented for all of a day or two, and the pattern started to repeat itself. Accordingly, after one particularly nasty night when Crandle refused to let anyone play anything but country and western music on the jukebox, which precipitated both a fistfight and the trashing of the jukebox, Dick was banned from the Officers' Club and ordered to seek counseling from the chaplain and the battalion physician.

"Major, I'll make the run with you," I said, much to the surprise of my fellow lieutenants. "But Mingus is right, sir, we'd be better off waiting till the perimeter patrol truck goes out to make the rounds. That way our jeep won't be as obvious."

"Sam, what about the gate guards?" Kaplan said, looking at me and shaking his head.

"Kaplan, don't sweat the small stuff. They won't say shit. They all love my ass," Crandle said.

That was probably very true. The troops did love his ass. They loved his irreverent attitude and his rough language. Most of all they loved the way he cut them all a lot of slack. He once drove a truckload of his men to a whorehouse and paid to get them all laid before taking them back to the field. That one escapade made him a legend in his own time within the First Marine Division.

"Well, I'll be damned! Let's go get 'em, Sam! Let's ride 'em all hard, switch around once or twice, and then put 'em to bed wet!" Crandle said, slapping me on the back and walking out the door.

"Major, what are you going to tell the sergeant at the gate? Buzzard just doesn't allow his officers to go out roaming around. It's not like it used to be, sir, with all due respect," Kaplan said, trying to present a voice of reason.

"We'll tell them we're going to see Beau Boden. It's not like I haven't thought this son of a bitch out. We're going to get a secret weapon Beau told me about," Crandle said, in a kind of huff.

"Secret weapon?" Kaplan said, eyebrows raised.

"That's right. Secret weapon. Beau's got him a couple of these new rocket pistols. And he said if I'd come over for a visit, he'd loan me one," Crandle said.

"Rocket pistol?" I said.

"Damn straight! Rocket pistol," Crandle said.

June 25, 1968: 2100 hours

The South China Sea lay calm, waves barely lapping the sandy shore. A full moon was rising. Tonight would be a good night to make a run, I thought to myself.

"Sucker's crazy," Mingus said.

"That's a big affirmative," I said.

"You know that we're going to have to stay out all night," Mingus said.

"Oh, absolutely. Once you slip out, you're home free. But don't come back until morning," I said.

"How many of these runs have you made?" Mingus asked.

"Who knows? Fifteen. Maybe twenty."

"And you never got caught?" Mingus asked.

"Well, that depends on who or what defines the word 'caught.' If you mean did the guards ever stop me slipping back in before daylight, the answer is yes. But they were so high on grass that they were just as glad as I was to cool it. Another time I had a date with this NSA nurse. It was all arranged. By the time Kaplan and I slipped out of here and got up to NSA, Crandle had beat me to her. Every time I called her after that, it seemed she had a date with some officer in this battalion. Some captain or major had already hit on her. From what I understand, she finally asked for a transfer just to get away from the officers of the Third Amphibian Tractor Battalion. So in a way I got caught by my fellow officers."

"And the commanding officer never made a stink?" Mingus asked.

"Hell no. Old Eight Ball, as we called him, was right in there with us. There were many nights he was slipping out the gate before Crandle, and that was hard to do. It got so bad that Eight Ball was catching his officers going out in broad daylight," I said.

"No shit."

"That's a big affirmative. Those were the good old days, until Crandle rolled a jeep one night. At the time I was the motor transport officer. I was acting for Kaplan who was on R & R. It was Kaplan's jeep that got rolled. Kaplan was pissed when he came back from R & R. He even had to do the investigation," I said with a laugh.

"And nothing happened to Crandle?"

"Hell no! At the time he was on a skivvy-girl run, bringing back some girls from the ville. The only people that got screwed real bad over that incident were some Vietnamese whores," I said.

"Lord have mercy, and me sweatin' my dumb ass out in the bush!"

"For sure. But don't feel bad, Mingus, somebody is better off for having you out there as an officer leading them. You saved lives, big guy. That's what its all about," I said, trying to make Mingus feel better.

"I don't know, man. I just don't know," Mingus said, gazing out at the South China Sea.

A light breeze was blowing through the clumps of cedars that bordered the shore. The breeze was coming off the land. It was that point when the day was finally giving way to all that which was the night. Thanks to the rising full moon, our ride up the beach to the Green Beret camp would be illuminated. The quick ride up the hard-packed sand would be no sweat.

"It's good to see you, Sam. I'm glad that you were able to make it back to battalion before I rotated home," Mingus said.

"Yeah, that worked out okay," I said.

Mingus and I had known each other back in Basic School, the finishing school each new marine lieutenant must endure before being assigned out into the Fleet Marine Force.

"But I don't know if I want to go tonight," Mingus said.

"What do you mean?" I asked.

"I mean I don't want to make the run," Mingus said.

"What the hell?"

The big guy sat down on the porch of the hooch. He picked up a stick and started to draw in the sand, aimless drawings with no recognizable shape.

"What's the matter?" I asked, sitting down beside him.

"You're gonna laugh at me, Sam, but the reason I'm not goin' with you is my mama," Mingus said.

"Your mama!"

"That's right. My mama. My sweet mama back in Sugar Creek," Mingus said, looking up at the moon.

"Hey, dude. That's okay. I'll tell Crandle you're not feeling good," I said.

"No. Tell him the truth. Tell him I don't want to go because I don't think that it's the right conduct for an officer, to go get laid in the ville."

"Say again." I was starting to get irritated.

"Don't get me wrong, Sam. I don't want to stand in judgment of anyone. Goin' on the run is just not for me."

"Well, you are standing in judgment," I added.

"Maybe so. Look, when I left home my mama asked me to do one thing, and that was to conduct myself in such a way that I would bring credit on the family," Mingus said.

"Sounds like a solid, middle-class value to me," I said with a smirk.

"Who the hell you think you are, puttin' down my mama?" Mingus shouted, startling me.

Mingus stood up and walked away toward the beach. I got up and followed. Mingus stopped under one of the cedars, looking out toward the South China Sea. A bright full moon stared back.

"I'm sorry, Mingus, I'm just a wise guy whose mockingbird mouth gets in the way of his hummingbird ass," I said.

"Don't tell Crandle anythin'. Just let me talk to you for a minute. I need somebody to listen to me just for a time," Mingus said, eyes watering.

"What's going down here?" I asked, wondering if Mingus had too much to drink.

"I've been faithful," Mingus said.

"What?"

"I've been faithful to my rank. I've been faithful to whatever cause we're here for," Mingus said, a single tear running down his cheek.

"That's true," I said.

"Damn straight it's true. And there were times, Sam, when some of the black folks looked at me with hate in their eyes," Mingus said.

"Hate?"

"Hate. Hate, it is, baby. Hate for the Uncle Tom mother who thinks he's better than they. That's hate, baby," Mingus said.

"Shit. I would have never thought."

"Some of those brothers hate me as much as they hate Kaplan, and believe me, they hate Kaplan," Mingus said.

"You can't make everyone happy, Mingus! Some . . . many of the men we have to lead are shitbirds," I said.

"Yeah, and some of them are the finest men in the world," Mingus said.

"You can't be all things to all people," I said.

"You know they hate me because they think that I think I'm better. But I don't think I'm better. They hate Kaplan because he thinks he's smarter and better,'' Mingus said, a kind of grin appearing on his face.

We were waiting for Kaplan and Crandle to arrive with the jeep. In spite of his better judgment Kaplan had decided to come along to look after his jeep.

''Hey, they don't hate me, do they? I get along with all the black brothers,'' I said.

''They don't hate you, Sam, they have a contempt for you,'' Mingus said.

''Say again?'' I was startled.

''You bend the rules as you see fit. They know that. There's nothin' honorable about you, Sam. To other officers you're an outcast. To the black brothers you're someone who will bend the rules. You don't bring credit on the officer corps. You don't observe the officers' code. You barely live up to the basic requirements for keepin' your appearance in order,'' Mingus said, looking up at the moon.

At first I felt anger. That emotion passed quickly. Then I felt pity. Pity for Mingus who was caught. Pity for myself because there was more than a grain of truth in what he said.

''I feel sorry for you if you believe all that, Mingus. You've been a good friend to me, and in a way—your way—I'm sure that you feel that your telling me the truth is part of being a friend. You're a good person. Killer Stud, you're a noble person, but right now you're upset, you're going back to the world. If the brothers have contempt for me, I'm sorry. That's the way it is, I guess,'' I said, not knowing what else to say.

''They despise you and they despise me. They would kill Kaplan and some of the others if they had a chance,'' Mingus said, now speaking very softly.

''Why? Why would they kill Kaplan?'' I asked.

''He's worthless as far as they're concerned. Kaplan doesn't care for them and they know it,'' Mingus said.

''Why wouldn't they kill me?''

''Who knows, maybe they would. You are worth somethin' to them I suppose. You're a kind of alternative officer. You may not live by the officers' code, and you may not be a credit to the officer corps, but you get people to do the right things, even when you're not there. Also, technically you've got your shit together. Everyone knows that. You've proved that in the field time and again, and people respect you for that know-how. And you've got guts. Everyone knows that.'' Mingus said, speaking very slowly.

"Well, it's important to know your strengths," I said with a smirk.

"You don't give a damn about what I said, do you?" Mingus said.

"Some of it I do. I just can't sort all this stuff out, Mingus. It's too hard to stay alive the way it is. If some of the brothers have a contempt for me, I need to know that. That knowledge might save my ass in a tight. But this stuff is nothing new to me. If you can't be specific about who despises me and why, it's all a bunch of generality. It's all bullshit.''

"Like this war," Mingus said.

"Sure, why not, like this war. What's so damn honorable about this war?'' I said.

"Some of the men who are fighting it.''

June 25, 1968: 2115 hours

Crandle, Kaplan, and I were through the gate and down the beach without a problem. Crandle told the guard we were running up to C Company, Fifth Special Forces, to see Major Boden, which was certainly part of the truth.

At about fifty miles an hour we passed Xom Son Tui, the little fishing village that lay between our camp and C Company. Kaplan was driving. That made me feel secure. The beach sand at the water's edge was hard packed and gleamed in the moonlight. Kaplan leaned forward over the steering wheel as he drove, deep in concentration. I was surprised that Kaplan had decided to come with us. I was equally surprised that Mingus, Crandle's fellow grunt, had decided not to come with us. I felt that his mama would be happy if she knew the circumstances.

I wondered about what Mingus had said as we drove down the beach. What Mingus called bending the rules, I called flexibility. What Mingus called infidelity to the officers' code, I called keeping my sanity. It was true that I played by many of my own rules. I called that common sense and good judgment. Maybe playing by my own rules made me an outcast, whatever that was, in the eyes of some of my fellow officers. But getting things done and the respect that I had from the troops was the effect of common sense and good judgment. To my mind that brought more credit to the officers' code than polished boots and brass.

I looked out into the South China Sea. Far out on the horizon the lanterns from the fishing junks sparkled like a string of carnival lights. To our immediate front a phosphorescence glimmered in the slowly receding water. It was a beautiful night to be alive. The full moon hanging over the sea was a cool blue color. It was glorious.

June 25, 1968: 2200 hours

Major Beau Boden held the rocket pistol to the light, looking down the barrel. From where I sat, the rocket pistol looked like a slim .45. Crandle was all smiles, clearly excited by the prospect of being one of the few chosen to field-test the weapon.

I was holding one of the little rockets in my hand. It was about the size of a .45 round, a smooth copper jacket with a small red hole at the back end. The principle of the rocket pistol was simple. A firing pin struck the small red hole, igniting the rocket propellant. The projectile gained velocity very quickly, but without a sound, exiting the gun barrel with barely a whisper; hence the value of the rocket pistol. While the rocket pistol was an experimental weapon that was very expensive to make and would probably never see widespread use, it was ideal for certain types of scouting and patrol activity where silence was crucial. Clearly it had captured Major Crandle's imagination. I flipped the little rocket back to Crandle. He smiled that shit-eating grin of his.

"I'm in love. I'm in love with both the idea and the chance to be a part of the testing. Hot damn, I feel that I'm making a contribution to something important again," Major Crandle said, putting his shoulders back and swallowing a shot of Jack Daniel's.

"You keep it for a few weeks. Use it as you wish. Shoot somebody with it if you can. I want a real field test," Boden said, grinning.

Beau Boden and Dick Crandle were from the same part of Texas. Their association went back a long way, even though they had served in separate branches of the armed forces. It seemed that their paths had crossed several times since boyhood: at Fort Bragg, when Crandle went to jump school; in Washington, when both men were assigned to the Pentagon; and in Vietnam, on a previous tour, during which both men served as advisers. The two men were bound together by shared experiences and common backgrounds.

"Hey, you ready for a little excitement, Dick?" Boden said, slapping him on the shoulder.

"What do you got in mind, Beau?" Crandle said, loading the rocket pistol.

"Let's head over to NSA and see them navy nurses. Maybe play a bit of that Merle Haggard they got on the jukebox," Boden said.

"Sounds like a plan," Crandle said, slipping the loaded rocket pistol into his shoulder holster.

"If I disappear on you, don't worry about me," Boden said.

"I'll just say the full moon made you crazy, Beau, just like it does to me every time I stare at it." Crandle gave a wink.

June 25, 1968: 2230 hours

I was fired up. We were sitting in the Naval Support Activity Officers' Club scoping out the area. This club was, in my opinion, the best hunting ground in Da Nang. NSA was close enough into Da Nang to be safe, yet far enough away from Division Headquarters so that none of the top brass came by to cramp your style. More importantly, NSA was staffed by doctors and nurses in the naval service who didn't stand on a lot of military protocol. They worked hard and they played hard, and everything in their club was first class. In spite of regulations to the contrary, the club often stayed open all night. Nurses and doctors would come in off their shifts in the middle of the night, their faces drained from the terrible stress of the operating rooms, to have a few drinks before hitting the sack. They all drank. It was a matter of burying their despair in alcohol and sex, and no one stood on ceremony. I once found a nurse drinking by herself at two in the morning. She picked me up and we skipped back to her quarters. Like I said, I was fired up.

It had taken me quite awhile to get back to NSA. I had been out in the field and had been rotated back to battalion to pull duty as pay officer for my company. Most officers hated being pay officer. I liked the duty because it gave me a chance to get back to NSA. However, I would have to be careful. My plan was a simple one. Find one of my former "friends," preferably a little redhead from Pella, Iowa, named Micky, if she was still around, and ditch Turkey Dick Crandle. As far as I was concerned, I was doing my own thing as soon as I got the lay of the terrain.

In the time that I had been gone, some changes had been made. There were now three places a person could drink. There was the patio, open to the night air and fragrant with a variety of blooming flowers, very pleasant and very relaxing. There was the old bar with its dance floor and jukebox, the jukebox having a wide variety of tunes ranging from country and western to rhythm and blues. The third place was new and very promising. It was a room of about twenty dark wooden booths, each shielded from the other by a high wooden partition, giving the occupants much privacy. The new room had an Oriental motif and was separated from the old bar by a beaded curtain. I began to prowl the area.

Much to my dismay, however, before I could slip through the beaded curtain and disappear, Kaplan grabbed a table in the old bar and ordered a round, yelling at me to sit down. Crandle was already grabbing at the ass of some passing nurse. Boden let out a kind of guffaw. I was afraid to acknowledge Kaplan lest I be identified with the individuals responsible for the loud, coarse outbursts already drawing the attention of the people throughout the bar. Guilt by association was my fear.

"Hey, Sam, come on and sit down. What are you, too good for us?" Crandle yelled.

"No way, sir, I was just looking for an old friend," I said, trying to remain inconspicuous.

"Don't back out on me now, like Mingus did. Don't let me down. I need you. I've been staring at the full moon and I feel crazy."

"Mingus didn't let you down, sir, he just wasn't feeling himself," I said, looking out through the window screens at the full moon.

"Beau, I don't know who to trust anymore, goddamn it! I don't know who to trust," Crandle said.

A rugged young sailor who was waiting tables brought the drinks. He set them down, four shots of Jack Daniel's and four bottles of ice-cold Budweiser. Budweiser was Boden's favorite beer.

"What happened to all your Vietnamese waitresses?" Boden asked.

"New commanding officer won't bend the rules. He says no more Vietnamese on base after 1800 hours," the sailor said.

"I'll be doggone! I was going to look for Lulu to get a blow job. What am I going to do now, Dick?" Boden said, an anguished look on his face.

"This new commanding officer runs a tight ship, Major. Those old days are gone. There's even talk of closing the club at 2400 hours," the sailor added.

"Where does he expect us to go to get a damn drink in the middle of the night? Hell, all Da Nang's off-limits now. You folks got the only good country and western jukebox between here and Saigon," Boden added, a worried look on his face.

"I'll be damned! First they get rid of the whores, then they crack down on the hours a man can get a drink. Damn, Dick, the war don't have no hours, do it?" Boden said, a smirk on his face.

A large black cat appeared at the edge of the window. It sat on the windowsill, staring at our table. I felt a chill, as if the arrival of the cat had brought another presence to our immediate area.

"Can't trust anyone anymore," Crandle said, staring at the cat.

"That's for sure," Kaplan added.

"What's troubling you, Kaplan?" I asked.

"Some of the men got busted today down in the motor pool," Kaplan said.

"Busted for what?" I asked, staring back at the cat.

"Grass," Kaplan said.

"Smoking or dealing," I asked, flipping a paper wad at the cat.

"Dealing," Kaplan said, rolling his eyes.

"Who busted them?" I asked, curious.

"I did," Kaplan said, looking into his drink.

"What the hell did you do that for? Who are you trying to impress?" I said, just missing the elusive cat with a beer can.

"Things were getting out of hand. One of the new black dudes was challenging my authority. He was openly dealing out of the motor pool. There was something almost defiant about what he was doing. Besides, I had no choice in the matter, the Buzzard had found out. He was on my case to do something," Kaplan said, obviously upset.

"Now you got to earn your pay, Kaplan. Be careful, though. Sons of bitches will turn on you," Crandle said, tossing his beer can at the cat.

"I wish Mingus and Peeples had come with us," Kaplan said.

"Why?" I asked, looking for the cat's whereabouts.

"To get out of the hooch," Kaplan said.

"Why would they want to get out of the hooch?" I asked.

"I found a frag grenade and a warning note on my bunk when I got back from dinner," Kaplan said.

"What did the note say?" I asked.

"It was a warning to me that I should lighten up," Kaplan said.

"Well, you best back off. You can't fight your own troops," I said.

"Too late, Sam. Besides, I couldn't do that. I won't be intimidated," Kaplan said.

"Wait a minute, is this the same Kaplan that I've known the last few months? What's going on here?" I asked, surprised by Kaplan's sudden moral certitude, wondering if the full moon had touched Kaplan.

"Peeples agrees with me. We have the same problem. We have to do something to gain control of the situation."

For a brief moment the cat appeared. Then he was gone.

"Peeples said that? Well, son of a bitch, good for him. Sucker's got some balls. And good for you, Kaplan, you slippery little Jew. I want to buy you a drink. I always knew you had guts!" Crandle yelled.

The word Jew drew a sudden silence from the crowd in the bar. A tall, distinguished-looking man rose from a table near us. He was wearing the white coat of a physician and as he approached our table he had a troubled look on his face.

"Excuse me. I'm Doctor Stein, and I find both your behavior and your language offensive. While in this club, it is incumbent upon all officers to model positive behavior and refrain from comments that have racial overtones. Please conduct yourselves accordingly. Otherwise I will have to ask you to leave," Stein said.

"Yes, sir," Kaplan and I said in unison; Boden and Crandle were too surprised to say anything.

The sailor who waited on us stood by the table. Doctor Stein nodded and then turned, saying nothing else.

"Who the hell was that?" Crandle asked the sailor.

"That was the new commanding officer, Doctor Stein," the sailor said.

"I'll put some tokens in the jukebox. Play "White Line Fever" by Merle Haggard," Boden said, rising and heading off to the jukebox.

"Major, let's cool it for a while, okay?" I said.

Crandle nodded in reply. At that point I noticed Micky coming into the bar. She saw me and waved. I waved back and got up from the table.

"I'll be right back," I said, making my move, having no intention whatsoever of returning, wondering if the full moon would make me crazy.

June 25, 1968: 2300 hours

The attraction between Micky Van Der Molen, and me was not something that had been instantaneous or even electric. We had met some three months before in a situation where all that had been required was some attraction, mutual openness, and a desire for intimacy. The fact that we were both from Iowa had given her great comfort and had contributed in many ways, I think, to our reaching both acceptance and the desire to please each other. I could make her laugh. That was very important. Our making love together, in spite of all the complications, just seemed to happen, no strings attached.

While Micky was glad to see me, she was in no mood to get it on. In the month that had passed since I had last seen her, she had lost weight. There were dark circles under her eyes and it seemed that when she spoke I could hardly hear her. She held my hand tightly, smoking one cigarette after the other with her other hand, her fingers trembling ever so slightly.

"It's been terrible. We had two major combat operations kick off in the last two weeks. This hospital is overflowing with the dead and dying. I haven't been able to get any sleep in a week. I keep waking up with these nightmares. It's crazy. I pop some pills and nod off for a couple hours. Then suddenly I'm wide awake, wired for some trip I can't seem to come back from," Micky said.

"Pills don't help?"

"Not that much. I've got some infection on top of that. You wouldn't want to see me, Sam, I'm a mess. I'm stressed. I've lost so much weight, I'm beginning to lose my tits," she said, laughing.

"Oh no, not those great tits!"

"Ah. They'll be okay. Once I get out of this filthy place and back to the rolling green hills of Pella, Iowa." She smiled.

"You and Peeples ought to get together. That's all he talks about, going back to Atlantic to raise soybeans," I said.

"That skinny nerd around?" she said with a grin.

"He's such a silly shit you can't help but like him."

"How did he ever get to be a marine officer?"

"He can run forever. He's a track jock. The Marine Corps likes guys who are skinny and can run forever. Problem is, skinny guys like that are no good in bar fights or hand-to-hand combat. All you got to do is kick their legs out from under them," I said in my best smart-ass style.

"Have you ever killed anyone in hand-to-hand combat?" she asked out of the blue.

"No."

"What about that time you were overrun on Hill 112? Tell me about that hill. Did you know that the Seventh Marines are taking it again? Some of the men in my ward keep talking about it," she said, desperate for some understanding of the big picture that I was unable to give her.

For a moment I thought I saw the cat at the window. I wasn't sure.

"Let's forget about that," I said, thinking of how much I hated cats.

"Let's move out to the patio. I want to smell the flowers," she said.

We left the new Oriental room for the patio. The patio was empty but for Kaplan and Crandle. Boden had disappeared.

"Hey, Sam, why don't you and the lady join us?" Crandle said.

The evening was cool and the morning glory–like flowers made the air fragrant. Micky and I joined Crandle and Kaplan, all of us having met on several previous occasions. Micky knew what to expect, I thought, and if Crandle got too obnoxious, we would just go somewhere else.

"Hi, Micky, did you miss me?" Crandle said, smiling.

"You know how I feel about those boys from Texas," Micky said, winking at Crandle.

"Sam, you're a lucky man, you know that. Prettiest little gal in NSA and she takes a shine to you," Crandle said, putting his feet up on the table.

"Yes, sir, I'm very lucky," I said, putting my arm around Micky.

"Micky, honey, don't you trust those boys from Texas?" Crandle said, affectionately rubbing his new rocket pistol.

"Sam and I are from Iowa, Major. We seem to understand each other. Something about Sam I trust."

"You and Sam got the same values. You trust each other like Beau and I trust each other," Crandle said.

"What happens if you don't have the same values, Major?" Kaplan asked.

"Don't get smart on me now, Kaplan," Crandle said.

"How about me and you, sir?" Kaplan asked, winking at me.

"Kaplan, I'm trying to talk to the lady and you keep distracting me. It's like this. Without the same values, you need indicators!"

"Indicators?" Kaplan said, boring in.

"You got to go through some shit together, Kaplan. You got to build that mutual respect," Crandle said, pointing the rocket pistol at the moon.

"Do you trust me, Major?" Kaplan said.

"Time was I didn't even like you. Tonight I let you drive, so I guess I respect you. But trust you?—I don't trust very many

anymore, Kaplan. Although I got to say I think that you're doin'
the right thing by bustin' that dope ring down in the motor pool.
Got to hand it to Peeples if he's backin' you. I didn't think
Peeples had it in him," Crandle said.

"Trust begets trust," Kaplan said.

"That's true, Kaplan. That's true until you've been betrayed," Crandle said, leaning forward.

"And you've been betrayed?" Micky said, suddenly into the
conversation.

"Yes, ma'am, I feel that I've been betrayed," Crandle said,
sighting down the bore of his rocket pistol.

"How were you betrayed, Major?" Micky said, her fingers
trembling.

"I was betrayed by my own stupidity. And I was blackballed," Crandle said, his voice shaking.

"Blackballed for what?" Micky asked. She lit a cigarette and
gave it to Crandle.

Crandle took the cigarette. He then leaned forward and took
Micky's hand. Crandle let out a deep breath and shook his head.

"Micky, honey, you look like you had a hard time these last
few days. Well, don't despair, honey, cause you still got your
pride. The way I feel, I should have been killed last time I was
in the field," Crandle said in a sober voice.

"Major, why?" Micky asked.

"I feel, I know that I should have probably taken my own life
for what I brought upon someone else that I dearly loved,"
Crandle said, holding both of Micky's hands in his own.

I looked over at Kaplan and raised my eyebrows. Kaplan
looked back at me and shrugged his shoulders. This kind of
behavior and talk was out of character for Turkey Dick Crandle

"What happened?" Micky said, her voice now trembling.

"I had an affair with another officer's wife while he was in
Nam. When he got word of it, he started doin' stupid things.
Some say he killed himself rather than come back to the States.
He was my friend and I snaked his wife. He was my brother
officer and I was unfaithful to him and my own code. I dishon-
ored him, his lady, and myself," Crandle said in a voice that
was barely above a whisper.

"There was nothing you could do?" Micky asked.

"No. I let it happen. Now I pay the price. Micky, honey, don't ever give up your pride. Do what's right," Crandle said.

It has always amazed me what the combination of fatigue and liquor can bring out in people in the wee hours of the morning. The last thing I wanted to hear was Crandle's confession. I wanted to give Micky my own form of comfort. She was upset and clearly not herself. Where Crandle's bullshit would take us was anyone's guess.

At that moment the black cat appeared on the wall that surrounded the patio. The cat settled itself on the wall and peered down at us, its large yellow eyes glowing. It was as if there were suddenly another presence among us. At the sight of the cat Micky jerked back.

"Oh, God, there it is," she said.

"Just a cat, Micky. No big deal," I said, bewildered by Micky's sudden reaction.

"No, Sam, that's not just a cat. We've been trying to kill that cat for days. I saw it under a table in the morgue, licking human blood. I see it slipping here and there in my dreams, drinking my blood. No one can seem to catch it. The sailors have even shot at it," Micky said.

"Everyone knows that sailors can't hit shit," Crandle said with a smile.

The rocket pistol uttered a barely audible whisper. A thin stream of smoke shot up at the wall and knocked the cat beyond our view. Crandle was up and over the patio wall after the cat.

"Holy shit!" Kaplan said.

I ran to the wall and pulled myself over. There, in the moonlight, Dick Crandle was holding the dead cat by its tail.

"Blame it on the full moon, Sam. This damn rocket pistol is something. But be quiet, Sam. I don't want anybody to catch me with this thing. I want to get the body back to Beau. He'll get a kick out of this! Son of a bitch!" Crandle said, grinning from ear to ear.

I looked back down at Micky. She was shaking her head, amazed. Kaplan stood beside her saying nothing, his mouth just hanging open. Overhead the full moon stared back at me like a single blue, violent eye.

GO NOI ISLAND

June 26, 1968: 0800 hours

THE WORD HAD come down at 0600 hours, and dust hung in the air over Hill 10 as two hundred–plus marines hurried about to pack their gear. No drill, this was for real. Ten twenty-five-ton amphibian tractors churned up from the tractor park, their driver revving the 810-horsepower V-12 Continental engines to gain speed as they climbed the grade to our assembly point. The word was that this was to be a short operation and that we were going to Go Noi Island. For sure, Go Noi was for real.

"Go Noi Island! That's decent! We'll see some action most ricky-tick, maybe get some kills. The grunts say Go Noi is high-octave evil and most bad!" Crosby said, pulling a red bandanna over his head.

I was glad to see that Crosby was getting high on all the action. Crosby seemed to be everywhere getting things prepared. For a few days his normally exuberant self, so full of high spirits and life, had been restrained and reflective as he tried to give some meaning to those we had lost during the last month. Now he was returning to the old Crosby that we once knew, a Crosby that was both emotionally explosive and an exhibitionist. My profound hope was that this latest shot of religion would have enough of an effect to keep him away from dope.

74

"Hey, dude. Maybe that's decent to you, but I'm too short for this shit!" Mother Africa said, tossing me my flak jacket.

Captain Lowy, who was waiting to board my track, just smiled. Warrant Officer Junge, Lowy's assistant, frowned and gave me one of those all-knowing glances. I ignored the whole thing, putting on my flak jacket and mounting the lead track, Zero Deuce.

No sooner had I returned from my home battalion, Third Amphibian Tractors, than I was greeted by Lowy and Junge. Both men had been working with some new program out of Da Nang. Their job was to link up with various line battalions in the area with respect to certain counterintelligence matters. It was said that they worked for the province senior adviser, no one knew for sure what the proper title was. The province senior adviser advised the province chief. He also had district senior advisers working for him at the district level. Lowy had said that he was heading up a special task group for the province senior adviser. Lukavitch informed me that Lowy really ran things for the province senior adviser, who preferred to keep in the background. The district advisers were left to do their own thing, Lowy picking up the "special projects."

It was Lowy who had first given me the word on my platoon's mission. That mission was to move Lima Company, Third Battalion, Seventh Marines, down Route 4 into a blocking position just below Hill 55. In the last day or so a situation had developed where the Seventh Marines and the First Marines had been directed to mount out a sweep in the Dodge City area north of Go Noi Island. As Lowy explained it, a large number of NVA had moved into the area. Division was now trying to capitalize on the opportunity at hand.

"Yeah, that's a big affirmative, Africa. Go Noi is most evil," Crosby said, pulling his track next to mine, the engine throbbing at low idle, making the very ground shake.

"That island ain't evil, dude! It's the little folk on it that make it evil. That island's just a piece of ground!" Africa yelled back over the hum of the engines.

Sergeant Holstrom boarded Crosby's track along with half a platoon of grunts. Lowy, Junge, and more grunts joined Africa and me on Zero Deuce. Africa would drive Zero Deuce as the lead vehicle. Crosby and Sergeant Holstrom, my platoon sergeant, would run last in line.

"You better chill out, Crosby. In about five you're going to be eatin' my dust," Africa yelled over to Crosby.

There was a healthy rivalry between Africa and Crosby. Both men were corporals and very salty. They took pleasure in ragging each other and, at times, Sergeant Holstrom.

Sergeant Holstrom had been preoccupied lately. Someone or something had a hold on his thoughts. He had grown very quiet and spent most of his free time reading his copy of the New Testament.

"What's the Sky Pilot say about evil, Holstrom?" Crosby yelled, still teasing.

"It's all in the Book of Job. The world contains not only good but evil. He judged it better to bring greater good to pass out of evil," Holstrom said, quoting scripture.

"Say what?" Africa yelled back even though the tracks were but three feet apart.

"The presence of evil enhances the good that exists!" Holstrom yelled back, leaning forward to make his point.

Lowy lit a smoke and smiled, obviously amused by the conversation. Lowy winked at me. Junge was still frowning. The last elements of Lima Company were moving down from Hill 10 to board our tracks.

"Man, that's cold!" Africa said, shaking his head.

"The ways of the Sky Pilot are often incomprehensible to man! Isn't that right, Holstrom?" Crosby was still taunting Mother Africa.

"That's a big affirmative. The problem of evil is a difficulty only to our finite minds, not to that of the Lord," Holstrom said, again leaning forward for emphasis.

"Holstrom, I do believe that you are stone serious. Here I am a short-timer and not only do I got to go down to Go Noi Island, I got to listen to this rap. How about it, Lieutenant, when are they goin' to cut us all a little slack?" Africa said, laughing.

"Africa, the Lord is both omnipotent and benevolent, and he's looking after you!" Holstrom said, still leaning forward.

"Shit. Short as I am, the only thing looking after this nigger is cold steel and my .50 cal. Who are you trying to shit?" Africa said with a tone of contempt.

The battalion commander of 3/7, Lieutenant Colonel Cheatum, sped by in a jeep. Lowy waved. Most of Lima Company had boarded the tracks. Junge was still frowning.

"Omnipotent and benevolent!" Holstrom repeated.

"Hey, wait a minute, Holstrom. I got one for you. If the Sky Pilot is so all powerful, say why doesn't he abolish evil?" Africa said, beaming.

"Because our faith needs testing," Holstrom said without hesitation.

"Then, hey, man, he's not benevolent. For he's responsible for the existence of evil just like he's responsible for my black ass and everything else. Therefore, he ain't benevolent, man. Shit! Short-timer that I am and he's sending me to Go Noi! Is that my reward? What the hell did I do?" Africa said with a smirk, pleased with his logic.

"I don't question divine prerogatives," Holstrom said, sitting back.

"Say what!" Africa yelled, still smiling.

"It's your payback man! You got to go to Go Noi because of your payback, and we all know that payback is a mother, Africa," Crosby said laughing.

For a moment Sergeant Holstrom said nothing. He was still serious, and he looked troubled.

"Maybe you will grasp what is best after you have passed through Go Noi. Maybe when you pass out of that evil, you will know the significance of the Lord. I will say a prayer for you, Africa," Holstrom said, putting on his communications helmet and pulling away as if what he had to say was the last word.

"Shit! I am sorry, Holstrom. You are truly a mystery to my finite mind!" Africa said, revving the engine of Zero Deuce.

We all laughed at that, even Gunner Junge, and over the engine noise I could still hear Africa laughing as he drove out onto Liberty Road, his Afro hanging out from beneath the edges of his communications helmet.

Junge turned to me and winked. There was something about Junge I could feel, a kind of presence, something threatening, almost sinister. It seemed to me that Junge was a person capable of doing great harm. Lukavitch said that he had a reputation among both the grunt officers and the district advisers as someone not to be messed with. He was devoted to Captain Lowy,

and, while the senior province adviser was someone who had
enormous power and latitude to do what he wanted, Lukavitch
claimed that this mysterious province senior adviser did nothing
without consulting Junge. Junge looked at me and smiled. It
was as if he knew some secret that he was keeping to himself.
I could see it in his eyes.

June 26, 1968: 0930 hours

We headed south on Liberty Road. The waning moon hung in
the sky until almost mid-morning. It was as if the pale, elusive
moon were marking our way, slowly dissolving into nothingness
as we headed toward our destination.

Liberty Road bustled with all kinds of traffic. Convoys from
Eleventh Motors passed by us on the left. Motor scooters and
overcrowded buses wove in and out of gaps between our tracks,
taking the lives of their passengers for granted as they passed us
recklessly. At one point a dusty, banged-up black Citroën full
of whores careened by us, its occupants waving and smiling.
"C'est très mauvais, mon cher!" one of the ladies shouted. I
couldn't tell if her comment was directed at me or Gunner Junge.

At Hill 37 two tanks from Bravo Company, First Tanks, joined
our column. The tanks took the lead as we moved east onto
Route 4. The second lieutenant in charge of the tanks impressed
me as a jingle-butt. I was grateful, however, that his vehicle and
not my own had taken the lead. Route 4 was notorious for mines.

June 26, 1968: 1000 hours

For some reason it became necessary to stop at a point on the
map called Giao Ai. If Giao Ai had once been a village, there
was nothing to show for it now. Apparently Giao Ai marked the
boundary between Dai Loc and Dien Ban districts. North of
Route 4 the ruins of a pagoda were shaded by a tall row of
mature bamboo. We pulled our tracks up under the shade of the
bamboo hedge and waited for further orders.

While Captain Lowy and the others left the tracks to relieve themselves, I monitored the radio. Battalion directed the grunts from Lima Company to disembark from the tracks and move into blocking positions along Route 4. My tracks were to wait at Giao Ai.

There was a nice breeze. Under the shade of the bamboo it was comparatively cool. I was grateful for that coolness as I watched the grunts file off into the heat of the day. Gunner Junge offered me a cigarette. It was a Gauloise, very strong. I declined.

"Do you believe in evil, Lieutenant?" Junge said with a smile. He was obviously referring to the earlier exchange between Africa and Crosby.

Crosby sat on the front of Zero Deuce. He had written "Cosby for President" on his helmet. Africa was putting the finishing touches on the back of his flak jacket. It read "GO NOI ISLAND may be MOST EVIL but MOTHER AFRICA is ALL BAD!"

"I believe in pleasure. I don't know if I understand what evil is," I said.

"Do you think killing is evil?" Junge said.

I had been warned that Gunner Junge was different. Junge had a reputation for being squared away. He drank very little and didn't screw around with the Vietnamese women. But at times he was hard to figure out. He asked a lot of questions. That made me nervous. The troops thought he was a little goofy. Of course, anyone who stayed in his business for any length of time was bound to be a little strange.

"Who knows? Killing can be right or wrong depending upon the circumstances, I suppose."

"You mean that in some cases killing is justified," Junge said.

"Sure," I replied, wondering where the conversation was going.

"It's the old ends justify the means," Junge said glibly, blowing smoke into the air.

"I don't follow." I sat up to give Gunner Junge my full attention.

"Ending this war while still meeting our objectives, that's the end we all seek. Don't you agree?" Junge asked.

Two choppers flew by. Seen through the overhanging bamboo, they looked like huge, cruel and abstracted dragonflies.

"Sure," I said.

"Then the right means to winning is to kill the enemy?"
Junge said.

"You ask a lot of questions, Gunner." Gunner was a little off
center.

"Sorry, Lieutenant, I like to know about the people that I
work with."

"A lot of this is self-evident, isn't it?" I asked.

"No. I don't think so anymore. Means and ends can become
relative and ambiguous as the experience becomes more complex."

"What are you driving at?" I asked, unclear as to what was
happening.

"Our men don't know what to believe. For example, many
call this a 'bad' war. Do you think that this is a bad war?"
Junge asked.

"I don't know. I guess I believe in what we're fighting for.
Certainly I believe that we need to allow the South Vietnamese
to have the chance to decide for themselves how they are to be
governed," I said, moving closer to Gunner Junge.

"Ah, then you view that particular end that we seek in this
war as good?" Junge asked, putting his cigarette out.

"Yes, I do," I replied, now drawn into the conversation.

"Then perhaps Go Noi is a means to further that end. Right?
I mean to look at things objectively. Don't you?" Junge said.

"I suppose," I said, slowly.

"You suppose. Don't you know what you believe, Lieutenant? If this Go Noi Island operation furthers our purpose, then
it is not an evil place; rather, it's a means to an end. Go Noi is
just a piece of ground. I worry about your men's perceptions,
especially Africa," Junge said.

Either Gunner Junge was a bright and philosophical dude or
he was a flake. Just then I was undecided. He certainly kept one
on his toes. The conversation had begun to fascinate me.

"Like I said, Gunner, I believe in pleasure. I don't think
going to Go Noi is going to bring anyone any pleasure, and as
for Africa, he's solid. Don't let his Afro hairdo fool you," I
said.

"What if you get some kills? Won't that bring you pleasure?
Won't that excite you the way it seems to excite your Corporal
Crosby?" Junge said, his eyes remaining fixed on mine.

I thought for a moment. I remembered Keyworth. I remembered the stench of the corpses when we had policed up several Marines dead who had been lost for several days, their bodies bloated almost beyond recognition from the heat. There was much in the war that was terrible and unpredictable that would consume us like the fireball from the mine that consumed Keyworth. And then there were the things that slowly consumed us, like the doubt and uncertainty that haunted me after Keyworth's death. Perhaps that was Keyworth's ghost.

"Killing has never given me pleasure, Gunner," I said, now understanding why the Gunner commanded the kind of respect that he did.

"Even when it's payback, like killing gooks who killed your own men?" Junge said, as if he were concluding some kind of test.

"It is a necessary evil. And like Crosby says, payback is a bitch. Certainly the mothers are the ones who pay," I said, gazing up at what was left of a waning moon that had slowly dissolved into nothingness.

"Do you think that you can depend upon Africa?"

"That's the second time you referred to Africa. Do you know something that I don't? Is there some reason why you have mentioned Africa?" I said, somewhat agitated.

"Well, I think that it's obvious isn't it? His manner and his general attitude do not inspire my confidence," Junge said, lighting another cigarette.

"What attitude is that?" I asked.

"It's the same attitude that you project, Lieutenant, an attitude of doubt and uncertainty. My feelings toward Africa have nothing to do with his Afro or the fact that he is black. My feelings are based upon my observations that both you and Africa are not certain of what you believe with respect to this war. Again, you project that uncertainty. By the way, that's a leadership problem." Junge rose and put on his flak jacket.

"Gunner, where have you picked up all this doubt and uncertainty?" I was angry but still outwardly composed because I found the conversation fascinating.

"The indications are not just in the way your men dress and speak, but a lack of leadership is indicated by their manner and the way that they present themselves to other marines. Oh, your track rats hang tough together, but they lack, I think, for want of a better term, some measure of self-respect,'' Junge said. He jumped from the top of the track to the ground.

The conversation had become too heavy for me. I looked around to see if others were listening. None were. ''Gunner, why are you telling me all this?''

''Cheatum, the battalion commander himself asked me to speak to you. He and I have known each other quite some time. Cheatum is concerned not just about your leadership, but about the way all his lieutenants lead. By the way, if I didn't share these things with you, no one would. Look at this conversation as simple feedback,'' Junge said, walking over to the bamboo hedge to relieve himself.

''There is nothing simple about this conversation, Gunner.''

I looked about. My men were scattered around the area. Most were in various stages of undress to keep cool. Weapons lay about unguarded, some clean, others not so clean. Holstrom had his grim face in a copy of the New Testament. Crosby was reading a *Playboy*. Clearly he had fallen from grace. Africa was studying himself in a mirror. In the distance, down toward the river that separated us from Go Noi Island, I could hear dull explosions. It sounded as if someone were blowing bunkers. I stood up on the top of my track, searching the direction the sound had come from for some indication as to what was going on. None of my track rats bothered to look up.

June 26, 1968: 1200 hours

The first tank had no sooner pulled off Route 4 than the ground literally shook from an explosion. I found it hard to believe that the tank lieutenant had driven his vehicle onto an old road that marked the boundary between Dai Loc and Dien Ban districts. The tank lieutenant had assumed that engineers had cleared the road. After all, he claimed, marines were walking down the road.

The fact of the matter was, marines were walking down the edges of the road. The grunt company commander had not asked for tank support so he had not taken the time to have the road swept by combat engineers. The grunt company commander simply had orders to be a blocking force. When Cheatum had directed that blocking force to move south, no one had made it clear who was responsible for directing tank support or sweeping the road. The tank lieutenant was too inexperienced to understand all of what was going on and had simply driven his vehicle onto a mined road. The whole incident made one wonder who was communicating with whom.

By the time the smoke and the dust cleared, the tank lieutenant was relieved of his responsibilities as platoon leader and sent back to Hill 37. He was unhurt but shaken up. The remaining tank was placed under my command by Cheatum, who then explained to me for the first time my track's role in the operation. Communications were not what they should have been. Cheatum had been counting on Captain Lowy and Gunner Junge to make things link together. But after talking to Lowy, it was apparent that Cheatum had not made his expectations clear to Lowy. It was all very confusing. The only thing that was clear to me was that we had lost a tank and the tank lieutenant had been made the scapegoat for the mistakes of others. Needless to say, the whole fiasco did not inspire the confidence of my track rats.

June 26, 1968: 1400 hours

Cheatum directed that my tracks be loaded with pallets of juice, food, and ammunition. As Cheatum put it, the effort was to be called a mechanized thrust. Once we arrived at our objective, the tracks would provide security as well as a means of transport. Cheatum was trying to run the operation like an amphibious assault.

Trucks from Hill 37 brought down the food and ammunition. No one thought about the labor needed to unload the trucks and stack things in an orderly and safe fashion inside the tracks. Everyone seemed to take it for granted that I could read minds. I had no idea of how Cheatum wanted things stowed in the tracks. When I asked the Lima Company commander, he just shrugged his shoulders. His grunts were already heading into the bush. As it was, my track rats had to unload the pallets of food and ammunition as best as they could. This caused a delay that brought Cheatum by to question me as to why there was such poor coordination.

"Where's Captain Lowy?" Cheatum asked, gazing at the long line of trucks strung out along Route 4.

"Some grunts blew a bunker complex earlier this morning. The combat engineers supporting the grunts later found a wounded gook. Lowy and Junge are checking the gook out, sir."

"Lowy needs to be here to assist and guide you. I'll speak to him about that. He is now attached to 3/7 for the duration of our effort. However, I expect you to assure proper coordination of all logistical and transport matters. Take the initiative to see that things are linking together," Cheatum said, waving his omnipresent green towel, clearly in a hurry to get on with his "effort."

"Yes, sir," I said, knowing enough not to question Cheatum.

Sergeant Holstrom just looked at me and smiled. There was no use in trying to explain anything to Cheatum. Cheatum had made up his mind on how things were to unfold. He counted on all his officers to make it happen. I doubted if Cheatum would have listened to what Holstrom and I had to say even if he did have the time. I smiled back at Holstrom and shrugged my shoulders.

June 26, 1968: 1500 hours

The wounded gook turned out to be an NVA sergeant. Lowy and Junge returned with the prisoner just as my track rats finished loading. Within five minutes two choppers landed and the whole area was filled with marine majors and captains, all of them wanting to see the NVA. By the time Cheatum had finished making the rounds with these officers, he was all pumped up. I wondered why all the fuss over one wounded NVA sergeant.

"What's all the fuss, Captain Lowy?" I asked.

"The NVA we picked up claims that there's a big bunker

complex just across the river on Go Noi Island, near An Quy-
en 2," Lowy said.

"An Quyen 2?" I said, getting out my map.

"Just a spot on the map. There's no longer a village there.
For that matter there isn't much left on Go Noi Island," Lowy
said.

"What's Go Noi like in terms of terrain?" I asked, spreading
my map out on the ground.

"It's pretty flat. West of the railroad berm that cuts the island
in two, there's a slight rise, maybe ten feet above sea level.
That's about it. The rest of Go Noi is either abandoned rice
paddy or elephant grass," Lowy said.

"How about all these villages noted on the map? Are they
still there?" I asked.

"No. All those villages have been blown away or burned to
the ground. Back in 1966 I moved through the area with my
grunt company. There were villages then, but not now," Lowy
said.

On the map Go Noi Island appeared to be twelve, maybe
thirteen kilometers long. It varied from two to four kilometers
wide. The Ky Lam river was the island's northern boundary.
The southern boundary was marked by a number of little rivers
that intermingled together. Go Noi sat in a wide rice plain just
above sea level.

"What does it look like from the air?" I asked.

"Like a no-man's-land," Lowy said.

"Is it wet? Are my tracks going to bog down if we cross the
river?" I asked.

"Parts of it are wet," Lowy replied.

"And I bet the whole area is one big mine field," I said, with
a sigh.

"Oh, that's most affirmative, Lieutenant."

June 26, 1968: 1500 hours

It was quiet. The air was still. The leaves of the bamboo hung
motionless. Off in the distance, far beyond where Go Noi Island
lay, a bird called. The call was like that of a dove.

The wounded NVA soldier lying on the ground answered with

a moan. He lay staring up at the sky, his eyes glazed from fatigue and pain. Moi, the balding Vietnamese from Dai Loc district Headquarters, squatted next to the NVA's broken leg. Moi chattered rapidly in Vietnamese to his counterpart, a fat, one-eyed Vietnamese captain. One-Eye gave Moi a brief reply. The reply needed no translation, for Moi promptly twisted the wounded man's leg. The NVA screamed. One-Eye giggled. Moi gave the leg another twist and a second scream pierced the silence.

Lukavitch, the battalion S-5 for the Third Battalion, Seventh Marines, and I listened from a distance of some fifty feet. Lukavitch and I were close friends, having gone through Basic School together. Both of us had a contempt for Moi and the one-eyed captain. Yet there was nothing that either of us could do. This questioning was part of the war's dirty business.

I noticed that at the first scream the many marine majors and captains departed. None found this kind of torture to their liking. All of us had heard of Moi, and no one wanted to appear to condone what was happening. Two choppers loaded with marine officers rose into the air and headed back to Da Nang.

The NVA passed out from the pain. One-Eye waved his hands in disgust and kicked the wounded NVA. Moi pulled his pistol and aimed at the NVA's head. At that moment, Lieutenant Holland, commanding officer of India Company, interceded, stepping between the wounded man and Moi. Moi just smiled, nodded slightly, and walked away.

"Did you see that, Sam? If Holland hadn't been there, that NVA would be dead right now," Lukavitch said.

"Come on, Lukavitch, that doesn't surprise you, does it?"

"What I saw here today was excessive, totally out of proportion to what was necessary. The cruelty was excessive," Lukavitch said.

"Happens all the time, Lukavitch. Where have you been? Damn! Some of our guys have been found skinned alive. It's sad, but it's the stone truth."

"That's evil, and I won't be a part of it," Lukavitch said.

"You're already a part of it. You think by walking some fifty feet away from what's going on, you're not a part of it? Come on, Lukavitch. Wake up," I said, somewhat disgusted.

"Some things can't be ignored. Just because others choose to remain unconscious doesn't mean that we have to. I've called a chopper to take the NVA back to the right people at NSA,'' Holland said, looking me dead in the eye.

''Tell that to all those majors and captains who were standing around while the guy was being tortured,'' I said, smiling.

''I think that the only humanity left in this war is the things that we as individuals do to lessen the pain and the cruelty. As for those officers from Division, they have to keep themselves distant from the dirty work. They leave it to Vietnamese like Moi and that one-eyed captain, who had his eye poked out by the Viet Cong,'' Holland said with conviction.

''Chad, that's bullshit,'' I said.

''Sam, that's the stone truth. Bullshit as it may seem, it's the stone truth.''

June 26, 1968: 1530 hours

Lieutenant Chad Holland was an Annapolis graduate. At twenty-seven he was about to make captain. A thin and wiry six-footer, Holland projected a no-nonsense attitude. Yet there was something genteel and polished about the tidewater Virginian. He was known as an excellent officer whose only indulgences seemed to be in his excessive reading and the macaque monkey that he kept as a mascot. Chad Holland didn't smoke, or drink hard whiskey. And he didn't go with girls who did things on the first date.

''That Moi, now there's an evil dude,'' Africa said.

''That's most affirmative, Africa. Moi is the clearest expression of man's inhumanity to man that I have found in my twenty months in Vietnam,'' Holland said with a smile.

''Moi found out what we needed to know,'' I said, matter-of-factly.

''That he did, Sam, and that was necessary, a necessary evil. A lesser evil, in fact, than getting our own blown away walking into the Go Noi. But we better not ignore Moi for what he is and what he represents,'' Holland said.

''What's that, Lieutenant Holland?'' Africa said, listening intently.

''Ignorance. Ignorance and cruelty. And when we choose to ignore what he is and what he represents, we forget that the ignorant who don't know who they are or what they are about can just as easily turn on us, or run out on us, or withhold from us what we need to know.'' Holland was looking off in the direction of Go Noi Island.

"But Moi is our ally. He's fightin' on our side, Lieutenant,'' Africa said.

A breeze picked up, swirling little dust clouds at the base of the amphibian tractors. The bamboo hedgerow began to sway in the breeze. Chad Holland's monkey sat up and listened, as if the slight weather change had brought a message.

"Moi is no one's ally. Moi is an animal. By the way, that's what moi means in Vietnamese, animal. Animal.'' Holland said, stroking his monkey.

Holland's monkey was named Mo Dickey. The monkey was a female and very affectionate. Holland had had his first sergeant back at India Company Headquarters start a personnel file with the name Mo Dickey. Recently Mo Dickey had been promoted to lance corporal.

At that moment Captain Lowy and Gunner Junge walked up. Mo Dickey bared her teeth and shied away.

"Looks like that monkey's afraid of you, Gunner Junge,'' Africa said with a smile.

June 26, 1968: 1630 hours

My track platoon linked up with India Company and we crossed onto Go Noi Island. Moi went with us to point out the locations that had been revealed by the prisoner. Moi also pointed out a spot to cross the Thu Bon River that would be advantageous to our tracks. The spot was called Phu Tay 2 on the map. It was a simple matter. A sandy beach led down to a broad shallows. Our tracks had no problems and we met no resistance. India Company crossed the Thu Bon on foot. At Phu Tay 2 the deepest spot was up to your waist.

June 26, 1968: 1830 hours

As Captain Lowy put it, we were capitalizing on an opportunity. The NVA had been the source of corroborating information according to Lowy. It was not so much what the NVA had revealed through the torture as much as what he confirmed about information Lowy already had.

Lowy and Holland appeared to work well together. Holland projected a sense of purpose as he moved from platoon to platoon. He was a good leader in that he gave direction and then let his platoon leaders and NCOs do their job. Holland also kept his people informed, insisting that Lowy meet each of the platoon leaders and their NCOs. Holland had Lowy describe in detail the importance of what we were doing and of the high priority Division placed on our little operation.

"Do you really think that Division knows what we're doing," I said, out of the blue.

"Division is like any big institution. It's a bureaucracy. It's overspecialized, overly formal, and too polite. It's a necessary burden we now must carry," Holland said.

"You're right, Chad. Back in 1965 we were more effective. We got more things done without the jingle-butts getting in our way," Lowy said, picking his teeth with a toothpick.

"Division is what we do to ourselves to keep from winning this war," Holland said.

The breeze was now blowing steadily. The high tops of the bamboo hedge just across the river tossed back and forth in the wind. All around us the elephant grass of Go Noi Island rustled. It was very pleasant and cool.

"We do it to ourselves, Chad. We make our own barriers, and it ain't getting any better," Lowy said.

"Just don't tell my troops that, Captain," Holland said.

"Oh, that's most affirmative, Lieutenant. We don't want them to think that we're just along for the ride," Lowy said.

"Well, that's exactly how I feel with you grunts. Most of the time I feel like I'm just along for the ride," I said, loud enough for Africa and Crosby to turn their heads.

"Careful, Sam, careful what you project to the snuffies," Holland said, petting his monkey.

The monkey gazed back at me with a look on its face that

told me I was in the same class as Junge and Lowy. The monkey tolerated me. Just so the damn thing didn't bite, I thought. I had seen Mo Dickey yawn. She had the canine teeth of a Doberman.

"I don't know where I fit half the time," I said quietly.

"Where you fit is where you place your faith," Lukavitch said.

Lukavitch had been sitting at the edge of my track's ramp. I had let the front ramp down so that we could all be more comfortable while we ate our chow, mostly combat rations with a few odds and ends thrown in like store-bought green chilies and Vienna franks. Lukavitch, our idealist, usually ate nothing but canned tuna fish or sardines. He was consuming Norway sardines in mustard sauce when he made his comment.

"Okay, Lukavitch, I'm asking for it this time. What do you mean by faith?" I said, trying not to be too much of a smart ass.

"You are never along for the ride if you know what you believe, Sam," Lukavitch said.

"Tell me more," I said, grabbing one of his Norway sardines.

"That's what keeps you from being along for the ride, knowing what you believe. It puts you in control."

"That's bullshit," I said, sucking the mustard off my fingers.

"I don't think it's so much a question of control as it is choice," Holland said, getting into the conversation.

"Choice?" I said, grabbing another Norway sardine.

"This conversation is too heavy for me," Lowy said, rising and tossing his C-ration cans into a hole.

The monkey glared at Lowy as the captain walked away. Holland stroked the creature to calm it. It seemed Mo Dickey sensed things that were beyond the conversation.

"Tell me what you mean by choice, Chad," I said, wiping my fingers clean.

"You underestimate yourself, Sam. You are here because of the commitment you made to the Corps. When all else fails, remember the choice that you made to be among the best, to be a professional marine officer," Holland said.

"I'm not sure that I have made that choice yet, Chad," I said.

"Well, the officer corps is where you fit, as Lukavitch would put it. Right, Lukavitch?" Holland said.

"I'm not so sure. I think that what you have said about Division is right on. Division is a kind of institution that we tolerate. It's a burden. I think that what sustains me though all this is the good that we are trying to accomplish. What sustains me is how we help the Vietnamese to help themselves. I believe in that,'' Lukavitch said.

"You would, Lukavitch," I said with a smirk.

"Yes, Sam, and that's a choice I have made. I want to work with the Vietnamese. My choice has put me in control. I'm not a pawn of fate. I am the master of my fate because I know in my heart that I'm making a contribution to the greater whole," Lukavitch said, intensely.

"It's a hole all right, Lukavitch. It's a black hole and you are being sucked in. By the way, don't let your Jesuit training get in the way of your good judgment. If I didn't like you so much, I'd ignore all your bullshit and let you get blown away," I said, smiling.

"I know where I fit, Sam, and I know what I believe."

"I know that I like your good-looking sister, Lukavitch, and that's enough for me." I threw my empty C-ration cans in the hole.

June 26, 1968: 2000 hours

Holland sent out his platoons to patrol the northwestern corner of Go Noi Island. He located his command up in the An Quyen area that was surrounded by the Thu Bon River on three sides. I pulled my tracks into a circle. Holland's weapons platoon set their mortars in the center of the circle.

June 27, 1968: 0600 hours

During the night the weather changed. The breeze picked up and a squall line blew in from the South China Sea. A light drizzle was falling as we began to sweep south through waist-high elephant grass.

India Company's first and second platoons led, covering a broad front of some five hundred meters. Third and fourth platoons followed in trace. My platoon of tracks brought up the rear, churning through terrain that seemed to bear the weight of the tracks with no difficulty.

June 27, 1968: 0730 hours

The drizzle was steady. The temperature was dropping. The damp seemed to chill all of us. Holland brought Mo Dickey to ride on Zero Deuce. The monkey just glared at me as if somehow I was the cause for the weather change.

Moi and the first platoon had found the bunker complex just where it should have been. While first platoon stopped to search the complex, second platoon pressed on. The elephant grass was now over six feet, high enough to cover paths that connected the bunkers. Movement along the paths was very slow. Moi found six booby traps in one hundred yards. All of us were very jumpy.

June 27, 1968: 1000 hours

Second platoon struck it rich at a place on the map called Phu Dong 2. What second platoon found was more than a bunker complex. Thirty fifty-pound bags of rice lay stacked in a pile next to one of the paths. Moi was excited. With three volunteers he climbed down into a tunnel complex only to emerge with news that they had found seven 122mm rockets. Everyone was elated and they began congratulating each other. The decision was made not to push farther south. Third and fourth platoons were to set up ambushes in the immediate area while first and second platoons finished searching the tunnels and bunkers.

June 27, 1968: 1400 hours

Holland was proud. He moved from platoon to platoon thanking his men for a job well done. That everyone was in high spirits was evident. Even Mo Dickey seemed to pick up. Holland had my tracks drive in circles to flatten the elephant grass. Mo Dickey rode on the front of Zero Deuce as we circled, hopping about the track, occasionally uttering a kind of curious little bark if Holland got too far away from the track.

"Lieutenant Holland's mighty proud of what we found so far," Sergeant Holstrom said.

"Nothing wrong with that, Holstrom," I said.

"Pride goeth before the fall, Lieutenant. That's what the Book says. I don't like this at all. It's been too easy," Holstrom said.

"Stay loose, Holstrom," I said, lighting a cigarette.

June 27, 1968: 1830 hours

Moi found a number of important documents in one of the tunnels. From what Moi said, the NVA had left before the documents could be destroyed. He also said that we needed to drop back to the northernmost point of the island where we would be surrounded by water on three sides. It was Moi's opinion that there were numerous NVA on Go Noi. What we had found was just scratching the surface.

After conferring, Holland and Lowy briefed the platoon leaders on the situation. The decision was made to fall back to the previous night's position, the only high ground that Go Noi Island had. If we were hit, we would have the advantage of clear fields of fire and water on three sides. We were in the process of moving out when the call came from battalion to stay put.

Holland, Lowy, Junge, Moi, and I met to discuss the situation. Holland called Cheatum on the radio. Cheatum was adamant that India Company stay at the site. Holland emphasized that 122mm rockets had been blown in place and the rice burned, and that as company commander of India Company, he felt that to remain where he was placed put the whole company in jeopardy. Cheatum refused to discuss the matter and directed Holland to set up a perimeter where he was.

Lowy and Junge gathered the documents Moi had found and sorted them into little piles. Lowy sat back after that was done and lit a long, dark cigar. The smoke from the cigar was rich and pungent. It must have been an expensive cigar. The thick smoke hung in the damp air.

June 27, 1968: 1900 hours

Lowy, Junge, and Moi flew out on a resupply chopper. They were gone before I knew it. Mo Dickey made a face as they left.

"Where's Lowy going?" I asked.

"Get those documents back to Division," Holland said.

The drizzle was picking up into a steady rain. My tracks had churned the terrain into muck. The grunts slipped and slid about. All of us were wet and chilled to the bone.

"Yeah, right. I'm going to take my own advice and stay loose," I said.

"Have the tracks pull in a circle. I'm checking coordinates for prearranged fire. When I'm done, I'm going to make you a copy, just in case," Holland said.

I had Africa start Zero Deuce. As the track turned, it churned up a skull. Holstrom picked up the skull and tossed it to me like a football.

June 27, 1968: 2215 hours

I buried the skull. I could tell that it bothered Africa. Africa kept staring as I buried it. Crosby was disappointed. He wanted the skull.

The rain had let up. Holland had pulled in his squad-sized patrols, setting out several listening posts around our perimeter. That the terrain was to our disadvantage was obvious. The platoons were strung out around Holland's command position in an irregular circle, with weapon's platoon mortars in the center of the circle.

"Damn! This place makes me jumpy, Lieutenant. They said Go Noi Island was evil and now I believe it. I can feel it!" Africa said.

"Stay loose, Africa." I looked over at Holland.

Holland smiled. He then rose and walked over to Africa. Holland's monkey followed, keeping right at Holland's heels.

"Corporal Africa, Go Noi is not evil. Go Noi may be isolation. Go Noi may be lost. But Go Noi is not evil. If you look around you, what do you see? You see a land that has been Rome-Plowed level," Holland said.

"I see nothing but mud and elephant grass," Africa said.

"That's most affirmative, Africa. So just stay loose," Holland said, rising and walking away.

"Lieutenant, it's what that mud and elephant grass is hiding that worries me," Africa said to me in a whisper.

I looked around at the grunts slipping and sliding in the black mud. The rain returned and the wind rose until the tops of the elephant grass began to wave back and forth in the dusk. Go Noi Island is a vast field of elephant grass, I thought. Moi called elephant grass American grass. American grass was our crop, and the fertilizer upon which that crop flourished were the villages and human beings that were crushed and ground up into the soil. While the grunts had dug in for the night, they had uncovered the skeletal remains of many more Vietnamese. It looked like Go Noi's vast field of elephant grass hid more than NVA bunkers. It appeared that a great graveyard lay just beneath the surface.

June 27, 1968: 2300 hours

Lukavitch, Holland, and I sat inside Zero Deuce. The red glow from my track's lights made for an eerie effect. I had dropped the track's ramp, for the rain had stopped.

"What do you make of all those bones the men found? Do you think that those are bones of dead VC and NVA?" Lukavitch said.

"Lukavitch, do you remember that old Marine Corps saying about the naked truth?" Holland said, grimly.

"No," Lukavitch said.

"How about you, Crosby? You heard about the naked truth. Tell the lieutenant here what the snuffies say about her," Holland said to Crosby, who was monitoring the radio.

"Yes, sir, the naked truth! You never want to get to close to the naked truth because she might screw ya!" Crosby said with a grin.

We all laughed. In the distance an artillery round fell. The round was part of our harassing and interdicting fire. Holland was dropping rounds all around Go Noi Island to keep the NVA on their toes.

"You still haven't answered the question, Chad," Lukavitch said.

"Careful, Lukavitch. This country will catch you. It will haunt you like a ghost if you get too close to it," Holland said, looking off into the darkness.

"Sounds like you're trying to warn me about something. What are you trying to say?"

"What he's trying to say is that this place is a nightmare. So what's new? Lukavitch, is there any doubt in your mind that this place and this war is a damn nightmare?" I said with disgust.

"What Lukavitch and I are talking about is more than that, Sam. You dismiss this whole business by calling it a nightmare. Well, that's not enough for Lukavitch nor, for that matter, is it enough for me. There's something more to be said," Holland replied.

"Didn't Crosby just say it all, about the naked truth and all that?" I asked.

"Sam, I'm just trying to clarify some things in my own mind. There are things that I want to know, about this war, about Go Noi Island, about what Chad Holland thinks," Lukavitch said.

"Well, that's easy, Lukavitch. Ask Africa. He will tell you that Go Noi Island is an evil place. I agree with him. Look at all the damn bones around here that testify to what took place here. As for Chad Holland, he has doubts just like you and me, just like Cheatum, especially when, just to please someone in Division, Cheatum refuses to let us move to higher ground," I said, raising my voice.

"Sam, no one in good conscience who really knows what has happened here and what continues to go on cannot have doubts. But it's a mistake to telegraph your doubt to the snuffies. And don't talk about evil, that's nonsense," Holland said curtly.

"Aren't you the one who just the other day was talking about the cruelty and shit and what we as individuals have to do to lessen the pain or something like that? Didn't you say that some poor dude who gets skinned alive is the victim of an evil?" I said, stirred up by Holland's comments.

"Sam, it was me who called torture evil," Lukavitch said.

"But I did say those other things and I still believe them. Sam, the heart of the matter is that you and I have a leadership role to play. It's going to be you and I who guide our men to where they need to go. It's you and I who have to accent the positives! Some things are best kept from the snuffies!" Holland said.

"Chad, who are you trying to fool? What do you think that you are hiding from the snuffies? You ain't hiding shit, Lieutenant! Let me tell you that! That's the stone truth! As for that leadership stuff, save that for Lukavitch. You been listening to Cheatum's rap. You and Gunner Junge!" I said, angry at being talked down to.

"I don't think that you understand, Sam," Holland said quietly.

"I guess not!" I got up and walked into the dark.

June 27, 1968: 2316 hours

The listening posts had been calling in movement for the last ten minutes. Mo Dickey had begun jumping around wildly, so much so that Holland brought out a leash from his backpack that he occasionally hooked to Mo Dickey's collar. Holland told Crosby to attach the leash to Mo's collar. When Crosby tried, Mo resisted and let out a kind of shriek, turning on Crosby and biting his hand. Crosby yelled and kicked the monkey. Mo Dickey rolled across the floor of Zero Deuce and cowered next to Holland.

At that moment there was a kind of whoosh overhead as an RPG-7 round struck Sergeant Holstrom's track. The RPG round must have been a signal, for all hell broke loose around the perimeter. Two or three more RPGs whooshed by, one striking Zero Deuce. The thin hull of the track was easily penetrated and hot slag spun about the interior of the track, hitting Crosby and Lukavitch. Holland and I were spared by a five-by-five-foot pallet of orange juice cans that absorbed the hot slag heading our direction.

As soon as it began, the firing stopped. Holland's marines had fire discipline. The encounter had apparently been only a probe of our perimeter.

Crosby and Lukavitch were lucky. Because the RPG had entered the track at an angle the slag had caught only their lower bodies. Both men were wounded badly but alive. Sergeant Holstrom had not been so lucky. The RPG round that hit his vehicle had spun hot metal through the interior, penetrating the head and chests of Holstrom and his driver. Both were dead.

Holland had gone up to the emergency radio frequency to get some assistance. Within minutes an army chopper from Black Cats up at Da Nang landed to pick up Crosby and Lukavitch. The army warrant officer didn't hesitate for a moment. He flew right into the landing zone as if it were broad daylight. I reminded myself to buy him a drink the next time that I got to Da Nang.

"That's two Purple Hearts, Lieutenant. Damn! They may not let me back in the field. What am I going to do, Lieutenant? I'll never make it back in Division. Damn, Lieutenant, do you think that you can have them send me back to the field, anyway? I'll never make it back in Division," Crosby said as we loaded him on the chopper.

"I'll see what I can do," I said, not sharing with Crosby the seriousness of his wounds.

Crosby was probably headed back to the States. His lower legs were ripped through, nickel-sized holes oozing blood where the hot metal had penetrated through the bones. Lukavitch had been hit in the ass. It appeared that the hot metal had passed through his buttocks for he had a single entry and exit wound. Lukavitch claimed it hurt like hell, but once we stopped the flow of blood, he seemed to rally. Both men were in great pain but lucid. For the moment, neither man seemed in shock.

"Lukavitch, you're going to be all right," I said as Africa and I carried him to the chopper.

"I know that. You are the one I'm worried about, Sam. You are still on Go Noi," Lukavitch said matter-of-factly.

The Huey rose and was gone. Within minutes Puff was on station, drilling the area surrounding our perimeter with thousands of rounds from its Gatling guns. Overhead four-deuce mortar illumination rounds dangled from little parachutes. It was like daylight, and Mo Dickey just stared up at the ghostly light of the flares and hissed, her great monkey teeth bared in a grimace.

June 28, 1968: 0600 hours

At first light, India Company blew the remaining bunkers. Cheatum flew down and agreed that it was time to move farther north on the island where India Company would be surrounded by water on three sides. Lowy had notified Cheatum that the documents Moi had found in the tunnels were responsible for a breakthrough relative to some sensitive intelligence matter. I didn't know if I believed that or not. Holland did, however, and he called his platoon leaders together to make a big deal out of it. My mind was on Holstrom and his dead driver, a little guy named Kirby, who had been in-country less than two months. My company commander said that he would take care of the letters to the next of kin.

June 28, 1968: 0900 hours

We moved north and east to the area called Bao An Tay on the map. It was an old ferry site. The plan had been to have the tracks cross back over to the opposite bank. The river at that point has a different name. It is called the Ky Lam and runs deeper than at Phu Tay 2 where we had crossed onto the Go Noi. Apparently Cheatum had seen that Bao An Tay was an old ferry site on the map and had just assumed that tracks could cross at that point. He was mistaken. If he had asked, any one of my track rats would have told him the situation. As it turned out, the river was too high to even contemplate a crossing. The rain of the last few days had turned what had been a broad and shallow, slow-moving river at Phu Tay 2 into a swift, deep-channeled torrent at the horseshoe bend at Bao An Tay.

Needless to say, Cheatum was angry and frustrated by what he thought was the refusal of the track platoon to be part of the team. I got smart this time and referred him to my company commander who happened to hold the rank of major. My company commander, who was already angry over the loss of Holstrom and Kirby, tore Cheatum a new asshole over the radio. Cheatum directed Holland to move back to An Quyen 2 and then head north to a position where India Company and my track platoon would be surrounded by water on three sides. It was the same spot that Holland had recommended the day before.

June 28, 1968: 1500 hours

Africa was acting platoon sergeant. He was driving Zero Deuce, so I drove Holstrom's track, training a new guy named Jim La Fleur. The terrain was so sticky from the rain I was afraid to let the new guy drive. As it was, two of my vehicles threw off track, and we had to stop while my men cleaned the track's suspension system and put the track back on. The thick, gumbo-like mud just collected under the track hull. Africa was at his best, however, telling everyone to watch how they steered so as not to throw off their track's suspension system, and even driving some of the vehicles through some of the rough spots. What amazed me was how well he rose to the occasion. I realized at that point that I had underestimated Africa. He was what Holland would call a leader.

June 28, 1968: 2000 hours

"Always keep in mind that in combat there are times when there is no book. No one knows what to do," Holland said.

"And this is one of those times, is that what you're saying?"

"I try to balance intuition and the facts," Holland said, smiling.

"And?" I said, waiting for the point.

"There is a time that you pick the lesser of the evils," Holland said.

"What do you mean evil? I thought that you didn't believe in evil," I said.

"Did I say that I didn't believe in evil or did I say nonsense? I think I said not to talk about evil because it was nonsense, nonsense in that the whole idea of evil relative to what we are doing is absurd and meaningless. It's absurd to talk about evil because this is war. It's meaningless to talk about evil here because these men wouldn't understand what you were saying. To them your concern for evil would be a sign of weakness. We, they, want and need leadership. That's what you must give them. Inspire them to leadership!'' Holland said, as if he were talking to an audience at Annapolis.

"Wait a minute, Holland, I don't give a shit about evil. You and Lukavitch were the ones who kept talking about it. Who are you trying to convince, for Christ's sake?''

For a moment Holland said nothing. Mo Dickey bared her teeth at me and hissed. I was beginning to hate that monkey.

"What I meant to say was that in a situation where there are no attractive options, one chooses the lesser evil, a choice which will do the least harm or which represents the least risk for all those concerned,'' Holland said, gravely.

I felt badly. Holland was struggling with some things, many things. The fact of the matter was that I wasn't being much in terms of support. I made a decision that I would try to be more supportive. After all, Chad Holland was company commander of India, 3/7. Who was I to shoot off my mouth? Chad Holland was a pro who had enough sense to make India Company one of the best grunt companies in the Seventh Marine Regiment. Holland had proven his coolness under fire and was one of the most technically competent men that I had known in Vietnam. More than that, he was a doer who got things done. His character and his courage were unquestioned. What was this compulsion to rage at Holland? Maybe he was just the target for my own confusion.

June 28, 1968: 2149 hours

They hit us with 82mm mortars, just walked them up and down our position for five minutes. Holland was clever enough to have his artillery coordinates down to where our supporting fire silenced the mortars. Holland had been hit during the mortar barrage. Even though he was hit, he stayed with the situation, his radioman and me assisting. Within minutes Holland had Puff overhead. We called in our listening posts and had Puff drill the area surrounding the perimeter. When Puff left, we dropped artillery around the area until morning, keeping what might have been a disaster to mere chaos.

June 29, 1968: 0600 hours

Holland was waiting to be evacuated. Lieutenant Henry, Third Platoon Commander, was acting for Holland. All told, the mortars had wounded twenty-five marines, fifteen seriously enough to be evacuated.

I lit a cigarette. I offered one to Holland. He declined.

The sun was coming out and it looked like the rain had left us. From my vantage point the river still looked swift, but that morning I was suddenly filled with some optimism.

"How many Purple Hearts you got, Chad?" I asked.

"Seven," Holland said, obviously in pain.

"Seven! Why do you keep coming back?" I asked.

"I'm one of the pros. Didn't I tell you that?" he said.

"What's a pro?" I asked, lighting another cigarette.

"A pro? Oh, I suppose a pro is someone who gets paid for what he's doing. Secondly, I would say that a pro is someone who is technically there in terms of what he needs to know, the state of the art and that sort of thing. Finally, I would say that a pro is someone who won't compromise certain principles of his profession, assuming the profession has principles or ethics," Holland said seriously.

I laughed. It was clear the son of a gun had thought about what a pro was. I didn't want an answer. I was just making conversation. Holland had taken me seriously. Of course, Holland was the kind of guy that took everything seriously.

"Sam, do me a favor and take care of Mo Dickey. I'll pick her up from you when you get back to Hill 55."

"For sure, Chad. You can count on it," I said.

I looked over at Mo Dickey, whom Holland had leashed. The evac chopper arrived and Holland got on it. Mo Dickey began to hop around and tried to slip her collar. When the chopper rose, Mo Dickey let out a kind of moan and covered her eyes. I walked over to Mo Dickey to give her a pat on the head. She hissed at me and bared her teeth. It was clear that I couldn't fill Chad Holland's shoes.

June 29, 1968: 0930 hours

Cheatum had given the word. The company was to be helilifted out at 1000 hours. My tracks were to proceed east along the Ky Lam River to the railroad berm, then turn southeast to the Korean Bridge. A marine squad would accompany us for security. Our estimated time of arrival at the Korean Bridge, some eight kilometers away, was 1800 hours. When Cheatum passed the word, I thought at first he was joking.

Cheatum choppered in to oversee the pullout. Lowy and Junge were on the same chopper. I had already called my company commander by the time Lowy and Junge came to talk to me. My company commander was livid relative to what was happening, but Cheatum wouldn't reply to his repeated calls over the radio. When I approached Cheatum to inform him that my company commander had been trying to contact him, Cheatum ignored me. Cheatum didn't say a word to me. Lowy saw that I was on the verge of exploding and pulled me aside.

"Hey, hoss, don't loose your cool. Stay loose. Isn't that what you always say," Lowy said.

"Son of a bitch is abandoning us, Captain! How are we going to cross Go Noi by nightfall, for Christ's sake?" I said, at the end of my wits.

"Listen to the old captain here. You just stay along the Ky Lam. In fact, I would follow the Ky Lam past the railroad berm to a bend in the river called Bac Dong Ban. Then I would shoot straight south. You go that way and it's only a couple kilometers to the Korean Bridge. No sweat," Lowy said with a straight face.

"Well, Captain, you should know. You've been that way before," I said, calming down.

"That's most affirmative. I been that way before," Lowy said, lighting one of his thick cigars.

June 29, 1968: 1330 hours

We were making good time. Lowy's suggestions were good ones. We had reached the bend in the river known as Bac Dong Ban and were about to head due south. At that point Go Noi

Island is only about two kilometers wide. Once at the south border of Go Noi, we had only two kilometers to go to the Korean Bridge, and those two kilometers were patrolled by the Korean marines. I was beginning to feel better.

If I was feeling better, my men were not. I then recalled what Holland had said about accenting the positive. Mask your doubts, Holland had said. Those words came back to me now as we headed into the thick elephant grass south of Bac Dong Ban. I turned back to the line of tracks and gave my men a thumbs up sign.

June 29, 1968: 1517 hours

Zero Deuce was mired in a pit. La Fleur had not seen the pit because of the elephant grass. The pit itself was filled with a kind of slurry rather than mud. When I got down into the stinking slurry, I found out that I was in a massive grave. Africa and I waded around waist-deep in the black slurry, stepping on bones and parts of decomposing bodies. The stench was awful. The more I moved around in the stuff, the more great, foul bubbles of gas rose to the surface to pop. I pulled a human femur that had been caught underneath the track's hull and flung it. Mo Dickey grunted, picked up the femur, and began to run along the edge of the pit, grimacing and uttering strange little barking sounds. I kept gagging on the stink.

Using bridge lumber, we built a firm foundation upon which to pull Zero Deuce out of the pit. Connecting four tracks in line, we were able to draw Zero Deuce out, my drivers revving the 810-horsepower V-12s to the point where I was sure someone would blow an engine. Slowly the four tracks pulled Zero Deuce free. Once out of the pit we all stripped down and threw our clothes away.

I stood there naked while Africa dumped water over my head. I gagged. If the NVA had wanted to hit us at that point, I would have been history. To save my ass I would have had to dive back into the charnel pit. As I pulled on a pair of pants, I noticed a large green frog had poked its head up from underneath the murk. Then I saw a second frog, its golden eyes blinking up at me. I lit a cigarette, drawing the smoke deep within. I closed

my eyes to gain my thoughts. When I opened them again, there
were more frog heads popping to the surface. As the tracks
pulled farther away from the pit, more frogs appeared. There
must have been a thousand frogs hiding in that pit.

"Africa, look at all these damn frogs," I said, amazed.

"One frag grenade would get them all, Lieutenant," Africa
said.

"That's most affirmative," I said, laughing.

Africa pulled the pin on a frag and tossed the frag into the
pit. There was a dull thump as the frag exploded. Dozens of
great green frogs floated to the surface, pale bellies upward in
the muck. Then it struck me that this pit was the quintessence
of Go Noi Island. This pit was both the essence and the metaphor for our ignorance, for what we had done to the land and
the Vietnamese, and for what we had done to ourselves. Africa's
killing of the frogs with a frag grenade was just another act of
cruelty vested upon the land, an expression of our own hate and
brokenness.

"Lot of frog legs, Lieutenant," Africa said without expression.

"Yeah. Let's get out of here," I said.

For about five minutes Africa and I tried to get Mo Dickey
up on the track. When Mo refused, I sent La Fleur after her
with a leash. Le Fleur couldn't catch her. Mo Dickey kept running back and forth along the edge of the pit, beating the human
thighbone against the earth.

June 29, 1968: 1811 hours

Our tracks arrived at the Korean Bridge without incident. All of
us were drained. When a Korean captain offered me a cold beer,
I almost forgot to thank him. He and I sat at the edge of the
bridge while the tracks crossed one by one. In his best broken
English he expressed his amazement that we had been able to
cross Go Noi the way that we had. I simply nodded, thanked
him again for the beer, and started to cross the bridge.

Africa stopped me halfway across the bridge. He and La Fleur
needed help. They were trying to catch Mo Dickey, who kept
running farther and farther out into the bald wasteland. At this

point on Go Noi Island the Korean marines kept the area clear of elephant grass with flame throwers, burning off all vegetation near the bridge. Africa and La Fleur stumbled across this landscape, trying in vain to keep up with Mo Dickey. When Mo Dickey reached the elephant grass, she was for all practical purposes gone. No way was I going to risk my men for a monkey, a mean monkey at that.

We waited for a time at the far end of the bridge. Mo Dickey never showed. Where she went was anyone's guess. I didn't really care. My mind was on Sergeant Holstrom. I could still see him. Only three days before he had sat beside me to clarify that the problem of evil is a difficulty only to our finite minds, not to that of the Lord.

SIPSY BLUE

July 1, 1968: 1000 hours

I HAD JUST got the word that I was to be sent to work with the province senior adviser's staff. Several special task groups had been formed to assist both the grunt battalions and the district advisers in the area. I didn't want to go. But no one had asked my opinion.

"Well, Lukavitch, this is what we call keeping our people informed," I said sarcastically.

"What do you mean, Sam?"

"No one tells you shit around here is what I mean!" I said, loud enough for the others in the Officers' Club to hear.

"Quiet, Sam," Lukavitch said. Lukavitch was the S-5 for the Third Battalion, Seventh Marines. His job was to work out in the villages with the Vietnamese, developing positive relationships and facilitating civil action programs.

"I wonder who I pissed off to get this assignment."

"Everyone gets rotated from time to time."

"Yeah, but I was just starting to click, Lukavitch. I was just starting to make things happen!"

"I understand," Lukavitch said.

"Do you? I wonder if any of us ever makes a lasting contribution to this place. I wonder to what extent any of us makes any kind of impact."

"You're talking about individuals."

"What?" I asked.

"Let's go take a walk in the ville," Lukavitch said.

We started down to the village called Duong Lam. The village was just south of Cobb Bridge, which spanned the Tuy Loan River. Lukavitch had been working with the village for some time, apparently with some success. He had been working with a district adviser and had some clue as to what I was in for. It seemed that this province senior adviser did his own thing. While he was viewed as unconventional by some, others said he was innovative. His district advisers spoke highly of him yet admitted that they hardly knew him. Much was delegated to Captain Lowy, Junge, some major down in Hoi An, and to a guy no one liked named Captain Watley. As luck would have it, I was to work for Captain Watley.

July 1, 1968: 1115 hours

"I would hate to see you loose your enthusiasm, Sam," Lukavitch said.

"What enthusiasm?"

"Oh, I detect a certain amount of inspiration in how you go about your business," Lukavitch said.

"More perspiration lately," I said.

We approached a group of Vietnamese who were yelling and screaming. Several marines were standing with them. Everyone's attention was centered on something in the middle of the crowd. Smoke from cooking fires hung in the air.

"What's going on?" I asked.

"They're fighting chickens," Lukavitch said excitedly.

"Fighting chickens?" I asked.

"Sipsy Blues," Lukavitch said, obviously proud of the birds.

July 1, 1968: 1210 hours

We watched the chickens fight for some time. Everyone seemed to be caught up in the excitement. There were a lot of bets and side discussions relative to the merits of each bird.

"Lukavitch, why did you bring me here?"

"I wanted to show how individuals can make a difference," Lukavitch said condescendingly.

"What are you talking about?" I asked, somewhat irritated.

"What I'm talking about is how a little know-how can make a big impact. What I'm talking about is how those individuals closest to the problems can sometimes come up with solutions that make the difference!" Lukavitch said intensely.

The chicken fights had started again. More Vietnamese were pulling up on motor scooters with little wire cages attached. There must have been almost one hundred people in the crowd.

"I hope no one decides to throw a frag grenade into this mess." I wondered how the idealistic Lukavitch had managed to survive so long in Vietnam.

July 1, 1968: 1234 hours

The crowd now must have been two hundred people. I noticed that several U.S. Army Green Berets had shown up with a cage. In the cage was a rooster. Then two sailors showed up from Da Nang. The sailors also brought a cage with a rooster.

I was pounding down cold Blue Ribbon beers, amused by the whole affair. It was quite an event for a small village like Duong Lam.

"How did you ever get this thing going, Lukavitch?" I asked, half in the bag.

"I have a corporal who works with me. Corporal Atrey. Do you know him?"

"Atrey! You mean Cottonhead! Sure, everyone knows Cottonhead. He's your typical redneck from Mississippi."

"Come on, Sam, give the man a chance," Lukavitch said.

"Cottonhead! He's the loudmouth that got himself shit-canned from Lima Company. Everyone knows about him. He refused to take down a rebel flag or something like that," I said, opening another cold Blue Ribbon.

"Everyone has a contribution to make, Sam. Don't be in such a rush to make a judgment. You know, you've been known to indulge yourself from time to time," Lukavitch said, confronting me.

Lukavitch was right. I had indulged myself from time to time. In fact, as I stood there in that crowd, watching all those attractive Vietnamese women, my mind wandered back to that indulgence.

At that moment I wished that I was back in my old battalion area south of Da Nang. That area, the Marble Mountains, with its huge limestone buttes jutting from the sand dunes at the edge of the sea, was the most beautiful place that I had seen in Vietnam.

During the day my friend Dao and I had walked in the cool shade of the big monolith known as Chin-Strap. We had climbed to the top of that great rock, and looking down, we had watched the folk in the village going about their business. Dusty little girls had splashed and bathed the water buffaloes. Quick little boys had herded their parades of ducks.

At twilight, on Chin-Strap mountain, we had watched the lights of fishing junks out on the South China Sea. At dawn, looking westward, we had watched high thunderheads moving through the mountain passes. Dao said that the clouds were moved by a great python, and when Dao spoke, those mountains seemed to be listening like so many of her dark kinsmen.

"Corporal Atrey. I'll be damned," I said.

"Atrey, come here a minute. I want you to tell the lieutenant what you developed here," Lukavitch said.

"Yes, sir. Glad to do that. Lieutenant, do you know anything about fightin' chickens?"

"No," I said. I drained my beer, highly amused by the whole affair.

"Well, back home in Neshoba County, we raise some of the best fightin' chickens in the world. Allen Roundheads. Grays. Red Fox Hatch. President Marcos of the Philippines bought some of my little stags."

"Stags?" I asked, not believing what I was hearing.

"Young roosters, sir," Atrey said.

"Have a beer, Atrey," I said, wondering if Division knew about "stags."

"Not right now, sir, got too much going on."

Atrey's refusing a beer surprised me. He was a hell-raiser.

"But the best fightin' chickens I had were my Sipsy Blues," Atrey said.

"Sipsy Blues?" I said, sipping my beer, still amused about stags.

"Feral chickens. They run wild back in the Sipsy Swamp in Mississippi. I captured some and crossed them with Red Fox Hatch out of Alabama. Those little stags can kick ass and take names. Boy, howdy!" Atrey said, his eyes blazing with emotion.

"Atrey was able to get several pairs of his birds over here through some contacts in the air force. Oh, I used some of my influence along the way. But the point is that we have the Vietnamese in this village hooked. We are already breeding Atrey's roosters into the local stock to upgrade their stags," Lukavitch said.

"Amazing," I said, certain now that no one in Division knew about stags.

"Yes, it is amazing. Atrey's made a lasting contribution to our civil action program that only he could make. As an individual, he's taken the Sipsy Blue project and is doing things that are unique to the civil action effort in terms of getting these Vietnamese to open up. He's unlocked the heat in a village situation to the point where I think we are truly making progress with these people. He deserves a lot of credit. But to me, Sam, Sipsy Blue is more than a project, it's an attitude. Individuals can make a difference," Lukavitch said, more than making his point.

"Okay. Okay, Lukavitch, get off your stump. I get the picture. Does Division know about this?" I said, feeling dizzy in the heat.

"I don't tell Division a thing! Hey, you okay?" Lukavitch asked.

"No. I'm not okay. I feel that I've just been shit-canned and I think I'm going to get drunk. You mind? I think I may have worms again. Probably picked them up on Go Noi," I said.

"I understand. Go ahead, pal. I'll drive you back to Hill 10 in a few minutes. I can get you some pills for the worms," Lukavitch said.

I didn't hear a word Lukavitch said. I was daydreaming of Dao. I was finally making progress with her. It was early evening and out on the South China Sea the lights of the fishing junks flickered on the horizon. Down in the village the roosters had stopped crowing. It was time for the watch to change. Time when the breeze coming off the water ceases. Backing-down time, when you take your last smoke before splitting to your ambush. Lull time before the wind coming off the mountains begins to draw seaward that heat locked up in the land.

Dao called to me. I rose and pulled off my shirt. Dao was standing with the South China Sea at her back, in the twilight her thick hair a waist-length shadow down her back and shoulders. She was taller than the other girls. No doubt the legacy of her Foreign Legionnaire father. Dao's long legs and long, narrow waist, those were European aspects. But the eyes, the hair, the clean, dusky slenderness—that was Vietnamese. Dao's spirit, her independence, the shrewd strength with which she dealt with me, that was just woman, and had no nationality.

"Why don't you let me bring you stateside?" I asked her.

"No can do. You get in big trouble. Dao say you number one sweetheart, but your mamasan, your Marine Corps, they no want Dao stateside," she said, holding my face in her slender fingers.

She wrapped her arms around my neck, pulling me down into the dark abundance of her hair. I trembled. A small moth fluttered up and became tangled in her hair. Brushing it free, I slipped my fingers down through that hair and around her waist. In the twilight something atavistic, something ancient and of the blood, was imposed, like a spirit, over the both of us. I could feel her opening up to me.

"You special, sweet Lieutenant. I make you come. I love you. When you go away, when I go away, I always love you, sweet boy. I always remember you," she said, running her hand down my thigh.

Her long legs came up to wrap around my torso. Her hair fell across both our faces. Somewhere out on the rice plains to the west an AK-47 cracked. I thought I heard return fire from a marine patrol. I wasn't sure. I was in my own lull time, hanging in the air like the wood smoke from the village cooking fires, Dao's perfume unlocking the heat.

"The first thing I want to do today, Lieutenant, is to make sure that you got your head and ass wired together," Captain Watley said, looking out the window.

"Yes, sir," I said, standing at attention.

"You may stand at ease, Lieutenant. While you stand at ease, make sure that you got your ears cleared out. This unit isn't a loosy-goosy field outfit like 3/7. Headquarters is not a shithole like Hill 10. Here we are wired together. We look good all the time. We stay out of Da Nang and don't chase whores. Officers who chase whores piss me off. And I know that you have seen plenty of officers, captains, and majors included, chase whores. But while you are in this unit, you will not chase whores. Is that clear?" Watley said, spinning around in his chair to look me in the eye.

"Yes, sir," I said, wondering who this captain thought he was.

"Now. You are probably wondering about me. Well, I will tell you all that you need to know about me. I know what's important and I know what I want. What is important is to make no waves and just do the job I tell you to do. What I want is to get my ticket punched. I'm on the fast track. And I'm going to eyeball you the whole time you're in this unit," Watley said, turning away from me to gaze out the window.

"Yes, sir," I said, now knowing that Watley was an asshole.

"Now, you are probably wondering about the unit. Well, I will tell you all that you need to know about the unit. We are not counterintelligence. Some think that we are counterintelligence or CIT, but we are not. Let them think what they want. We are not an intelligence-interrogator team or IIT. Some think that we are IIT. Let them think what they want. What we are is support to a new program. Some of what we do is counterintelligence. Some of what we do involves interrogation. Some of what we do is very dangerous and sometimes very dirty. We never tell people what we do! Do you understand?" Watley said, raising his voice.

"Yes, sir," I said, still staring straight ahead.

"Now, I'm sure that you have some questions," Watley said, rising from his chair and walking to the window.

Watley was short. His head was shaved almost bald. His camouflage utilities looked like they had been starched. Watley appeared to have a kind of rash around the back of his neck where his collar brushed the skin.

"Yes, sir, I do. Maybe you could give me some idea of the big picture," I said slowly, in a tone that tried to show respect.

"There is no big picture that you need to know. What I will tell you is that you will be planting sensors. When you plant those sensors it will not be in downtown Da Nang. One of our people who was planting sensors out on the edge was caught by some VC. Those VC or whoever they were skinned that man alive. I know. I found him while there was still life in him. The bastards didn't even have the charity to put a round in his head. They let him suffer. They let him suffer after they cut off his balls and shoved them in his mouth. Who knows what he told those people before they cut off his balls. He spoke fluent Vietnamese. I understand, Lieutenant, that you speak some Vietnamese. I understand that you also get on quite well with the Vietnamese. Is that right?" Watley asked, inches from my face.

"Yes, sir, I speak good gook. I have lived in the ville," I said, not believing Watley's bullshit story for one minute.

"You have lived in the ville. You have lived in the ville. Well, who knows what you might tell the VC if they catch you. Here is as much of the big picture that you will get. Keep in mind the reason that I must withhold some information is to protect others. Suffice it to say that what you will be doing is very dangerous and very important. Your individual effort could effect the outcome of things much greater than yourself. But have no illusions. There is nothing rational that I can give you in terms of a big picture. What control we have of what we do varies. Sometimes I call my own shots. Sometimes I'm told what to do. When I send you out on the edge of things I guaran-god-damn-tee you that it will be a situation filled with unknowns," Watley said, looking down at the floor.

"Who will I be working with, sir?" I asked, hiding my disgust for Watley's condescending tone.

"A good group. A damn good group. By the way, our unit is one of several in I Corps. Sometimes we link up with others. Captain Lowy runs a unit similar to ours on the western and southern edge of the Dai Loc map sheet. There is a SEAL officer down in Hoi An who we work with from time to time. Mostly we just exchange lists of names,'' Watley said, matter-of-factly.

"Lists of names, sir?'' I asked, not liking what I had just heard.

"Much of what we do is track down people on the lists. In order to do that you will at times be working with the provincial recon unit out of province headquarters,'' Watley said, wiping his face with a white handkerchief.

"You mean the PRUs, sir?'' I asked, playing dumb.

"Yes, the PRUs. And have no illusions about them when you do work with them. For now you will be taking a little hike with Warrant Officer Musto and a small team from First Recon,'' Watley said with a smile.

"Hike, sir?'' I asked, getting a sick feeling in my stomach.

"Yes. According to my information you know the western edge of the Dai Loc map sheet fairly well,'' Watley asked, smiling a second time.

"Yes, sir,'' I said, the sick feeling in my stomach turning to fear.

"For this job I needed someone who had been through the Dai Loc map sheet enough to make his way on the ground and in the dark. I also needed someone with grunt experience who spoke Vietnamese. I also prefer men who have demonstrated coolness under fire, ideally big, strong men who have had the opportunity to blow someone away or cut a throat or two. Based upon my information you fit that picture, not that you should be proud of it,'' Watley said with a sneer.

"I understand, sir,'' I said, controlling my fear and anxiety.

"Do you understand? I hope that you do. For we have a job to do here and lives are at stake. If you do your job right, you have the opportunity to make a difference and save American lives. If you screw up, expect the worst, both from me and the enemy. I know that you drink too much and border on the intolerable in terms of your conduct with Vietnamese women. However, I cannot fault you about that because some of our senior marine officers have failed to provide the proper example, much to my disappointment. What I will do, though, is save you from your own ignominy. I will offer you a chance to make a difference,'' Watley said, all puffed up with his own self-importance.

"A lasting contribution," I said. I was thinking about Lukavitch and Atrey.

"What was that?" Watley asked.

"You are talking about making things happen that make a difference, about things that make a lasting contribution. Is that right, sir?" I asked slowly, hiding my contempt.

"Damn straight! That's exactly right. I'm talking about things that can change the course of this war. I'm talking about you making the difference in American lives. I'm talking about grabbing a hold of this snake and shaking her to death before she can bite you," Watley said, shaking his fist in the air.

"Snake?" I asked, thinking that Watley might be a little crazy.

"Damn straight. It's a snake. In fact, you just got your radio call sign," Watley said, sitting down in his chair and picking up a pen.

"Snake, sir?" I asked, wondering how many marines Watley had gotten killed.

"No. Habu. Ever seen an Okinawan Habu, Lieutenant?"

"Yes, sir. One almost bit me once up in the north end of Okinawa," I said, now beginning to understand just how much trouble I was in.

"Well, they are big, thick, dark, and ugly, just like you. Aren't they?"

Watley wrote "Habu" across the cover of a folder in big, bold letters.

July 2, 1968: 1400 hours

I drew my gear and headed down to my hooch. I debated turning my shotgun in for an M-16. I decided to keep the shotgun. But I did draw another .45 automatic and some steel-jacketed rounds for insurance. It was my understanding that I was to be on my way in the morning. I was to be ready at first light. When I asked where I was going, Watley said that I was going to the edge, wherever that was.

July 3, 1968: 0715 hours

A thunderhead boomed over Ba Na Ridge, spreading its hood like some great cobra. The snake cloud was a welcome end to what had been a hot week, where the dust and grit had hung in the still air making sleep impossible on my grimy bed and comfort just a memory.

The thunderhead boomed again. Below the neck of the snake cloud I imagined breasts and the outline of slim hips. My mind wandered back to Dao. In the rapidly changing cloud forms, I could see Dao's hair falling waist-length down her back and shoulders. I could smell the wood smoke within that hair.

"Three hundred eighth NVA Regiment is up on that ridge line, Lieutenant," Knight said, smiling.

"I bet they're down inside their caves and bunkers eating hot rice," I said, wiping my face with a towel, feeling somewhat dizzy.

An artillery round burst down on the valley floor. I looked for a wisp of smoke. I had a clear field of fire to the valley's floor, a moonscape of blasted trees and craters. The moonscape was called Happy Valley, and if I spotted anyone moving across that space during daylight, they were history. I had been in this valley before and could sound off map coordinates for artillery fire in my sleep.

A second round impacted the valley floor. This time a thin column of smoke rose above the blasted scrub. Stirred by the wind, the column of white smoke blended into the dark clouds of the approaching storm.

A third round fell into the moonscape. This round burst much closer to our position, sending up a shower of dirt and bits of vegetation. I picked up Knight's binoculars and scanned the moonscape.

"Don't look too hard, Lieutenant. You might find something," Knight said.

Our unit, as Watley liked to call it, was scouting the trails that ran along the southeast edge of Happy Valley. Corporal Knight and two marines from First Recon who had worked this area before were attached to Watley's program until our mission was complete. Our mission was to find a particular trail walker who scouted the area for the NVA. Direction was to come from War-

rant Officer Musto, an Australian Special Air Service type who
had been an adviser to the ARVN Hac Baos, better known to
the marines as ARVN Black Panthers. Musto had been tracking
this little guy all over I Corps.

A fourth artillery round impacted on the far slope, just at the
edge of the moonscape where a patch of jungle remained. I
scanned the area with field glasses. I knew from Musto that a
trailhead could be found near where the artillery round landed.
The spot was easily marked from our position by a great rock
cairn known to Musto as the Bee Hive.

I looked up at Ba Na Ridge through the field glasses. The
cloud buildup now covered the ridge. Soon clouds would mask
our position. Occasional big drops of rain began to patter on the
foliage. My stomach was churning. I refused to think about
Watley. He was a bullshit artist. I would keep my mind on Dao.

July 3, 1968: 1030 hours

Corporal Knight had two tours under his belt. His first tour had
taken him all over I Corps on large scale operations as a grunt
squad leader. Knight's second tour found him with First Recon,
patrolling actively west to the Laotian border. Davy Knight had
just extended six months onto his second tour for something
"different," as he termed his connection with Watley's program. At twenty-four, he was only a year younger than I was.
But twenty-four was old for a grunt in I Corps, and Knight had
a kind of wisdom far beyond his years. I liked his calm and
collected manner. When he told me that he had just got the word
that he was to get his sergeant's stripe, I was gratified. Knight
represented the best the Marine Corps had.

In contrast Warrant Officer Musto had rarely taken part in any
large scale operations. His experience with the Hac Baos had
been as a training adviser. Though usually referred to as the
strike company of the First ARVN Division, the Hac Baos were,
in reality, a Ranger unit. While Musto had been on many ambushes and worked many small unit patrols, he had found working with the Black Panthers lacked something.

What was lacking with the Black Panthers, Musto found
working with Mike Forces, attached to C Company, Fifth Spe-

cial Forces. Led by Green Beret advisers, Mike Forces moved rapidly through the jungles west of Da Nang with a minimum of support, meeting the enemy on his own terms and on his own turf. Musto had patrolled with small units of the Mike Forces west to the Laotian border and beyond.

Musto, a stocky man with a broad, hairy chest and thick, muscular forearms, squatted down and started to draw in the dirt with a stick.

"Lieutenant, here's the Bee Hive. Here's our current position. This trail twists and turns, but it runs from the Bee Hive to the scrub just below our present position." Musto threw his stick into the direction of the Bee Hive.

I looked on the map. A little stream called Lo Dong ran from Ba Na Ridge down into Happy Valley. At the spot where the Bee Hive should have been was the name Mang Chua. Under that name the word "abandoned" was printed.

"That's where you think this little guy's going to be?"

"That's right, mate. He's been spotted before." Knight said.

"What's the significance of the Bee Hive?" I asked.

"It is believed to be an old Cham ruin," Musto said.

"Cham?" Knight said, shaking his head.

"The ancient Chams. In Da Nang you pass the Musée de Cham every time you go get shit-faced at the White Elephant Bar. Those big stone heads that you see out in front of the museum, they're from the old Chams, who lived here before the Vietnamese," Musto said, blinking his eyes.

"I never drank no beer at any White Elephant Bar so I wouldn't know," Knight said.

"I have," I said.

I had seen the great Cham heads that Musto mentioned. They were made out of the same dirty brown rock that made up the Bee Hive. I had even taken a leak on one of the Cham heads after a night of beers at the White Elephant. I had been with my little friend, Micky Van Der Molen. Later we had made love in a borrowed room at the Naval Support Activity. The next day Micky had ignored me, saying it was all just an impulsive, one-night stand. Then she gave in. I wondered what she was doing with her evenings. I made up my mind to drop in on her when I got the chance. Maybe a few more months in the Nam might make her appreciate me more.

"So tell us more about this little dude that we're looking for," Knight said.

"Oh, he's a clever one. He's a Katu. Katu live along the Laotian border in the valleys of Ashau, Aloiu, and Tabat. However, I believe this man may be one of the lowland Katu who once lived in a place called An Diem," Musto said, looking out into the valley.

"Never heard of the place," Knight said with a smile.

"An Diem was at the edge of these mountains. Some of our people tried to work with these Katu. It didn't work out," Musto said.

"What happened?" I asked, curious relative to this part of the war.

"An Diem was abandoned. Later, the few Katu that remained were harassed into oblivion by the VC," Musto said.

"So exactly what is the value of this guy?" I asked.

"He's a Katu. We know that by what we have seen him wear and by behavior that we have observed. This man is a trail walker for the NVA. Katu may not be good fighters, but they know every trail between here and the Laotian border, I would guess. We want to snatch him up and see what he can tell us. That's all. It's quite simple."

The other members of the team were listening. Happy Valley had been unkind to First Recon. Quinn and Botke, two lance corporals, had heard the worst. Both men had also seen some of the worst. Quinn and Botke were veterans of patrols from the Que Son Mountains to the An Bang foothills and Base Area 112. They could be depended upon.

"Simple?" I asked with a cynical tone.

"Keep in mind that this Katu may have information that may shape some decision. We have watched him for some time now. He is somewhat predictable, as if he were following some pattern. Snatching him away gives us an important intelligence gain," Musto said.

The team was silent. Then Knight nodded. His nod was followed by a thumbs-up sign. Deep within the foliage, a cicadalike insect buzzed. My stomach was still upset. I was still having dizzy spells. I nodded back.

July 3, 1968: 2030 hours

The early dark of the jungle twilight had settled in around us. I leaned against a rock, waiting for Quinn and Botke to slip away into the darkness. For about an hour it had drizzled, just enough to soak us to the skin. Then the storm had blown seaward. A half-moon now peeked through the broken cloud cover, creating shadows between the clumps of elephant grass and scrub to our front. Overhead there was a strange, chattering sound.

"That chattering that you hear is only the nightjar chasing after insects," Musto whispered.

"What's a nightjar?" Knight whispered back.

"A kind of night-flying swallow," Musto said.

It grew quiet. In the silence we all watched the valley below. Several times I could have sworn that I saw movement, that the quiver in the vegetation was not a dream. I was glad that I was not down on the trail with Quinn and Botke. Then I heard the nightjar again.

I looked back down at the valley. I tightened my belt. My stomach growled. I was losing weight again. I probably had worms. What if I should die of some internal parasite that I picked up in these hills? For a moment I wondered who had recommended me for this program. How in the hell had I managed to get myself in Happy Valley? This whole thing was a mystery no less profound than the existence of the elusive nightjar that now circled unseen in the darkness, high above our heads. I looked hard into the darkness. I could almost see the great rock cairn of the Bee Hive rising like an ancient tower from the surrounding jungle.

July 4, 1968: 0400 hours

I was dreaming of Dao. She and I had slipped away to a part of Nui Kim Son just under the shadow of Chin-Strap mountain. We were making love in a secluded clump of bamboo. I was on my back, looking up at the swaying tops of the bamboo.

"Lieutenant, wake up," Knight said.

"What's up?" I asked.

"Quinn and Botke clicked the handset on their radio. We got

all kinds of movement on the valley floor,'' Knight said in a whisper.

July 4, 1968: 0500 hours

It was getting light. I fixed my gaze on the vegetation and watched shadows turn in the density of the leaves. Time was passing slowly. There had been no communication from Quinn and Botke since 0430. Knight kept looking over at me as if he expected me to do something. I wondered what he would think of me if he knew about my relationship with Dao.

Down in the valley I heard the sound of laughter. A fog blanketed Happy Valley. In another hour or so the fog would start to lift. For a moment more laughter came from the valley. Then all was silent. I got down on my knees and threw up, screening myself from the rest of the men. Knight just watched, saying nothing.

July 4, 1968: 0630 hours

Musto and I moved ever so slowly down the trail. From our immediate left came a hiss. Both of us ducked, then rose slowly from a squatting position, our weapons pointed in the direction of the hissing sound. Must be a big snake, I thought.

A large, white-throated swallow-like bird lay next to the trail on its back. Its wingspread must have been three feet. Musto was quick and pinned the bird to the ground with his boot. The bird hissed and struggled to free itself from what appeared to be a game net strung between two large trees. Musto cut the bird free, but one of its wings seemed damaged.

But for its white throat, the bird was black. It reminded me of a large bat. The eyes were a yellow-gold. There was hardly any beak to speak of, just a wide, ugly pale white mouth set into a thick neck that hissed back at Musto whenever he touched the bird.

''Just look at that ugly mother, Lieutenant. Look at that ugly mother,'' Knight said, shaking his head.

"Nightjar. I believe it *is* a giant nightjar," Musto said in reply.

July 4, 1968: 0900 hours

Knight had impaled the nightjar on a stick. The bright yellow-gold eyes had faded in death to olive. Occasionally the long black tail would twitch.

Musto was watching the fog rise up from the floor of the valley. While our side of the valley was scrub with a few clumps of elephant grass, the opposite side of the valley, stretching above the rock cairn, was jungle that somehow had been spared.

The cicada-like insects were starting to sing in the foliage. From high atop a tree one would start to buzz. Another would answer from across the slope. Soon the valley was vibrating from their collective buzz. The buzz gave me a headache. I threw up again. I didn't think that I had anything left to throw up.

July 4, 1968: 0930 hours

It was as if the valley were a pool of clouds. Out of that pool wisps trailed up the slopes through the brush and trees. The cicadas' singing through the fog was unsettling. The tip of the rock cairn poked through the dissipating fog. Bits of vapor trailed off the tip of the rock cairn like separate spirits of the long-dead Chams. The dizzy spells were increasing in frequency and I was getting chills. My mind wandered. I heard laughter rising from the valley.

July 4, 1968: 1000 hours

Dao kept creeping into my thoughts. Both she and I were caught between the reality of our situation and the rules. There had been no doubt on my part. I knew what my emotions told me. But for Dao there was indecision as well as fear. I didn't know what to do, let alone how to do it. I did know that a person is never whole when fear leads him. I felt that was why Dao had left me. But then again, this was Vietnam. I wasn't really sure why. In Vietnam things are never quite what they seem. Like the nightjar I thought was a snake. Or like Captain Watley with his bullshit stories. One didn't know what to believe or who to trust.

July 4, 1968: 1014 hours

Botke and Quinn clicked their radio handset. Three clicks followed by a single click. The man we were looking for was coming down the trail.

Squat and bandy-legged, the Katu coming down the trail couldn't have been five feet tall. He carried only a stick, walking with a kind of funny little hop, always scanning the trail ahead.

He was fifty feet from us when he suddenly stopped, sensing something was wrong. The Katu wore a dirty orange rag around his head. Around his waist was a sarong that was the same dirty orange color as the head rag.

Botke burst from the vegetation like a linebacker and tackled the little Katu. Quinn and Knight were beside Botke in a second. The three recon marines simply picked the little guy up and carried him off. The Katu didn't struggle.

July 4, 1968: 1100 hours

When I quizzed the Katu in Vietnamese, he seemed to have no problem understanding, nodding frequently. When he smiled, you could see teeth that were filed to points.

Musto called in, notifying Watley that our mission had been successful. Watley directed us to move to a prearranged checkpoint for extraction.

At that moment a bell began to ring somewhere on the opposite slope. It reminded me of the old farm dinner bell that used to call me to supper back in Iowa.

July 4, 1968: 1115 hours

Our checkpoint for extraction was a boulder field. In order to reach that checkpoint, we had to move five hundred meters through brush and elephant grass. I scanned the area with field glasses. I saw nothing unusual. I was beginning to feel better.

Then Musto tapped me on the shoulder and pointed down into the valley. I directed my field glasses toward the Bee Hive. Three men were standing on the top of the rock cairn. All three men appeared to have field glasses and were studying our portion of the ridge line. Two of the men were clearly NVA by way of their stature and their uniforms. The third man was very large and was wearing black.

"What do you make of that?" I asked, amazed that the men would be so bold as to expose themselves.

"I think that we're about to have guests," Musto said.

"Who do you suppose that big dude could be? That one in black," I asked.

"Oh, I don't know, Lieutenant. Out here on the edge anything goes. For all I know, he could be the Devil!" Musto said.

An AK-47 cracked. Everyone ducked. Then we heard a whistle. The Katu began to laugh a sinister, monotone laugh. Knight turned around and slapped him on the side of the head with his M-16. The AK-47 fired a second time.

Botke and Quinn returned fire, but it seemed that the whole slope erupted in automatic weapons fire. Botke and Quinn disappeared into the brush, departing to prearranged rally points. Knight and Musto provided covering fire as I slipped into the foliage and made for the rock outcropping that was to be our departure point, dragging the Katu behind me.

July 4, 1968: 1220 hours

The insects had stopped singing. The smell of the firefight hung in the air. I sat looking at the Katu. The sullen, glazed eyes stared back at me. I fashioned a noose and slipped it around his neck. I tied the rope end of the noose to my belt. Down on the valley floor the fog had all but disappeared. The dark structure of the Bee Hive now manifested itself like the shell of a great tortoise. I resisted the impulse to call in artillery on the ancient ruin. I didn't know where the rest of my unit was. For all I knew, they could have been forced to move in the direction of the ruin.

July 4, 1968: 1400 hours

I had been clicking my radio handset for two hours with no response. After the initial firing there had been a lull. An eternity passed until there was one more frantic burst of firing farther down the slope. The silence that followed was broken by a scream. The scream grew into a raging, insane, wailing howl of someone at the threshold of unbearable pain. The howl ended in a shriek. Then I heard Vietnamese on my radio, speaking obscenities into the handset. Botke and Quinn were probably dead. My hope was that Musto and Knight were still hiding in the brush.

July 4, 1968: 1430 hours

I lay crouched among the great boulders. I gagged the Katu. All around me I could hear the Vietnamese. There was a strange taste in my mouth, as if I were sucking a penny. My eyes burned. I tried to drink from my canteen only to find that I could hardly swallow.

July 4, 1968: 1440 hours

I had made up my mind. When and if I got out of this, I was going to give Dao one of Atrey's Sipsy Blues. She would like that. Vietnamese are big on fighting chickens. I shouldn't have been so quick to stand in judgment of what Lukavitch and Atrey had done in that village. They were winning the hearts and minds of the people. Maybe I could use one of those Sipsy Blues to win just one heart.

The little Katu was trembling. He was sweating like a pig. Strangely enough I was calm. Stay loose, I said to myself. Think about Dao. My sickness seemed to have passed for the time being. The chills had stopped and I hadn't had a dizzy spell for quite a while.

July 4, 1968: 1500 hours

I could hear our choppers coming in. I broke radio silence as the gunship passed overhead through the low, broken cloud cover. I popped a yellow smoke grenade. It was the only color I had.

A CH-47 dropped through the cloud cover, a naval cargo net hanging below its belly. The door gunners worked their machine guns up and down the slope. Still no Musto or Knight.

From the jungle to my left small arms fire opened up. The door gunners returned fire. Leaves fell along the edge of the jungle as if it were autumn. Rounds pinged and clanked against the belly of the CH-47.

The chopper continued its descent. The cargo net touched the boulder and I sprung for it, slapping my D-ring on the woven rope. For a moment it seemed that the Katu was trying to resist. I yanked the noose tight and secured him to the net.

"Let's go," I screamed into the radio, but it wasn't necessary.

The chopper rose quickly, rounds from the jungle pinging and banging into its belly. The door gunner was wearing a bright surfer shirt. I must get one of those for Dao, I thought. It would be good to see her. I wondered if she would ever hold me again. She had said that it was over, but in Vietnam I had learned that things are never what they seem.

I looked down into the valley to see hundreds of green muzzle flashes. From my height I could see Musto's body at the edge of the boulder field. It had been stripped naked. Knight's body as well as two others were lying farther down the slope. Oh Lord, what has happened here! What has happened to these men! The reality that I alone survived hit me like a bullet. Then we were in the clouds.

COTTONHEAD

LIMA COMPANY, THIRD Battalion, Seventh Marines, found
the cornfield. It lay in a little ravine tucked back into a corner
of Happy Valley where run-off from Ba Na Ridge trickled down
to form a stream to keep the field well-watered and lush.

Captain Watley, my new commanding officer, had been curious when news of the corn field reached Division. Watley and
a local CIA case officer were tight and discussed the cornfield
at length over breakfast. The next thing I knew, I was assigned
to implant special sensors in the ground in the immediate area
of the cornfield.

My new job was somewhat of a mystery. All the district senior
advisers were U.S. Army personnel. They all had staffs and ran
according to a set procedure. Our province senior adviser, to
whom all the district advisers were to report, was a Marine
officer. I was told that this was an experiment, and that while
there were Marine officers in other jobs in this new program,
there had never before been a province senior adviser who was
a Marine. I found this interesting. Of course, there had been
Marine officers who had served as province psychological warfare officers, and there were Marine officers who were working
with the regional and popular forces. So it came as a surprise
to me that there had never been a Marine officer who had served

as a province senior adviser. What Captain Watley and I were about, however, was a "special task team."

What this special task team did seemed to vary. Watley talked a lot about the newly announced Phoenix or Phung Hoang Program. Actually, the program had been around for a while. It just hadn't been advertised for the obvious reasons. It seemed that the Phoenix Program involved more than met the eye. I was told that I would be hearing more about the program as well as the parent organization, CORDS. CORDS stood for "civil operations and rural development support." It was clear that much was going down in a very short time and that there were a lot of changes taking place. I would just have to stay loose, I told myself. Staying loose went with the job. I had to keep telling myself that, even though I could see that all these changes were creating a lot of ambiguity. I was quickly learning that ambiguity came with change and was part of the nature of this war. Watley's special task team wallowed in ambiguity.

If there had been any doubt on my part about the cornfield mission, my doubt was nothing to that being experienced by my 3/7 contact, Cottonhead Atrey. Atrey was fuming. He considered our being in Happy Valley both a waste of time and a dangerous risk.

The fact that Lima Company was sweeping the valley made no difference, for checking out the cornfield required us to hike into the ravine from the floor of Happy Valley with only a squad of Marine grunts for security. Now we had found something that was to complicate all our lives. Across the ravine, among the rocks and scrub just above the cornfield, lay a body wearing the tiger-striped uniform of the Fifth Special Forces.

July 15, 1968: 1100 hours

Lima Company was sweeping the moonscape of the valley floor. One platoon was moving along a trail that ran directly through the valley. Another platoon was working a trail that swung up the slope of the far side of the valley. The two remaining platoons hung back as reserve, for Lima was seeking contact with elements of the 308th NVA Regiment.

July 15, 1968: 1105 hours

"Well, Cottonhead, we got a for-sure body out there," I said.

"It'll be all right, Lieutenant, I'll take a fire team and be back before you know it," Atrey said, calm in spite of the firing that had broken out up-valley.

"Maybe we ought to plant the sensors and get out of here, Atrey. That body could be a trap." I was remembering Watley's instructions to get in and out as soon as possible.

"Sir, we can't leave that body there. There's no tellin' when a marine company's gonna get back up this way, by that time it could be buzzard bait," Atrey said.

Cottonhead Atrey was a thin, wiry corporal who carried a tomahawk in his belt. You looked into his eyes and you knew that he was crazy. If you spent five minutes talking to him, you knew that he was full of bullshit. What was worse, he believed his own bullshit. He had no doubts. For him there was nothing ambiguous about the need to get the body back. As far as Atrey was concerned, it was his duty to get the body back. To Atrey, getting the body back served a higher purpose than planting sensors in a cornfield.

July 15, 1968: 1300 hours

Watley was on my ass. He couldn't believe the situation report that I had given him. Watley, of course, had no choice, he would have to sweat it out like the rest of us.

Down in the valley things were heating up. Lima Company had all of its platoons committed. India and Mike Companies were being choppered in. It was going to be a hot afternoon in more ways than one.

July 15, 1968: 1514 hours

The body turned out to be that of an American. Atrey and his fire team had brought the body out without incident. Upon our return to Hill 10 we were informed that we had the body of a

Special Forces Mike Force lieutenant who had been separated
from his men during a firefight the previous week.

July 15, 1968: 1830 hours

"You compromised the mission," Watley said.

"Shit happens," I said, very tired.

"In this business we keep our shit together or we're dead,"
Watley said, blowing a smoke ring into the air.

"I put my faith in this Cottonhead. He may be a little crazy,
but I felt he could pull it off," I said, searching for something
to say.

"In this business life is short and death is certain, and I haven't
got time for crazies."

"This Cottonhead is an individual. Individuals make a difference. He thought what he did served a higher purpose," I
said, still searching.

"That's bullshit. Don't disregard my orders ever again.
There's no room for individuals in the way I do business. Here
we all roll with the punches and do what we are told. That's the
way it is." Watley blew a second smoke ring into the air.

FROG HAIR

July 20, 1968: 0900 hours

"WELL, ARTEY, THE lieutenant says that you say this so-called Anglo known as Frog Hair actually does exist," Watley said, a kind of all-knowing look on his face.

"Sir, the name is Atrey, and the answer is a big affirmative. Frog Hair does exist. He may be rare as frog hair, as the saying goes, but I done seen him twice. Second time I had a clean shot at him. Should have dropped him," Atrey said, nodding as he spoke.

T.T. Watley, just looked at Atrey with contempt. Both men were from the South. T.T. Watley wore a college fraternity ring. Cottonhead Atrey wore an eagle, globe, and anchor tattoo. But the division between the two men seemed to be more than a matter of social class and rank. It seemed to me that Southerners were harder on each other when it came to making certain kinds of judgments. Not being a sociologist, I couldn't put my finger on exactly what was going on. I could only feel it. What was going on had to do with power. It also had something to do with dignity.

Watley was a son of a bitch to work for. He had been shit-canned from a platoon leader position because his troops had tried to frag him. Moving Watley to Division had saved his life. Much to my misfortune, however, Watley was a senior lieuten-

ant who soon found himself a captain. Good captains are hard
to find. Captains with political connections like Watley, and who
couldn't make the grade for whatever reason, usually found
themselves doing motor transport or supply work. By some twist
of fate, Watley had landed in a program everyone was reluctant
to name. Very soon those who had placed Watley where they
did were beginning to have regrets.

Watley didn't communicate. He didn't interact with the troops.
Moreover, he had no desire to do so, even when coached by his
higher-ups. By his own admission, Watley had fallen short in
that area. One night after a few beers, rare for Captain Watley,
he said that he felt it was beneath him to interact, to get too
close to those under his command.

"Under no circumstances do I want this Frog Hair blown
away. If we are lucky enough to catch him, I want him alive. In
fact, I think I'll go up to Division and get us a good sniper.
We'll nick him in the leg or something. But I don't want him
blown away. It's in the national interest. Besides, I'd like to get
inside this dude's head," Watley said in a manner both condescending and arrogant.

"That's a big affirmative, sir. Credit goes to Atrey here for
spotting this Anglo," I said, trying to be upbeat.

Atrey had spotted the Anglo crossing the road. It wasn't for
sure if the guy had been marine or army. All that we knew was
that he was fighting on the side of the Vietcong and that he had
been a part of successful ambushes. Several lucky survivors had
told of seeing a blond Anglo shooting prisoners caught in the
kill-zone of an ambush. I had talked to those marines myself
and I felt the emotion and conviction of what they had said. So
it was with some embarrassment that I listened to Watley query
Cottonhead Atrey who, in his own redneck way, demonstrated
the patience of Job.

"Atrey, Lieutenant here says that you been in Nam a long
time. Says that you are on your second extension. Why does a
man want to stay here and do what you do?"

"Sir, with all due respect, I am here for personal reasons,"
Atrey said, somewhat shaken by the question.

"That's not good enough, Atrey. To me it's a matter of human
reliability that we know why we stay in this country. We need

to be united and of one mind as to why we are doing what we are doing!'' Watley said, as if he had achieved a victory.

"Beggin' your pardon, sir, I don't know how to answer that question. All I know is that I'm here to be a good marine. And if you say Frog Hair is of more value alive, that's the way it will be.'' Atrey's voice was shaking.

"Very good, Atrey. I just wanted to be sure that we had an understanding,'' Watley said, putting his feet up on his desk.

"Atrey, all we can ask of you is that you be a good marine. Just trust your judgment. I will,'' I said, holding back the personal rage that I felt for Watley, for the crude arrogance of power with which he played with the dignity of Atrey.

Watley just glared at me, saying nothing. The little sucker, who was barely five feet, four inches, maybe one hundred and thirty pounds, rose from his desk and brushed by me. I wanted to break his fingers.

July 21, 1968: 0413 hours

We were in a village called La Chau 5. La Chau 5 lay at the edge of a little river called the Yen. The country was flat, with a few bamboo hedgerows and rice paddy dikes to offer cover. Watley, Atrey, Cruiser, our Vietnamese Kit Carson scout, myself, and a sniper named Stovall had worked our way carefully up the little river to a point where we could observe the village. We had been very lucky.

Apparently Frog Hair had a girlfriend. For the last three weeks he had been traveling regularly in the vicinity of La Chau. Cottonhead Atrey and Cruiser had been clever enough to catch that there had been movement down a certain path to the river every night.

Cruiser and Cottonhead had spread goose feathers and duck down on the trails leading into La Chau 5. After several nights they had been able to track the leading players by way of the duck down. Since the Vietnamese in La Chau raised ducks, this method drew little attention. When I asked Atrey where he had learned such tricks, he said that it was only trail savvy, and that he had hunted all his life along the Pearl River in east central Mississippi.

It came as a profound revelation to T. T. Watley that Frog Hair did exist. He and I watched as an Anglo in black pajamas, carrying an AK-47, walked calmly into La Chau 5. The Anglo was tall and thin. His sparse, shoulder-length hair was blond in the moonlight.

July 21, 1968: 0447 hours

Frog Hair left his girlfriend and headed toward the Yen river. Soon it would be daybreak. With the moonlight and the early sunrise, our sniper had plenty of light with which to get off a good shot.

Sergeant Ben Stovall from the First Marine Division Sniper Platoon didn't need much light. He raised the Remington 700 BDL with its Redfield scope and brought Frog Hair down at less than one hundred yards. It was simple business for Stovall, who was used to dropping men at five hundred yards or more. There was no wind to speak of, and Captain Watley's only request had been a leg shot when Frog Hair got to open ground. Stovall squeezed the round off and Frog Hair leaped when the round struck him, throwing his rifle high into the air.

July 21, 1968: 0516 hours

Frog Hair lay on the ground looking up at us. Stovall's round had cut the femoral artery. Frog Hair was in shock. Watley seemed unconcerned, smoking his cigarette. Stovall, Atrey, and I stared in amazement as Frog Hair whispered to Cruiser in Vietnamese.

Our Anglo was not an Anglo. Whoever Frog Hair was, he wasn't American. The high cheekbones, the slanted eyes, one of which was blue, the other brown, spoke to history. Our Anglo was at best a Eurasian, a dying Eurasian at that.

Watley had been speaking to the Division G-2 for the last half hour via a special radio frequency. He nodded occasionally, his body language suggesting that for him this was a kind of victory. Once he raised his voice, shouting a question in Vietnamese to Cruiser. Cruiser queried our prisoner and replied in Vietnamese to Watley. At no time did Watley seem concerned about Frog Hair's welfare. At my own initiative, feeling a kind of shame, I applied Frog Hair's web belt as a tourniquet to stop the flow of blood. Cottonhead assisted me.

"Look at that, Lieutenant. Dude's got one blue eye and one brown eye," Atrey said, peering into the dying man's eyes.

"Show's over," Watley said, approaching with a swagger.

"What's going on, Captain?" I asked, concerned about the dying Frog Hair.

"This is Dai Loc, for lack of a better name. He actually has no name. Division tells us that he is the offspring of a French/ Vietnamese woman named Mai and a Legionnaire of German extraction who served at Dai Loc in 1949," Watley said with some satisfaction.

"How did you find all that out, sir?" I asked, giving Frog Hair a sip of water.

"He is the bastard son of a whore and a former Nazi who fled to the safety of the French foreign legion," Watley said, lighting a cigarette.

"Damn!" Atrey said.

"His sister is an administrative officer for the province chief. Someday I will point her out to you. She is very beautiful, by any standard. I always wondered if her blond hair was natural," Watley said jokingly.

"You lost me, Captain. What's the point here?" I asked, wondering if I had missed something.

"What do you mean, Lieutenant?" Watley said, glaring again.

"Your humor seems to have changed. I understand that you view this as a success, but we have a dying man here, a man who you have said that you want to keep alive. Remember, you said that you wanted to get into his head," I said.

"Oh, that's true. I did say that. But that was when I took Atrey here at his word that this man was an Anglo. Obviously he is not an Anglo, and the point here is that I will be very happy to point out to Division that this man was not a marine, but a Vietnamese bastard out of some German. I find that good news, Lieutenant, don't you?" Watley asked, getting to within inches of my face.

"What do you want me to do, Captain?" I said, already knowing what Watley's answer would be.

"Atrey!" Watley said.

"Sir!" Atrey said, snapping to attention.

"Frog Hair is your mistake. You take care of him," Watley said, looking off toward the little river.

"I thought you said it was in the national interest to get into Frog Hair's head," I said.

"He's a gook. He's a gook that's got a sister that's the squeeze to the province chief. Division says that it's in the national interest to snuff him," Watley said.

"Who said that in Division?" I asked.

Watley was in my face in a second. He glared at me, as if he wanted me to try something stupid. I looked back at him. I was ready to kill him out of dislike. My code as a marine officer was keeping me from doing that. I had not followed that code to the letter, but for now it was keeping me from being the animal that would cut Watley's throat. It was also the code that was concerned for the welfare of Frog Hair.

"You dare to question me!" Watley hissed.

"You just ordered Atrey to snuff a prisoner. That's bullshit and you know it. What's going on?" I asked, my hand at my razor.

In the silence that followed, one could hear the breeze pick up off the river. The breeze turned the slim leaves of the bamboo upward. The breeze made a rustling sound as it wove onward through the tall grass surrounding the open ground on which we stood.

"Frog Hair," Watley whispered, turning to the dying Vietnamese.

"Let's go," I said to the men, sensing what was about to happen next.

"Atrey!" Watley yelled.

"Yes, sir," Atrey replied, in a shaky voice.

"I want you here. The others can go, but I want you here!" Watley yelled.

"Yes, sir!" Atrey said, looking at me for help.

I shook my head. Things were going on here that I did not understand. My experience in Vietnam up to this point had already shaken my beliefs about things like human dignity, honor, and the presumption of some higher purpose. I just didn't know what they meant anymore. I would have to redefine everything. It would take a lot of time.

"And Atrey, I want to know one thing!" Watley yelled.

"Sir?" Atrey said, puzzled.

"Back in Mississippi, did you ever see hair on a frog?" Watley said, grinning.

"No, sir," Atrey said, staring at the ground.

A single pistol shot rang out. Watley blew into the smoking barrel of his .45 and walked away.

HABU

AT FIRST LIGHT squalls drove inland from the South China Sea, bringing a damp chill that shook me from my drowse. Mortar Valley lay wet and dripping from the squall line, occasional big drops of rain falling through the foliage.

"There's something on the path," Cruiser whispered.

"I don't see a thing," I whispered back.

The Kit Carson scout smiled in the gloom of the bamboo hedgerow and pointed. I still saw nothing. To our front, on the high ridge line that separated Mortar Valley from Happy Valley, swallows were beginning to circle in the early morning light, stirring from deep within the honeycomb of the ridge line's rock wall.

"Show me again. I still don't see anything," I whispered again.

"By the cistern," he said.

The large, concrete cistern was about all that remained of the village of Phuoc Nhan. It served as a catch basin for the runoff from Charlie Ridge, the massif that imposed itself at our backs, rising some four hundred feet from sea level in about two kilometers.

Then a movement caught my eye. Numb from the cold, a fifteen-foot python, thick as a human thigh, was slowly uncoiling from a tangle of vegetation at the edge of the path.

"Do you see that, Weathers?" I asked.

Sergeant Weathers, one of the two snipers with our killer team, shook his head.

"Damn, Lieutenant, I don't see shit," Weathers replied.

"You watch," Cruiser grinned.

Without a sound Cruiser moved down the path. He leaned to within inches of the sluggish snake. With his long braid he tickled the snake's head. Slowly the python drew back. Over all the dripping sounds within the vegetation I could hear the python's hiss. Cruiser made a funny face and slipped quietly back into the foliage. Above, the cave swallows began to whistle, greeting the new day and the sun, which was now beginning to break through the cloud cover. There must have been five hundred swallows circling in a swarm over Mortar Valley.

October 1, 1968: 0700 hours

Our first night had passed without incident. No doubt we had been lucky. All of us on the team had worked that area on different occasions in the past, and each of us had a horror story to tell about the sacrifices that had been made.

Weathers and Odum were marine scout snipers who had carried out a number of successful Stingray patrols during Operation Mameluke Thrust. As marine scout snipers, they had used stealth and, when appropriate, the deadly accurate fire from the Remington 700 BDL. Cruiser, of course, had seen the ground from two sides. As a Kit Carson scout, he was a former North Vietnamese Army (NVA) soldier who had rallied to the South Vietnamese government.

I had worked the area as a platoon leader with the Third Battalion, Seventh Marines, my tracks carrying marines and material through the valley. That operation had started out as a simple exercise. By the time we were done, we had lost two men and were almost overrun. We got out of the valley after a series of running firefights.

"Lieutenant, why don't you let me and Odum skin that son of a bitch out. I'd just love to show that hide back in Lusk, Wyoming," Weathers said, trying his best to charm me.

"Sorry, Weathers. We can't risk exposing ourselves on the trail. You know that," I said.

Weathers had been trying to dominate the team since we had been given the go-ahead back at Hill 10.

"Well, okay, Lieutenant, you're the boss." Weathers smirked.

We were set in just above a trail junction that overlooked what had once been Phuoc Nhan. Below us the trail junction split, one branch running down to the bottom of the valley, the other branch running east toward Da Nang, out into the flat rice paddy country known as the Khuong My Plain. Where the two trails came together, they formed what Odum and Weathers called the Speed Trail.

The Speed Trail was well traveled. It was the only trail that ran from the bottom of Mortar Valley over the top of Charlie Ridge. While Speed Trail was well marked on the Dai Loc map sheet, for some reason it was only in the last year that the trail had been closely monitored. As Habu One, monitoring the Speed Trail was our mission. Like the thick and deadly Okinawan habu, we would set along Speed Trail and observe. If the right opportunity arose, we would strike.

Weathers called it "snoop and poop." My boss, Captain O.D. Lowy, head of the special task group, also hoped that we would have opportunity for what he called a "snatch and run." The ideal candidate for that snatch was one Pham Van Tra who traveled the Speed Trail.

One couldn't help but like O. D. Lowy. He was entirely different from his predecessor, Captain Watley. Where Watley had been rigid and inflexible, Lowy was open and actively sought the opinions of his men. Watley had been removed from his position. There had been a power struggle of sorts and the province adviser had made Lowy his "deputy." Lowy's new authority allowed the province senior adviser time to do the important "liaison" work so necessary to his job. Lowy ran the special task groups. For the most part Lowy left the district advisers alone. Lowy was interested in his projects. First priority was Habu. Second priority were the various activities of the Cold Steel Crowd. Third priority were the boys from Hoi An who linked with various groups and at times chafed under Lowy's authority since their leader was a major.

Within our working area there were a number of districts, including Hieu Duc. The day before we departed, someone at the Hieu Duc District Headquarters had fingered Pham Van Tra to the captain.

Pham Van Tra was old enough to be my grandfather. He lived out in the Bo Bans, a hot VC area that bordered the Hieu Duc and Hoa Vang districts. When Captain Lowy came up with a picture of the old man, I was impressed. The picture showed Pham Van Tra as a schoolteacher standing next to the class that made up his one-room school. His shock of thick white hair would make him easy to spot.

While Pham Van Tra may have been an old man, he possessed stamina and was remarkably fit for his age. At five feet he was thin and wiry, and barely over one hundred pounds. Yet, it was apparent from our intelligence that during the day and night he ranged widely throughout the northwest corner of the Dai Loc map sheet. Captain Lowy felt that he ran the Speed Trail over Charlie Ridge into Mortar Valley, carrying information from the Bo Bans to the base camps in the mountains.

"Come on, Lieutenant. Take us five minutes to skin that son of a bitch out," Weathers implored.

The python now lay sprawled in the sun on top of the concrete cistern. Probably built by the French, the five-foot-high cistern was about thirty feet long by about ten feet wide. Its breadth and length allowed sun through the wall of bamboo hedgerow that bordered the trail. Clearly any involvement with the snake risked exposure.

"For the last time, Weathers, that's a big negative."

Weathers shrugged his shoulders and nodded.

We had been lucky coming into the valley. Amphibian tractors had dropped us off in the mouth of Mortar Valley. With the rain providing cover, we had slipped into the bamboo hedgerows of what had once been Phouc Nhan.

As a result of having participated in the Stingray operations, Odum and Weathers had received commendations. Already confident, each of them had developed a sense of independence. Weathers, in particular, had a reputation as a lone wolf. My presence on the patrol probably ran against the grain of that independence. My refusing to let Weathers kill the snake only served to highlight the problem. I was sure each man would have preferred to run his own killer team.

October 1, 1968: 0800 hours

By my own estimation I was anything but a boot lieutenant. I had almost a full tour in Vietnam, serving all of that time either as a rifle platoon leader or as an amphibian tractor platoon leader. I had lost count of the ambushes and patrols that I had been a part of. I had mired my tractors in the mud of Go Noi Island and had choked in the dust of the Arizona Territory. First Marines, Fifth Marines, Seventh Marines, I had supported all three regiments in the field.

Weathers glanced my way. Blond and blue-eyed, he was a rugged, clean-limbed six-footer who had been born and raised up near the Yellowstone in Wyoming. I could sense his irritation. Lowy had alerted me to Weathers. At times in the past, Weathers had resisted being part of the team. Under pressure he had a reputation for being critical. On a number of occasions he had overstepped his prerogatives.

Yet, although overbearing to some, Weathers was the kind of marine one needed for this job. The very qualities that irritated my fellow officers were the core of Weathers's forceful character. Quick in thought and action, he undertook his responsibilities with a can-do attitude. As a marine scout sniper, he sought out opportunities and got results where others would have backed off. In short, he had guts. He also had more confirmed kills than any other marine scout sniper in the First Marine Division.

Odum settled under the bamboo hedge to my right. Weathers had relieved him from the trail watch. Short, dark, and wiry, Odum was a contrast to Weathers. Odum smiled and winked as he slipped the Remington off his shoulder.

"How about it, Lieutenant? Don't you wish you were back in Da Nang drinking a cold brew?" Odum said, still smiling.

"Hell no, Odum. This is where all the action is. I like to get high on the action," I said, sounding like a smart ass.

"You and I both, Lieutenant. Who would want to be back in the rear, those hot meals, showers, and all that Vietnamese pussy," Odum said, a smirk on his face.

If Weathers was a loner, Blade Odum was just the opposite. Open and friendly, Odum was Captain Lowy's favorite. He came across as optimistic, a people-person.

"How long you and Weathers been working together?" I asked.

"About six or seven months, on and off," Odum said.

"He wants to go out and skin that snake."

"Yes, sir. That he does," Odum replied.

"Don't you think that's a little crazy? Out here where we happen to be?"

"Crazy, sir? Out here, what is crazy? I'd like to have that python hide myself. Take a guy like Weathers. What's crazy to some may be normal to him. Weathers is used to being his own boss. That's why he liked to stay out in the bush. No bullshit. You can kill your snake and take time to skin it out if you're so minded," Odum said, as always with a smile.

"What got you interested in being a sniper?" I asked, changing the subject.

"Well, I didn't want to grunt anymore. I didn't want to go back to the world. The routine back at Headquarters in Da Nang was getting to be too much spit and polish and lifers, so I volunteered. I like variety. Like Weathers, I like the freedom. And we get around a lot. I got a couple of girlfriends out in the villes. You know how it is, Lieutenant."

I did know. I thought of Dao. I thought of how she had once given me her warmth and comfort. At that moment I wondered where she was. I wondered if she ever thought of me.

"Yeah, well, old Weathers is okay, Lieutenant. It's just hard for him to get used to having an officer around." Odum winked.

Blade Odum was from east-central Mississippi. With his Southern accent and easy manner, he had the tact and charm lacking in Weathers. It would be hard for me not to favor Odum.

The blade Odum carried was a kukri, the weapon of the British Gurkhas. The kukri is a bolo-style knife with a blade over a foot long. The bolo curve maximizes leverage and chopping power. A kukri will split a skull or sever a spinal cord with one blow. My marine K-Bar seemed impotent by comparison.

"So you would risk your own skin for that snake's hide. Is that right, Odum?" I asked.

"Yes, sir, that's a big affirmative," Odum replied.

"That important," I said.

"Sir, did you ever hear of the Holiness Church?"

"No, I haven't," I replied.

"Sir, my daddy is a snake-handling preacher in the Holiness Church. When I saw that snake, all I could think of was my daddy and Mark sixteen, eighteenth verse," Odum said.

"I don't know that one."

"The verse says that they shall take up serpents; and if they drink any deadly thing, it shall not harm them; they shall lay hands on the sick and they shall recover. I would love to bring home that hide to my daddy. You see he has a zeal so fundamental that he believes every word of the bible, literally."

"Taking up serpents," I said.

"Yes, sir, they shall take up serpents," Odum repeated.

"You still think I should have let Weathers kill and skin that snake, don't you?" I asked.

"For Weathers it's a matter of pride. For you it would be an act of faith in him. My daddy believes that taking up the serpent is a pronouncement of victory over evil." Odum gave me another wink.

October 1, 1968: 0915 hours

"Movement down the trail," Odum whispered.

Weathers and Cruiser lay to my left, keeping visual contact with Odum and me.

"There you go, Lieutenant," Odum whispered, obviously excited.

A single NVA soldier led the group, distinctive in his faded and worn pith helmet. He was followed by three boys, none of them more than ten or eleven years old. An old man with a great shock of white hair brought up the rear. The old man appeared to be Pham Van Tra.

From our left Weathers drew his finger across his throat. I signaled negative, shaking my head slowly. Patience is the hunter, I thought. The look on Odum's face told me that he was clearly disappointed.

The group approached the cistern. The NVA soldier greeted the sprawled python as if he were an old friend. The python drew back into a great mass of coils. The old man smiled and jabbered something to the boys about his "watch dog." My Vietnamese wasn't good enough to catch all the meaning. One thing I did catch. This old teacher, dignified in his own way, had walked either his pupils or his grandchildren into our team's kill-zone.

October 1, 1968: 0930 hours

They had been resting in the clearing next to the cistern for about fifteen minutes. All the while Pham Van Tra was the teacher. The three young boys listened to his every word as he spoke of what had once been the village of Phuoc Nhan. Pham Van Tra spoke of the Frenchman who had helped him build the cistern and of the road that once ran down the center of Mortar Valley. At one point he walked to a tree that grew beside the cistern that he had planted before the boys' fathers had been born. Pham Van Tra touched the tree with affection and let out a sigh.

All this was apparently too much for the NVA soldier. He interrupted Pham Van Tra's lecture with his own concerns. Taking the boys to one corner of the great cistern, he lifted what appeared to be a concrete slab camouflaged with foliage. Below the slab there clearly was a tunnel entrance. After discussing the entrance briefly with the boys, the NVA soldier disappeared into the mouth of the tunnel. One by one the boys followed, Pham Van Tra quietly bringing up the rear. A pair of strong, brown arms reached up and pulled the slab back into place.

Weathers and Cruiser were at my side within a minute.

"Why didn't we zap them when we had the chance?" Weathers asked bluntly.

"I thought it best at this point to take it slow. As they say, patience is the hunter."

"Who says that! We just missed some quick kills!" Weathers said, making a face at Odum.

Odum was looking down at the ground, chewing his gum rapidly. Only Cruiser seemed to agree, nodding slowly.

"What do you think, Cruiser?" I asked.

"They're training little boys to be messengers. Tough marines don't kill little boys," Cruiser said, making his funny face.

"Bullshit! We'll catch them and we'll cut their little nuts off, won't we, Odum?" Weathers said.

Odum smiled and gave me a wink.

"Weathers always gets results, Lieutenant," Cruiser said, and this time there was no funny face.

Two years earlier Cruiser had defected from the NVA up in northern I Corps. Sensitive and well educated by Vietnamese standards, Cruiser's father was a French mining engineer that the North Vietnamese had allowed to remain in North Vietnam because of his open sympathy for the communists. Cruiser's mother was a white Thai his father met·while working in the Con Voi Mountains north of the Red River.

The only thing Cruiser retained from this background was a silver bracelet. For Cruiser loved all things Western. His hair grew down to his shoulders, now woven into a long braid for bush travel. At Headquarters he always seemed to have a transistor radio plugged into his ear.

Cruiser was quick and bright to the events around him. Sometimes he would play the fool, hence his "funny face." That it was a gesture or expression without words was obvious. What was never clear to me was if the face were meant to be comic or tragic.

At Headquarters Cruiser's behavior seemed to alternate between periods of furious activity and lulls when he would appear overwhelmed. Behind those bright eyes I sensed that Cruiser was looking for something. Behind those same bright eyes I also sensed much doubt. It was evident to even the most casual observer that Cruiser tried to please everyone, even Weathers, who held him in contempt.

"Well, did we do right, Cruiser, sparing those little boys?" I asked.

"Patience is the hunter," he said.

October 1, 1968: 1015 hours

My orders were clear. Since we weren't to rendezvous with the amphibian tractors until the following day, we would wait. We would wait beside the trail like the thick and deadly habu that was our namesake. If neither the boys nor Pham Van Tra ever reappeared, so be it. We would booby-trap the area and boogie on down the trail back to our rendezvous point. My intuition told me that we would see the old man again. Anyway, it was clear to me that we had preserved our stealth. Our stealth was our advantage. The knowledge earned from that stealth was our gain.

At the very least we were certain that the cistern was a way station or resting place along the Speed Trail. That information Captain Lowy would find invaluable.

Weathers, however, persisted in demonstrating his impatience. "Damn, Lieutenant, we had them in our sights. Could have blown them away and been home for lunch."

"Too many constraints, Weathers. They may have had friends around. The little boys."

"The boys! Those little boys are gonna be hard-core VC!"

"Yeah, I know that, Sergeant," I said, looking away.

"Lieutenant, what would you say if I told you that Odum was willing to go into that tunnel after them," Weathers said.

"That is crazy," I replied.

Taking up the serpent, I said to myself. His daddy back in Mississippi may handle snakes, but he has no corner on his son when it comes to taking risks. I had seen it before. One could call it the "point man" or the "tunnel rat" syndrome. Status went with each endeavor. I viewed such compulsions with sadness and suspicion, for those who volunteered were clearly out to prove something that in the end would make no difference in terms of the "big picture." Then again, who was I to pass judgment? We all had our different rewards.

"Yeah, Lieutenant, that is crazy. I agree with you. Figuring how crazy is the problem," Weathers said.

"I'm listening."

"I know you are, sir," Weathers said.

October 1, 1968: 1130 hours

If Odum's reward for being here was some sort of prestige or recognition, Weathers's reward was running his own show. In his own lone-wolf, cowboy way he was just trying to do his part. Somehow I sensed that we hadn't given him enough of something. That something may have been guidance or clear direction. Maybe that something was just control. Once you give a guy like Weathers the freedom to perform a job that he deeply believes in, it's hard to take back that freedom. I knew that I didn't have full control. I would just try to point Weathers in the right direction.

If Odum were out to prove something and if Weathers were out of control, Cruiser was a mess eager to please. I couldn't help but see them all as adrift, one driven by faith, another by a violent fidelity, the last by luck. I recalled Okinawa and the first time I stumbled upon a habu. We were crossing a stream and the snake had slid into the water. Suddenly it was just there beside me, without a sound, floating its own dark weight.

October 1, 1968: 1200 hours

At high noon, almost to the minute, the swallows that darted back and forth over Mortar Valley became agitated, chirping and chattering, clearly disturbed by something in the valley below.

"Got movement in the valley, Lieutenant. Something or someone is stirring those birds," Weathers said."

"You're right. What do you think it could be?"

"Could be rice carriers. If it were up to me, I'd check it out," Weathers said.

"What about booby traps on the trail?"

"Luck of the draw, Lieutenant. Odum and I got enough trail savvy. Don't worry, Lieutenant, we'll just read the sign and boogie on back."

"Call it an act of faith," I whispered to myself.

"What was that, Lieutenant?" Weathers asked.

"Nothing, I was just talking to myself. All right. You and Odum go ahead," I said, letting go.

They were off in an instant, and I drifted into my thoughts. My God I thought, what act of faith had brought me here? What was I doing extending my tour in Vietnam? Hadn't I seen enough death, needless sacrifice, and betrayal?

I had long ago given up any thought of orderly progress in the war. But after seeing my friends suffer and die, I felt that I needed to come to terms with my own insufficient contribution. Everyone said to go home, but like Weathers, I wanted results. It was vengeance for the loss of my friends and what seemed to be our inability to accomplish anything lasting that drove me. I would drink too much and then brood to the point of self-destruction over a friend's sacrifice, heaving my guts out on the ground. I would wake in the night with pounding headaches and wild impulses. I would have blown away those little boys.

October 1, 1968: 1230 hours

Mintues passed by without event. From time to time the python would move on the cistern, seeking shade where part of the bamboo hedgerow overhung it.

Then, at about 1230, they began to come up the trail in a long line of twos and threes, more than a hundred NVA regulars in the span of about thirty minutes.

They weren't logistical support troops. They were infantry. What bothered me most was the ease and confidence with which they marched past us, smiling and joking. Two separate groups paused to fill their canteens and water bags at the cistern.

At 1245 Weathers and Odum appeared at my side, having made their way silently through the foliage. I felt both relieved and calm. While it may have been an impulse that brought me to my present situation, I knew that in the past weeks I was learning to control that energy. More than that, I was truly beginning to trust myself, and, given the circumstances at hand, I would pace both myself and the situation. If at all possible, I would not kill any kids. Perhaps I could even inspire the confidence of Weathers and Odum. After all, that was what leadership was all about.

October 1, 1968: 1645 hours

At 1645 Pham Van Tra emerged from the tunnel with two of his boys. He spent a few minutes speaking to the remaining NVA. The sound of female laughter came from the tunnel and I was astounded as two Anglo women appeared. Both women were wearing the light blue smock of the German missionary nurses at An Hoa. The two women embraced, saying something in German. The younger woman then returned to the tunnel entrance. The older woman turned and followed Pham Van Tra and the two boys down the trail that led to the floor of Mortar Valley and out onto the Khuong My plain.

October 1, 1968: 2000 hours

Twilight brought the cave swallows back, circling in the dusk, preparing to enter that deep honeycomb within the rock face of the ridge line's wall. For the first evening in two weeks there were no rain clouds to hide the mountains to the west, and for the last twenty minutes the Speed Trail had been quiet.

The python had crawled slowly off the top of the cistern and lay like a great coil of harbor rope at the fork of the Speed Trail. When Pham Van Tra's third boy appeared from the tunnel, he sat at the edge of the cistern, looking up at the sky.

A voice called to him from deep within the tunnel. He answered that he would only be a minute, that he wanted to watch the last of the roosting birds and the first of the evening stars. The voice from the tunnel acknowledged. It was an accented, woman's voice, certainly that of the German nurse.

The boy would never answer her. In a single, graceful move Weathers slipped across the cistern and snatched the little boy. Simultaneously, Cruiser was on the downhill trail setting booby traps. The uphill trail was mine. I quickly set two separate fragmentation grenade booby traps, placing the live grenades into ration cans. Someone hurrying down the trail would catch the trip wire, pulling the frag grenade from the can.

Odum covered the Speed Trail where it forked, his attention riveted on the left fork, our escape route. The little boy went limp in Weathers's grip, a simple "sleeper," I had said. Then it happened that the woman's voice again came from the tunnel. There was a singsong quality to the voice, as if she were preparing a child for bed.

I could barely see her in the dusk as she rose from the tunnel. She never had a chance to utter a sound. With two giant steps Blade Odum crossed the clearing from the trail fork, and, since there was no helmet to contend with, the blow was a simple vertical chop to the top of the skull. Odum reacted upon impulse, knowing that splitting the brain immediately destroys the capacity for speech. He also reacted without seeing clearly.

There was no time to search her body. Odum returned to his former position at the trail fork. Cruiser left her body at the tunnel entrance, booby-trapped with a frag grenade. At that point there was a thrashing at the trail fork as Odum came upon the python. In the dim light the python's body was tossing about the clearing.

I signaled the men and we were gone, down the left fork of the Speed Trail. In ten minutes we were out onto the valley floor and heading toward Hill 10.

October 1, 1968: 2200 hours

"Sardine Actual, this is the Habu Actual, over," I said, breaking radio silence for the first time in two days.

"Habu Actual, this is Sardine Actual," came the reply.

"Roger, Sardine Actual, request pick up at Checkpoint Lima, over."

"We copy, Habu, see you in twenty, out."

Moving out onto the Khuong My Plain, we could hear the booming engines of the amphibian tractors coming to pick us up.

Before long, four-deuce mortar illumination popped overhead, turning the evening into day. I saw the silhouettes of four of the twenty-five ton amphibian tractors lumbering across the plain.

Weathers was sitting on the ground, clearly exhausted, with the boy on his lap. When the boy looked up at me, his eyes were bright with both fear and fatigue. In time I hoped he would be able to tell us much about his teacher, Pham Van Tra. Perhaps he knew where the German woman had come from.

Odum was crouched, Vietnamese style, to my right. He was holding the great python's head in the flickering light of the four-deuce illumination, muttering to himself. No doubt the signs found in Mark 16: 16–20, as with the taking up of serpents and speaking in tongues. No doubt Odum's faith was as strong as the blue steel of his kukri.

Cruiser, calm and relaxed, looked up at me and gave me his funny face. I wondered if he believed as Paul wrote, that the last enemy that shall be defeated is Death.

THIRD PRINCE OF
THE LOTUS

THERE WAS NO doubt that the dead woman in the middle of Liberty Road was an Anglo. She had been a healthy, beautiful woman. Her naked body lay bent backward so that the full expression of her womanhood lay exposed, adding to the final indignity.

"Nice tits," Sergeant Weathers said.

Odum and I said nothing in reply. None of us had slept since last night's action. We were all so wired by the events of the last two days that sleep seemed impossible.

"Hey, Lieutenant, stay loose," Weathers said, winking and cracking his chewing gum.

Weathers pissed me off with his give-a-shit attitude. I had made up my mind that when we got back to Da Nang I was going to have a talk with Captain Lowy about getting him off my team. What I first thought was nonchalance and a casual indifference toward officers in general, I now knew to be impertinence. Weathers was an insolent son of a bitch who not only seemed to hold officers in contempt, he also apparently had no respect for the dead.

October 2, 1968: 1515 hours

We had been on Hill 10 when Lieutenant Lukavitch called me
about the body. Since my team's mission was counterintelligence, he felt that I should know that a dead Anglo woman lay
naked in the middle of Liberty Road. As battalion S-5 for the
Third Battalion, Seventh Marines, Lukavitch had charge of civil
affairs for the area surrounding Hill 10. My team had been operating in and around his area for more than a week. I'm sure
that he called me out of professional courtesy. He couldn't have
known the truth.

Odum was now dealing with the truth. He squatted by the
body, staring at the woman's head. Her skull had been split
down the middle. The blow had been a simple vertical chop to
the top of the skull.

I looked around for Lukavitch. He was nowhere to be seen.
A squad of marine grunts sat on the opposite side of the road
from the body, gazing with indifference at my team and the
small group of Vietnamese that had gathered to gape at the
scene.

"Who's in charge here?" I asked.

A thin black arm rose above the heads of the marine grunts.

"I am, Lieutenant," a young black marine said.

"Why haven't you pulled that body off the road?" I asked.

"Sir, Lieutenant Lukavitch said not to fool with it till he got
back. He said the body might be booby-trapped. Might have a
105 round buried underneath," he replied.

"That's a big affirmative, Lieutenant. No use killing good
marines over some dead squeeze," Sergeant Weathers said, still
smirking.

I looked at Weathers. He was standing behind Odum who was
still staring at the body. Weathers winked again and nodded at
Odum. I got the drift.

"Odum. Go back to the jeep and watch the kid. Tell Cruiser
to come here," I said.

My mind raced back to last night's patrol. Odum knew who
it was lying in the middle of Liberty Road. Cruiser and Weathers
also knew. This was the German nurse that we had killed by
mistake on last night's patrol. Where she had come from, we
could only guess. Officially, the German Mission was neutral.

However, from time to time some of their people had been spotted way out in the field, far from where they would have been considered safe. Maybe this was one nurse who had traveled too far. Killing her had been an accident, Odum said. He had not seen clearly and reacted to her movement. It was all a terrible mistake.

October 2, 1968: 1520 hours

Keep your cool, I thought. Right now the most important thing is to keep the emotions under control. I watched Weathers. He was jumpy. Odum sat by the boy, still distant and preoccupied.

The boy reminded me of a chipmunk or some other small rodent. Probably eleven or twelve, he sat quietly, bewildered by all of the events about him. There was a space between his two buckteeth. He had a thick shock of black hair that stuck out in all directions. His fat cheeks were a contrast to the lean and hungry look one would expect of a Vietcong messenger.

A number of Vietnamese had now gathered from the ville to view the dead woman. Looking over their heads, I noticed that the body had been dumped at the entrance to a walk that led to the village pagoda, a particularly beautiful structure with sliding doors that opened to the road. Those doors were open, and looking down the stone walk I found myself looking into a shrine where Buddha stared back at me, flanked by two lesser shrines. The musky scent of burning joss sticks filled the morning air.

"You wanted me, Lieutenant?" Cruiser asked.

"That's right. This thing is weird, Cruiser. Totally weird."

"Weird?" Cruiser asked, not knowing the word.

I kept forgetting Cruiser's language limitations. The Kit Carson scout winked at me and smiled as if he understood what I was thinking.

"Something's very strange here," I said.

Cruiser simply nodded.

"Did you get anything out of the boy?"

"Only his name, which is Trin, and that he is a prince," Cruiser said, smiling.

"A prince! What do you mean a prince?"

"His birthday is May 27. That is a day marked by daylong

festivities by the Chinese in my home province. It is the birthday of a child-God worshiped as a hero and a miracle worker. He is known as the Third Prince of the Lotus." Cruiser said.

"That boy told you this?"

"No, sir. The boy only told me his name and his birth date."

"And what did you tell him?" I asked.

"I told him that he was very lucky."

October 2, 1968: 1530

I looked toward the jeep to see Weathers and Odum in deep conversation. Weathers was shaking his head in a manner that suggested to me that he and Odum were having more than a dialogue. As I approached, both looked up in silence.

"Find Lieutenant Lukavitch yet, sir?" Weathers said.

"That black corporal said he's on his way down from Hill 10 with a body bag. I want to hang loose until he gets here. Maybe we can take the body back to Division. I want to get the spectacle over," I said.

"Cruiser show you the sign that he found, Lieutenant?" Weathers asked.

"Sign?"

Cruiser pointed to a cardboard sign that I hadn't noticed. The sign lay at the edge of the road. Something in Vietnamese was written on the sign, painted on in large white letters.

"What does it say, Cruiser?" I asked.

Cruiser hesitated. His eyes flickered from side to side, never looking at me.

"We better take that sign with us, Lieutenant," Cruiser said.

"What's the sign say?" I asked.

"It says marines gang-rapists and woman killers."

I picked up the sign and tore it into several pieces. I threw the pieces into the brush along the side of the road. Weathers smirked and shook his head.

"Weathers, take Cruiser and scout around through the area. If you find any more of those signs, police them up. Tell those grunts that I want that crowd of Vietnamese out of here. The public show is over," I said.

"Yes, sir, consider it done."

Odum sat in the jeep staring out toward the mountains. I felt that I should say something to him, but I didn't know how to begin. My feelings were getting the best of me. It was Odum that broke the ice.

"Well, am I going to get court-martialed over this thing, Lieutenant?" Odum asked.

"Odum, I don't think anyone knows who killed that woman but the team."

"Weathers says I'll get busted for sure, maybe do some hard time. Weathers said Division already sent some grunts to hard time for killing a couple of civilians. Just my luck they'll grab my ass for this. No telling what they'll give me for killing a white woman," Odum said with a kind of sad smile.

Odum wanted me to tell him how I was going to handle the situation. The fact was that I didn't know. What Odum didn't know was that more than a few marines had been charged and court-martialed for acts committed upon the civilian population in the last few months. It was Captain Lowy's opinion that Division was trying to send a clear message to the grunts in the field to watch their step.

Captain Lowy would know how to handle this thing. He was someone everyone looked to for advice. The province senior adviser let him run the show, confident that Lowy could work with all levels of command within the province from the district advisers to the various battalion commanders. Lowy had helped me in the past with some difficult issues. I trusted his varied experience and his insight to help me through this mess. For sure, Captain Lowy would get us out of this shit.

That we were in deep shit was obvious. Sooner or later I would have to file my report. In addition, we had this kid. When Lukavitch and Captain Vilks got word of this kid, they would want to pump him for information. Vilks was the S-2 for Third Battalion, Seventh Marines. He handled their intelligence. He was a good guy but he spoke fluent Vietnamese. The kid could tell him anything, provided the kid had the big picture. How much did the kid know? That was the real question, the answer which would determine the breadth and the depth of the shit in which we were all about to wallow.

"Wonder what they would do to you, Lieutenant?" Odum said.

What would they do to me? I recalled Captain Lowy telling me of a marine company commander who had killed a badly wounded NVA prisoner. The NVA was suffering and it appeared that there was no way to evacuate. The company commander simply put a round through the man's head. Later, when the company returned to the rear, a doper who had a grudge against him blew the whistle. At this very moment that officer was facing a court-martial.

Overhead a wild crane passed by, its large wings beating rapidly. The great bird's legs trailed out behind him. His long neck was extended full length. I thought of my own neck.

"Look at that, Lieutenant, wild crane. Down in the ville the gooks call that good luck," Odum said.

I snapped out of my thoughts and tuned in Odum. Then it hit me. Here I was preoccupied with my neck when my real job was staring me in the face. Here I was worried about what kind of support I would get from Division when the immediate need was to make Odum think and feel as if he had the support he needed.

"Odum, I'll tell you the truth. I'm not sure what we are going to do right now. One thing you can depend on for sure is that I'm behind you. This whole team's behind you."

"Lieutenant, Weathers is shaky. He don't have any confidence in you or anything connected with this team. All he wants to do is to go back and do his own thing. He wants out of this team. You need to sit down and talk with him," Odum said.

"What do you mean, me? I'm not the issue here, you are. We need to pull together. If this thing gets out, we all got to have our stories straight."

"Lieutenant, I think you're missing the point. I'm not worried about Weathers backing my story. He'd go to hell for me. What I'm worried about has to do with the team. I want to hold this team together. Weathers and I already talked and he knows that I'm behind the lieutenant one hundred and ten percent. But holding that team together, Lieutenant, there's some things we might have to do to make that real," Odum said.

"What do you mean?"

"The boy," Odum said.

"What about the boy," I said.

"What if the boy knows, Lieutenant. What if the boy tells?"

"Odum, the boy probably doesn't know a thing."

The boy sat in the back of the jeep. He was blindfolded, and I was sure that Weathers's "sleeper hold" had kept the boy from seeing all of last night's events.

"Weathers wants to snuff him, Lieutenant."

Slowly it began to dawn on me. I had totally misunderstood the situation. I was worried how Odum was handling the guilt. Now it was apparent that he and Weathers had discussed murdering the boy. It was also apparent that I had not only misread Odum, but I had profoundly underestimated him. His statements about holding the team together were no more than a veiled threat.

"You would kill that kid! What on earth would Weathers gain by killing the kid," I said, feeling my emotions welling up.

"Silence. And it's sorta like insurance for the team. You know, all I think Weathers wants is insurance that he'll be able to stay out in the ville, without officers or lifers—no offense, sir—getting into his shit. That's all it is, Lieutenant. And like Weathers says, there's no telling what the kid saw or what the kid knows, but why take a chance. If Captain Vilks gets ahold of that kid, and that kid starts talking about that nurse . . ."

"Odum, would you kill that boy?" I asked, barely under control.

"I don't think that it has anything to do with me, Lieutenant. I think it has to do with the burden that we carry. As Matthew said, we are all heavy laden."

"What the hell are you talking about?" I yelled, losing it.

"As Matthew said, 'come unto me, all ye that labor and are heavy laden, and I will give you rest.' I regret what happened. I truly regret it. But perhaps it was meant to happen and I was just the Lord's instrument. I hope that the spirit of that German woman is resting with the Lord. Maybe this boy's spirit needs to rest."

I would have to watch both Odum and Weathers very carefully. I would have to direct their every move from now until we got back to Captain Lowy. Captain Lowy would know what to do.

"We're taking the boy back to Lowy. I don't believe that the boy knows or understands all of what has happened. Even if he did know and comprehend all of this, I wouldn't kill him," I said, calmly.

"You have taken on the burden, Lieutenant."

"Then that is where I must place my faith." I looked at the little boy, the one Cruiser now called the Third Prince of the Lotus. Cruiser was right. Today that little boy was very lucky.

WHEN I GET
TO THE GRAND HOTEL

October 2, 1968: 1600 hours

LIEUTENANT LUKAVITCH ARRIVED with the body bag
and we zipped in the dead German nurse. Lukavitch had no idea
of our involvement with the corpse. He speculated that the dead
woman was either an army nurse from Da Nang or a Red Cross
worker from farther south. Apparently both had disappeared
during the last two weeks. "You know VC have kidnapped
American women before," Lukavitch said.

I nodded, saying nothing. I was watching our young prisoner
for his reaction. We had been lucky snatching this boy. I wanted
to observe him.

"But my gut feeling on this one is different. I'd bet some of
our people are involved in this," Lukavitch said.

"There it is!" Weathers said, winking at me.

"What do you think, Sam?" Lukavitch asked.

"I don't know, John. The navy will handle it, I guess."

I directed Odum to borrow a trailer from 3/7 so that we could
haul the body. I instructed Odum to keep the boy blindfolded
and under guard.

"Somehow, Sam, I thought this body would concern that new
group that you're working with," Lukavitch said, watching
Odum and the boy depart.

"How so?"

"Don't you folks in CIT deal with these matters?" Lukavitch asked.

"CIT is the first Marine Division's counterintelligence team. Our mission is better described in terms of countermeasures. It's a new idea, and though I call it counterintelligence, in fact, it's many things."

"Countermeasures?"

"Yeah, countermeasures."

"Countermeasures against the VC, I assume?"

"Actually we call it VCI or Vietcong infrastructure. It's the political apparatus we're after. And errand boys, like this young prisoner."

"Could have fooled me, Lieutenant," Weathers said, smiling.

I ignored Weathers's remark. Turning away from him, I started walking toward the spot where the body had been lying. A group of chickens had gathered on the road, pausing at the dark stain where the body had been. First the rooster, then the hens began pecking frantically at the blood-filled earth.

"Get out of here," Weathers yelled, kicking at the chickens.

"Is that boy part of the countermeasures?" Lukavitch asked.

"More or less," I replied.

Lukavitch was probing. That made me nervous and it pissed me off.

Lukavitch turned to Sergeant Weathers. "How do you like working with this new group, Sergeant Weathers?"

"We're all a bunch of gook lovers, Lieutenant Lukavitch. We go out and try to sniff them out. But we don't do nothing. Just kind of hang out in the ville. You know, Lieutenant, like you folks in the S-5 shop."

"That's enough, Sergeant Weathers," I said.

At that moment someone struck a bronze gong in the pagoda across the road from where we were standing. The Vietnamese had opened the pagoda's sliding doors to Liberty Road. A shrine of Buddha overlooked all of us as we stood by the body bag.

"Prayer gong. It's getting late," Lukavitch said, using the sound of the gong to change the subject.

The gong sounded again. This time the sound seemed to echo in the thick overhang of the bamboo. It was a sound that drew you to reflect, a sound that drew you into introspection.

"You seem real tired, Sam," Lukavitch said.

"I'm very tired, John. These last few days have exhausted me."

The gong struck a third time and this time I found a kind of comfort in the sound. In the quiet of the late afternoon, under the thick overhanging bamboo, with the mountains at our back like great shadows, I felt myself drifting in spite of the body bag at my feet. Fatigue, I thought. For a moment it was as if I were out of my body, hovering, looking down at the whole grisly scene.

"Well, Lieutenant, do you think this lady found Buddha?" Weathers said. This time there was no smirk on his face. His question brought me back to reality. I was tired, very tired. Weathers probably picked up on me drifting off. I got to get my shit together, I thought.

"In her last moments I'm sure she found some truth," I replied.

"It's really a shame. Let's hope that NSA will be able to find something out. I've called in the details. They will perform an autopsy, I suppose. Check dental records. That sort of thing. I really appreciate your dropping the body off," Lukavitch said.

"No problem at all. I've got to swing by Da Nang to see Captain Lowy. As soon as we debrief him, we'll make the run to NSA," I said.

NSA had a morgue that was on my way back to Headquarters. It was just south of Da Nang. NSA was just north of the village of Nui Kim Son where Dao lived. Dropping off the body was a favor I was more than glad to do. I would try to look up Dao.

"Sergeant Weathers, round up Odum and tell him that we're ready to go," I said.

"Yes, sir!"

Weathers was a case. One minute he was full of impertinent remarks. The next minute he was eager to serve.

"How do you like your new job, Sam?" Lukavitch asked.

"It's okay. It's where the action is. That's what I told them at Division. I wanted back in the action."

"What's the skinny on Sergeant Weathers? Is he loony or what?"

"John, he probably is a little loony. He's a sniper. In fact,

I'm sure that he would much rather be off on his own, doing his own thing. The same is true for Odum."

"Why are snipers so important to this new group of yours?"

"Come off it, John, you know the answer to that!"

"I was hoping that you'd tell me."

"What do you want to know, John?"

"What's the story on the kid?"

"He's a VC errand boy who got snatched from him mama. But John, aren't you the one who should be giving me the answers? Aren't you the one who went out to live in the ville and found Buddha?" I was tired of Lukavitch's prying.

"If you're asking me if I found the truth about the Vietnamese out in the ville, I'll have to say yes. Of course, that truth has to do with how I feel about the Vietnamese. I guess that I would have to admit that I'm one of those gook lovers that your Sergeant Weathers is talking about. Maybe that's why I'm concerned about that boy you have."

Lukavitch and I had gone through Marine Officer's Basic School together. We were both from the Midwest. Before going overseas, we had met in Chicago and hit all the good bars on Rush Street. He was much too sensitive to be a grunt officer. In spite of his height there was something delicate about him. Maybe that's why the Seventh Marines made him an S-5 and put him into civil affairs. Good application for his Jesuit training, I thought.

"So you're a gook lover. Is that right, Lukavitch?"

"That's a big affirmative."

"Well, I won't hold it against you," I said, smiling.

"What's your Buddha, Sam? Where did you find it? That is, if you have found it."

Buddha. Lukavitch was using the term like the troops. Used that way, the word meant truth and had little or nothing to do with the religious leader who founded Buddhism. Finding Buddha was slang for finding some aspect of your philosophy, whatever that philosophy was. I had heard grunt marines say that they found their Buddha in ways too numerous to be counted. Finding Buddha was finding a kind of enlightenment, however banal, however spiritual or introspective.

"I don't know, John. I guess I found my Buddha on Go Noi Island, the night Mike Company, Third Battalion, First Marines, was overrun. I survived that nightmare. I don't know. Maybe I'll find Buddha tonight when I get to the Grand Hotel," I said, yawning.

I thought for a moment of Dao. I had met her at the Grand Hotel. I had made her laugh and now I found comfort thinking about her. I could see her standing with the South China Sea at her back, her thick hair a waist-length shadow down her back and shoulders.

"Yeah, there it is, John. I'll find Buddha when I get to the Grand Hotel," I said, repeating myself.

"What will the boy find, Sam?"

"What are you trying to do, John?"

"I just want you to keep me informed. I'm sure Captain Vilks would also like to know if the boy reveals something important. After all, Sam, you folks were, technically speaking, in 3/7's area of responsibility."

"So that's it. We're on your turf!"

Lukavitch looked down at the ground and shook his head. Behind him the sun shining through the bamboo hedgerows cast long shadows across the road. "Turf has nothing to do with it. My concern for the boy has to do with the personal responsibility I take as civil affairs officer for this area. What do you think these villagers are thinking? What do you think they are feeling?"

"Feeling! You take yourself too seriously, John. You're a lieutenant, not a shrink. You always were idealistic. Vietnam is no place for idealists."

"On the contrary, sometimes I think that I don't take myself seriously enough. As for idealists, we need more of them. And we need more good ideas. Everyone is . . ."

"Everyone is what? What we needed here today was someone who could stand the stench to put what was once a beautiful woman into a body bag. We need to get the hell out of this country, Lukavitch. We need to get you, my team, and all the damn civil affairs officers out of this country!"

"I know that when you have some rest you will think differently."

"I don't know. I really don't know about that. But I do know one thing."

"What's that?"

"When I get to the Grand Hotel, I'm going to take a hot bath, drink about six cold Sapporo beers, and get some of that rest. I may even turn into a gook lover for one night."

"Say again."

"You heard me. When I get to the Grand Hotel, I'll get a shack job."

Lukavitch was seething, but at least we were off the subject of the boy. His curiosity about the boy unnerved me. It was dangerous.

"You amaze me. One minute you're talking body bags and the next minute . . ."

"Let me tell you, John, about a little truth I felt this afternoon. I was looking at that dead woman. I was looking at her body, John. And John, even though the sun had started to bloat that body, I felt myself getting hard!"

"Mother-of-God!"

"Yeah, say a prayer for me, John."

"You have to remember that you're an officer. Hell, I love this country. It's beautiful. I think that its women are beautiful. But no matter how much I am compelled by that beauty, I've got to set an example of restraint," Lukavitch said.

It was as if, in trying to convince me, Lukavitch was convincing himself. We all had our doubts about the war, the price being paid by all those involved. Being part of the pacification effort, Lukavitch had seen first hand and in great depth the extent of the war's impact on what he called the innocent. How innocent the boy was I didn't know. I knew only that Lukavitch cared deeply for the common folk out in the villages. Long hours of working and living in the villages had slimmed the tall, rugged Lukavitch I had known in the states to about one hundred and forty pounds. His clothes hung baggy and loose on his six-foot, three-inch frame.

"You've got to watch your appetites, Sam. You still have no check on your appetites."

The intense blue eyes gazed back at me. He was right. I had no check on my appetites. I was compelled by all the beautiful things in this country. More than that, I hungered for the things that were elusive, like Dao, like the enemy. Most of all I wanted to know—that was my greatest hunger. If there was an appetite that consumed me, it was trying to know the answers to the unknown, like the identity, the true identity of the beautiful dead woman. I wanted to understand the terrible contradictions left unexplained. I wanted to blurt out to Lukavitch that this woman was no American. I wanted to shout that this woman may be a German nurse, Lukavitch, you dumb shit! And my team, which is supposed to have its shit together, killed her last night by mistake. And no! I don't know how or by what process or method she came to be on this road! The answer to that is as elusive and unknown as any of the Vietcong's terrible secrets.

Odum drove up with the jeep. The team was packed closely, the boy who we had captured the night before sitting on top of the gear, the body bag rode in a trailer behind the jeep. The boy was still blindfolded. He sat with his face upward as if he were listening. Then I heard distant explosions coming from the west. Artillery rounds dropping in the area of Mortar Valley, the area my team had patrolled last night.

I looked down the long tunnel that was the road to Da Nang, a shady tunnel lined with tall bamboo. At the far end of the tunnel it seemed that I could see little children, figures not much different from the boy who sat blindfolded behind me.

I found myself trembling slightly. Deep within I could feel a terrible, dark weight. I needed to lift that weight. Fatigue, I thought. I would lighten up when I got to the Grand Hotel. "Let's go find our Buddha, Odum."

Odum hit the gas pedal and we were off.

THE SKULL GAME

October 2, 1968: 1800 hours

EARLY EVENING BROUGHT a fog down from the mountains. It crept through the bamboo hedgerows and into the low places along the road to Da Nang, swirling around our legs while we waited beside the body of the dead German nurse.

Cruiser, our Kit Carson scout, grew increasingly agitated, concerned about what the fog might hide while we waited, exposed along a road known for frequent ambushes. Captain Lowy had insisted upon meeting us outside Da Nang. Now that rendezvous had been delayed, Lowy calling at the last minute to complete some business at Division Headquarters.

To placate Weathers's growing impatience, I let him buy a six-pack of Falstaff at Cobb Bridge. Weathers was already three beers into that six-pack and testing me, throwing two of his empty beer cans at the boy who was our prisoner. Each time the cans had just missed the boy's head.

Odum and I sat in silence, watching the fog move through the hedgerows. Weathers crushed the third empty beer can. There was a smirk on his face.

"Is that what you call doing your duty, Sergeant Weathers?" Odum said, sparing me the embarrassment of having to say something.

"That's my form of baby-sitting. Got to keep the kid's attention. Not that it means anything. What do you care, Odum? You turning into a gook lover on me?''

"Shit. I don't want that boy around any more than you do, but since we got to tote him around, I don't see any sense in bullying the kid.''

My concern was much more than that. Here we had a little boy, a civilian noncombatant. More than that, Lieutenant Lukavitch, the civil affairs officer of Third battalion, Seventh Marines, was concerned over the kid's welfare. It didn't seem to matter to Lieutenant Lukavitch that the kid was probably a messenger boy for the Vietcong. I called him the Little Prince.

"Odum, for all you know that kid could have been out setting booby traps. Who knows how many marines got their balls blown off because of that little sucker," Weathers said.

"That's enough, Weathers," I said. Tempers were short. The past two days had brought out both the best and the worst in all of us.

"Enough of what, sir?"

"I don't want you drinking any more beer until we get to Da Nang.''

Weathers frowned.

"Lieutenant, when I get to Da Nang, I want to talk to Captain Lowy about getting reassigned," Weathers said.

"That's fine, but for now, no more beer," I added.

"As for my duty, Sergeant Odum, I'm not sure what that is anymore. I thought I was here to kill gooks, not baby-sit them," Weathers said.

"Your duty ain't bullying that kid," Odum said.

"Don't shit me, Odum. You were willing to snuff the Little Prince this afternoon," Weathers said.

"I wouldn't shit you, Weathers, you're my favorite turd," Odum said.

"That's enough!" I yelled.

"Lieutenant, with all due respect, we should have snuffed your Little Prince in the mountains. We wouldn't have had anything to worry about," Weathers said.

"Weathers, I didn't think that you worried about anything," I said.

"Lieutenant, when your Little Prince starts spilling out the whole story back at Division, how are we going to defend ourselves? We screwed up. We killed that German nurse. And for what? I'm not even sure what the mission of this team is supposed to be. Two days after I join this team, I'm off in the middle of Mortar Valley with no support. And when we find gooks, we can't do what we are trained to do. I am a sniper. I like knocking down at long range! No thank you! I was recruited, I volunteered for a sniper team, not a baby-sitting job.''

How ironic that the Little Prince made Weathers, the bully, feel defensive. As I thought back over the last few weeks, it occurred to me that Weathers had always been a bully. Whether it was picking on the emotionally weak, like Cruiser, or the physically weak, like the Little Prince, Weathers derived satisfaction from threatening others. His impertinence and general insolent behavior toward me, I assumed to be contempt for officers. Yet, at times there was something in his attitude toward me that was meant to intimidate. I was glad that he wanted to talk to the captain about getting off the team. I wanted him off.

October 2, 1968: 1915 hours

By the time Captain Lowy arrived, the fog totally blanketed the road to Da Nang. A long convoy of trucks from Eleventh motors passed by, headlights on in the foggy dusk. I had never seen that kind of fog at dusk. It was as if a cloud had descended with the setting of the sun, the sun creating strange afterglows through the fog. Strange weather by any standard.

Captain Lowy and Gunner Junge pulled their jeep to the side of the road, waiting for the convoy to pass. Taking the initiative, I crossed the road and joined them in their jeep.

"Beer, Lieutenant?" Lowy asked, offering a cold Budweiser.

Against my better judgment, I took the beer. It went down fast. By the time I brought the two of them up to date with the past two days events, I was on my third beer.

"What we need here is an organizational time-out to think this through," Lowy said. "Trouble is there are no halftimes in Vietnam. Even the cease-fires are phony."

Captain O.D. Lowy from Sulphur, Oklahoma, used a lot of football jargon. At forty he looked like he could still play linebacker. Lowy had been a legend in his own time with the Quan-

tico teams. He had once remarked that he had made football his
career in the United States Marine Corps. At six feet, two inches,
two hundred and thirty pounds, he must have held his own. I
had seen him walk across the dance floor of the Grand Hotel on
his hands. The men loved him for it, and they were quick to
point out to me that Captain Lowy was the best officer that they
ever knew.

What made him the best officer that they ever knew was a
question that I had often asked myself. It wasn't simply a matter
of Lowy's openness. What made him such a good officer was a
combination of things. For one thing there was an aspect to him
that was larger than life, something exaggerated yet real. What
Captain Lowy said was important, *was* important. He wasn't
a phony who would say one thing and then do another. Lowy
wouldn't sweat the spit and polish. His attention to detail always
seemed to concern matters related to getting the job done. His
know-how was unquestioned and he was a person who was there
to give you support. I'm sure it was Captain Lowy's know-how
that impressed the higher-ups. What I think impressed the average Joe about Lowy was his ability to treat the lowest scumbag
with some sort of respect. He had a tolerance that he claimed
was born of his own lowly beginnings. Character, know-how,
the fact that he was a doer, these were all very important. But
it was the patience and the humanity with which he went about
his business that were, to my mind, his greatest qualities.

"So you say that Odum and Weathers are scared?" Lowy
asked.

"Yes, sir, they think that we're all going to burn on this one.
Weathers has been off the wall."

"Be specific."

"He's been impertinent. Bullying. In general, he's a smart
ass."

"He'll calm down if we handle him right." Lowy said.

"What does that mean, sir?"

"Well, we will have to see what it means. Weathers has been
out in the field too long. He's been in Vietnam too long. We
should have sent him home a long time ago. Trouble is, he don't
want to go home, and the fact of the matter is that he's the best
sniper in the First Marine Division. If he gets a little squirrelly

on us from time to time, well, that's what you and I get paid all this money for, Lieutenant, to keep him from going bad.''

"Think he's going to go bad on us?'' I asked.

"Bad. No, well, let's put it this way, I hope not. He's a damn good marine. He's doing exactly what we trained him to do and he's done everything we asked him to do, which is to kill people. Of course, then we complicate his life by telling him that we are going to work with people like Cruiser who are former NVA and we tell all that this war now has something called 'rules of engagement.' Then, after a guy like Weathers, who has spent mucho time in the bush, gets frustrated or squirrelly, we say he's got a bad attitude. The point here is that I just want to protect Weathers from himself. I don't want him to do something stupid because he's drunk a case of Falstaff,'' Lowy said.

"What about Division, sir? What's going to happen when the word gets to them that one of their hit teams killed a German nurse by mistake?''

"First of all, don't use that term 'hit team.' That sets some of the jingle-asses up at Division on fire. A hit team is exactly what it is, but we don't want to call it that.''

"What do we call it, Captain?''

"We're a support team. We're a support team to both the intelligence and counterintelligence efforts,'' Lowy said.

"Sounds okay,'' I said.

"Listen, Sam, when I first came to Nam I met the guy who started counterintelligence in this area. We were drinking one night up at Division. I asked him what his program was like, and he laughed. He said that when he reported in to assume his new 'command,' they sent him to a room where they said that he would find all that he needed to run a good counterintelligence program. Do you know what was in that room?'' Lowy asked, a wry smile on his face.

"Got me, Captain.''

"Three things. First of all there was a map of the Da Nang area on the wall. The map had a lot of little red pins stuck at various locations around Da Nang. The rest of the room was bare, but for a big table and a few chairs. Do you know what was on the table?''

"Got me again, Captain,'' I repeated, wondering if this was twenty questions.

"The other two things. A shotgun and a list of names."

"Simple program. Sounds like a hit team to me," I said.

"You got it. But the point that I want to make is that we have come a long way from a shotgun and a list of names. Another thing. Maybe killing that nurse wasn't a mistake at all."

"Say again, sir?" I asked.

"I said maybe snuffing the nurse wasn't a mistake. What the hell was she doing there in the first place? But that has yet to be determined. Hopefully, the boy will know. At any rate, right now you and I need to buffer the men from any Division contact. That's a decision I'm making."

"Buffer," I said, wondering what that word meant.

"Yeah, buffer. And I also want them to feel that you, me, and Gunner Junge are absorbing all the heat and the risks from the situation."

Lowy may have been an old knuckle-dragger, but he was also one smart son of a bitch.

"What do you think, Gunner?" Lowy asked Gunner Junge.

Gunner was the Marine Corps title used to address warrant officers of Junge's rank. Like Lowy, Rolf Junge was a former enlisted man. He was old enough to be my father and had served in the Korean War and in China. He was particularly proud of his China service. The term he used to describe himself was "China Hand." But the most interesting thing to me about Rolf Junge was that he had once been in the German army. As a youth, he had fought against the allies in France. After being captured, he was sent to Louisiana. When the Second World War came to an end, Junge was one of those who found that his former home had become part of East Germany. Upon returning to West Germany in 1946, Junge found that his sister, the only member of his immediate family to survive the war, had married an American GI and was living in New Jersey. Through his sister, Junge was able to get back in the States as a displaced person. Once in the States, Junge joined the Marine Corps.

"So what do we do with the woman?" Gunner Junge said, the German accent still evident in spite of his years with the Marine Corps.

"Gunner, I want you to dump her at the Naval Support Activity. Who knows? They may never sort this thing out." Lowy said.

Captain Lowy looked at me out of the corner of one eye and smiled. His flattened nose had been broken so many times that he could barely breathe through it. Consequently his mouth always seemed to be hanging half open, usually with a toothpick to one side. Toothpicks cured his tobacco craving, so he said.

"What you're saying, Captain, is that we're not going to report this thing to Division. Right?" I said.

"Look. All we know is that a German-speaking woman was in the wrong place at the right time to buy the farm. For that matter, how do we know the woman's a civilian, for Christ's sake?" Lowy continued.

"We know," I said.

"Bullshit! We're guessing. And the fact that we're guessing relates to our mission," Lowy said.

"I don't follow, Captain."

"I'm treating this as an intelligence matter. Again, it's my decision and I'll take the heat. For the record, I'll justify my decision by saying that it would be premature to volunteer anything to the Naval Support Activity. Some jingle-ass might compromise our mission," Lowy said.

"Do we tell the team that?" Junge asked.

"Yes. Given the situation, Odum reacted as any prudent person would have acted." Lowy added, shifting the toothpick to the other side of his mouth.

I opened another Budweiser and took a long pull. I was shaky, but the beer seemed so good. That detached feeling came over me again. I felt as if I were heading down the wrong road but that there was nothing I could do about it. A tank churned past us, appearing out of the fog, its diesel exhaust like the hot breath of some great beast.

"What do we tell Lukavitch and Captain Vilks?" I asked.

"I don't know. Let's think about that one. Lukavitch is a do-gooder whose sympathy is misplaced. Vilks is a kind of jingle-ass. Oh, basically Vilks is okay, but he'll turn into a hot dog on you if you don't watch him," Lowy said.

"Hot dog?"

"Vilks grandstands. He's always looking to look good. That can get into the way of good judgment real fast," Lowy said.

Another tank churned by. A squad of marines rode atop that tank. One of the marines waved as the tank went by.

"Captain, what you say Cruiser and I take the body back to the Naval Support Activity. It's getting dark. That will give you time to talk to the team," Junge said.

"Sounds like a plan to me, Gunner. I'll see you back at the Grand Hotel."

Gunner Junge and Cruiser loaded the body in the back of Captain Lowy's jeep. Junge also took the Little Prince. He placed the boy on his lap, removing both the blindfold and the gag. The boy blinked, saying nothing. Gunner Junge offered the boy a drink of water from a canteen. The boy drank heavily, water spilling down the front of his shirt. Cruiser then cranked the jeep and they were down the road and into the fog.

October 2, 1968: 1930 hours

Captain Lowy brought me up to date on the various events happening around Division. Clearly it was a time of transition. Lowy's boss, the province senior adviser, was a full marine colonel by the name of Schuster. Schuster, who I had yet to meet, had been caught up in the politics of the transition. The province senior adviser linked with the province chief in order to assist with emerging needs. The general idea was to take these emerging needs and turn them into opportunities for gain. It was very complex. The province chief had two lines of authority, one military, a second political. Progress had been slow, but certain. Now this progress was to be affected by a number of new programs controlled by the CIA.

"Captain, tell me more about what you had in mind when you were talking about a buffer. I still don't follow what you mean by buffer."

"Oh. I suppose I mean a number of things. One thing for sure is too keep Odum and Weathers away from Division. I don't trust the Division pogues looking into the way this old mustang does business. There's more than one of them up there that would like to take a chance and run this program," Lowy said.

A mustang was an officer who had been an enlisted man. With the increase in the size of the Marine Corps due to the Vietnam War, many staff noncommissioned officers had been commissioned. Lowy was a former gunnery sergeant.

"Another thing is to take the pressure off. Buffer them from as much bullshit and unnecessary pressure as you can. Another thing you want to do is get to the root of their gripes," Lowy said, opening a can of Budweiser.

"Gripes? I was always told that a bitching marine is a happy marine."

"Won't deny that, all I'm saying is that it's good to sit down once in a while to have a tailgate meeting at the back end of the truck. Just listen to what they have to say, and that will carry you a long way toward earning their respect," Lowy said.

"Tailgate meeting."

"Yeah, you talk to them. Either one-on-one or in a group," Lowy said.

"Is that what you plan with Odum and Weathers?"

"Oh. I don't know. I'll just give them the old skull game," Lowy said.

"Skull game?"

"The old skull game is that you never deny anything, you affirm a higher good," Lowy said,

"Sorry, Captain, don't follow you."

"Well, what I mean is that you appeal to the fact that we're all part of a team. Or you can appeal to the men themselves, their abilities. You can affirm the special nature of your mission. For those that will believe you, you affirm God and country. When in doubt, always affirm the Marine Corps—it may stop loving you, but it will never stop screwing you," Lowy said with a laugh.

The toothpick went to the other side of the mouth. The battered, hooded eyes softened. Captain Lowy pulled on his Budweiser and flecks of foam tipped his mustache. "You see, Lieutenant, it gets the men in a frame of mind that takes attention away from you or the problem and onto something that they believe in or respect."

"Are you saying that the men don't respect me?" I said, startled.

"Oh. No offense, Sam. But from what you have told me so far, there's no doubt about that," Lowy said.

I was trembling. I looked out into the foggy gloom of the bamboo hedgerows, and I couldn't stop trembling. Get your shit together, Lieutenant, I said to myself. Captain Lowy looked away to where Odum and Weathers were having a smoke.

"Another thing. The fact that you change their frame of mind for the moment doesn't mean that your problems are solved. What you have done, if you're lucky, is buy time. What you want to think about then is how to isolate your problems if you can. If you can't, you might even want to involve the team in coming up with some solutions and solving the problem for you. That's also part of the skull game," Lowy added.

"Sounds simple," I said.

"It's not. You'll need my support in this. I'll be the silver-tongued devil when we talk to Weathers and Odum."

"When will we do that?"

"As soon as we get them to the Grand Hotel. Right now we're running out of beer. By the way, the bottom line in the skull game is sometimes convincing yourself. In football it's the difference between winning and losing."

"But what if you're not sure?"

"Lieutenant, in the skull game nothing is sure. Nothing is sure," Lowy said, draining his beer and throwing the empty can into the ditch beside the road.

October 2, 1968: 2030 hours

Ground level at the Grand Hotel there was a restaurant that opened onto a wide veranda. On that veranda one could sit around any of thirty or so umbrella-covered tables in an over-sized cane chair and watch the night lanterns of the fishing boats out on Da Nang Bay. Marble balustrades bordered the veranda. Broad stairs led down to a long pond where Madam Ti, owner of the Grand Hotel, grew lotus and kept several large golden carp. Beyond the pond was the aviary where Ti kept a variety of exotic birds. There also was where one would usually find Gunner Junge, sitting in the shade of the large, ancient bamboos that overhung the aviary.

Downstairs at the Grand Hotel there was gambling, another bar with a dance floor, and some of the finest dancing partners in Asia. If you were an officer, Madam Ti would let you run a tab at the bar. Accordingly, it was there that Captain O.D. Lowy liked to hang his hat. Since he spent considerable time there, Lowy jokingly called the Grand Hotel his real headquarters. When Madam Ti sat on his lap, Lowy called her his adjutant. The truth of the matter was that we probably got more accomplished in that hotel with the many contacts we developed than we did with our actual field work.

Captain Lowy, Weathers, Odum, and I sat down at a table in a far corner of the downstairs bar. The bar was almost empty save for the bartender, one of Ti's bodyguards, and a couple of bar girls. It was early in the week. Even in Da Nang business was slow early in the week.

"Slow night," Captain Lowy said.

"It may pick up later, you never know," Weathers said.

Captain Lowy ordered a round of Sapporo's, his favorite beer, and offered each of us one of the fine Upman number nine Havana cigars that were his trademark. We all lit up and soon the wonderfully mild smoke of Cuban cigars hung in a haze over our heads.

The cigars and the Sapporo began to take effect. I found myself relaxing.

"Spent some time in Cuba, before Castro. Acquired a taste for good Havana cigars. In fact, my first old lady was Cuban. Married while on liberty in Havana. Had known her three days. After three years and two kids she kicked me like a bad habit. Took me ten years to get over her. I guess I'll never get over good Havana cigars," Lowy said, smiling.

"Captain, did the lieutenant tell you that I want off the team?" Weathers asked.

"He did."

"How about you, Odum?" Lowy added.

"Don't know yet, sir."

"Weathers. What's on your mind?" Lowy asked.

"Well, sir, I'm a sniper. When you folks recruited me for this team up in Division, you said that I'd be doing my trade, knocking them down at three hundred yards or better. Right now I don't know what this team's all about. I don't know where I fit. Sir, I guess I don't want to whore around."

Weathers was using the word whore the way the troops used it. The way he was using the word suggested not just selling one's talents, but also wasting one's time on some useless effort.

There was also the connotation of being exploited by whatever you were "whoring" with. Needless to say, whore was one of Weathers's favorite words.

"How about you, Odum? You think you're some kind of whore?" Lowy asked, a somewhat perplexed look on his face.

"No, sir. I ain't no whore. But, Captain, after killing that woman, all I could think of was Revelation and the fall of Babylon," Odum said, taking a big draw from his Sapporo.

"Babylon," Lowy repeated, raising his eyebrows.

Here we go, I thought to myself.

"Yes, sir, Babylon. As I remember, it goes that the kings who lived luxuriously with her and who committed fornication with her will weep and lament for her when they see the smoke of her burning," Odum said.

We all sat in silence. Even Weathers had nothing to say for once.

"Sir, I had a vision of this here Vietnam and how her judgment will come," Odum continued.

"Oh. How will that judgment come?" Lowy asked, amused.

"In the blood of all those that are slain," Odum said without hesitation.

"I see," Lowy said quietly.

For several moments nothing was said. Lowy was obviously reflecting upon what Odum had just said. So much for Lowy the silver-tongued devil, I thought to myself. A passing bar girl ran her fingers through Lowy's hair. Finally Lowy straightened up in his chair and leaned forward.

"Well. A lot of this is my fault. The way things came together so fast when you men came on board. That was unfortunate. I don't deny that I should have taken more time to give both of you the big picture," Lowy said, starting to warm up.

"That's okay, Captain," Weathers said, draining his Sapporo.

"No, no. Let me say this. If you both want out, I'll see to it in the morning. I want all volunteers. But let me say this before you decide. This program has a special mission. More than that I need men with your guts and experience. This thing that happened with that woman is history. I'm not going to report the matter since I choose to judge it an intelligence opportunity yet to be developed! And that's that! Those jingle-butts at the Naval

Support Activity are nothing to worry about, I'll see to that!''
Lowy said, motioning for another round of Sapporo beers.

"What about the Little Prince?" Weathers asked.

"He's with Gunner Junge until we can figure out the details,"
Lowy said.

"What are you going to do with him, sir? What if he talks?"
Weathers said.

"What do you want me to do with him, Weathers, wire his
mouth shut? I suppose that we'll send him south, way south, so
south that even Lukavitch can't find him," Lowy said with a
smile.

Odum and Weathers laughed. The round of beers came. The
bar girl ran her hands through Lowy's hair a second time. Things
were beginning to lighten up.

"With all due respect, sir, I think Weathers is right on. What
if the Little Prince did talk?" Odum asked.

"If the boy talks, he talks. So what? We don't deny a thing.
We just affirm that a German nurse, or whatever she was, bought
the farm because she was where she wasn't supposed to be.
Anyway, where I'm going to send that kid, no one will listen to
him anyway. Trust me!" Lowy said, obviously wound up and
on a roll.

"It would help me, Captain, if I knew where you was talking
about," Odum said.

"I've got some old buddies with C Company, Fifth Special
Forces. We'll send him out into the highlands. Let the Little
Prince clean latrines for the Green Berets!" Lowy said.

We all laughed. Captain Lowy ordered another round of beers.
He then grabbed the ass of one of the bar girls as she passed the
table. We all roared. People passing by outside of the bar began
to peer in.

"Captain, I still don't understand how I fit into this whore,
or as you put it 'the big picture,' " Weathers said.

"You gonna stay? If you stay I'll tell you—and let me assure
you that it will blow your socks off in a Hong Kong minute, and
that's the fastest minute in the world!" Lowy said.

We all laughed again. More people peered into the bar.

"I'll stay," Odum said, eyes glazed.

"Hell, so will I," Weathers said.

Damn! I thought to myself. Here I had thought I was getting rid of Weathers.

"Well, let me share with you things that I have yet to tell the lieutenant here. Things have happened so fast. Lieutenant, you have probably heard of Robert Komer?" Lowy asked.

"No, sir," I said.

"Since May 1967, he has been President Johnson's special ambassador for pacification. The man is former CIA and no bureaucrat. They call him the Blowtorch and he has started in motion a number of important things that affect us personally. We will have to roll with the punches. We will be working with the PRUs," Lowy said.

The PRUs, or Provincial Reconnaissance Units, were formed from old counterterror teams whose mission was selective assassination. We all nodded.

"Well, until late 1967 there was no organized effort to target the Vietcong infrastructure. In other words, no one was going out in any kind of systematic way to disrupt Vietcong support, the errand boys, the pay masters, the mama-sans hauling rice, that kind of thing. Well, that's all going to change. PRUs will be focusing their efforts to target the Vietcong support structure. Our mission is to link up with them and other intelligence operations in an effort to share gathered intelligence so that we or the PRUs can take action," Lowy said, clearly excited.

Lowy's eyes were blazing. If this was the skull game, he was convincing. Of course, what Vietcong support meant was more women and kids would be targeted because women and kids supported the VC effort. If I had a headache over the kid we had just snatched, by definition a civilian noncombatant, what did I have to look forward to with this new program? By changing a few words, did we really change the status of kids and women? I was concerned. Just by keeping the Little Prince I felt we were breaking the law because we were holding a civilian noncombatant against his will. But I wasn't sure what was kidnapping and what was war. Everything was blurring together. Lowy's skull game made everything even more ambiguous and vague.

"You men need to be part of this program. Whatever you believe, believe me when I say that this effort, your effort, will save marine lives and shorten this damn war!"

"Captain," Odum said.

"Yes, Sergeant Odum," Lowy replied.

"Captain, sounds like Revelations to me!" Odum said.

"Revelations?" Lowy said.

"Yes, sir. 'And the ten horns which you saw on the beast, these will hate the harlot, make her desolate and naked, eat her flesh and burn her with fire!' " Odum said, slurring his speech.

"I see," Lowy said, sipping his beer.

"How about you, Sergeant Weathers?" Lowy asked.

"Sir, I just want to kill gooks."

October 2, 1968: 2200 hours

Captain Lowy, Weathers, Odum, and I moved out onto the veranda. On the way out we passed Madam Ti, a beautiful Eurasian woman who was said to be in her forties. I couldn't tell. To my mind she was exquisite with a kind of delicate beauty that I was never to possess.

Madam Ti had lived in Sydney, Australia, and Paris, France. During the day she usually kept to the back wing of the hotel, where a spiked iron fence enclosed the hotel's courtyard. Her afternoon tea was taken under a large flamboyant tree next to the aviary. After tea she would stroll by the lotus pond while Sandman, her huge Chinese bodyguard, watched from his drowse, half-lidded eyes gazing without blinking. Evening would find her sitting on the veranda over a glass of Pernod, socializing with journalists and officers. She was always the last to turn in for the night, usually after a nightcap with an old French paratrooper who Sandman ushered to the great teak door, all of them singing Piaf's song, "Non, je ne regrette rien."

Madam Ti nodded as we passed. I thought for a moment that her eye caught my eye. Fatigue, I thought. Fatigue and too much to drink.

Weathers dumped Odum in the jeep, Odum being all but passed out. Before I could ask Weathers if he was okay, he was gone, on his way to some convenient hiding place.

Captain Lowy had his own hiding place. It was the Grand Hotel. The province senior adviser, Colonel Schuster, had several. To say the least, Schuster was very secretive. Some called him paranoid. Unlike other province senior advisers, he didn't believe in keeping an office or a staff. He was always on the move, delegating operational necessities to his deputy, Lowy. I had yet to meet Colonel Schuster.

Captain Lowy and I sat down in the big cane chairs on the veranda to enjoy the cool night. Da Nang has always been a port city famous for its spice, and that night the spice was in the air.

"Well, what do you think?" Lowy asked.

"I'm real tired, Captain."

"What do you think of Odum's babbling about Babylon?" I added with a smile.

"Oh, he's nuts. Weathers is just a little crazy, but Odum is nuts!"

I then began to laugh. I couldn't help myself. They were nuts! I wondered if what made them crazy would make me crazy. I was tired, very tired, but somehow in spite of my fatigue, I found myself laughing. Lowy just smiled.

That evening thousands of delicate lacewinged insects swarmed around the hotel lights. Madam Ti and the new girl they called Sky Lady approached our table, apparently amused by my laughter. The marines called her Sky Lady because she always seemed to be high. Sky Lady put her hand on my shoulder. Ti's bodyguard, Sandman, rushed up to sweep some of the lacewings from the glass top of our table. With his red scarf Sandman then swept off the seat of a chair for Madam Ti. Sandman gave me a wink. He then leaned forward and whispered:

"You like Sky Lady, Lieutenant. Relax and enjoy. All who come to the Grand Hotel gonna find their whore."

Oh yeah, Sandman, nothing's for sure, I thought to myself. In this skull game, nothing is for sure.

CHINA HAND

WE WERE SMASHED on Sapporo beer and sitting on the veranda of the Grand Hotel. We were having fun with two of the most beautiful women in Da Nang, and while I was fairly certain Captain Lowy wasn't serious about Madam Ti, who was sitting on his lap, the old French paratrooper, Madam Ti's great admirer, was not so sure. The Frenchman sat in the spot reserved for those French who still maintained a presence at the Grand Hotel. His thick hands clutched a tiny glass of Pernod into which he gazed, occasionally glancing up to glare at Captain Lowy like a wounded steer.

The old Frenchman was given to extreme highs and lows. I had watched him in the past, one minute bellowing out an Edith Piaf song, the next minute brooding because he felt that the exquisite Madam Ti was not paying enough attention to his small, Francophone corner of the veranda. Oh! How he hated these Americans!

I, on the other hand, was in love. After a night of beers, Sky Lady had captured both my imagination and my heart. Sure, she was a whore. But what was that Captain Lowy had said about the old skull game? Never deny anything, always affirm some other purpose! Sky Lady seemed as gentle and benevolent as she was beautiful, and she smelled great. Hers was a comfort that I had not expected in this place. I was taken unaware, and I had convinced myself. Even Gunner Junge, that sour old China Hand, so aloof and judgmental treated Sky Lady differently. Most of the girls Junge ignored. Junge seemed to tolerate Sky Lady to the extent that they would share conversations. To me that was amazing.

Captain Lowy placed much confidence in Gunner Junge. While the two men were clearly different in style and temperament, they respected one another. On occasion I had heard Gunner Junge express disgust for Lowy's drinking and general permissiveness with the troops. That was, however, the exception in what appeared to be a very effective working relationship. Certainly there was no doubt in Captain Lowy's mind. Many times I had heard Lowy refer with affection to his guardian angel, his "Old China Hand." However, there was some doubt on my part.

If I was a kind of whore, and Lowy, my captain, was a kind of pimp, where did Junge fit in? For the moment Junge was gone on some errand. Maybe upon his return I could get some answers. Much was vague and undefined.

All this doubt on my part was as dangerous as it was ambiguous, like the situation that was developing with the Frenchman. Lattre, the Frenchman, rose from his table and walked to the jukebox on the far side of the veranda. Lacewinged flies swirled around the light over the jukebox. Lattre waved them away with a sweep of his hand and dropped a coin in the jukebox. Fats Domino's "Blueberry Hill" was the selection.

"Hey, Lieutenant, that's one of the all-time greats! Where were you when that came out?" Lowy asked.

"I was in high school. No! I was in junior high. I was in goddamn junior high school," I replied.

"Well, I was a buck sergeant in Havana, Cuba, and I was in love, l-u-v, with my first old lady. Married her after three days, for Christ's sake!" Lowy yelled.

"Yes, sir. You've told me the story before."

"Ti! Dance with me, you lovely thing! Dance with this old broke-dick dog from Oklahoma," Lowy said, loud enough for Lattre to bristle.

"Where's that?" Sky Lady asked me, breathing into my ear as she whispered the question.

"North of Texas," I replied, running my hand through her long, waist-length hair, the thickness and weight of which is still unique in my memory.

"I know Texas. Many GIs I meet from Texas," she said with a smile, rapt and enigmatic, a smile that accented her lithe grace and gentle charm.

I wondered how many of those GIs Sky Lady had loved with her subtle blend of serenity and sensuality, this slant-eyed beauty so high on life in the balmy evening air. How many of those GIs were then swallowed up by the jungle, never to be found? How many were consumed by fire?

The chic and cosmopolitan Ti, so different from the gentle and delicate Sky Lady, rose and accepted Lowy's invitation to dance. Lowy, lost in some Oklahoma folk memory of his past, began to sing along with the song as they danced, pulling Ti close to his chest with his powerful linebacker arms. Ti seemed catlike. Her bare shoulders gleamed like bronze, illuminated by the floodlight above the jukebox, as Lowy spun her ever so slowly, kissing her lightly on the cheek as the song ended.

I was leaning back in my chair trying to kiss Sky Lady, when Lattre blindsided Captain Lowy. Lowy went down and Lattre hit him again on the back of the head with what appeared to be a large sap similar to those used by the Navy Shore Patrol. Anxiety stabbed me in the chest. In less than a second Sky Lady was off my lap and I was in a dead sprint across the twenty or so feet that separated me from Lattre.

I tackled the Frenchman and knocked him through the jukebox, momentarily knocking the wind out of the old man. I was instantly on my feet. I picked up the sap and threw it out somewhere on to Doc Lop Street. I paused, thinking the fight was over and began to attend to Captain Lowy who was out cold. That was a mistake.

Lattre scrambled to his knees and grabbed for my balls. He was big for a Frenchman, a thick, barrel-chested, two-hundred-and-thirty-pound man. But his closure on my balls was just a feint. Somehow he knocked my legs out from under me and got me to the ground. With his superior weight he managed to get a scissors hold around my middle and began to squeeze the breath out of me. When I tried to punch him, he jabbed his finger into my eye and began to pull it out. I screamed, and countered by going for his eyes since I couldn't get a clear punch. Unfortunately for me he could get a clear punch and he knocked my lights out with two quick hooks to the point of my jaw.

When I came to, Lattre was putting the boots to me. Instinctively, in my semiconsciousness, I had curled into the fetal position. I was still gasping for breath when I heard a loud crack.

Lattre went down across me like a fallen oak, but he scrambled to his knees, uttering some obscenity. Then Gunner Junge hit him again, only this time square in the back, in the process breaking the baseball bat he was using.

Before Gunner Junge could hit Lattre again, Sandman, Ti's bodyguard, stepped between them. Where was Sandman when Lowy was blindsided, I wondered. For that matter, where was Sandman when I was getting the boots put to me?

Lattre scrambled to all fours and plunged into the night and safety, shouting profane oaths in French as he disappeared into the darkness.

October 3, 1968: 0130 hours

"Well, where is this Frenchman?" Lowy asked, holding his head in his hands.

"He ran into the garden behind the hotel," I said.

"Sandman will find him and send him home," Ti added.

"You will have to be careful, Captain. The last thing we need is something like this," Gunner Junge said, shaking his head. Clearly he was disgusted by the incident.

"Gunner, thank God for an Old China Hand. Lieutenant, you got to have an Old China Hand like the Gunner here backing you up," Lowy said, obviously hurting.

Lowy leaned back onto a couch and into the arms of Madam Ti.

"Goddamn right. You got to have an Old China Hand," Lowy said, drifting off.

I winked at Madam Ti. I then motioned to Gunner Junge. Together we quietly left the room. Sky Lady was talking in whispers to Madam Ti.

"Gunner, it's too late to go back to Divisio. We'll stay for the night."

"As you say, Lieutenant," Junge replied, giving me a dirty look.

"Madam Ti gave me the keys to her room," Sky Lady said quietly, holding the keys up for me to see, a gleam in her eye.

"Sounds like a plan to me," I said, smiling.

I had crashed at the Grand Hotel on a previous occasion. That time I had been too drunk to get it up. Now, after the exhilaration of the fight, with the carefree Sky Lady smiling back at me, I was suddenly wired, ready to indulge in whatever ecstasy Sky Lady could create.

"Let me touch base with the captain," I said.

I walked back into the room. Lowy had already nodded off in Ti's arms. Ti looked back at me with a sense of calm. There was something about her gaze, almost serene. A breeze off Da Nang Bay blew through the curtains.

"You and Sky Lady enjoy my room," she said.

I nodded, saying nothing. I carefully closed the door behind me.

October 3, 1968: 0140 hours

"Sandman can't find the Frenchman," Junge said.

"So what. I wouldn't sweat that. He probably crawled into a hole somewhere," I said somewhat impatiently.

Sky Lady and I were arm in arm. She slipped her hand down under my ass and gave me a little pinch.

"We shouldn't take this Frenchman for granted," Junge said.

"What do you want to do, Gunner, go out there and look for him?"

"That's exactly what we should do," Junge replied, looking me directly in the eye.

"Come on, Gunner. Lighten up. I want to hit the sack."

"Very well. As you say. But I think I will sit in the garden for a time. I will keep Sandman on his toes," Junge said, glancing over at the big bodyguard, who had fallen asleep in one of the large wicker chairs.

"Where are Ti's other security people?"

"There are only two still here, and they're in the bar watching the bar girls. There are some army types amusing themselves with the bar girls. No matter. That kind of security is useless anyway," Junge said.

"Well, Gunner, it will be a comfort to know that I got an Old China Hand out there watching out for my hide," I said, heading up the stairs.

"Is that so?" Junge said.

Marines cling defiantly to a vast pantheon of heroes and primitive myths. Myths like Belleau Wood, Mount Suribachi, and the Chosin Reservoir provide the foundation for Marine Corps tradition. The greatest heroes, men like Chesty Puller, take on a spiritual quality, especially late at night in bars when old enlisted men relate with a tone of reverence tales of personal sacrifice, hardship, and courage in the face of adversity. Of the highest order in the pantheon are the China Hands, those inexorable few who served in China before and after the Second World War.

The stories of these China Hands had grown with the years, from the intrigues and special missions up the Yellow River to the barroom yarns of lying naked in the dim glow of an oil lamp, young girls massaging and kneading one's body with their feet. It was difficult to separate legend from fact. One thing, however, was certain. That certainty was that there was no nonsense about Gunner Junge. He had served in Shanghai, Tientsin, and Tsingtao. In the late forties he had ridden the trains inland, guarding the diplomatic mail. On two occasions he had traveled deep into central China on special missions and returned. Gunner Junge was a true China Hand.

"Goddamn right. You got to have an Old China Hand," I answered, mimicking what Captain Lowy had said earlier.

Junge smiled. The breeze off Da Nang Bay was picking up. Leaves rustled in the thick bamboo beyond the veranda.

"Sleep well, Lieutenant," Junge said, walking off into the darkness of the garden.

October 3, 1968: 0200 hours

At the edge of Madam Ti's great marble tub someone had etched the last line from one of Edith Piaf's great songs: "Je me fous du passe"—"I don't give a damn about the past." I had seen it written as graffiti in other places throughout the Grand Hotel. It was written on the walls in the men's room. It was scratched into the soft stone at the edge of the pond where Madam Ti kept her golden carp.

I thought of the old French paratrooper for a moment. I remembered him bellowing out Piaf's songs like they were some obsession. I hoped that the Frenchman would forget about tonight. I must make an effort to reconcile matters with him, I thought.

Outside the window, the heavy tops of the thick bamboo tossed in the breeze coming in off the water. Sky Lady walked to the window and pulled the floor-length curtains together, the light on the veranda below silhouetting her form against the curtains. I lay soaking in the tub, up to my neck in bubbles, having poured a whole bottle of finely scented soap beads into the hot water. I flipped the light foam at Sky Lady. It caught her slim, naked belly. She scooped it off with her finger and blew the bubbly foam into the air, where for a moment it drifted.

Such times may never come again, I thought. I was wired. Sky Lady and I had made love the first time as soon as we were through the door. I had come almost instantly. Within five minutes I had showered and we had made love again, this time with her on top. But that second time had been rushed and full of randy passion. What we were into now was ecstasy, the slow and careful sharing of each other through the senses.

I felt the weight of her thick, waist-length hair on my stomach as she leaned forward to take me in her mouth. I touched the smooth shadow of her slenderness in the dim light, trembling as her mouth slid over me. Reaching forward, I cupped the fullness of each of her breasts in the palms of my hands. She bit down on me ever so lightly. Wonderful pain! With my right hand I reached around to her ass and slid my middle finger down the crack between her buttocks until I found the surprising thickness of her bush. She worked me so wet and slippery with her lips that I couldn't help myself any longer. Rapture.

October 3, 1968: 0300 hours

Sky Lady had fallen asleep in my arms. For a while I had dozed. The sound of helicopters flying overhead or the mere putt-putt of a passing Honda motorbike was enough to wake me; and I was troubled by recurring and traumatic dreams. Always I was pursued, friends dying all around me. In spite of my restlessness, Sky Lady slept soundly, the cool breeze of the Da Nang Bay almost chilling.

I was about to light a cigarette when I saw someone out on the balcony. When he parted the curtains, I was sure. Lattre! The Frenchman had returned as Junge said he might.

Quickly assessing the situation, I knew that Sky Lady and I were in the darkest corner of Ti's bedroom. Could he see us? I would have to move before Lattre's eyes adjusted to the darker bedroom.

The bed creaked. Sky Lady let out a sigh and turned in her sleep. Like a bamboo cat, Lattre was across the floor. He grabbed wildly, catching Sky Lady around the waist. Sky Lady started to scream but Lattre shoved a cloth to her mouth. Sky Lady kicked enough to throw Lattre off balance. With all my weight I pushed them back toward the window. Lattre slipped on the slick tile floor, throwing Sky Lady back onto the bed.

Lattre then grabbed my arms and charged. This time I was ready, and using both his weight and momentum, I ducked under his arm and slammed him into the marble balustrades that surrounded the small balcony.

The Frenchman jumped to his feet, swinging a straight razor in a wide arc that caught Sky Lady on the cheekbone, cutting a thick tress from her waist-length hair. Two quick thuds from a semiautomatic came from the next balcony, some ten feet away. Lattre paused mid-stride. Two more quick thuds slammed into his chest and he fell.

"Mon Dieu . . ." Lattre whispered; then he died.

October 3, 1968: 0305 hours

"Let me in. It's Junge," the gunner whispered.

There was blood everywhere. I was still naked, as was Sky Lady. She sat in a chair holding a towel to her cheek, uttering an occasional sob.

"Where's Lattre?" Junge asked.

"Here! Why on earth did you have to waste him? One shot was enough to disable!" I asked, confused.

"The Frenchman is an agent for the Vietcong," Gunner Junge said.

"For sure?" I said, amazed.

"For sure, Lieutenant. For sure he hates Americans," Junge added.

Junge went through Lattre's pockets. He then turned the shower hose over the tile floor. In the dim light the dark stain on the floor slowly dissolved and began to disappear into the floor drain. I looked at the graffiti etched in French on the marble tub. *"Je me fous du passe."* From now on that line would take on a new meaning. As would the haunting voice of Edith Piaf.

"Help me heave him over the balcony," Junge said.

"What then?" I asked.

"The pond, of course," Junge said.

"What of the security?"

"They're pigs. Sleeping pigs. Why else do you think this happened," Junge said.

Lattre's body fell with little noise. Junge turned to Sky Lady, who had slipped on a chemise.

"Let me see how bad," Junge said.

"It's not bad," I said.

"Ah! Only a nick. You were a lucky bitch, Mona. Say nothing of this to anyone, even Lowy," Junge said.

"Mona?" I said.

Gunner Junge picked up the thick tress of Sky Lady's hair that had been cut off by Lattre's razor.

"Here, Lieutenant, I souvenir you," Junge said.

"Mona?" I said a second time.

"Lucky for you Mona is one of my agents, otherwise we would have had also to kill her," Junge said.

"Mona," I said again.

"Yes, now let's go find something to hold him down," Junge said.

October 3, 1968: 0400 hours

The water in the lotus pond seemed ice cold after the warm bath that I had taken earlier. Fish nipped my legs as I waded toward the pond's center, where the water's depth was greatest. The pond itself was about a thirty-foot circle. Lotus and water lilies grew around the edges.

"It's going to take two of us," I croaked, up to my knees in silt.

"Shit," Junge said.

We had wrapped Lattre in rope weighted down with several large stone elephants, each close to eighty pounds. One by one we had attached the elephants to Lattre's body. Even with the combined strength of Gunner Junge and myself, it was very difficult. Now we were pulling this weight into the deep silt. We would never make it to the center of the pond. We paused to gain our breath, both waist-deep in the chilling water.

"What's Madam Ti going to say when she finds her elephants missing?" I asked jokingly.

"Least of our worries. Anyway, they were probably stolen," Junge said.

"What was stolen?" I asked.

"These elephants," Junge said.

"The elephants are stolen," I said.

"Probably. The elephants are relics from China. Relics from the old imperial burial grounds. Part of the ancient burial temples. I think of China often, especially when that north wind blows down across the South China Sea from mainland China. China was good to me. I look back at my time there with much fondness."

"We can blame it on those army dudes if anyone bothers to ask," I said, somewhat surprised by his rambling over China.

I was already chest-deep and sinking deeper. Then one of Madam Ti's large golden carp glided by, inches from my face. Even in the dim light I could make out the golden orange color through the murk. The fish passed by me again, almost glowing, this time brushing my bare arm with its tail.

"Let's pause again. I got to get my breath," I said.

"This is deep enough," Junge said.

Halfway to the center of the pond we pushed and stomped Lattre's body into the thick sediment.

"Will he stay down?" I asked.

"I hope so. I opened his belly so that his gas wouldn't bring him to the surface when he bloats. Even with all that weight, I wasn't sure. And, of course, there are the fish," Junge said.

"So bets are that he'll stay down?"

"Who would know for sure, Lieutenant," Junge said as we reached the pond's edge.

Several of the large golden carp glided past me. Others followed, slowly moving from the far end of the pond toward the spot where Lattre's thick body lay beneath the surface. The golden carp soon formed a great, glowing school, circling slowly in the gloom.

THE CRESTED ARGUS

October 3, 1968: 0500 hours

THINGS WERE CRAZY. I knew that I was out of my element.
If I could have returned to a marine grunt battalion I would have
gone in a Hong Kong minute, and that was the fastest minute in
the world according to Captain Lowy. Well, I thought to myself,
I wanted to get into the action. Now I had all that I wanted. I
just wondered where I fit and how this was all going to end.

"There's a lot going down at Division," Junge said.

"What do you mean?" I asked.

"Big shake-up. It will probably impact what we do. We will
probably be working for the CIA before we are through. There's
a move to control province senior advisers all over South Vietnam. CIA wants to run the show," Junge said, sipping his coffee.

"What do you think about that?" I asked.

"I think that our Colonel Schuster won't like it. I suspect that
Schuster is doing all he can to retain what control he has. But
it's not just the CIA that he's worried about. He's worried about
doctrine. That kind of thing."

I moved to the edge of the lotus pond and watched the small
bubbles rise to the pond's surface. Just beneath the surface of
the water the school of golden carp swam in a slow circle.

"I don't know anything about doctrine. And I don't give a shit about doctrine," I said, lighting a cigarette.

"Schuster thinks Division isn't fighting the war the way that they should. He says that there is too much emphasis on amphibious doctrine. Schuster has made some enemies. That's why he spends all his time with the politics and has to let Lowy run the show."

"What does Lowy think about doctrine?" I asked.

"He seems indifferent." Junge yawned.

"What does Lowy think about the CIA trying to take over the show?"

"Lowy likes that idea. He thinks that all efforts need to be coordinated better. The National Police do their thing. The PRUs do something else. Most do nothing. Lowy's right. Things need to be coordinated better. Of course, remember that Lowy once worked with the CIA as part of the Naval Advisory Detachment attached to the SOG based in Da Nang," Junge said.

"What's SOG again?" I asked.

"Studies and Observation Group," Junge said, disgusted.

"I'm sorry, Gunner, I don't know all these different groups and the politics. I'm still bothered by the Frenchman we snuffed," I said.

"Forget it, Lieutenant. Stay loose and forget it."

"Just like that, just forget it."

"That's right. Just like that," Junge repeated.

For a minute I said nothing. We sat in silence at the edge of the lotus pond, drinking the coffee Sky Lady had brought for us, facing the large aviary where Madam Ti kept her collection of tropical birds. It was getting light, and soon the sun would break the horizon on the South China Sea.

"Gunner, I just can't believe what's happening. And I don't for the life of me see where this whole thing is going. I don't know where I fit."

"It's the nature of the business," Junge said.

"What business?"

"A business that you are expected to know nothing about," Junge said.

"More riddles. I don't know, Gunner. I'm out of my element. At first I was uncomfortable. Now I'm scared. Oh, I know that I've got to get my shit together, and I will. But I got to tell you that this whole thing has got me rattled," I said, lighting another cigarette.

"Patience is the hunter," Junge said.

"I've heard that before."

"Let's take a walk through the aviary. I'm very fond of Ti's aviary. She has an incredible collection of native birds, some of which are very rare," Junge said, lighting a cigarette as he spoke.

The aviary covered almost an acre, with large cages on either side of a U-shaped walkway. Ancient stone elephants made out of gray marble, priceless mandarin relics from China, bordered the walkway. Mature bamboo rising some thirty feet surrounded the entire complex, shading the aviary during the day and providing cover from prevailing wind and rain during the monsoon season.

We rose and started down the walk. In the predawn light the doves had begun cooing. Occasionally another, unknown bird would utter a kind of warble.

"Doves. I like that sound. Reminds me of the doves back in Iowa," I said.

"Those are wood pigeons. Imperial wood pigeons. Doves don't make any sounds until much later," Junge said.

"Know your birds, Gunner?"

"It's an interest. Come on. I'll take you on a tour," Junge said.

We approached the first of several cages, cages twenty feet long and at least six feet in height. Dark shapes the size of chickens scurried back and forth without a sound, obviously upset by our presence.

"These are Ti's pheasants. Silver pheasants and Siamese firebacks. It's not light enough to appreciate them. You must see them during the day, and then you must wait patiently for them to appear from their hiding place under the shrubs. These are shy. They are very shy, but very beautiful. Well worth the wait," Junge said, pausing at the cage of the Siamese firebacks.

The sun was poking up over the China Sea. With the sun, several finches in the next cage began to chatter. Their chatter grew into a chirping as we approached their cage.

"These are finches. Right?"

"Let's see. Yes. There are some finches. There is also a white-eared jay in there somewhere. But yes, these are finches. Scarlet finches and rose finches,'' Junge said, moving to the next cage.

The scarlet finches reminded me of scarlet tanagers in Iowa. For a brief moment I was back there in my mind, sitting along a creek with an old girlfriend. It was May, a beautiful spring day. The girl and I were making love. A scarlet tanager landed on a branch above us and warbled a song. I tried to remember the girl's name. I couldn't remember her name even though in my mind's eye I was holding her in my arms.

As the sun continued to rise, a kind of canary joined in with the finches. I couldn't see them, hiding back in their cages within the protective shrubs. But their melodious songs seemed to blend in a chorus.

''What are those?'' I asked.

''I'm not sure. Several kinds of birds, I believe,'' Junge said.

Larger birds now began their varied calls. Even I recognized the shrill whistles and piercing shrieks of the cockatoos. A large parrot screeched, flapping its wings wildly as we passed its cage. By now the sun was above the horizon and the sounds of the birds had grown into a cacophony.

For several minutes the cacophony continued. Then, quite suddenly, the birds ceased. The only sounds were a low, booming grunt and an occasional, strange rustling sound, as if someone were shaking the tail of a rattlesnake.

Gunner Junge pulled out his bottle of Lilac Vegetal and splashed some of the liquid over his face and arms. Lilac Vegetal, made by Pinaud, was a cheap scent from Paris that smelled like lilacs and was supposed to keep away the bugs. It kept the bugs away. It also made Junge smell like a whore.

''Give me some of that, Gunner. If I'm going to be a whore, I might as well smell like one.''

''Bugs bothering you, Lieutenant?''

''Lots of things are bothering me. It's like Sergeant Weathers said to Captain Lowy. At first he felt he was just wasting his time. Then he got the feeling that he was being used, or did he say exploited. No. Weathers wouldn't use a word like exploited. He probably said used. In fact, he may have said used up. I know he said whore,'' I said, testing Junge.

''Exploited?'' Junge said.

''Yeah, exploited.''

"Exploited in what sense?"

"Exploited in the sense that one is being used unethically for someone else's benefit or for some other purpose than they should," I said.

"With all due respect, Lieutenant, that's a crock of shit," Junge said, agitated.

"Gunner, we're killing civilians and snatching kids. I can see why Weathers thinks he's a whore," I said.

"It's not that damn simple. And if you feel that way, why did you volunteer for this program?"

We moved down the U-shaped walk to the next cage. The rustling, shaking sound grew louder. There was a booming grunt. We turned the corner at the cockatoo cage. The cockatoos whistled and shrieked at us as we passed.

"I guess I didn't know any better."

"Oh!" Junge said.

"And I guess I wanted to do something more than I had done. I had heard that counterintelligence was interesting. Actually, I wanted to work with the team that I had met out at Mike Tower," I said.

"Mike Tower. You are talking about the Cold Steel Crowd," Junge said.

"Yes. Like the Cold Steel Crowd. But again, I wanted to do something more than what I had done."

"Now you have done that," Junge said.

"What, by snatching kids and snuffing some old Frenchman?"

We moved down the walk and under the cover of the overhanging bamboo. I heard the booming grunt again. The shaking and rustling sound grew louder.

"What the hell is that, Gunner?"

"That's the sound of the crested argus," Junge said.

"Crested argus."

"Yes. The crested argus. But let me say again that the old Frenchman was the real whore. He sold himself and information to the VC. There was nothing neutral about him. If we had not killed him, the Green Berets in Special Operations Group would have soon enough."

We reached the cage of the crested argus. It looked like a kind of giant peacock with its great tail. It made a low sound as we approached, half boom, half grunt. Turning, the crested argus extended a wing cover with blue and green "peacock eyes," and shook it so that the vibrating feathers made a rustling, shaking sound like a rattlesnake's rattle. When the bird moved out into the middle of the cage, the size of its enormous tail became apparent. The tail feathers extended at least twelve feet.

"Does it have a mate?"

"No," Junge said.

"Strange bird."

"It's the only known crested argus in captivity," Junge said.

"Wow!" I said.

"Ti would sell it, but for the hope that she has of finding a mate for this bird," Junge said.

"This is a male?"

"Yes."

At that point the bird rushed the cage, startling me. I fell backward, tripping on the stone walkway and landing on my backside. The crested argus turned in the mottled shade of its cage. The wing trembled and shook again.

"Where do these come from, Gunner?"

"The mountains."

"I bet this one's worth some bucks."

"The tail feathers are priceless to some collectors," Junge said.

"Well, I'd give all of those tail feathers just to know the truth about that German nurse we snuffed."

Gunner Junge lit another cigarette. In the stillness of the early morning air the smoke seemed to hang in front of him. "A word about the nurse to put your mind at ease," Junge said.

"Shoot," I said.

"When you said that you heard her speaking German, I feared that you might have killed one of the Maltese," Junge said.

"Maltese?"

"Order of St. John," Junge said.

I looked at Gunner Junge blankly. We turned the corner at the bottom of the aviary's U-shaped walk and started back toward the lotus pond. The cages that we passed were all empty.

"The German nurses at An Hoa are part of the Order of St. John, Knights of Malta. They are often called Maltese," Junge said.

"Oh. Sure, I know now what you mean," I said, very interested.

"Well, I made some inquiries. My little errand last night was not only to drop off the young boy that you snatched. It was to see if any of the German nurses were missing."

"And?" I asked.

"None are missing," Junge said.

"So?"

I could see Sky Lady approaching down the walk. She was bringing more coffee. She had pulled her long hair into a bun-ponytail combination. Surprisingly the Band-Aid on her cheek was sufficient to cover the nick she had taken from the Frenchman's razor. Smiling and radiant in spite of last night's circumstances, she was more than beautiful, she was an inspiration.

"Beautiful," Junge said.

"Yes. Rare and beautiful. Like the crested argus, she's one of a kind," I said.

"I agree," Junge said, drawing on the cigarette.

"About the nurse," I said.

"She might have been an East German," Junge said.

"East German!" I said.

"Maybe an East German agent," Junge added, blowing smoke up into the air in little circles.

"Can I share that with Weathers and Odum?" I asked.

"Not yet."

"Why? It would ease a lot of pain!" I said, excited.

"It's not time," Junge said, sitting down at a table by the lotus pond.

Sky Lady set her tray down on the table. She winked at me as she poured the coffee. Back in the aviary two finches began squabbling, chattering and making curious snapping noises.

"What do you mean, it's not time? When will it be time, for God's sake?"

"When the captain tells us," Junge said.

"When the captain tells us based upon what?"

"Based upon their need to know, Lieutenant."

"I think that they need to know right now!" I shouted.

At the sound of my voice the finches stopped chattering. The whole aviary grew silent. I looked into the lotus pond to see the large golden carp circling near the spot where we had buried the Frenchman Lattre. Occasional bubbles rose to the surface.

"It would help them see how things are fitting together. Shit. That's important!" I said.

"We'll talk to the captain about that," Junge said.

"What other secrets are you keeping, Gunner?" I asked, sitting down next to Sky Lady.

Sky Lady moved her chair closer to mine. Our knees touched under the table. My body responded as any young marine officer's might. I wanted to get away from the Gunner and put my arms around Sky Lady once more before I had to leave for the field.

"Like what, Lieutenant?"

"Like Sky Lady, for example. Or should I say, Mona?" I said, kissing her lightly on the cheek.

"That was to keep you out of trouble, Lieutenant," Junge said.

"Trouble?"

"Lieutenant, with all due respect, you are a tough, rugged young officer, but you drink too much and it is well known that you have no check on your desire," Junge said.

"You've been talking to Lukavitch," I said.

"I don't need Lieutenant Lukavitch to tell me what I can see for myself," Junge said.

"And what is that?" I asked, somewhat amused.

"That you are fond of Vietnamese women," Junge said.

"So what? So's the captain."

"That's true and that's a shame," Junge said curtly.

Sky Lady pinched my ass.

"So what's the difference between me and the captain?" I said.

"The difference between you and the captain is that he is a man of much experience who will unselfishly sacrifice for both his men and the cause we're for. You, on the other hand, are a self-centered lieutenant who is struggling with doubt and uncertainty."

"Does it show?"

"Only when you drink too much," Junge replied, lighting another Gauloise cigarette.

Somewhere in the aviary a parrot screeched. Sky Lady stood

up beside me and began to massage my shoulders. Out on the pond a lotus was beginning to bloom, opening up into the bright morning air. A dragonfly hovered over the blooming lotus like a small gunship.

"How about it, Gunner. Do I have any good qualities?" I said, having taken the hook.

"You have guts, are physically very strong, and have demonstrated on more than one occasion a coolness under fire. And I must admit, you have a good mind. That's probably why the Marine Corps puts up with your childish excesses." Gunner Junge flicked a cigarette ash into the pond.

A big golden carp rose to the surface and swallowed the ash.

"You keep mentioning all these excesses, Gunner. What's so big a deal about that? A lot of marines are like me," I said, swallowing the gunner's bait.

"Lieutenant, if you survive Vietnam, I believe that someday you could make a fine officer," Junge said, leaning back in his chair.

Sky Lady's massage had started with my neck. Now she had worked her way down to my shoulders. I turned in my chair to allow her more of me to work on. She blew into my ear.

"Let's go back into the hotel," she whispered.

"That's beautiful, Gunner. What a put-down," I said, ignoring Sky Lady's request.

"It's not meant to be a put-down. Certain things are just a function of experience," Junge said, matter-of-factly.

Sky Lady sat down next to me. Junge offered her a cigarette. I lit the cigarette. Sky Lady sat back and inhaled. She seemed nervous. The smoke from the Gauloise cigarette was strong, very strong.

"Well, it was beautiful, a beautiful put-down," I said.

"You mean it had the ring of truth," Junge said, blowing another smoke ring.

"Yeah, Gunner. It struck a cord."

"Actually there was nothing beautiful at all about what I said. You talk about how things fit. You talk about where you fit. So I just say what I say," Junge said.

"I don't believe that for a minute," I said with a challenging tone.

"Suit yourself, Lieutenant."

For a moment there was an uncomfortable silence. Sky Lady looked away as if she were avoiding my eyes. Gunner Junge shifted in his chair a couple times. The dragonfly hovered over the sugar bowl on the coffee tray. Sky Lady quickly brushed the dragonfly away with a wave of her hand. I winked at her. She smiled and moved closer to me.

"What excesses do you have, Gunner?" I was hungry for more.

"Philosophy. I am fond of philosophy as you are fond of beer and Vietnamese woman."

"That's beautiful," I said.

"No. That's the truth. You keep confusing the two notions," Junge said with a wry smile on his face.

"I'm not a philosopher. I'm a lieutenant of marines," I said quickly.

"Are you?" Junge snapped back.

Sky Lady looked down at the ground. She took another cigarette and lit it herself before I could light it for her.

"What do you mean?" I said intently.

"Lieutenants of marines have the integrity to master their appetites. They take personal responsibility to honor the code that they live by," Junge said, blowing smoke across the table in my direction.

I could feel my face getting red. Sky Lady got up and walked to the edge of the lotus pond. My right hand started to tremble slightly.

"What do you mean by integrity?" I asked, once again returning for more punishment.

"A sense of yourself in relation to the whole," Junge said.

"You lost me," I said.

Sky Lady sat down on my lap. She whispered in my ear a second time. "Let's go. This is stupid."

"Give me an example of what you're talking about," I said, raising my voice somewhat and ignoring Sky Lady.

The crested argus boomed at the far end of the aviary. The bird's strange shaking, rattling noise followed for almost a full minute.

"It's like that bird, the crested argus. Do you think that the bird is beautiful, Lieutenant?"

"I don't know. I suppose. Why? What does that have to do with integrity?" I asked.

"I think that the bird's true beauty is a matter of where it belongs. It's a matter of where it fits in the true order of things. We take it out of its natural element and it loses something. We corrupt it. It doesn't fit. Its wholeness and completeness are impaired. It doesn't behave as it should," Junge said.

"Your point is that I don't behave as I should. Is that it?" I asked.

"The point is that the bird fits in the wild where it can fulfill its purpose," Junge said, showing some emotion for the first time in the conversation.

"Noble idea, but what does that have to do with this green mother called the Marine Corps?" I asked, tired of Junge's bullshit.

Sky Lady put her arm around my neck as if to calm me. She wrapped one of her beautiful, slim legs around my lower left leg. Her warmth was hard to ignore, but the conversation had grown too intense.

"It has to do with where we all fit. Anyone can be fairly certain of this war when they're fighting some enemy who is shooting back at them. When it all fits some notion of form and function, Marine Corps doctrine, black or white, honor, duty, that sort of thing," Junge said, eyes glazing over with intensity.

"Hey, I like that, Gunner!" I said.

"Yes. I imagine that you do. For you are like that crested argus in that you fit back in your natural order. You belong back in your own jungle, where there is a clearer pattern that connects and where you don't feel like a whore, Lieutenant," Junge said, almost out of breath.

"Where is your jungle, Gunner?" I asked.

"My jungle is here, where things fit with difficulty, like the Frenchman we snuffed," Junge said.

"And your integrity?" I asked.

"I fit into the mission. That's what the corps wants."

"What do you want?" I asked.

"To confirm what I believe," Junge said.

"Riddles again, Gunner."

I sensed what the gunner was trying to tell me. But it was difficult for me to understand how all these abstract ideas really meant anything to anyone else but him. Integrity. Natural order. Those things were fine if one was a philosopher.

"My integrity has to do with my commitment to the corps. I have no damn doubts! My personal standard cuts no slack. When things are no longer pretty, when they no longer fit some neat little organization chart up at Division, I'm the kind of glue that fits it together. And since what we do is by its very nature a thing that goes against the rules, at times we have to make our own rules to make it work," Junge said with great vehemence.

At that point the dragonfly landed on the top of Junge's head. For a while Gunner Junge said nothing, as if this last intense outburst had drained him. The dragonfly then hopped to another point on his long, gray-blond head. Sky Lady noticed the dragonfly and smiled. There was something ridiculous about the whole conversation that seemed to reach the height of its absurdity as the dragonfly hopped from point to point on Junge's head, unnoticed to Junge.

"Did you say 'making this work'?" I asked.

"Sometimes you put the crested argus in a cage. Sometimes you create a new order," Junge said sternly.

A new order. Where had I heard that before? The idea rebounded and glanced around in my head like a ricocheting bullet. Then it hit me.

"Do you know what the argus wants, Gunner?"

"What do you mean what does the argus want?" Junge asked.

"I think that you're right. I am like the argus. In more than one way. But what does this bird really want? What does any bird in this damn aviary really want?" I said, smiling.

The gunner thought for a moment and then smiled. The dragonfly was gone.

"Perhaps what the crested argus wants is to escape," Junge said softly.

"Let's let that big mother go," I said.

The gunner sat back in his chair as if he had been struck. There was a strange gleam in Gunner Junge's eye. He smiled and nodded his head. The smile became a grin, and before I could say another thing, the gunner had risen from our table, striding toward the cage of the crested argus, bewitched by an impulse to make his own rules.

"And for what greater purpose shall we claim this act was done?" Junge called back.

"Your new order. How about that, Gunner, a new order," I said, laughing.

Gunner Junge reached the cage of the crested argus and broke the latch. He then swung the door open and backed away. For a time the only crested argus in captivity stared at the opening, barely moving, its eyes glancing back and forth from the gunner to the open door.

Then with an explosive flutter of wings, the crested argus rose above our heads, the vanity of its great tail glinting in the sun. All through the aviary there were murmurs and wing-beats. The crested argus soared over the back wall and was gone.

All the while I had my arm around Sky Lady. Pulling her closer, I had slipped my hand down around her ass. She had a great ass. It was a beautiful ass. It fit just right.

NIGHT ZEN

October 3, 1968: 0800 hours

IT WAS A glorious morning. Everything seemed very still, and the South China Sea lay calm and gleaming, waves breaking easy on the broad beach just east of Da Nang. I jogged from the beach back to the hotel. The trees overhead cast a mottled shade on the street, and because it was Sunday morning, there was hardly traffic for me to dodge.

When I got back to the hotel, I knocked on Captain Lowy's door to see what the order of business was going to be. Sunday was like any other day for us, and by now I was sure that Lowy would have his plan of action together. To my surprise Madam Ti answered my knock, opening the door a crack to whisper that Lowy was still sleeping. Ti's kimono was half open and I couldn't help but notice the fullness of her breasts. She noticed that I noticed and, smiling, blew me a kiss as she slowly closed the door.

I stood on the balcony at the end of the hallway and looked down the street. Two months ago a Lieutenant Hardy and I had stood on the same balcony after a night of hell-raising. We had slipped away from Division Headquarters to have an orgy of sorts. But we got to drinking and got so drunk and crazy that we never did justice to the girls that we picked up. We had stood on the balcony and watched the girls walk away.

When Hardy returned to the field, he lost both his legs to a booby trap. He was medevaced to Naval Support Activity Hospital where he lingered for several days before dying. I was on my way to see him when he died. I got there just as the priest was giving Hardy the last rites.

My friend Hardy had been working with the Mike Company off of Hill 10. Like myself, he had extended in Vietnam because he felt that he was saving lives through the contributions that he was making. He felt that his job was one that was fairly safe, and it was a job that he found interesting. He knew the Vietnamese as well as any officer that I'd ever met, especially their customs and religious beliefs.

One night after much beer and discussion we were talking Zen, which to him was enlightenment sought through introspection and intuition. Not knowing much about Zen or for that matter about religion or philosophy, I found the conversation both interesting and a source of support. In the last months I had seen many young marines die. The effect of those experiences seemed to be catching up to me. One night I would drink myself into oblivion; the next night I would sit by myself, reflecting over my copy of the New Testament.

That night, after much discussion, we invented our own religious perspective. It was called Night Zen. Hardy felt that the only real truth he found in Vietnam, the only real enlightenment, came to him at night, whether that truth came through a well-sprung ambush or a good piece of ass. Jokingly, he claimed that the process through which he found both himself and reality was always at night, in darkness, usually with his hands, either interrogating or caressing. Hence the term Night Zen.

When I thought of Hardy, which was often, I tried to remember his pleasures rather than how he died. He was an artist who painted watercolors and sketched. Now I stood on the balcony sipping my coffee, looking out at the South China Sea. Strange how the outcome of events should bring me back to the same balcony.

Sky Lady joined me. At that moment the wind seemed to change direction, picking up speed. To the north, over the dark headland called Monkey Mountain, a line of clouds was coming in.

"China wind," Sky Lady said.

"What's that?" I asked.

"China wind blow down from China very hard. Not good. Bring weather change. Not supposed to happen this time of year. China wind come too early," Sky Lady said.

"Stay loose, Sky Lady. It will be gone before you know it."

"Americans like China wind. Blow very hard in one direction for a while. Then sure to change."

China wind. Hardy would have liked that, comparing Americans to the China wind. He would have liked Sky Lady. If he were alive, I wondered what he would have thought of the situation I was in.

I walked back into the room. I lit a joss stick and watched the musky smoke curl into the air. The smell of burning joss had been one of Hardy's favorite things. He was always leaving burning joss sticks stuck here and there. This morning I lit the joss stick for my friend and for the profound revelations of the previous night. Sky Lady just smiled as if she understood.

October 3, 1968: 0900 hours

Sky Lady was in the shower. I stripped and joined her, soaping her back and breasts. We rinsed and toweled dry.

"How long have you worked with Junge?"

"Three months," she said, combing out her long, thick hair.

"Where did you first meet him?"

"Saigon," she said, running the comb through the hair on my chest.

"You're from Saigon then?" I ran my fingers through her damp hair.

"Yes. That was where I first found out about Americans," she said, smiling.

"And what did you find out?"

"That you all dinky-dau." She laughed.

"How did you get into this business?"

"Air force major show me," she said, winking.

"Air force major!"

"He take my cherry. Screw very hard. Scare the shit out of me," she said, laughing again.

"Are you kidding me?" I said, surprised.

"He kinky. Like to play with my shit," she said, clearly trying to shock me.

"I think you dinky-dau! What happened to him?"

"He go Stateside, back to his fat wife. I gave him the clap to take back to her," she said, giggling.

What a wonderful woman Sky Lady was. I laughed with her and picked her up in my arms. I was growing fond of her. The fact that she was a whore made no difference. My feelings for her were genuine.

October 3, 1968: 1000 hours

Captain Lowy seemed to be hiding. His expression was opaque, giving nothing away. It was clear to me that he had no clear, thought-out objective with respect to the problems we were facing. It was as if he had suddenly found oblivion. Lowy seemed like an artist staring at an empty canvas. I wondered if the crack on the head he suffered from the Frenchman had done some damage.

"Every law creates an outlaw. Ever hear of that saying?" Lowy said.

"No, sir, I don't think that I've ever heard that before," I said, wondering where the conversation was going.

Junge and I had met the captain for coffee. Junge and I had hoped that we would get some direction. The events of the last evening weighed heavy on us. As yet we had not told Lowy that we had snuffed the Frenchman that cracked him on the head. It was apparent that Lowy was oblivious to all that was going on around him. He seemed dazed and distant.

"Do you think that this is all a bunch of smoke and mirrors?" Lowy said.

October 3, 1968: 1400 hours

At 1306 hours Captain O.D. Lowy died of brain injuries suffered from a blow to the back of the head by a large sap. As we left our morning coffee, Captain Lowy had collapsed unconscious on the street outside the Grand Hotel. He never regained con-

sciousness. By the time we reached the Naval Support Activity
Hospital, Lowy had stopped breathing, forcing us to give him
over to the naval corpsmen.

We reported his death as the result of an encounter with a
suspected hostile agent believed to be in the service of the Vietcong. Junge notified both Division and the province senior adviser. Division put out word concerning the Frenchman to the
military police. Colonel Schuster informed Junge that I now had
oversight of both the Cold Steel Crowd and the Habu effort.

October 3, 1968: 1416 hours

"What a waste. What a damn waste," I said, opening a Beck's
beer.

"That depends," Junge said, pulling the jeep in front of the
Grand Hotel.

"Depends on what?" I asked.

"It depends upon if you think he died in relation to some
purpose," Junge said. "His purpose was counterintelligence.
His new passion was this Habu effort. It was very important.
The Frenchman was one of the inevitable targets of that program, depending upon how one looks at the situation. Do you
think that that is true?" Junge asked.

"Sure," I said, sipping the cold Beck's.

"Well, look at it this way. The captain's injury gave rise to a
series of events that brought an end to the Frenchman," Junge
said.

"Let's refer to him as an agent. I feel more comfortable with
that. I have some good friends that are French," I said.

"Oh, is that right. Well, that's too bad, Lieutenant," Junge
said.

October 3, 1968: 1600 hours

Madam Ti kept to her room. Junge had felt it important that we
return to the Grand Hotel. Odum and Weathers and the Cold
Steel Crowd were told to scout the area for the Frenchman. I
put Sandman, Ti's bodyguard, on notice that if I had any trouble

from anyone, especially him, I would use my new authority to close the Grand Hotel and drag him down to the Da Nang Special Sector. He kissed my ass when Weathers appeared on the scene. For some reason, probably a good reason, Sandman had a healthy respect for Weathers.

"Gunner Junge, what have you got against the French? They're neutral in this war," I said, putting my arm around Sky Lady.

"No one in this country is neutral."

"Did Captain Lowy feel that way?" I asked.

"Captain Lowy drank too much and made his own rules, yet he had an astonishing lucidity of mind when it came to this business that we are in. He was precise and intelligent. Losing Captain Lowy the way that we did was both tragic and stupid. It was to my mind an unnecessary loss. But it doesn't surprise me. No, it doesn't surprise me. You see, Lowy gave away a kind of middle ground. He let that Frenchman close to him even though he knew that he was an agent." Junge shook his head.

"Why?" I asked.

"Who knows? He got high on that kind of action, but there is no way of knowing for sure what was in his mind. He was intuitive. He played hunches, and of course, he was a mirror for the conflicts and anxieties of his age," Junge said, lighting up a Gauloise cigarette.

"I don't understand," I said.

"He was an individual, a rugged individualist that is, in a large organization that demanded a certain amount of conformity in return for what that organization provided. He loved the Marine Corps, but hated some of its rules. Under the guise of official Marine Corps business he pursued his own goals. To him the rules of engagement reduced his freedom. That's why he found his way into this business after running a grunt company. Yet he was afraid. He was afraid that someone in Division would figure out why he was so effective. And he felt guilty," Junge said.

"Guilty of what?" I asked.

"Guilty of taking the lives of the innocent, guilty for his mistakes, whatever they were, and guilty of not being honorable to the corps to which he had promised fidelity."

"Gunner, I think that you're full of shit! Captain Lowy was one of the best men that I ever knew. I don't even want to hear this crap about Lowy, ever!'' I said, grabbing Sky Lady by the hand and walking away.

October 3, 1968: 2200 hours

I lay next to Sky Lady in the quiet of the room. Outside the night sounds of Da Nang worked their way in, the putt-putt of scooters, the cough of a diesel, the blare of a radio in a passing car. On the ceiling various colored lights flashed. I got up and lit a joss stick. The musty scent filled the room.

"You need to relax," Sky Lady said, rubbing my shoulders as I sat down on the bed.

"Hard for me to relax, but I love how you touch me," I said, thinking of what my buddy Hardy had said about Night Zen and a caress, how an affectionate touch once brought him to a kind of enlightenment.

"How do you relax?" I asked.

"I let things unfold," she said, now rubbing my arms.

I lay back and thought of how hard it was to relax in the presence of either fear or desire. Holding her and touching the way we did helped me reconnect. It helped me center myself in the midst of all that was happening around me.

"I try to relax, but I can't," I said, stroking her hair.

"Push too hard. All dinky-dau Americans push too hard. Push less. Open out. Let happen," Sky Lady said, lighting one of her strange-looking cigarettes.

"You want smoke?" she said, offering whatever it was to me.

"What is it?" I asked.

"Get you high. Relax you good," she said.

"No. I want to know what's happening. Don't want to get caught up in that shit," I said, waving it away.

"The more you let go, the more open you become. The more open you become, the more easy you will know what's happening," Sky Lady said, smiling.

"I need more than that," I said.

"Let go of what you have and you will receive what you need. Let go of what you are and you may become what you might be," Sky Lady said, a gleam in her eye as she relit her smoke.

In the light of the match there was something deep and inscrutable about her face. I had taken Sky Lady for granted. I thought I had understood this woman. Now I was uncertain.

"Think of how Captain Lowy died. How stupid and what a waste it was. What I am really afraid of is that I will die a stupid and useless death like that. How can I relax or let go?"

Her kimono fell open, revealing her breasts, as she lit another match. The flame of the match cast shadows on the wall. Sky Lady lit a candle by the window and shed her kimono. Picking up a comb she began to brush out her hair in the candlelight.

"Aren't you afraid of death?" I asked.

"Death is not frightening because I know how to let go," she said, sliding into bed next to me.

The day had ended. There hadn't been a cloud in the sky all day and the South China Sea still lay calm, waves breaking easy on the beach. Soon the night traffic would disappear and the only sound would be that of the breeze rustling in the trees.

I thought of my artist friend and tried to remember his pleasures. I thought of the rugged Captain Lowy and of his good nature, and of how much he had brought to me. That night with Sky Lady I found both part of myself and a new reality as I lay there in my introspection. I found that reality in darkness. I was touching. It was called Night Zen.

THE COLD STEEL CROWD

October 4, 1968: 0600 hours

SKY LADY WAS brushing out her hair on the balcony. I sipped my morning coffee, distracted by the sheer beauty of her motion. She looked at me and smiled, pulling out long strands of her hair from the comb.

"Hey dinky-dau! What you thinking about?" Sky Lady asked, putting down her comb.

"I was thinking about how beautiful you are, and I was watching you, thinking about how lucky I am," I said with a sigh.

"What the matter?" Sky Lady asked, putting her arms around my waist.

"I can't get Lowy off my mind. When I look at you, I feel great. But then, when I think about what happened, I feel guilty. I feel that I should be out doing something, but I don't know what to do," I said, draining my coffee.

"You want me to leave?" Sky Lady said, hugging me.

"Absolutely not. I'm just confused. Something Lowy said keeps coming back to me," I said, stroking her hair.

"What's that?" She twirled a strand of her hair.

"He asked me if all we were doing was nothing but smoke and mirrors," I said, picking up several of the long strands of her hair that had fallen to the floor.

Sky Lady picked up her comb and began to brush her hair.

She walked to the edge of the balcony and looked out at the South China Sea. The fishing junks were coming in with the night's catch. The promontory known as Monkey Mountain jutted out into the sea from our left, a great, dark headland shrouded in fog.

"Then you must see through the smoke and see beyond the reflection in the mirror," she said, turning and smiling, still brushing out her hair.

"What are you talking about? You dinky-dau!" I said, tossing the twisted strands of her hair in her direction.

Out of nowhere a little bird landed on the balcony, snatched up the twisted strands of hair, and flew off into the trees. Sky Lady just smiled and continued to brush her hair. A light breeze stirred the leaves, and for a moment I found myself breathing easy.

October 4, 1968: 0630 hours

I was still sitting on my balcony watching the fishing junks when Gunner Junge came by. The fog surrounding the headland was lifting. I wondered how the fishermen found their way through the fog. I also wondered if I was falling for Sky Lady. Maybe my feelings for her were simply a matter of needing someone due to the emotional strain of the last few days. I wasn't sure. I only knew that the events of the last few days had changed me. More and more I found myself hanging on to the moment, and there was something about Sky Lady that compelled me.

The breeze coming in off the water brought the smell of fish. I breathed in and out slowly, deep into my thoughts, knowing that my affection for Sky Lady involved more than just physical pleasure. I gathered up the loose strands of Sky Lady's hair and slipped them into my shirt pocket.

"What are you doing?" Junge asked.

"Saving some of Sky Lady's hair," I said sheepishly.

"Are you in love, Lieutenant?" Gunner Junge said with a cynical tone.

"I'm confused. I know that," I said with all honesty.

"Watch it, Lieutenant, she can be like a drug," Junge said, pouring us both a cup of coffee.

"Well, I'm addicted to Sky Lady, whatever it is, and how I came to this state of affairs I'll probably never figure out. And Gunner, maybe it doesn't matter if I ever figure it out." I rose and walked to the balcony.

"This is not good," Junge said.

"Ever been in love, Gunner?"

"Twice."

"Tell me about it," I said, lighting a cigarette.

"Are you sure that's what you want?"

"Actually, I'm not sure what I want. I know what's important, but I'm not sure what I want."

"If that is the case, then you are in more trouble than you realize," Junge said, sipping his coffee.

"What are you saying?"

"What you should want is to be an effective leader. What you should get out of your head is a whore who is on our payroll and who would probably turn double agent on us if the offer were made and the price were right," Junge said.

"Double agent!"

"It's only a matter of time. Once they know your appetites, once they know what you like, they've got you," Junge said.

"Who's they?" I said, somewhat irritated.

"Who else! They are the enemy, both within and without. By the way, one thing is for sure, if you continue on your present path, I guarantee one of our enemies will soon find you. If that happens, the bait will be too sweet. One of our enemies will take it," Junge said with a smirk.

"What enemies? Do you mean the VC?" I asked, blowing a smoke ring into the air.

"VC. Division. Have no illusions, Lieutenant, there are those up on Freedom Hill sitting in some Division job who would jump at the chance to make an example of a lieutenant who traffics with a whore."

"You traffic with her. You pay her to do things that could get her killed," I said with contempt.

"She is a means to an end," Junge said.

"You're dangerous, Gunner," I said, flicking an ash off my cigarette.

"The real problem we have to face today, Lieutenant, is not your love life; rather, it is what we have to do to put you in charge. Right now your image is shit. You best take some action with the Cold Steel Crowd or you will just be along for the ride. Lowy's death has left a vacuum.''

I took the hair from my pocket and began to twist the strands. I sipped my coffee, lit another cigarette, and formed the twisted strands into a ring.

''Ride?'' I said.

''They'll take you for a ride, Lieutenant, just as Sky Lady is taking you for a ride.''

''What are you saying?''

''If you are going to lead the Cold Steel Crowd, then you must know what you want. Otherwise, you will just be along for the ride,'' Junge said.

''What should I do?'' I asked.

''Do you want to talk about love or do you want to talk about what you should do?'' Junge said.

''Tell me what you would do with the Cold Steel Crowd,'' I said.

''I would spend the next two or three days watching what they do. Start with Cernich. He is an opinion leader. Also watch Klepper. Keep in mind that there is tension between the two men.''

''Tension over what?''

''Watch and judge for yourself. For now that is best,'' Junge said.

''I know Klepper is a communications jock. Lowy liked him. I know that Lowy just looked the other way when it came to some things,'' I said.

I set the little hair ring down on the coffee table. My bird thief friend suddenly appeared on the balcony. The bird must have been watching, waiting in the trees for me to leave so that it might gather up all of Sky Lady's hair. Perhaps it wants the hair for a nest, I thought.

''I'll work with them for a few days. Watch what they do,'' I said.

''You will find that they do many things,'' Junge said, raising his eyebrows.

''Lowy said that they were active with the boys from Hoi An. He also talked of this new Phoenix program that's supposed to kick off.''

"That program may get us all into a new way of thinking. But that has yet to be determined. Right now the Cold Steel Crowd spends a lot of time with these sensors. They are also trying to track down some wild information about hand-held surface-to-air missiles called SA-7s," Junge said.

"What are SA-7s?"

"Heat-seeking missiles that weigh only twenty-two pounds. I have heard them referred to as 'Strelas' and as 'Grails.' NVA infantry units are said to have been trained in their use. As you might imagine, this information is highly classified. Again, Lowy claimed to have a lead," Junge said.

"Probably just wild stories. Lowy was given to bullshit. He also said that you folks had some agents."

"We have one agent. A whore named Sky Lady," Junge said.

"I'll spend some time watching the men," I said, ignoring his comment.

"That's fine. And again, keep in mind that a month ago Lowy had these men on some hot projects. Things sort of dried up on Lowy. He kept waiting for this so-called 'Phoenix' program to give him direction. At any rate, I want you to form your own opinions," Junge said.

"Could have fooled me, Gunner."

The gunner tossed the hair ring in the direction of the little bird. The bird snatched the hair ring in midair and was gone.

"Do you still want to talk about love?" Junge said.

"Sure" I said.

"I have been in love twice. Each time for different reasons. The first time was with my sweetheart back in Germany. I was seventeen. It was during the war. We made plans, but we were realistic. We knew that we would have to wait. Yet, we had it all figured out, the marriage, the house. I would work with my father in Leipzig. Then I was in the army. I came home on leave and got her pregnant. A month later I was captured in the Battle of the Bulge. Next thing I know, I'm in the States, the war is over, and Saxony is part of East Germany. I joined the corps to forget because there was no way to track her. My family was dead, all the brothers killed but me. My one sister married to an American GI. I never knew until years later what became of her," Junge said, looking off in the direction of the headland.

"What became of her?" I asked.

"She became a whore," Junge said.

"And the child?" I asked.

"I don't know. To this day I don't know. I could never bring myself to follow up and find out," Junge said.

"How do you know this whore business?"

"My sister finally told me after I came back from China."

The little bird returned to the balcony. It flitted to the floor and gathered up another strand of Sky Lady's hair. It hopped to a second strand of hair, wound it around its bill, and then flew into the trees.

"Tell me about the second time. How was that different from the first?" I asked.

"Oh, it was in China. I had a kind of housemaid, a mere girl. At first I treated her very badly. But then I grew to love her. Our love was different in that it grew out of particulars. It grew out of a lot of little things that we did together. The day that I was leaving China was the day that I finally realized that I loved her," Junge said.

"What happened? What became of her?" I asked.

"Oh, I had to leave her behind," Junge said, still looking out toward the headland and the fog.

"You lost touch," I asked.

"Yes. I was young. I didn't realize what was happening," Junge said, standing and walking to the balcony, all the while his eyes seaward, as if he were scanning the horizon.

"What are you looking at, Gunner?" I asked.

"Oh nothing. I was just distracted for a moment," Junge said.

"Distracted?" I asked softly.

"Yes, I was trying to make out the headland through the fog," Junge said.

October 4, 1968: 0800 hours

Joe Cernich was from Waukegan, Illinois. He had worked in the wire mill in North Chicago for two years before joining the Marine Corps. One week before going to Vietnam, he had married his high school sweetheart in Holy Family Church just five miles from that same wire mill. Joe's father and one of his uncles had been marines in World War II. Joe had grown up on tales of "the Canal" where his father had served with the immortal Lou Diamond.

Cernich was tall and well-built. He had a rugged good looks, his big, Joe Palooka chin almost too square and perfect. Well proportioned, Cernich's big neck and chest were balanced by long, athletic arms and legs. He had been a football player and a wrestler. His clean, athletic good looks had made him the Cold Steel Crowd favorite. Cernich knew this and took advantage of his favored status. Then again, Cernich had earned his due. For Cernich had two hearts acquired as a grunt out in the Arizona Territory west of An Hoa. Those two hearts had made Cernich a young man who seemed always on edge. He would jump at any sudden sound or movement. His fingers always seemed to be trembling slightly.

Joe Cernich wanted one thing and that was to go home to his wife and son. When I talked to him he seemed much older than twenty years. He wore a rosary around his neck, the black cross of the rosary dangling over the spot where an NVA soldier had tried to bayonet Joe while he lay wounded in the kill-zone of an ambush. Joe had snapped the bayonet off with his bare hands when it hung up between two of his ribs, pulling the NVA soldier down to break his neck with some kind of wrestler's hold he had learned at Waukegan Township High School, a high school always noted for producing good wrestlers through the Sixties.

Joe didn't drink too much. For when Joe drank he got mean, and Joe Cernich was no one anyone would mess with. Those big arms and thick hands that had snapped a steel NVA bayonet were fast as well as powerful. He could lash out like a snake, quick as an Okinawan Habu.

"What's the plan, Joe?" I asked, following Junge's advice by trying to get to know Joe.

"I figured that we'd head out to Captain Lowy's favorite spot and show you the project Klepper's been workin on, sir," Cernich said.

"Project?" I asked, popping a cold beer.

"An underwater acoustical device that we had Klepper rig up. Isn't that right, Klepper?" Cernich said.

The pudgy and bulky Klepper was a contrast to the handsome Cernich. Rolf Klepper gazed back at me through thick, wire-rimmed glasses. Klepper was from southern California but he didn't fit the image of the surfer. Quite the contrary, Klepper was a communications type who could jock around with radios and electronics to eavesdrop on just about anything you could imagine. Lowy had discovered Klepper at Mike Tower and offered him the opportunity to work on his teams. Klepper jumped at the chance to work with someone as laid back as Captain Lowy. Klepper was your basic smart son of a bitch. Rolf was a kind of genius who would do anything to please his hero Lowy.

What Lowy had Klepper do was wire Division for sound so that he could listen in on his own superiors. When I thought about to what lengths Lowy went to eavesdrop on his fellow officers, it made me wonder. What was Lowy afraid of? Why this compulsion to send his people to spy on our own? Lowy not only had a contempt for Division—he didn't trust them to the point that he felt it necessary to spy upon them. Klepper was his indispensable tool to do this. Klepper knew his value to Lowy. Accordingly, when Klepper sold his dope to various navy and air force types, Lowy looked the other way.

"Is that right, Klepper? You folks got something special?" I asked, totally ignorant of this realm of technology.

Klepper put down the science-fiction paperback that he was reading and picked up something that looked like a beer can with an antenna.

"Do you know what PSIDs are, Lieutenant?" Klepper asked.

"No," I said, sipping my beer.

"Patrol seismic intrusion detectors. The PSID. Picks up ground vibrations. I also use EMIDs, electromagnetic sensors. A lot of this stuff is classified," Klepper said.

"I wouldn't understand it. I don't know a thing about this kind of business," I said.

"Well, Captain Lowy did, sir. He thought that Klepper was a genius for what he invented," Cernich said.

"What did you invent, Klepper?" I asked, draining my beer. It was getting warm and the beer was starting to go down real good.

"I wouldn't dignify what I did by calling it an invention. I tinker. What I tinkered with was an underwater device that attracts fish," Klepper said, taking the beer that I offered.

"Fish?" I said.

"Yes, sir, fish. You see, Captain Lowy was a bass fisherman. He fished the southern U.S.A. for smallmouth bass, and he had a theory that when he retired, he could make a living fishing bass tournaments," Klepper said.

"So? I don't get the point," I said.

"The point is that this project of ours attracts fish. It hums! It has great commercial potential," Klepper said, somewhat disgusted by my lack of understanding.

"You mean to say that this project that you were working on was to help Captain Lowy catch bass when he got back to the States?" I said, with a tone of disbelief.

"There it is. Oh, there's some spin-offs to the people that we work with, like the SEALs, but I haven't worked out all the bugs yet. Like Captain Lowy said, each war generates a technology that changes private industry. That's part of what makes America great, he used to say," Klepper said.

"Fishing for bass. You got to be shitting me," I said, beginning to feel the effect of the beer.

"Got to understand this, sir. Captain Lowy sure liked to fish. That's why he had me keep this boat. He felt that just because he had to go to Nam didn't mean that he had to give up fishing, if you know what I mean," Cernich said.

"Bass fishing," I said, making certain that I was hearing correctly.

"Any kind of fishing, sir. But Captain Lowy was going to make it rich fishing for bass that were attracted by Klepper's little invention," Cernich said.

The fog had lifted and the sun was beginning to show through the broken clouds. Fishing. Apparently we were going fishing. I hadn't been fishing since I was a kid. I thought of Sky Lady and what she had said about letting go, about just letting things happen and becoming more open. I also thought of what Gunner Junge said about being along for the ride. I decided to let go. It seemed to me that the more open I became with Klepper and Cernich, the more I would know what was really happening. I needed to know. As Sky Lady said, by letting go I get what I needed, by letting go I might become what I might be.

October 4, 1968: 0830 hours

We skimmed across the open brightness of the South China Sea. The boat was a Boston Whaler that Ruiz and Cernich had acquired in a swap with some sailors up at Camp Tien Shau. Cernich had mounted two big twin Johnson motors on the boat. He was quick to point out that the twin Johnsons had been made in his hometown of Waukegan.

"So all you have been doing is fishing and taking care of the boat, is that right?" I asked.

"Yes, sir, that's about it. Klepper and I kind of been taking a vacation since our little trip down to Hoi An. That's been three weeks. But that's the way this war goes. Things get hot for a while and then cool off. Captain Lowy used to say everything seems to go in cycles, especially this war," Cernich said.

"Lowy would say that. Made you wonder if he had it all figured out," I said, lighting a cigarette.

We were sitting in a little cove just inside the reef which separated the cove's shallows from the deeper water off the headland. The sun kept trying to peek through the cloud cover. Little squalls were gathering in the distance, far to the south toward Hoi An.

"I think he did have it all figured out, sir. He had it all under control as far as the men were concerned. He knew what was happening. He knew what we had to do to stay out of trouble," Cernich said.

"If he was so together, how come he got wasted the way that he did?" Klepper said, cleaning his glasses.

"Hey, dude, that was a fluke. Lowy was a righteous captain who tended to business. What happened to Lowy could have happened to any one of us," Cernich said, somewhat agitated.

"If what happened to the captain was such a twist of fate, then he didn't have it all under control, that's all I'm saying," Klepper said, nodding to me.

"Hey, dude! He was always good to you. You didn't have to sweat shit. If it wasn't for Lowy, you would have still been fixing radios in some communications hooch," Cernich said, now clearly agitated.

"Hold it, Joe. I'm not bad-mouthing the captain. I think that his getting killed was a real bummer. He got me out of hot water boo-coo times,'' Klepper said.

"He let you skate right through this war, Klepper. Don't you ever forget it. He kept Division from nailing your sorry ass to the wall,'' Cernich said.

"Oh, and I suppose that you never did anything wrong or that you shouldn't be ashamed of,'' Klepper retorted.

"What are you talking about?'' Cernich replied.

"A lot of things. How about Mama-San?'' Klepper said.

"What about Mama-San?'' Cernich came to his feet.

The boat began to rock. Cernich was clearly angry.

"Sit down, you're rocking the boat,'' Klepper said.

"What about Mama-San?'' Cernich repeated.

"You are the one who skated that one. You skated that one big time!''

Cernich sat down. He picked up the acoustic device that Klepper had been working on and threw it into the sea.

"Come on, Joe! What's the matter with you? How am I going to get that back?'' Klepper said.

"Dive for it. Dive your fat ass over the side and get it like I been getting for you for the last two weeks,'' Cernich said.

"Who's Mama-San, or shouldn't I ask?'' I said.

"Mama-San was an old lady we spotted planting mines in the road. When Captain Lowy told Division, he got word that he was to leave her alone. Division said to watch her for a while and make sure. Division wanted to make some big study project out of it. When Lowy told us, he said he would leave it up to us,'' Cernich said.

"And?'' I said.

"We had lost some men to those mines. The team thought that we should snuff her. Captain Lowy said that she was getting special treatment from Division for some reason. The team felt that any special treatment given to Mama-San might cost more marine lives. Like the Captain said, Division was a rock and we were the hard place. Division had all these official goals and reasons why. Down at our level we had to operate. To operate we kill the enemy,'' Cernich said.

"So your team killed Mama-San,'' I said.

"I killed Mama-San,'' Cernich said.

"And then there was Babi-San. Tell him about Babi-San," Klepper said.

"Babi-San?" I asked.

"Boy, did you skate that one, Cernich. Tell the lieutenant about that one," Klepper said, picking up a Swedish K submachine gun and wiping it down.

The Swedish "K" fired 9mm rounds. The one Klepper carried was fitted with a sound suppressor similar to the Bell Laboratory design which I had seen mounted on the M3/A1 grease gun.

"Who was Babi-San?" I asked.

"She was a fifteen-year old whore who used to flirt with Joe. Followed him around all the time. Joe was always slipping off in the middle of the night to rendezvous with her. We had to cover Joe's ass. Then one night Junge catches her outside the back door of the Grand Hotel with this Swedish 'K' that's got a silencer on it. Joe's off waiting for her to show up at some other spot. It didn't look good," Klepper said with a smile.

"All we know was that she was snooping around in the dark!" Cernich said.

"Still trying to defend her, aren't you, Joe?" Klepper said.

"She was okay. I know she was okay. Everybody overreacted," Cernich said.

"You're the one that lost control, Joe," Klepper said.

"What are you talking about?" Cernich said.

"You lost control of the situation. You lost control of the situation just like Captain Lowy lost control of the situation the night the Frenchman cracked him on the head. It happens, Joe. Forget it. It happened to the lieutenant here the night his team snuffed that German nurse by mistake. It happens all the time," Klepper said, still smiling.

I lit another cigarette and looked Klepper directly in the eye.

"How do you know about that, Klepper?" I asked.

"Handled Captain Lowy's communications. It was just something that I picked up in doing my job. No cause for worry, sir, your secret is safe. It's just like Joe says. Division is a rock and we are the hard place. Division may say all this official stuff, but down at our level we have to operate," Klepper said, opening a beer.

The sun had once again broken through the cloud cover and

the sea became bright and shining. Bits of foam sparkled in the water that slapped against the side of the boat. How clever this Klepper was. The sunlight reflecting off his thick glasses hurt my eyes.

October 4, 1968: 0900 hours

Below us we could see what appeared to be hundreds of fish. While they varied in size, most seemed to be over a foot long. We were drifting in only about ten feet of water. The water was very clear. The wind had died down so that the surface of the water seemed like green glass.

"They just circle the device. It's almost as if they're hypnotized," Cernich said.

"In a way they probably are," Klepper said.

"How does it work, Klepper?" I asked.

"I'm really not sure, to tell you the truth, Lieutenant."

"You must know what's involved, the principle, that sort of thing."

"Not sure, really. This is something that was discovered by accident. Some sailor discovered it. I just fine-tuned it so that this particular kind of emission attracts the fish, or for that matter, low forms of life. One day we had two sea turtles that kept circling the thing," Klepper said.

"What do you call this thing?"

"I didn't know what to call it, so Captain Lowy named it. He called it the Sirens' Song. He'd get so damned excited when he saw all those fish. He said it reminded him of that myth where the Sirens lured sailors with their singing."

"I know the myth. The Sirens did lure the sailors with their singing. They lured them to their deaths," I said.

October 4, 1968: 1600 hours

I showered and sat out on the balcony. Sky Lady brought cold Kirin beer. The bustle of Da Nang's late afternoon was beginning to slow down. I looked for my little bird friend, but the bird was nowhere to be seen.

"What did you do today?" Sky Lady asked, rubbing my shoulders.

"I followed your advice," I said.

"My advice! You dinky-dau!" she said, laughing.

"No. I followed your advice. I let go," I said.

"No. You bullshit Sky Lady. You never let go. You like control just like you always want to be on top when we make love. You never let go!" Sky Lady said, running her hands across my chest.

"I swear. I just let things happen. I went out to get to know Cernich and Klepper. Junge kind of scared me so I had to go try to get to know them. I had to find out what they were all about," I said.

"And what did you find out?" she asked, blowing in my ear.

"A lot," I said kissing her lightly on the cheek.

"You ready to let go again?" she asked, humming a melody in the same ear.

"What do you mean?" I asked, pinching a nipple through her kimono.

"You ready to let me be on top," she giggled, her tongue now in my ear.

"Sure. What difference does it make? I'm already out of control," I said, running my hand up her leg as she opened her kimono.

October 4, 1968: 1700 hours

I drifted around the bar where the Cold Steel Crowd were having their beers. From my vantage point I saw that each one reported to Gunner Junge as soon as he entered. Gunner Junge sat and checked things off a list. It was amazing the way he kept the Cold Steel Crowd busy. Lowy may have been a master of the skull game, but Junge was the paperwork guru.

I noticed that Ruiz was finishing up some paperwork. I sat down next to him and bought a couple of beers. "What are you working on, Ruiz?"

"You know, sir, the regular stuff. Carrying paper. I had to report up to CORDS and turn in some paperwork," Ruiz said.

CORDS, or the Civil Operations and Rural Development

Support Program, was the umbrella organization that now had oversight of all pacification programs. Province senior advisers were to take much of their direction from CORDS. Schuster, who was the only province senior adviser who was a Marine officer, seemed to have a problem with this. Most province senior advisers were U.S. Army and were assigned by the Military Assistance and Advisory Command. Also, while Schuster may have had a problem with the way the Marine generals were fighting the war, he seemed to have a greater problem with CORDS; Schuster struggled with where his loyalty should be placed. That was one problem I wasn't going to let get to me. There was already too much politics in this mess. If CORDS was who I had to work with, so be it!

"What do these programs do, Ruiz? I mean, you folks seem to spend a lot of time shuffling paper."

"Big Boss doesn't believe in having an office. He spooks around like he's some CIA dude or something. Maybe he is, sir, I don't know. What I do know is that our office is the backseat of a jeep and that I gopher around for all kinds of things. You name it. Everything from pigs to fighting chickens!" Ruiz said, laughing.

"Fighting chickens?"

"Yes, sir. That Lieutenant Lukavitch and some goofy redneck had me fly in fighting chickens for some kind of civil action effort. I don't know how I got the duty, to tell you the truth." Ruiz shrugged his shoulders.

"Sipsy Blues?"

"You got it, sir. That was the name of the project. Just so some district adviser could make some district chief happy. Lieutenant Lukavitch did all the wheeling and dealing, though. Really amazing the stuff we get into."

There was something about Ruiz that I liked. He was upbeat and down to earth. He did his job with minimum bitching, and he stayed away from drugs. Ruiz had a tough, no-nonsense attitude that one had to admire.

"Ruiz, did you ever wonder how all this shit fits together?"

Ruiz looked at me out of the corner of one eye. He smiled, shook his head, and pushed the paperwork that he was working on out in front of him. "Lieutenant, I know what my job is. I don't know exactly how what I do makes the difference in terms of the big picture. But I haven't got time to worry about all that. I do my job. I think if you get caught up in all the bullshit of trying to figure out what this war's about, it will drive you rabid-ass crazy. Look at Klepper. Look at Cernich. In different ways they are both messed up. Well, not me, Lieutenant. I got my shit in one bag," Ruiz said, drinking his beer.

"I see."

It occurred to me that I should take a lesson from this little corporal. His belief in what he was doing was inspiring. Ruiz was firm in his conviction. Perhaps this certitude could be used to the group's advantage. Talking to Ruiz had made me feel better about the Cold Steel Crowd. In the future I would seek out Ruiz for his opinions.

"How about a drink, Lieutenant!" Gunner Junge said, approaching the table with a bottle of cognac.

"How are you doing, Gunner? Go ahead, sit down. Ruiz was just giving me his point of view on some things," I said, winking at Ruiz.

"Ruiz is a good marine, Lieutenant. Of course, you don't need me to tell you that," Junge said, pouring three shots of cognac.

"What's happening, Gunner?"

"I got word from Schuster that our show may be over."

"What does that mean, Gunner?" I sipped my cognac.

"As the colonel put it, we are about to experience the first phase of the transition. He's a bit bitter because the lines of authority are about to change purely for political purposes, but he seems to be resigned to the upcoming change. Here's to the colonel," Junge said.

"Bitter. Did you say bitter?" I asked, pouring another cognac.

"Yes, Lieutenant. He's bitter about the years that he put into this program and now its all going to change, just as he is beginning to see progress. That's the way it happens. Stay loose, Lieutenant. Stay loose." Junge threw down another cognac.

October 4, 1968: 2000 hours

I had Joe Cernich take me and Sky Lady for a boat ride just off Camp Tien Sha. Four or five other boats were out there doing the same thing. It was safe enough. The water was very calm and we were close to the shore.

Joe tied Klepper's sensor to a stick and hung it over the side. Within minutes several glowing shapes, each about a foot long, appeared. The shapes, never more than two or three at a time, moved very quickly, hovering just beyond the edge of the boat where Joe had dropped the sensor.

"What kind of fish are those, Joe?" I asked.

"Not fish, Lieutenant. They're squid, luminous squid, attracted by the sensor."

October 5, 1968: 0800 hours

Colonel Schuster met us down at the Naval Support Activity. He was in his late forties with a full head of gray hair. Tall and slim, he reminded me more of an executive getting off a commuter train in a Chicago suburb more than a Marine Corps colonel.

"Sorry about not meeting you sooner, Lieutenant. We seem to be experiencing a number of changes at this time. It's all political. Things get complicated in this business. It's not like running a grunt battalion, if you know what I mean."

"You will have to help me out on that one, sir. Captain Lowy didn't share too much with me."

"And that's how it has to be. Most of the Cold Steel Crowd don't know the big picture. That's by design, I'm afraid. I've taken great pains to maintain security, while at the same time giving my district advisers the authority to act when and where they feel it is necessary. One does a juggling act in this business. At times one deals openly and closely with the activities. At other times it is necessary to keep one's distance. If I didn't have to spend so much time convincing our own people of the worth of what we are doing and of our approach, I would have more time to spend on the operational side of things. For now, I want you to do what Captain Lowy was doing for me. Junge will assist you."

Schuster and I continued to talk for some time, drinking much black coffee. The Cold Steel Crowd was to be moved out of Da Nang as soon as possible. To stay in Da Nang after losing Captain Lowy would only draw attention, especially from other marine officers at Division. Schuster was paranoid about security.

"Maintaining a cover is important. I want our own people to think that you do some kind of counterintelligence work, but I don't want them to know exactly what your mission is. Not that your mission will stay static for very long anyway. It won't. This new Phoenix thing is going to change that. Right now I know that you don't understand how all the things fit together. For that matter most of us working with this thing find that it changes almost constantly. There is no certainty that I will be your commanding officer one week from now. By the way, from now on you will be Habu Six. I want you to begin to merge your Habu team with the Cold Steel Crowd. The plan will be to reorganize the Cold Steel Crowd," Schuster said.

"I think that I'm beginning to get the picture," I said.

"I'll be moving around a lot, but I'll keep you informed," Schuster said.

"What do you want me to do besides getting the men out of the Grand Hotel?"

"Give them a good party," Schuster said with a grin.

"A party?"

"That's right, Habu Six. Since I can't meet with them due to the circumstances, give them a party for me. Generate a little team spirit in the process if you can. By the way, Habu Six, be prepared to dump your little friend, Sky Lady. You look like you're too smart to let that get in the way of your job," Schuster said, still grinning.

October 5, 1968: 1300 hours

The wind had picked up during the morning. A gray scud of clouds lay low on the horizon over the South China Sea, promising a weather change of some magnitude. I watched a fishing junk coming in, its prow carved, two eyes painted on the bow. Perhaps Lowy's death had brought a weather change.

We had returned to the quiet cove of the day before to cook some steaks and drink a few beers. Navy Swift boats patrolled the area regularly. I was comfortable with the spot, but just to be sure I had my Kit Carson, Cruiser, snooping about the brush just behind the beach. Odum had volunteered to go with him, since he was curious about the area.

Weathers was trying to fish. He sat in a little rubber raft, drifting around the cove. He had Klepper's sensor in tow, hanging about six feet under the water. Klepper had suggested that he lower it farther, but Weathers had his own ideas.

Klepper, Cernich, Ruiz, and several others were eyeballing me. They had been given the word that the Grand Hotel was a thing of the past. They weren't happy. The only smile that I got was from Ruiz.

Ruiz was a scrounge artist without par. It was Ruiz who had picked up the steaks in trade for some poncho liners. When I asked him what his job had been with the Cold Steel Crowd, he said that he swapped stuff and spread rumors. He also said that he carried special communications. I asked him to find Sky Lady. He was to tell her that she and I would have to be apart for a while.

The men were not happy. Schuster had said to give the men a party in order to raise their spirits. In fact, the men were probably hoping that I would go away. I knew only that I was going to miss Sky Lady. I was truly letting go. I was giving her up for something I wasn't sure of.

In Schuster's eyes the Cold Steel Crowd had fallen from grace. They were sloppy. I wondered how Lowy had been able to link them together effectively. The Marine Corps was good at making that happen. When it happened "right," each man had the technical respect of each other, and each backed the other as necessary, in spite of the diversity. Lowy's shoes were size twelve D. They would be hard to fill by any standard.

I liked being called Habu Six. I liked the idea of merging Habu with the Cold Steel Crowd. So did Weathers. He decided to get to know the other members of the Cold Steel Crowd. This was a change for the lone wolf we knew as Weathers. Cruiser, however, was saying nothing. With the exception of Odum and myself, Cruiser eyed everyone as if from a distance. Yet I was beginning to see some spirit in his sad eyes. Perhaps Lowy's death had taken away part of Cruiser's strength and conviction.

My job was to bring these men together. I thought that steaks and cold beer would help that. The weather had not been with me, however, and it was as if the spirit of Lowy had come back from the dead to haunt my efforts. The sudden drop in temperature, the strange wind direction—under the best of circumstances, these things portend the ominous to the Vietnamese. Combined with the death of such a strong spirit as Lowy, these natural events seemed to signify something greater, as if my men and I were at the edge of something evil. It was the evil of the unlucky and the disastrous. I could sense the feeling within my men.

The fishing junk drew closer to the mouth of the cove. Two Vietnamese on deck were struggling with what appeared to be a tangled net. The motorized junk was clearly laboring, dragging a great weight astern. The men were cutting the net, all the while gesturing wildly. As the junk came abreast of the cove, the net came free, and the junk turned in a wide arc and headed south toward Hoi An.

Weathers paddled about in the middle of the cove in his rubber raft. Our other two boats were beached. From where I stood, all that I could make out was what looked like a great lump floating in the mouth of the cove.

"Hey, I got a strike," Weathers yelled.

Weathers pulled his line in, but at the end of the line where a fish should have been was a sea snake as big around as his forearm: an ivory-and-black striped snake about four feet long that slapped its tail wildly on the surface as it attempted to escape. Weathers cut its head off in a single frantic swing of his K-Bar combat knife. Then he screamed.

The lump at the mouth of the cove seemed to come alive. It was a seething mass of sea snakes, which seemed just to flow off the floating lump and head for Weathers.

"Sea snakes! They're attracted by the sound of the sensor. I've seen them hanging around before. They're deadly poisonous," Klepper said.

"Let's go get them," I yelled, running for the boats.

There must have been thousands floating in that one great mass like a huge clump of floating seaweed. When we got close up, this clump of seaweed sprouted heads. Klepper opened up with his Swedish K, pumping magazine after magazine into the floating lump. I opened up with my shotgun, using double-ought buckshot. Everyone was yelling. Weathers never stopped howling the whole time, his rubber raft swarming with snakes.

The snakes dove to get away from our fire, but there were so many that it was hard not to hit them. Odum and the others joined us in the second boat, spraying the area repeatedly with M-16 fire. Occasionally snakes surfaced beside our boats or made some attempt to climb in. Odum went crazy, swinging his kukri from right to left as if he were cutting cane in his native Mississippi.

Klepper and I pulled the wild-eyed Weathers from his rubber raft. Once aboard we cut Klepper's acoustic transducer free from where it had wound around his leg during the confusion. Weathers then threw it as far as he could toward the dark headland that jutted out into the sea behind us.

The men were still yelling and occasionally firing. Though the snakes had all but disappeared, the men kept yelling and waving their knives as if they were out of control. It was as if that wind that had come in during the afternoon had picked them up, and tossed them about like so many fishermen on the South China Sea, carrying them on through a change.

And through this change I found the true Cold Steel Crowd. They were a wild and violent bunch; all of them were different, and all of them seemed driven. Each had an agenda, yet each was willing to make a contribution when the chips were down. The craziness, the drinking and drugs, the doubt that festered within some like a cancer, these things could be overcome. I knew what I had to do and that was to bring the group together as a team. That was my job. It was clear.

As they all gathered around to gape at the still wide-eyed Weathers, who had somehow come through unscathed, I knew what kind of legacy Lowy had handed down to me. At that moment there was a flash as a bolt of lightning struck far out at sea. The squall line was heading in, and for a time the wind coming off the water seemed to change direction. Sky Lady had once said that as Americans we were like the winter wind that came down from China, blowing hard in one direction, yet guaranteed to change with the season.

The men grew silent as they regained control of their emotions. Then I gathered myself together. I believed in this team, and I hoped that the truth of the Cold Steel Crowd was that they were like the China wind, given to great extremes, yet destined to change.

AN ACE YOU CAN HOLD

October 6, 1968: 0630 hours

LIEUTENANT LUKAVITCH HAD called running "a cleansing discipline." The tall, lanky Lukavitch could run forever. He was on my mind as I ran down the beach east of Da Nang sweating out all the beer that I had consumed in the last three days. I hated running, but it helped get my head together. Lukavitch had once said to me that you must believe that there is a pattern that connects. In the last few months I had been struggling to find that pattern. For that matter I had been struggling to find myself.

The last few days had been full of emotion for me. Yet, it was as if I had crossed a threshold so that a curious calm had come over me. Lowy's death and the circumstances that surrounded his dying had begun to make a deep effect on me, one marked by a resolve to pursue a new direction. I had decided that I was going to "get my shit together" as an officer. Maybe by working on my personal integrity, I would find the pattern that the philosophical Lukavitch was talking about, the pattern that connects.

Another thing was clear to me. That was the realization that I had the ability to pull the team together to make all our efforts more productive. But in doing that, I wouldn't go off on any of Captain Lowy's wild projects. I would keep things as simple as possible. My first commitment to simplicity was that I was go-

ing to get the Cold Steel Crowd out of the Grand Hotel and back
in a secure area. That was going to be tough.

Tougher yet was going to be Sky Lady. Keeping my distance
from her was not something that I was doing easily. I cared for
Sky Lady. I had a passion for her. But I had made a choice. If I
was to lead the group, and Schuster had given me the chance to
do that, I had to set an example of restraint.

"Hey, big guy!" someone shouted.

I turned to see Chad Holland in a pair of tiger-striped shorts.

"Chad—thought that you were out of the country."

"Well, I'm back. Couldn't stay away. I'm not one of those
who came to get his ticket punched. You know that," Holland
said, smiling.

Getting your ticket punched was a term used to describe how
some officers got their combat time for career purposes. It was
said that there were really only two kinds of officers in Vietnam;
those who were there to get their tickets punched, and those who
were there to play for real. Holland was back to play for real.
Though I was confused about many things concerning the war,
I had extended my tour because I, too, believed in "playing for
real."

My old gunnery sergeant out on Hill 10 had a slightly different
way of expressing his opinion on ticket-punching. The Gunny
had said on more than one occasion that the problem with this
war was that we were more interested in looking good than
being good.

"Well, Lieutenant Holland, do you want to just look good or
do you want to be good?"

Holland laughed.

"Hey, big guy, I'm one of the pros, or did you forget about all
that once they moved you up to Division?" Holland replied.

I laughed. It was good to see Chad. He was one of the best
officers I had known. Chad Holland was a former company
commander highly respected for his leadership and his know-
how. Chad went by the book. How would he respond to the
world that I was now living in?

"Did you hear about Captain Lowy?" I asked.

"Yes. That's a shame. Lowy was capable. That's too bad,"
Holland said.

"Where did you hear about Lowy?" I asked, concerned.

"Up at Division. G-2. That's where I'll be working. I understand you have the group now."

"The group?" I said, playing dumb.

"Yes, that counterintelligence group or whatever it is that you do. All I know is that Schuster has oversight, and it's all hush-hush. You must be involved in some important things."

"Yes," I said, showing no emotion.

"Well, Lowy was certainly a loss. Quite a capable individual."

"Capable. Oh yes, he was capable all right."

"He seemed to adapt better than most officers. From what I saw he seemed to get results," Holland said.

If only Chad Holland had known the truth. I thought of the Little Prince, the German woman, the Frenchman. How strange that I would have to withhold information from someone I liked and trusted as much as I did Holland.

"What will you be doing with G-2?" I asked.

"They said that I'll be liaison to a number of different programs with the Vietnamese, Schuster's among them. The truth of the matter is, most of us have to look for things to do up at Division," Holland said.

"I see." The sweat was dripping off my forehead and into my eyes. The run had been good. Seeing Holland had been even better. Old memories and feelings from experiences shared on Go Noi Island flooded back into my mind. As I listened to Chad Holland, I could feel all the poison that I had been putting into my system flowing out of me. I had bad body odor. I stunk. I needed the workout to cleanse myself.

October 6, 1968: 0715 hours

Da Nang was already clogged with traffic of all descriptions. For want of a breeze, diesel fumes hung in the morning air. A convoy of trucks, turbochargers whining, roared by on the way north through the Hai Van Pass.

Holland waved. I jogged back to the Grand Hotel, feeling good about the start I had on the day. Holland had once told me that I was too preoccupied with myself. I laughed at the time. I figured that he had been talking to Lukavitch. Now I knew that he was right. What I feared was that I saw myself as venal, as someone opened to a kind of corruption by the events of the last few weeks. It was not a good feeling. It was clear that I lacked Captain Lowy's guile and skill in dealing with the men. I could never do business the way that Lowy had. Holland waved again. I waved back.

Holland disappeared over the hill. There was something about Holland. He was so certain. I wondered how much of that certainty he was going to retain up at Division. Division had a way of changing lieutenants who had grown confident in the field. Many seemed to loose their enthusiasm and commitment. It was as if there were two enemies. One that we found in the countryside, and one which we found internally in our own acquiescence to the forces at the Division rear. Perhaps Chad Holland, who had so admired Captain Lowy for his ability to adapt, would rise above what Junge called the great leveling force of mediocrity one found in the Division rear, a force that seemed to beat down those hard-charging lieutenants who had the will to speak out.

October 6, 1968: 0830 hours

"Gunner, I saw Chad Holland at the beach. I told him about Lowy," I said, sipping my coffee.

"What did he have to say?" Junge asked.

"He said Lowy was a capable man."

"Why do you smile? He was capable. He was capable and imaginative. He used surprise, deception, and mobility. But that was not his greatest strength," Junge said, lighting a Gauloise.

"Okay, Gunner, what was his greatest strength? I know that you will tell me anyway even if I don't ask."

"Lowy's greatest strength was that he had the will to act where others would not. He had a great will. That will was not always rational. It was not always intelligent. But it gave him the force of character that made him a leader," Junge said, gazing back at me as if he were waiting for my reply.

I said nothing. I felt that Gunner Junge wanted me to reply, but I said nothing. I just waited. My wait was rewarded.

"Do you know what Lowy's greatest weakness was?"

"What was it, Gunner?" I asked, still smiling.

"You don't take this conversation seriously, but you should. His greatest weakness was his lack of control and restraint, which I might add is something that you need to work on now that you are to lead this group."

"I'm going to work on that, Gunner. But tell me, what do we have to do to square this group away?" I asked, pouring myself another cup of coffee.

"Too much slack, Lieutenant. It's the same thing that we had back on Go Noi Island. Captain Lowy, God bless him, ran a loose ship. You need to run a tight ship. But tightening up is always harder than loosening up, as I am sure you are aware." Junge flipped his cigarette butt into the pond where only a few days ago we had buried the French agent.

Madam Ti appeared on the balcony above us. She was wearing black. I waved. She waved back. In the pond one of the large golden carp rose to the surface and swallowed Junge's cigarette butt.

"We need to get the men out of this hotel," I said. "If the higher-ups at Division knew how we lived down here, the shit would hit the fan. The men have developed an attitude that they don't have to follow rules that are standard procedure for any combat outfit. When I was out in the field running my platoon, I wouldn't have dreamed that enlisted marines were running around Da Nang and shacking up at the Grand Hotel."

Madam Ti descended the stairs and walked to the edge of the pond. She picked up one of the large lotus flowers and walked back to her aviary. A kind of parrot screeched from the bamboo hedgerow that overhung her aviary. Junge and I watched her. Ti seemed distant, distracted.

"Have you talked much to Ti?" I asked.

"There is nothing to say," Junge said.

"It just all catches up with you, doesn't it?"

Junge said nothing. He watched Ti. I could feel the tension in the air. Junge had never liked Ti. Ti, in turn, had no love for Junge.

"Gunner, how did Lowy ever let things go this far?"

"In defense of both the men and Lowy, I would say that this kind of business differs from field combat. I won't dispute for a moment that Lowy let things go too far. And I want to stress that I am pleasantly surprised by what appears to be a change in you. Yet Lowy had good reasons for running things the way that he did. While I didn't agree with his methods all the time, I am the first to admit that he accessed many sources of information. He was indeed capable and imaginative. All things considered, he made few mistakes," Junge said, still staring at Madam Ti.

"How about the Frenchman?" I asked.

"That is a tough one. Did the Frenchman attack Lowy because he was jealous over Madam Ti's attention to Lowy, or did the Frenchman really know who Lowy was? We may never know for sure." Junge shrugged.

Ti turned under the shadow of the overhanging bamboo and looked in our direction. Sandman joined her from under the shadows. Both stared in our direction for a time. Sandman gave me the creeps.

"What other things can we do to pull the men together?" I asked.

"We need to do something about the little boy," Junge said.

"Oh yes, the Little Prince," I said.

Ti and Sandman began to walk toward the lotus pond. They stopped at the edge of the pond. Ti threw scraps of bread to her golden carp. Soon the water was boiling with feeding fish. The feeding frenzy continued for some minutes during which time Junge said nothing. He just watched Ti and Sandman. It was as if he were trying to see inside their heads. I could feel the tension mount. Finally I broke the silence.

"What about the Little Prince?" I asked.

"He's down at C Company, Fifth Special Forces. But we can't keep him there too long. Sooner or later someone will ask questions about him. The sergeant who's watching him for us can't promise much," Junge said.

"Let's send him south. Let's send him to Lowy's friends down in Hoi An. You know, the boys from Hoi An," I said.

"Not so loud. I don't want Ti or Sandman to hear," Junge whispered.

"You don't trust them, do you?"

"Do you, Lieutenant?" Junge asked with a smile.

"No," I said, beginning to make the connection that Junge had already made.

"I think they must know about the Frenchman," Junge whispered.

"How do you know?" I whispered back.

"I feel it."

Sandman and Ti walked past our table. Ti nodded politely. Junge and I smiled back.

"So let's send the Little Prince down to the boys from Hoi An," I said, watching Ti and Sandman climb the stairs and disappear.

"Good idea, Lieutenant," Junge said.

As a special task group, the boys from Hoi An would be the perfect place to keep the Little Prince till things cooled off. The boys were part of the new program. The boys could be trusted, for sure.

I had once heard Lowy describe three levels of effort going on relative to these new programs, especially this Phoenix business. There were the official goals, which the command structure at First Marine Division endorsed, and which I am sure most marine higher-ups truly believed were legitimate. Then there were the operational goals that each field unit had. Finally, there were what Lowy called the "real" or "operative" goals—they were what Lowy's unit was all about.

According to Lowy, these real goals were concealed from Division. In order to do what he had to do effectively, it was justifiable in Lowy's mind not to conform to accepted rules or standards, like messing around with the boy we called the Little Prince, or like making his base of operations the Grand Hotel.

"We will need to pick up the boy," Junge said.

"Okay, I'll go with you. It will give me a chance to see Major Crandle down at Third Tracks. He and Lowy were tight," I said.

"Good. I know Crandle. He's crazy, but the way things are going, he may be of use to us one of these days."

"How's that?" I asked.

"Crandle is a good resource," Junge said.

"Gunner, do you know something I don't know?"

"No, but Crandle is someone we can depend on. Let's work it some."

"What else do we need to do, Gunner?"

"Two things. We need to know where this effort will lead. Oh, I don't mean the Little Prince business. I mean the group; where this group is going. We will need more direction from Schuster on that. Schuster was content to let Lowy do his thing. We need to know about Phoenix and if we are going to go with it. By the way, our men need to know that also. The other thing that we need is a success story. We need a success story so that you have an ace you can hold when Division catches up with us."

October 6, 1968: 0900 hours

Junge dropped me off in front of Third Amphibian Tractor Battalion so I could give Crandle the story of what had happened firsthand. I spent ten or fifteen minutes walking through the battalion area. Things hadn't changed much since I had been gone. I found Kaplan down at the motor pool, his feet up on his desk, reading *The New York Times*.

"Well, looks like you've got things under control," I said, glad to see my old friend.

"Hey, it's all an illusion. Have no doubts, I'm just along for the ride. Need any parts?"

"No. I came down to talk to Crandle. My commanding officer got killed. He and Crandle were chums," I said.

"Too bad. Crandle's been having a hard time lately. Right now he's up on Chin-Strap chasing gooks. Been doing a lot of that lately. Chasing gooks and having a hard time," Kaplan said.

"Still drinking a lot?" I asked.

"Are you kidding? You know better than that. For a while he was trying to hold it to a six-pack a day. Now he's spends most of his time in Nui Kim Son where he does what he wants to. The CO can't get rid of him. Division won't take him. So Crandle and the CO cut a deal. The deal is that Crandle either stays up on Chin-Strap or in Nui Kim Son when he drinks. No drinking in the battalion area at all," Kaplan said with a smirk.

"Crandle probably loves that," I said.

"That's most affirmative. Crandle stays out all the time. Word is that Chin-Strap mountain has some sort of gook hospital deep down inside. Crandle takes a patrol out every chance he can.

He's got the CAP working with him, too. I think he's gone loco myself," Kaplan said.

I looked up at Chin-Strap mountain. There were plenty of places to hide up on that huge monolith. Various boulders stuck out from it like great, gray gargoyles. There was something fantastic and unreal about it. I feared it and I found it fascinating. Dao and I had rendezvoused in a cool, shaded spot deep within the mountain. Who knows what chances I had taken? I wondered if a Vietcong had ever watched our lovemaking.

"How are you doing?" I asked.

"I'm working my ass off. Of course, I fight a different kind of war. I run this motor pool, cum-shaw parts, do investigations. Keeps me busy," Kaplan said.

"What happened to those dopers you were having problems with?"

"Cut a deal with Division Legal. The whole mess came to a head. Our CO backed off at the last minute. Got cold feet because of some death threats. Then Legal pointed out that everyone who had been charged was black. Everyone accused me and the CO of being down on blacks. CO said that he didn't want it to appear that he was racist. Truth of the matter was that he was scared someone would frag him," Kaplan said.

"What happened to those who were charged?" I asked.

"Sent them all to Okinawa. Charges were dropped. They all got off scot-free and got out of Nam at the same time. I made out because I got rid of a bunch of wild men. Legal was happy because it saved them a lot of work. CO was happy because he didn't have to write letters to various black congressmen explaining why all those charged were black. Like I said, I'm just along for the ride," Kaplan said, giving me a wink.

October 6, 1968: 1000 hours

Crandle and members of the CAP platoon from Nui Kim Son were descending Chin-Strap mountain when I found them. The Combined Action Platoon, or CAP, as it was called, was made up of experienced marine grunts who had volunteered to live in the ville and work as a "combined" force with local Popular Force Militia. The big surprise for me was seeing Cottonhead

Atrey. He had made sergeant and had extended again to work with the CAP in Nui Kim Son. Crandle and Atrey. What a combination.

Crandle had already heard about Lowy. He shook his head when I related the details. I wanted to share with him the story of the Frenchman and how Junge and I had buried Lattre in the pond; I didn't dare.

"Lowy was one of a kind. They broke the mold when they turned him out," Crandle said, examining his rocket pistol.

"You had a chance to use that thing yet, Major?" I asked.

"Damn straight. Tell the Lieutenant, Atrey," Crandle said.

It was clear that Atrey was an admirer of the major. That was to be expected. Both were action people, committed to going out and facing the enemy.

"Major's got three notches cut on the grip of that pistol. I saw two of them go down myself. That there is the kind of technology that we need. Thing don't make hardly a sound. Knocks them down every time!"

"How did you get that close?" I asked.

"Up on the mountain, Lieutenant. Just me and three men. A quiet little night patrol. I'm finally doing something here, Lieutenant. I'm finally back to where I think I'm making a difference. Battalion leaves me alone. I leave battalion alone. Just stay out here either in the village or on the mountain and try to make a difference. That right, Atrey?" Crandle said.

"That's most affirmative, Major. Just quiet little night patrols," Atrey said with a smile.

I wondered what fate had in store for Atrey and Major Crandle. It seemed to me that it was only a matter of time before their numbers were up. The gooks were too smart to let this business go on for too long. So far Atrey and Crandle had survived on experience and luck. But Kaplan was right. What they were doing was crazy. It was crazy because it was predictable. It was crazy because they were looking for trouble. In this business there were too many variables to tempt fate.

October 6, 1968: 1100 hours

The Little Prince looked fine. I bought him some ice cream on our way up to Division. I was standing next to the jeep eating an ice-cream cone when Schuster came up and said hello.

"We were on our way to see you, sir," I said.

"Is that the kid?" Schuster said, having been filled in by Junge.

"Yes, sir," I replied.

"I've made arrangements," Schuster said.

"Arrangements, sir?"

"Trust me, Lieutenant," Schuster said, looking me in the eye.

"Yes, sir. By the way, I was hoping that you could come down this evening and say a few words to the men. This is our last night all together in the Grand Hotel. Tomorrow I'm sending half of them to Hill 10. The rest I've got to find homes for. I thought that your presence would give them a lift; they don't want to go back to a more controlled environment, if you know what I mean," I said.

"I know what you mean. Sure, I'll say a few words to them. But it will be brief. I don't want any Vietnamese linking me with your group. We will all look like a bunch of amateurs if that happens," Schuster said.

"I understand, sir. If you could come by at 1600 or so that would be nice."

"Count on it, Lieutenant." Schuster nodded and walked away.

October 6, 1968: 1200 hours

I found Chad Holland waiting in line for chow. I grabbed him and suggested that he come down to the Grand Hotel and meet Schuster. Holland was excited by the idea. It looked like his job up at Division was going to be nothing more that a series of one Article 15 investigation after another. Maybe Schuster could use his influence to find a job that used Holland's experience and know-how.

October 6, 1968: 1530 hours

When I got back to my room at the Grand Hotel, Sky Lady was waiting for me. She was wearing a miniskirt and a halter top. She looked great.

"Hey dinky-dau, don't you love Sky Lady no more?" she asked with a smile.

"I love you more than ever. But now I've got to be careful. Things have got to change," I said, not really knowing what else to say.

"I know. Now you big honcho. Don't have time for this babi-san," she said, pinching my ass as she walked by.

"You will always be my babi-san. You know that."

Sky Lady smiled and winked as she walked out the door. For a moment I could feel the weight of her thick, waist-length hair against my nakedness. I trembled slightly and started to call her back, but she was already gone.

October 6, 1968: 1745 hours

Schuster, Junge, Holland, and I sat on the veranda overlooking the lotus pond. Schuster had talked briefly to the men, explaining that change was needed, and that their cooperation was necessary for these changes to take place. It was all very stiff. The men were not happy. Klepper appeared stoned. Weathers seemed drunk. Odum was the only one with anything to say. As usual what he said concluded with a quote from Scripture. I was glad when Schuster suggested that we get a beer. That had been an hour ago. In the meantime Holland had arrived. I was glad to introduce Holland to Schuster. I could tell Schuster had been impressed with Holland's background.

"Sir, I just hope I don't go crazy up at Division. It's not what I'm used to," Holland said, drinking a beer. That was unusual for him.

"Yes, the demands are much different from the field," Schuster said.

"I prefer the field," Holland said.

"We all do," I said.

"Speak for yourself, Lieutenant," Junge said.

We all laughed. Madam Ti moved by gracefully. She waved. Sandman followed behind her with a scowl, saying nothing.

"What is it you prefer, Gunner?"

"I prefer action. You don't have to be in the field in our business to have action."

"Action. Yes, I buy that. I like action anywhere you can get it. How about that, Chad? You got any action up at Division?" I said.

We all laughed again. People at the other tables glanced over at us. Sky Lady was at one of the tables, hustling an air force captain.

"I don't know what we have, to tell you the truth," Holland said, taking another beer.

"What do we have up at Division, sir?" I asked the colonel.

"Ambiguity. Contradictions and ambiguity. Absence of a higher purpose or goal. That's what you have right now. We are caught in a change and we don't know where that change is taking us. When I run across officers who tell me they are interested in amphibious assaults, I laugh," Schuster said.

"That's the way the men feel," I said.

"That's the way we all feel," Holland added.

"That's the way anyone in good conscience feels," Schuster said, draining his beer.

"What about those who don't have a conscience?" I asked.

We all laughed a third time, only this time the laughter was not as loud, nor did it last as long. Sky Lady glanced over at me and winked. I blew her a kiss. Junge saw me and made a face.

"Do you have a conscience, Lieutenant?" Junge asked me.

"For some things."

"For what things?" Junge continued.

"For the things that I give a damn about," I said in a loud voice.

The veranda grew quiet. Sky Lady was still looking over at me. For a moment Sandman poked his ugly face over the balcony. I stuck out my tongue at him. Sky Lady saw me do this and began to giggle.

The beers were going down easy. I was surprised to see Holland drink. He had always abstained before. Perhaps the last months had made him a beer drinker. Clearly he was a novice. After four beers the tall, thin Holland seemed woozy.

"What if you don't give a damn about anything? What if you don't feel anything?" Holland said, slurring his speech.

"That happens. Some don't have a conscience. Some are just too self-centered to care. Some are stupid. Some never have a chance to really get in touch with what's going on. And through no fault of their own. Some don't adapt when they need to. That's my big beef with the higher-ups in Division. But they won't listen to me," Schuster said.

"Why? Why is that, sir?" Holland said. His eyes had glazed over.

"It's the nature of the beast, Holland. For the effort to succeed, for us to be more effective, the feelings and sentiments of officers like yourself and Captain Lowy need to be given a chance for legitimate expression rather than to be suppressed. Division doesn't want to hear what they don't want to hear. Division is controlled by a bunch of old men who fought in World War II and Korea. By the way, they are still fighting there. They have never arrived in Vietnam," Schuster said.

Schuster had made a connection. He had linked feelings and thoughts that I had but could not quite give form to. I understood now why Schuster allowed Lowy to run the group the way he had. Lowy had been big on interacting with his men, getting them to express what they felt and saw, and then acting upon that information to the greater gain of the group. Lowy and Schuster had the same style. It was connecting for me. Things were still very complicated, but something about what Schuster was saying really made sense. Yet I could see why Schuster was viewed as a radical by some and as an innovator by others. I could also see how a guy like Schuster would scare the hell out of the more conservative types up at the division level. For Schuster apparently was questioning basic Marine Corps beliefs like amphibious doctrine and the way the war was being fought. That was heresy. It occurred to me that his attack on the "old men" back in Division was a bit unfair. Those old men may have just been the target for Schuster's frustrated ambitions.

Then it hit me. In taking the men out of the Grand Hotel, was I working against the openness and freedom of expression that Lowy had fostered? I needed to perform a balancing act; that was clear. I needed a balance between openness and some kind of structure. It was clear that there was no formula. But I now had another ace. Why had I never realized this before? It seemed so simple.

Holland and Cernich had served in the same company. Holland thought highly of Cernich. Accordingly Holland excused himself from our table and began to drink with Cernich and Weathers. Schuster also excused himself, saying that he had enjoyed the company and that the drinks had been a good idea. I suggested that he meet us the next day and follow us out to Hill 10. I pointed out that we were guests on Hill 10 and that there might be some advantage in his meeting briefly with Lieutenant Colonel Cheatum about our mission. Schuster agreed to meet us the following afternoon. At this point Madam Ti came by our table to thank Schuster and express her great sadness about Captain Lowy. At that point I slipped away and joined Holland and the others at the bar.

October 7, 1968: 0800 hours

Holland was hung over. Cernich and he had stayed up till almost 0300 hours drinking beer and sharing yarns. The teetotaling Chad Holland I had known was no more. For a while I had listened in on their conversation. Holland kept pounding down the beers, as if he were trying to make up for all those years he had been a teetotaler.

"How's your head?" I asked.

"Not good," Holland answered, rubbing his eyes.

"Well, Chad, if you're going to drink beer with this crew, you better learn to pace yourself," I said, laughing.

Junge joined us. He carried a Swedish K like Klepper's, but without the silencer.

"Got yourself a K? I'd like to get one of those," Holland said.

"We get out to Hill 10, I know someone who's got one that he might swap or sell. I'll ask him for you. Can you meet me back here this afternoon?" I asked.

"No sweat. I'm my own boss after 1300," Holland said.

"Let me work on it for you. I'll try to get you a silencer for it like Klepper has. Then you can impress all those dudes up at Division," I said.

"I'd like that. Got to run now. Catch you back here later. Got any time in mind?" Holland asked, rising to leave.

"Yeah, around 1600 or so. Schuster will be here, too," I yelled after him.

Junge kicked me under the table.

"Quiet, Lieutenant. There's too many ears around this place," Junge said.

"I agree. Sorry, Gunner," I said, waving to the waiter for more coffee.

As I motioned the waiter over, I noticed three people standing by the entrance to the veranda watching Gunner Junge and myself. The first two I recognized with no problem. It was Lukavitch, the battalion S-5, and Captain Vilks, the battalion S-2, for the Third Battalion, Seventh Marines. Then it struck me. Standing between them, his white shock of hair a dead giveaway, was none other than Pham Van Tra, the local Vietcong paymaster that had been the object of our search these past weeks.

October 7, 1968: 0930 hours

The world had turned on end. Lukavitch and Vilks had not only brought in Pham Van Tra, they had brought new insight into what Lowy and I had been doing in their area of operations. The source of that information had been none other than Pham Van Tra, who turned himself in so that he might once again see his only grandson, the boy we called the Little Prince, the same little boy that only the day before we had considered sending south to the boys in Hoi An.

Vilks and Lukavitch had also been told about the beautiful German nurse who was not a nurse at all, but an East German technician for some weapon.

Things were getting too complex. There were too many variables.

Several other changes had also occurred. Lukavitch was now the battalion S-2 for the Third Battalion, Seventh Marines. His responsibility included intelligence matters. Moreover, it was Lukavitch who somehow had been able to bring Pham in and sway him to our side. That is, if you believed all of what Pham had said. Gunner Junge did not.

* * *

"So tell me, Pham, what is it that made you want to rally to the cause of the South Vietnamese government? You, who have been a member of the Vietcong these many years! You, whose sons have all been killed by the same South Vietnamese government you now hope to serve," Junge said mockingly.

"I no longer have much family left. You hold my only grandson," Pham said in almost perfect English.

Pham had been a schoolteacher for many years. He was well-educated by any standard, having traveled as a young man to France and China. How delicately I would have to handle this business. Even though the woman had been an East German technician in a combat zone, questions were bound to be raised as to why Lowy, Junge, and I withheld certain information. Even though the boy had been tagged a member of the Vietcong infrastructure, why had Lowy, Junge, and I chosen to send him to the special forces in order to keep him secure? If Pham, who was a very intelligent man, wasn't asking these questions of himself, I was sure Lukavitch was asking them.

"Tell Gunner Junge what you told me this morning, Pham. Tell him what you told me about how tired you were of this war," Lukavitch said.

"It's true. I am very tired, and it is only by yielding that I endure. When I give of myself to you, maybe I become more for my grandson, whom you already have," Pham said, looking at the ground.

"Well, that's real fine, Pham. But what's in it for us?" Junge said, with a smile.

"I came here to save lives. I came here not only to save the life of my grandson, but to save your lives. You and your men, Lieutenant, you have been targeted. You must leave this hotel as soon as possible," Pham said.

"Targeted when and how?" Lukavitch asked.

"I don't know the when and how, I only know the why," Pham said.

"The why?" Lukavitch asked.

"These men killed the Frenchman, Lattre," Pham said.

Vilks and Lukavitch looked at Junge and myself in disbelief. Things were getting very complex. I wondered if Lukavitch would be able to find the pattern that connected all the madness.

October 7, 1968: 1000 hours

It was decided to get the Little Prince back from Division. Cernich and Klepper left in Junge's jeep in order to make that happen. Weathers and Odum took my jeep and headed out to Hill
10. I had made up my mind to pull all of the group over to Hill
10, and, since Weathers and Odum were most familiar with that
area, I sent them ahead to work out the details. I was acting
quickly. I wanted the Cold Steel Crowd out of the Grand Hotel
as soon as possible.

The Cold Steel Crowd was not happy about leaving. I called
the group together one last time and briefed them on where we
were going and what I had hoped the outcome might be. In
talking to them, I remembered what Gunner Junge had said
about an ace that you could hold. I mentioned to the men that I
viewed Pham Van Tra as our ace. Pham had revealed to Vilks
and Lukavitch information about a large bunker complex and
an as yet unspecified weapon. We were all going to destroy that
bunker complex and secure that weapon. I stressed to the group
that we could do something to impact Vietcong activity throughout the whole Dai Loc map sheet. Although Gunner Junge com-
plimented me on what I had said to the men, somehow I felt
that I hadn't got the message across.

October 7, 1968: 1300 hours

By noon the plan was outlined. Vilks and Lukavitch would return with Pham Van Tra to Hill 10. Vilks would brief Cheatum,
the battalion commander of Third Battalion, Seventh Marines,
on the information Pham had provided. Vilks insisted that
Schuster be notified. Vilks also wanted to include the Habu team
in his plans because Gunner Junge had a lot of credibility with
Cheatum. By involving Junge, Vilks hoped to sway the increasingly cautious Cheatum into mounting an operation into the
Sherwood Forest area where the bunker complex was supposed
to be located. Cheatum had not been very successful in the past
several months of his command. Like me, he needed a success
story. Cheatum needed an ace you could hold.

October 7, 1968: 1400 hours

Schuster was livid. He said that his role as province senior adviser had been compromised. He shouted that we were all a bunch of amateurs and that he had expected more from Gunner Junge. He shook his head a lot, saying that now that we had the whole world involved, we had no choice but to go along with Vilks. Schuster ended by directing me to meet him at 1600 hours outside the Grand Hotel as planned, from there we would all head out to Hill 10 and sort things out with Vilks and Cheatum.

October 7, 1968: 1530 hours

On the way back from Division, Junge and I met Odum, Weathers, and Ruiz. They were all drunk, saying that they had got caught up in a going-away party that Madam Ti had decided to throw. I didn't like the sound of what I had heard. I directed Odum to drive to Hill 10 and headed out toward the Grand Hotel.

October 7, 1968: 1545 hours

We got hung up in Da Nang traffic. While waiting behind a long line of trucks, we found Chad Holland hitchhiking down from Division. He appeared to have been drinking.

October 7, 1968: 1615 hours

We were a block away from the Grand Hotel when we heard the explosion. By the time we got to the scene, the truck that I had secured to take the Cold Steel Crowd to Hill 10 was a fireball topped by a plume of ugly, black smoke. Bodies and marine combat gear lay strewn all over the street. Cernich lay in an awkward, twisted position on the front of the truck. Colonel Schuster lay sprawled in the street. Both were dead.

Holland and Junge were speechless. None had survived. I felt a rage welling up within me, and I began to tremble. The Cold

Steel Crowd had tempted fate. And fate, provoked, had taken its measure.

October 7, 1968: 2200 hours

"I can't understand what all these guys were doing here," the marine M.P. lieutenant said.

"They were part of a special group," I said without emotion.

"You would have thought they'd be smarter than to all load up like that, especially down here in this part of Da Nang," the M.P. said.

The last of the bodies was gone. I stood with Gunner Junge and studied the charred and twisted mess that had been the truck. All of the Cold Steel Crowd were dead except Ruiz, who had left with Odum and Weathers. The Little Prince, who had been sitting in the cab of the truck, was dead. Sky Lady, who had stood in front of the Grand Hotel blowing the men a kiss as they were about to leave, was dead. Madam Ti and Sandman, her bodyguard, were nowhere to be found. Both had disappeared when the truck had blown up.

"So you think it was Ti," I said, wiping off Klepper's Swedish K and checking the silencer.

Somehow the Swedish K had been blown clear. It appeared to be in working order.

"I'm certain that she's behind this. Where is she? Where is Sandman? Didn't you ever ask yourself why Ti didn't alert us to the gravity of Lowy's injury the night that he stayed with her? Didn't you ever ask yourself why Sandman didn't go to your aid when the Frenchman had you down during the fight? And where was Sandman the night that we snuffed the Frenchman? Sandman was probably watching us the whole time that we were burying the Frenchman in the pond. Then, someone probably overheard us discussing our plans last night. They knew that we would have this truck here at 1600 hours. Doesn't it all connect?" Junge said, lighting a cigarette.

The Marine M.P.s had shut down the hotel. I looked at the building in the darkness. There was no telling where Ti and Sandman had gone. For all I knew, they could still be somewhere in the building or on the grounds of the hotel.

Chad Holland was sitting on the steps of the hotel. He had been drinking one beer after the other. He was very down about Cernich's death. "You okay, Chad?"

"No. No, I'm not okay," he replied.

"Well, come with the Gunner and me. We're going to check out the pond," I said.

October 7, 1968: 2230 hours

In the darkness I waded out into the pond. The golden carp brushed against my arms and legs as I moved out into the water. The body had been weighted down with stone elephants and partially submerged in the muck. It would be easy to find if it was still there. But another element in the pattern had connected for me. How had Pham known about the death of the Frenchman? How had Pham known enough to warn us about the danger of the Grand Hotel? I crossed and recrossed the pond, at times almost chest-deep in the water. After a quarter of an hour it was apparent that the body was gone.

From the pond I walked to Madam Ti's aviary. One by one I opened all the cages. The birds were gone. All the birds were gone. She had taken the birds with her. The pattern was connecting. It was a pattern of betrayal.

October 7, 1968: 2330 hours

"Do you think that they are somewhere in the hotel?" I asked, still numb from the shock.

"I doubt if Ti's still here. Sandman might be. Then again, who knows. Holland's out of his mind, though, I know that," Junge said.

At that moment there was an explosion on the second floor of the hotel. The explosion was followed by a great whoosh as the whole upper balcony erupted in flames. Against the firelight we could see Chad Holland carrying a gas can. Holland waved at us.

"He needs to get off that second story. Sandman had weapons

and explosives stored on the second level of the hotel,'' Junge
yelled.

"Are you certain?'' I yelled back over the noise of the flames.

"Most affirmative, Lieutenant!'' Junge screamed.

But there was no time. Holland's arson had been too effective.
The whole second story of the hotel seemed to lift with the shock
of a second explosion. Junge and I were knocked to the ground.
I looked up at the balcony where I had last seen Chad Holland.
What was left of the balcony was a wall of flames.

October 8, 1968: 0200 hours

Junge and I reached the top of a hill outside of Da Nang where
we knew we would be secure. From our hilltop we had a good
view of the fire. Junge and I watched it burn for about an hour.
It seemed such a simple matter burning down the Grand Hotel.
Holland was able to do it in a matter of minutes. Who knows?
Maybe he needed an ace that he could hold. I was filled with a
great sadness. I sat down in the wet grass on that hilltop and
listened to the sounds of the night. It was all I could do to keep
from crying.

WALL OF FLOWERS

THE LINE OF broken hills and scrub that was known as the Sherwood Forest stretched about four kilometers along the south bank of the Tuy Loan River. At one time the Sherwood Forest had actually been a forest of tall hardwood trees; combat operations during the last two years had reduced the forest to scrub.

The western edge of the Sherwood Forest was dominated by a ridge line known as Hill 112. It was about two kilometers long. The steep slopes peaked to a crest that was barely one hundred feet wide. Hill 112 was a limestone razorback of a hill pitted with caves and crevices. Piles of boulders lined either side of the razorback, making the slopes of Hill 112 even more difficult to any proposed frontal assault.

To the north of Hill 112, overlooking the Tuy Loan River, were two knobs called Hill 36 and Hill 39, little more than a kilometer apart. They were both denuded of vegetation and thus served as good observation points for what was going on throughout the Sherwood Forest.

Between Hill 36 and Hill 39 lay the ruins of a pagoda and a length of ancient wall. The ruins of the pagoda and the wall were located in an area known as An Nhon 2, for the village that once stood there. The wall served as a landmark for operations in the area. One could sight a compass off the wall and get a reading on his position relative to the high ground of Hill 36 and Hill 39.

The origin of the wall was lost in history, although Lukavitch agreed with Pham Van Tra that it was probably built by the Chams, a race displaced by the Vietnamese sometime during the Middle Ages. Thick vines covered the wall. Large trumpet-like white flowers grew on the vines, and at night, when the flowers opened, they made the night fragrant with their scent. Under the full moon, with all the flowers open, the wall of vines seemed luminous and alive, hundreds of large, nectar-eating moths flitting about like hummingbirds until morning.

The beauty of the flowers failed to move me, however. For the last day I had been numb. Except for occasional outbursts of anger, I was devoid of sensation, preoccupied with thoughts of the loss of Sky Lady, Holland, and the Cold Steel Crowd. When I could feel the anger rising within me, I knew that I needed to repress it. I was directing my hostility toward getting things done relative to the mission. For me the world had abruptly divided into two camps: those that were the target of that mission, and those that were helping me get to the target. The target had to do with this wall. The wall was the site of the NVA supply dump Pham had told us about.

"These flowers are beautiful," Lukavitch said, picking one of the morning-glory-like blooms.

I was glad to hear Lukavitch speak. He had hardly said a thing in the last twenty-four hours. He had taken the loss of Holland and the Cold Steel Crowd particularly hard. When I described what had happened, he blamed himself, rambling on about being at the mercy of events. Since then he had seemed distant. When Vilks and I talked to him, he had trouble concentrating. When I asked him what the problem was, he simply said that he was depressed by the loss of Holland in particular. He added that he was beginning to think that all of what we were doing was hopeless.

Part of me wanted to say to Lukavitch that he was finally coming to terms with the reality a lot of us had been living with for some time. But Lukavitch wasn't a grunt. In fact, he hadn't lost a lot of close friends.

Another part of me saw the whole situation as a confirmation of all my suspicions about the Vietnamese. Weathers and I had openly talked of cutting Pham's throat, each of us certain that he had hidden motives. Junge picked up on the conversation and talked us out of it. But Weathers and I were still hypersensitive to Pham, ready to counter any move he made in the flicker of an eyelash.

"Beauty. Beauty is often illusory. It may hide the truth," Pham said, almost in a whisper.

There was a philosophical quality to Pham Van Tra. In spite of the fact that he was our prisoner, he kept the challenge in his voice. One couldn't help but respect his learning and his stamina. The loss of his grandson must have crushed him. Yet he kept right up with the effort to work with us. His knowledge of English amazed me.

Junge had taken the opportunity to exercise that knowledge. Junge had grilled Pham without mercy, preoccupied with the most trivial details. Since the loss of Holland and the men, Junge had turned inward, unable to relax, and almost obstinate in his insistence that we take time to get our plans sorted out. His swing to extreme meticulousness was too much for Vilks, who wanted to act immediately based upon what information we had. Junge, Weathers, and I were defensive and warned Vilks to be on guard.

Unfortunately Vilks was in love with the opportunity that he saw in Pham. Vilks seemed unaffected by the loss of Holland and the Cold Steel Crowd. He plunged on with what seemed to me to be a lot of bright ideas and philosophy. Those bright ideas could get one killed, and I, for one, was disgusted with philosophy. Both Pham and Vilks were full of philosophy. Weathers called it bullshit and openly expressed his contempt for the way Vilks and Pham interacted and dialogued endlessly on political matters. I understood that was the way it had to be. Vilks was working Pham, and although I shared Weathers's feelings about all the talk of politics and philosophy, I knew that was part of the game. For that matter, I also knew that I needed to be reminded of what to believe in. And I needed to know how to believe. The events of the last day or so had taken my general attitude of disenchantment and turned it into one of fear and distrust of just about everything and almost everyone. In the meantime I had made up my mind to maintain. I would keep control and stay loose. I would work on how to believe.

"Did you say illusory?" Lukavitch asked.

"Yes, illusory in the sense of the unreal or misleading appearance, like a beautiful woman who is a whore," Pham said.

Weathers looked at me and shook his head. He drew his finger across his throat. I thought I saw him wink in the moonlight.

October 10, 1968: 0330 hours

Sometime during the next two days Pham claimed that a number of rice carriers would arrive at the wall to pick up rice and some kind of weapon. When that happened, marines of Lima and Mike Companies of Third Battalion, Seventh Marines, would be strung out through the area to interdict, and, if possible, secure this weapon of unknown significance.

"These vines may be hundreds of years old. If you look closely at how each one has climbed the rock wall, it tells a story," Pham said.

"Yeah, right," Weathers said with a snicker.

At that moment Pham grabbed my arm and pointed to the far end of the wall. There, out of a crevice, one could see a form, thick as a man's forearm, rising some six feet in height.

"What the hell is that?" Weathers whispered.

"King Cobra," Pham said.

Under the moonlight the huge snake turned toward us as if he had heard Pham speak, the great hood suddenly spread wide in warning.

October 10, 1968: 0600 hours

The rippling, thumping sound of chopper blades told me that Vilks was coming in to pick us up. The flowers had closed up with first light, but their fragrance still hung in the morning air. The king cobra had slid back into his crevice and was now probably sleeping deep within the ancient Cham wall.

My mind drifted from Sky Lady to Holland, and from Holland to Schuster. Vilks and Junge had been working the problems arising from the aftermath, and, to a certain extent, I had to admire how Vilks had managed to keep the momentum going with Cheatum and Pham Van Tra, while Junge handled the administrative details connected with the deaths of Colonel Schuster and the Cold Steel Crowd.

The flak rising from the death of Schuster, the province senior adviser, had been considerable. Although no one in Division, or in III MAF for that matter, was sure what the province senior adviser did, everyone knew Schuster, recognizing that he was a fine officer whose know-how was unquestioned and a polished stylist sensitive to the varied politics that existed.

Schuster had been able to impress both the Marine Division Staff and such varying constituencies as the press, the Vietnamese, officers in other branches of the service, the CIA, and civilian do-gooders. From the airless universe of the Third Marine Amphibious Force compound, with its Mandarin-like atmosphere of Marine General Staff and high Vietnamese muckymucks, to the raunchy brothels of Da Nang, Schuster had moved with both autonomy and anonymity in the process performing what he called his "liaison" work. I wondered what sins he had forgiven. I knew what evil he had embraced. It was becoming clearer to me now that as province senior adviser, Schuster had been the driver for Lowy and his Cold Steel Crowd. Lowy responded to Schuster's needs either for information or action. Accordingly, Lowy had opened his kimono to get Schuster what he wanted and needed.

In retrospect I was also beginning to understand Lowy much better, his craving for activity and excitement, his exploitiveness. All this was driven by his efforts to keep Schuster happy. His excessive self-dramatization was part of trying to impress Schuster. It was clear to me now that Lowy operated in a world of his own, a world where much of what he did was based on hunches and intuition. Lowy's world was one governed by a very high element of risk, where men and resources were needlessly squandered. Yet there was no doubt that Lowy had the ability to inspire and to create momentum. In that way he and Vilks were very much alike. Vilks and Lowy had the power to invigorate and revitalize.

There was little doubt that Schuster also had that power. The vacuum left by his death had Vilks and Junge responding to numerous calls from people who needed reassurance that all was well. Since my working knowledge of the situation was lacking and because certain higher-ups had to deny knowledge of the nature of much of what Schuster did in his liaison work, Gunner Junge had to respond. Junge was known in that end of the business and was able, through his experience and credibility, to maintain some semblance of continuity in the minds of the callers.

Junge maintained continuity in a number of ways. First of all he delayed, saying that "Habu Six"—me—"is heavily involved in the follow-up to Schuster's demise," and that Habu Six would get back to them. Junge also delegated authority, giving those who needed it the reassurance to proceed. By then it was apparent to Junge and me that Schuster had a lot of irons in the fire. The fact that he had no backup was amazing to me. So Junge and I became his backup with advice from Vilks, who had worked closely with Lowy and Schuster. The third thing Junge did was link up with Vilks—he had no choice but to do so. As a marine captain, Vilks was able to facilitate things that Junge and I were not able to do. When necessary, Junge intimidated. There were those that he simply told what to do. Finally, there were those whom he ignored, among them the boys from Hoi An.

The boys were one of Schuster's hot irons. At first they refused to accept the fact that Junge was functioning in any capacity as backup to Schuster or the mysterious Habu Six, so Junge got Vilks involved because none of the boys from Hoi An wanted to try a hostile interrogation of a Marine Corps captain. All we were doing was, of course, a bluff and a ploy to gain time.

In the meantime the highest levels had no knowledge of all this confusion. The district advisers continued on. The fact that one of the key men in the province had been killed seemed to make little difference. A number of things became very clear quickly: Division placed little value on what Schuster had been doing; failure to understand all of what Schuster had been doing was an oversight by someone; the individual temporarily appointed to fill Schuster's position had no knowledge of what was going on or what he needed to do. His main concerns were that there were no files, there was no office to speak of, and there was no clerk to handle the administrative work.

Colonel Stuart was right on all those accounts. There were good reasons for not having files, a high-profile office, and a clerk. The fact that he didn't understand this was indicative of his level of understanding about the true nature of Schuster's liaison work and the nature of this war.

Colonel Coe Stuart was a soft-spoken man whose grayish white hair gave him a distinguished look. He looked like a colonel of marines. The evening of October 8, 1968, at 1900 hours, he had received word that he was to ''fill in'' for Schuster. By 0800 hours, October 9, 1968, Stuart, Junge, and I were meeting. Luckily we had brought Vilks with us to update Stuart on Pham Van Tra and our proposed effort in Sherwood Forest. Stuart, eager not to upset what he thought was an action based upon some systematic analysis, gave his blessing. Stuart was particularly impressed by the computer printouts Vilks kept referring to that suggested there had been much movement of late in the Sherwood Forest area. Stuart was smart enough not to mess with what he didn't understand. On the other hand, if he did understand, he was smart enough to steer clear of all the complexities and ramifications. He could simply deny knowledge of what had gone on. Whatever the truth, Stuart was savvy. I could tell that we were going to get along just fine.

That there were to be ramifications in lieu of Schuster's death was inevitable. Even Lukavitch had picked up on the rumblings about the province senior adviser. These rumblings had begun surfacing the morning after Schuster's death and smacked of professional jealousy. To quiet these rumblings, Vilks and Lukavitch fed rumors from their side of the operation that Schuster had been on to something very big with Habu. They mentioned Pham Van Tra as key. All this was fed to Cheatum, who of course swallowed it whole and ordered preparation for ''Operation Bench Mark.''

Had I not been so intent on taking action, all of this would have scared the shit out of me. As the Vietnamese say, we were riding the tiger and there was no getting off. There was no doubt that we had fooled them for the time being. Yet, there was also no doubt that Junge and I and what was left of my Habu team were just along for the ride. I couldn't decide if the tiger was Vilks or Pham, and I hoped that we weren't fooling ourselves.

I looked at the wall. It seemed quiet and benign. I wondered if Stuart truly believed that Schuster's work had been a matter of gracious liaison with our Vietnamese allies. Who really knew what Schuster and Lowy had uncovered? Who knew what paybacks, messups, and travesties Schuster had chosen to overlook as he fulfilled his role as province senior adviser. Deep inside the wall of flowers a king cobra lurked, ominous and baleful. Who knew what malignancy Stuart might uncover if he tried to look for answers in the program Schuster and Lowy had built?

Pham Van Tra approached. He offered me a cigarette. Like Junge, he smoked Gauloise. The smooth, dark brown rock was marked by graffiti in several places. At one spot someone had carved "Camargue," 1953. Beneath the date was the name "R. Trinquier" and what appeared to be the letters GCMA.

"Pham, what was GCMA?" I asked, lighting a cigarette.

"French. Groupement Mobile 100. Very elite," Pham said matter-of-factly.

"Never heard of them," I said, sucking the smoke deep within.

"We wiped them out," Pham said with a kind of smile.

Pham Van Tra was a strange bird. Weathers and Odum questioned Pham's motives. They wondered why Pham kept up the effort to work with us now that his grandson was dead. Perhaps it was because Pham had no place to go. I made up my mind to keep a close eye on Pham Van Tra.

October 10, 1968: 0800 hours

"Odum, you should have seen this son of a bitch. He rose up eyeball to eyeball with me and the lieutenant here. That old hooded head must have rose six feet up in the air. Ain't that right, Lieutenant?" Weathers said, excited.

"That right, Lieutenant?" Odum said.

"That's right," I said.

"Damn! Wish I'd been there to see that," Odum said.

"Would you stand eye to eye with evil?" Pham said, with a kind of sneer on his face.

"Yes, old man, I would stand face to face with that thing whatever it be, for therein lay the truth," Odum said.

"Holy shit, Lieutenant, you got to get Odum out of the field before he does something crazy," Weathers said, shaking his head.

"Hell, I'd give up three confirmed kills just to go hand to hand with that snake," Odum said.

Off in the distance we could hear the tracked vehicles bringing in the marines from Lima Company. Lima Company was to occupy the high ground of Hills 36 and 39. The amphibian tractors should have no problem transporting Lima to those positions, I thought to myself. During the night artillery fire had prepped the avenue of the tractors' approach thoroughly. There had been a number of secondary explosions, suggesting to me that a number of land mines had been detonated.

Farther to the south Mike Company was moving in on Hill 112. According to Pham, Hill 112, or Nui Dong Chua, was the site of an NVA bunker complex. This complex was supposed to contain a hospital and was to serve as a staging area for movement into the low rice plains west of Da Nang. Mike Company was to surround Hill 112 and, at the direction of Cheatum, the 3/7 commanding officer, seize and destroy the bunker complex.

October 10, 1968: 0830 hours

Drops of rain were beginning to fall. Rain clouds had moved in during the early morning. The sound of the drops on the leaves almost lulled me to sleep.

"Lieutenant, can Odum and I talk to you a minute?" Weathers asked.

"Sure."

"We made up our mind that we want to snuff Pham no matter what happens," Weather said, a little shaky.

"So, what do you want me to do. Give you my blessing? I don't trust him any more than you do."

"We just ask that you look the other way, Lieutenant, when the time comes," Odum said in a hoarse whisper.

"You don't have to whisper, Odum, no one can hear you," I said.

"Then you'll support us?" Weathers asked.

"You didn't ask me to support you. You just asked me to look the other way," I said.

"You don't care if we snuff him?" Odum asked.

"Go for it," I said coldly.

October 19, 1968: 0900 hours

I gazed at the wall through the large telescope. From Hill 36 I could see the whole length. The great power of the telescope allowed me to view the wall as if I were standing next to it. Vilks had cumshawed the powerful instrument from the navy for four camouflaged poncho liners worth less than a hundred dollars. The telescope's lenses alone were probably worth several thousand. There was a rash boldness about much of what Vilks did. Junge told me that Vilks's last name was Latvian for "wolf." That was appropriate, I thought.

"You like that scope, Lieutenant?" Vilks asked.

"Most affirmative. Looking through this thing is just like standing next to the wall."

"That's my spyglass. In fact, that's my new call sign. I got a little project I'm working on with those boys from Hoi An. I think I'll call it Spyglass, after my radio call sign. You do good on this out here, Lieutenant, and I'll let you tag along. You see I plan to get into the business that your old boss was in," Vilks said with a smile.

"What business is that?" I said coyly.

"The business of making things happen, Habu Six. You know about that. You worked with Lowy too long. Can't fool me," Vilks said with a wink.

Rex Vilks sat on the ramp of the amphibian track drinking C-ration coffee. It was drizzling and the low cloud cover offered little promise of any break in the weather. Thunder rolled in the distance. "Something on your mind, Habu Six?"

"I was thinking about Holland and what a damn shame it is. I just don't understand what happened, sir," I said.

"Couldn't cope. That was the word that I heard," Vilks said in a cocky, matter-of-fact way, as if he had all the answers.

"Hell, I don't know if I can cope half the time, Captain," I said.

"Don't let the men see that side of you."

Vilks played the part of a marine captain well. In spite of his arrogance, I respected him. I liked his sense of humor and his confidence. While he was at times narcissistic and could bore one to death with his long, one-sided, philosophical ramblings, he had poise and a definite military presence. Barrel-chested, with powerful shoulders and arms, he seemed a younger, more intellectual version of Captain Lowy. When one first met Vilks, he inspired confidence. He might had been only five feet, eight inches, but he appeared much larger due to his massive build and the fact that he was covered all over with dense, medium blond hair.

"Coping has to be learned, Lieutenant. Sometimes it helps to have someone who will listen."

"Not in this man's Marine Corps, sir."

"Not so. Everyone needs someone to confide in. By the way no one said your job was easy, or Holland's job for that matter," Vilks said.

"Okay, Captain, what does it take?" I asked.

"Coping?"

"Yes, sir, coping."

"Well, I think that you first have to take in information and see it for what it is. Don't fool yourself."

"I agree with that. I think that Chad may have had a problem that way," I said.

"I think so. Then I think that you need flexibility to make the changes that are demanded. Have to adapt. Sometimes one has to compromise."

"Chad didn't do that. There were some things that he wouldn't compromise."

"Well, that's a choice he made. Chad didn't learn to juggle," Vilks said.

"What?"

"I think that to cope you have to recognize that you are always juggling many things. Lowy was a good juggler," Vilks said.

"I think that Chad was overwhelmed. He should have never come back to the Nam," I said numbly.

"Holland didn't reevaluate. Have to do that if you're going to cope," Vilks said, draining his coffee.

"That's all very good, Captain, but I think that you left out a big thing."

"What's that?" Vilks asked.

"Freedom from the internal threat," I said.

"What are you talking about?"

"You can't be worrying about Division coming down on your back, for one thing," I said.

"Lieutenant, I don't think that you know what you're talking about," Vilks said.

"Captain, I'm just looking for someone who'll listen," I said.

October 19, 1968: 1000 hours

I was fascinated by the telescope. It helped take my mind off the loss of Sky Lady, and although I still felt overcome by a great feeling of despair, I was beginning to accept the fact that Sky Lady was gone. I sensed that some of my old ways of thinking and feeling had changed. There was a new, cold seriousness about me. I felt under control. In spite of what I had said to Vilks about coping, I knew that I wasn't going to go off the deep end. I could cope.

Strangely, I also felt that I was letting go, that I was going with the flow of events. Maybe my acceptance of what had happened was somehow directing me. No doubt I was seeing things through a new perspective. I knew what I had to do and what I wanted with a greater clarity than I ever thought I would have.

"Tell me again what you meant by internal threat," Vilks asked.

"I wasn't sure of what I was trying to say. I just know that one can never trust Division. You never know what they are going to do."

"You know that or you feel that?"

"I feel that, I guess," I said.

"You speak as if Division had some conscious will," Vilks said with a smirk.

"I would say that, generally speaking, there is an attitude that represents Division. It's a cover-your-ass attitude. It's a get-your-ticket-punched attitude,'' I said.

"That's bullshit, Lieutenant. 'Division,' as you call it, is made up of different people, individuals. If you ever sit in on any high level meeting, you will be able to see that there is no such thing as 'they' when you speak of Division. In fact, most of the colonels I know are in competition with each other,'' Vilks said.

"Then they aren't a team? Is that what you're saying?'' I countered.

"Well, that's a tough one," Vilks said.

"Captain, I say that there's an attitude at Division that puts down the experienced lieutenant when he comes in from the field. I felt it. Chad Holland felt it. Lukavitch has felt it.''

"That's more bullshit. You need to get your head out of your ass and remember that our common purpose here is to kick the enemy's ass," Vilks shouted.

"I'm not so sure, Captain," I said.

"What's that?''

"I had a captain tell me once that he was here only to get his ticket punched. He was my commanding officer and he sent me on a mission with a team where I was the only one who came back alive. There are a lot of people here who are here only to get their tickets punched. They don't give a shit about you or me!''

"There you go again using 'they.' Who in the hell are 'they'?'' Vilks laughed.

"I don't know who they are anymore. I just feel that they are there, just like I feel the presence of gooks when I go out in the middle of the night, or when I feel the presence of something evil," I said.

"Well, guard your feelings then. Guard them for the sake of the men and for your friend Holland. Now is the time when we need to rally and take it to the gooks," Vilks said in a loud voice.

Our conversation had attracted the attention of Lukavitch and Junge. They approached from an adjacent track where they had been seeking shelter from the drizzle. Pham Van Tra followed them.

"Speaking of gooks, Captain, why don't you or someone carry that message to the ARVN? They're the ones who need to rally. They're the ones who need to build their national will," I said hotly.

"You're the one who speaks of national will. I don't believe in such a thing. If you say national purpose, I'll buy what you are saying, but I don't believe in such a thing as national will," Vilks said.

"Just words, Captain," I said.

"No, it's not just a matter of words."

"Captain, you don't think that our being over here is an expression of our national will?" Lukavitch asked, his old idealism evident in the tone of his voice.

"Get real, Lieutenant. That's romantic nonsense," Vilks snorted.

"Ho Chi Minh talks about national will. I bet that the NVA don't believe it's nonsense," Lukavitch countered.

"What you're talking about is culture. You know, shared values and beliefs. That sort of thing unites people. It's not national will," Vilks continued with a know-it-all tone.

"Ask Pham. How about it, Pham, do you believe in a national will?" I asked.

"Of course," Pham said, brushing back his thick shock of white hair.

"There it is," I said.

"Look, I won't deny that some might believe in such a thing as national will. In fact, given the level of intellectual development of the average NVA soldier, national will probably means something to them," Vilks said.

"Sounds like you're putting the NVA down, Captain. The NVA have kicked the ARVN's ass. Something gives them direction," Lukavitch said.

"They want to unify their country. Maybe that's what national will means to them," I added.

"You believe in national will, Gunner?" Lukavitch asked.

"As a young man I remember the fall of Germany. I remember many boys taking up arms to die for their country—my three brothers, for example. They didn't believe in Hitler, but dying to protect their country was something that they did freely. I suppose our national purpose or national will, whatever, was one of survival."

"What's your point?" Vilks asked.

"Maybe the meaning of all this exists in its consequences, maybe one believes in the notion of national will when one's country's survival demands it," Junge said.

I gazed for a moment through the telescope. I thought I saw movement in the crevice that was the lair of the cobra.

"I don't know. To me national will suggests some absolute. I don't believe in absolutes," Vilks said, throwing the remainder of his coffee in the mud.

"What do you believe in, Captain?" Pham asked with a cynical tone.

"I believe in making comparisons. I believe in making choices based on those comparisons," Vilks said with a smile.

"The NVA soldier compares a unified Vietnam with that of a divided Vietnam. It's that simple. That's what gives him direction," Pham said.

"In the long run my bets are on the NVA. The NVA seems to always kick the ARVN's ass," I said.

"Well, Habu Six, the meaning of that statement is always relative. A good ARVN unit will stand up to a good NVA unit," Vilks said with disgust.

"What I think this all boils down to is whether or not we are going to win this war. Captain, do you think that we are going to win?" Lukavitch asked.

"Sure. We will win. We will win if we don't lose our humanity and abandon these people. We will win if both our leadership and that of the ARVN can articulate clear and purposeful goals, goals that are free from contradictions," Vilks said, almost eloquently.

"What do you think, Gunner?" I asked.

"That's an ideal," Junge replied.

"Yeah, I know, but what do you really think about this stuff, about this ideal, national will, or whatever?" I asked again.

"I think that when man in his imperfection tries to create such ideals, he is running counter to the great leveling process inherent in the nature of this country," Junge said.

Vilks got up and spat on the ground, his arms on his hips. "If you believe that, why do you fight, Gunner?"

"Oh, that's simple enough. I fight because I am a marine and a professional."

I had spotted the king cobra through the telescope. The king cobra seemed to be black with gold and cream-colored markings. I was captivated. Pham walked over to me and offered a cigarette. I refused the offer. While there was much about Pham to admire, I didn't trust him. His hanging around made me nervous.

"Pham, what do you think?" I said, making conversation.

"About what?" Pham replied.

"Oh, I don't know. How about Captain Vilks. What do you think about Captain Vilks?"

"Captain Vilks says that he does not believe in absolutes. I think that he may not believe in a higher being than himself. If he does not believe in a higher being—a God—then I feel sorry for him," Pham said.

I looked up from the telescope. Pham stood there smoking a cigarette, nodding slightly.

"I see. But you can't say that he's not committed. Maybe that's what he's all about," I said, focusing the telescope as I spoke.

"No doubt. Vilks is smarter than most, but there is a certain arrogance about him."

"So there is," I replied.

I got the impression that Pham wanted to talk to me. It was as if he were reaching out. But I didn't want to talk to him.

"Sometimes I think that he doesn't understand," Pham said.

"Understand what?"

"Why he is doing what he is doing."

"What do you mean?" I asked, knowing that Pham had me.

"He is fooling himself, playing a part," Pham said with a wry smile.

I could see why Weathers wanted to kill Pham.

"I don't know about the captain, but I've felt that way," I said, humoring Pham.

"I know," Pham said.

"What do you mean, 'you know'?" I asked, raising my voice. Pham was beginning to aggravate me.

"I know what Dao told me," Pham said, watching for my reaction.

For a moment I stopped breathing. Pham had said Dao. What did he know of Dao? More than that, what did he know of Dao and me?

"Dao? Is Dao VC?" I asked, looking Pham directly in the eye.

"No. She is someone who, like all of us, is trying to survive."

I said nothing in reply, letting the silence do its work. I looked through the scope to see that the king cobra had risen to its full height, its hood spread wide and taut, the embodiment of evil. Then I felt it. I felt as if I was to see clearly for the first time what was really going on. I looked over at Pham. He was the enemy I had known. He was staring back at me as if he knew what I was thinking. I knew that I only had to ask and he would tell me the truth.

"What did she say?" I asked, trembling slightly.

"She said that you were confused."

"I admit that. I was then. I am not now, but I know that I could be again. There are many of us who are confused. There's much to be confused about. What else did she say?" I was feeling a strange confidence beginning to build within.

"She said that you loved only yourself."

"That bitch. I loved her. She knows that. What else did she say?"

"She said that you have a big appetite," Pham said, now looking down at me.

I sat down at the edge of the track's ramp and peered back at the king cobra. It lay coiled in front of its lair.

"Yeah, I bet that she did say that. Well, I seem to have lost some of that hunger, Pham," I said, my confidence returning.

"How about your friend Holland? Do you ever think of him?" Pham said.

I thought for a brief moment of reaching up and breaking Pham's skinny neck. I restrained myself and decided to continue to play Pham's game; that night Weathers and Odum would be playing a game of their own with Pham Van Tra.

"Yes. How did you know that?"

"I watch, and listen. And you are a person who is easy to read. On your sleeve you wear the grief for your comrades," Pham said.

"Yeah, Pham, I do. It's all part of it."

I looked back into the telescope. The king cobra still lay coiled. More lightning flashed in the distance.

"Did you ever hear the notion that capitalism destroys so that others are born?" Pham said.

"What?"

"The deaths of young men like Chad Holland are part of the price your country pays to renew itself through exploitation," Pham said, blowing smoke into the air.

I felt an urge to kill Pham. I knew that he wasn't there to help us, that the business of his grandson was a ploy. I maintained. Stay loose, Habu Six, I said to myself.

"Exploitation? I'd say that we're here to help the Vietnamese at their request," I said.

"Do you really believe that?"

"Yes."

"Then I hope that you are a very smart young man. You will need to be," Pham said.

"Oh?"

"You will have to be very smart, indeed, in order to live with such ideas. Because such ideas as that are contradictory to the reality that surrounds you. Maybe that is what happened to your friend Holland," Pham said.

"How do you mean?"

"Maybe he woke up one day and could no longer make the adjustment," Pham said.

"Adjustment to what, specifically?"

"Who knows! The contradictions. The guilt. The mentality of a high command with a Word War II outlook."

I looked through the telescope to see that the snake was moving back into his lair.

"You lost me, Pham. You plumb wore me out with all your bullshit," I said.

"Your high command abandoned the only program that had a chance of working, that was pacification, living down in the villages, living with the people," Pham said intensely, trying to get a rise out of me.

"I don't know, Pham. See that computer printout that Captain Vilks is reading? That's a program that works. It's telling us who moves where and how often. It's a summary of data collected by these little sensors,'' I said, tossing the special sensor Klepper had made to Pham.

I had been carrying Klepper's sensor around with me. I had made up my mind that I was going to learn more about its application.

"What is this but a piece of metal?'' Pham said with a sneer.

"It may be the competitive edge,'' I said seriously.

"Habu Six, one has to be close to the people and the land. People are the competitive edge,'' Pham said.

Pham dropped his cigarette to the ground and crushed it out. He turned and walked away without saying another word, having sown his seeds of doubt and uncertainty. It is clear that evil has many forms and that there are many ways to cause harm and pain, to inflict injury upon another. It wasn't so much that Pham Van Tra was evil as he was bitter and unlucky. He had lost all his family and had betrayed his lifelong cause only to lose his last remaining relative, his grandson. Pham had struck a bargain with fate, and fate had walked away from the trade. I realized then that I could not kill the old man. I pitied him. In a manner of speaking, Pham's spirit had already perished. For him there was no longer anything to hope for, and for Pham there would be no personal peace. Perhaps that is the greatest evil and the most profound cruelty.

I looked through the telescope to see the king cobra. The snake was gone. There was only the mottled green and brown of the ancient, vine-covered wall.

October 10, 1968: 1300 hours

The rain was now coming down in torrents. At the suggestion of Lukavitch, we had decided to set up inside my old track Zero Deuce. Two platoons of Lima Company and a section of five tracks were to be located on Hill 36. Those platoons were now moving in, the wind whipping their rain gear wildly and making their lives all the more miserable.

Inside the track Vilks was tinkering with the sensor Klepper had made. Vilks was heavy into the technical side of things. Yet with Vilks, one always had the feeling that he wasn't telling all that he knew. I probed while Vilks tinkered.

"What do you think, Captain?"

"Klepper was a genius. Say, can I take this with me and see if I can have one of the communication jocks duplicate it?"

"Sure, Captain, long as I get it back."

"I wonder who and what resources were wasted producing this thing," Vilks said.

"I don't know, sir, but I guarantee you that it attracts fish and sea snakes."

"Truly amazing, the things that Lowy would do just to please Schuster," Vilks said.

"Think that's what it was?" I asked.

"You bet. Schuster was a big fishing jock, just like Lowy. Some people play golf with their boss; some people bowl and drink beer. Schuster and Lowy were fishermen, big time bass fishermen. You forget, Habu Six, I knew these folks back in the States," Vilks said.

"Did you know Lowy's friend Dick Crandle?" I asked with a smile.

"You mean Turkey Dick! Hell, Turkey Dick was once my company commander, if you can believe that!" Vilks said.

"I worked with him back in Third Tracks," I said, grinning.

"You have my respect and admiration. Did you ever get over it?" Vilks said with a smirk.

"It takes all kinds, Captain," I said tactfully.

"Well, Lowy and Crandle were two of a kind. Last I heard, he was having trouble at Third Tracks."

"Yes, sir, but you know, from what I can see, he doesn't care about criticism. It's almost as if he's indifferent. That is, except when you get him drinking, then he's downright aggressive," I said, again trying to be diplomatic.

"Sounds like he hasn't changed much. I heard through the grapevine that he was getting worse. The term I heard was 'estranged.' "

"Yes, sir—he is definitely one who keeps to himself when it comes to his fellow officers. He'll mingle with the troops, especially grunts. But for the most part he's pretty withdrawn when it comes to other officers," I said.

"I hear that he's going out at night on Chin-Strap mountain with some kind of rocket pistol that doesn't make any noise when you fire it. Word is that he's freaked out."

"That's too bad," I said.

"I don't know, Habu Six, it's real easy to lose sight of what we're doing. You know that," Vilks said.

"Yes, sir, that's what my old Gunny used to say right here inside this track. Zero Deuce was his favorite track. He called it lucky. But he would always add that it was lucky because it was good. What was it he also said . . . oh, I remember. He always used to say that there's a difference between looking good and being good," I said.

Vilks stopped his tinkering for a moment and looked up at the ceiling of the track. Outside the sound of thunder rolled like a B-52 air strike. We were snug and warm inside Zero Deuce. I felt sorry for the grunts huddling outside against the side of the track, trying to keep out of the wind. That cold China wind was blowing hard.

"Listen to that, Habu Six. We may need some of that luck of Zero Deuce yet," Vilks said with a frown.

October 10, 1968: 1600 hours

Cheatum called on the radio to give Vilks the word that he was calling off the operation because of the torrential rains. When Lukavitch and Junge heard that, both cautioned Vilks that letting up now was probably a mistake. Junge urged Vilks to protest. Backing off would only allow the enemy to gather themselves, spoiling any element of surprise that we had. Vilks agreed. He called a chopper to take himself and Pham Van Tra back to Hill 10. Halfway to Hill 10 lightning struck the chopper. The craft fell to the ground like a stone. There were no survivors. When Junge, Lukavitch, and I heard the report over the radio, we just sat in stunned silence.

October 10, 1968: 1800 hours

It was official. As of 1800 hours Operation Bench Mark, as the effort was known, was called off. Things had ended before they began.

October 10, 1968: 1900 hours

Cheatum had choppered out to Hill 36. He ordered Lima off the hill, leaving two squads for security to cover the tracks. I began to protest on behalf of the tracks, but Cheatum ignored me. Since the rain had momentarily let up, Cheatum thought it advantageous to move his grunts out. The tracks, however, were, for all practical purposes, marooned until the water surrounding Hill 36 drained into the Tuy Loan River.

October 10, 1968: 2000 hours

The rain began again. A battalion of North Vietnamese regulars could have passed within fifty feet of our position and we would have never known.

October 11, 1968: 0700 hours

The Tuy Loan River had risen during the night. It spread out of its banks, working its way through the low places of Sherwood Forest until much of the land lay beneath water, varying in depth from a few inches to several feet. Here and there the high spots were islands, two of the highest being Hill 36 and Hill 39. The wall also became an island, and I scanned it through the telescope wondering what had become of the king cobra.

Cheatum ordered the tracks to stay put on the high ground. Junge, Lukavitch, and I succeeded in convincing Cheatum that when the water receded, we needed to follow up on the information Pham had given us about the wall. Cheatum agreed reluctantly, claiming other priorities had come down from Division. In effect, we were on our own with what we had. What we had was five tracks and two squads of grunts. That amounted to ten tracked vehicle operators and twenty-eight riflemen.

October 11, 1968: 1300 hours

The rain continued and, at times, came down in sheets so thick as to obscure men walking ten feet in front of you. My skin grew wrinkled and began to slough off in little bits. Our only relief was to huddle inside one of the tracks. The men took turns at this, cramming together inside the tracks, their bodies steaming.

"Lieutenant, do you think that those rice carriers will move in this rain?" Odum asked.

"If it lets up a bit, I'm sure they will. The rain provides cover for their movement. What do you think, Gunner?"

"They will move. I'm certain," Junge said.

"Lieutenant, why don't we ease down to the wall and wait for them?" Odum asked.

"What do you think, Gunner?" I asked.

"It might be worth a try. We should take half the grunts. We should move out in the dark, using a compass azimuth to guide us to the wall," Junge said.

"I think it could be done. Let's do it!" I said.

As Vilks had said, it was time to rally and take some action. We knew that the enemy would be at or near the wall some time that evening. We also knew the approximate location of the cache. If we didn't rise to the occasion and firm up a plan, we would lose an opportunity. It was clear what we had to do. Now it was my responsibility to make something happen.

October 11, 1968: 2000 hours

The people left on the hill were not happy. But we had worked out a plan that seemed to take into consideration just about all the things that we imagined could happen. I kept the plan from Cheatum for I was sure that he would veto it. Junge agreed with me.

The rain had lightened to a drizzle. We set out in single file, Weathers at point. I was next in line. Ruiz followed me, carrying the radio. Gunner Junge and a good grunt sergeant brought up the rear.

About three hundred yards out we paused and waited until

darkness. There was less water than I expected. The depth of the water varied from ankle deep to mud. We had to move slowly, and there was much slipping and sliding due to the poor footing.

Junge played out a long nylon cord about a quarter inch thick. The track operators had supplied a great length of cord so that our path back to Hill 36 was marked, should return to the hill under the cover of darkness be required.

October 11, 1968: 2300 hours

We reached the wall and set in a perimeter, each man facing out. I thought of the king cobra as we moved through the darkness. The white flowers had opened and their fragrance filled the air. The cold China wind had stopped blowing. It had become very still.

October 12, 1968: 0100 hours

One of our worst fears became reality. Hill 36 was being hit. The dull thunk of mortars could be heard coming from somewhere near the base of Hill 112. The NVA mortar men walked their mortars back and forth across Hill 36. I took it upon myself to order the men off the hill. The tracks offered too concentrated a target. It was better to abandon the tracks and save the lives of the men.

Those on Hill 36 followed the cord down the hill as they were instructed. I sent Weathers and Odum to guide them into our position. One by one the NVA took out the tracks on the hill with what must have been RPGs and satchel charges. Zero Deuce seemed to burn the brightest.

October 12, 1968: 0330 hours

The wall was much higher than the rest of the terrain. Footing was firm, and I had the men set in ambush position so that they might fire freely to either side of the wall. Several men climbed to the top of the wall, including Weathers. Odum and Ruiz stayed

with me, Ruiz taking the radio. After assuring Cheatum that
there were no wounded, we maintained radio silence. I thought
I could make out NVA back on top of Hill 36, their figures
illuminated by the burning tracks. I wondered what they were
thinking.

October 12, 1968: 0400 hours

I couldn't believe what I was seeing. Across the rice paddy south
of the wall, at least thirty Vietnamese were hustling toward the
wall. All were in shorts. A few were wearing the pith helmets
of NVA regulars. They were moving so quickly that I almost
didn't react. All were carrying entrenching tools. Only a few
had weapons.

I waited until they reached the wall. Without pausing to rest,
they began digging immediately. They were within thirty feet
of an M-60 machine gun. For a few seconds I watched them dig
frantically. Then, as two of them with weapons began to move
toward the wall, Odum opened up. The NVA screamed and dove
for cover, some of them reaching the rice paddy before they
were cut down. In less than a minute it was over.

October 12, 1968: 0500 hours

Odum and I counted twenty-seven bodies. One or two may have
managed to crawl off in the dark to the deeper water of the rice
paddy. Weathers was ecstatic. Junge was pleased. Lukavitch
said nothing. I felt drained and empty. Was this it? Was this the
payback for Sky Lady, Holland, Lowy, and all the rest that we
had lost?

In the early light the flowers were still blooming. The sweet
smell was almost sickening in the heavy, wet air. Odum and I
walked over to the crevice where the king cobra had been spotted. We checked the narrow opening, but could find nothing.
Odum was disappointed.

"Lieutenant, I wanted to stand eyeball to eyeball with that
thing," Odum said, smiling.

"What was that Pham said to us, something about standing eye to eye with evil?" I asked.

"I don't know, Lieutenant. I think I did that about 0400 hours this morning."

I looked over at the wall whose origins were lost in history. I looked at the thick vines that covered the wall, vines that were hundreds of years old. I thought about what Pham Van Tra had said, how if you looked closely at how each one climbed the rock wall, it told a story. I wondered what past bloodshed the wall had witnessed. I wondered if it had seen Vietnamese beheading Chams, or if it had been a wall against which the French had stood Vietnamese before firing squads. I was afraid to look too closely. For I was afraid that the great snake might be looking back at me through the density of the leaves with its wicked, yellow eye, its great hood ready to spring suddenly through the vivid green of the wall of flowers.

THE BOYS FROM HOI AN

October 13, 1968: 1600 hours

COLONEL STUART LOOKED concerned. It appeared that he had learned a lot about the nature of Habu in the last two days. He drummed his fingers on the table while he thought.

"You are very lucky, Lieutenant. My first impulse was to call for a fact-finding. Then, upon reflection, and after discussing the matter with Lieutenant Colonel Cheatum, we both came to the conclusion that a full fact-finding would not be a service to all those concerned. Also, there will no longer be any special task groups. The district advisers will work with me more closely. Things will be more controlled and we will work with Division to ensure that their needs are met. Do you understand?" Stuart said.

"Yes, sir," I said, smiling.

"Lieutenant, I take exception to your flippant attitude. Cheatum warned me that you were confused," Stuart snapped.

"Sir, I may have been a little muddled in the past about things, but I knew what I had to do on Hill 36. That was to save lives. So a few tracks were lost to save those lives. I had no doubts. I made a choice based upon what was happening at the time. I'll stand by that choice. It's a matter of judgment."

"You mean you made a decision, however ill-advised," Stuart said.

"Sir, I didn't ask anyone's advice but Junge's. There wasn't time!" I said, raising my voice.

"That's exactly my point, Lieutenant. This whole question of why the tracks were abandoned without a fight seems to be answered by your attitude toward authority. Who authorized what, relative to Habu? I'm afraid if I probe further, I may not like what I find. I'm afraid that you are viewed at this point as a loose cannon, Lieutenant," Stuart said, shaking his head.

I looked around Stuart's new office. Outside there were two clerks, not one. In the adjacent room the two clerks were filing in what appeared to be new filing cabinets. The walls were covered with maps of I Corps. The maps were loaded with little red pins. A gun rack hung on the far wall. There were three shotguns in the gun rack.

"Loose cannon?" I asked.

"Yes, loose cannon. Do you know how they used to handle loose cannons on those old sailing ships, Lieutenant?"

"You lost me, sir. I don't follow what you are saying," I said.

"I'm extending the metaphor, Lieutenant. Loose cannons!" Stuart said.

"Oh, I see, sir."

"The way you handle a loose cannon is that you tie it down or take away its wheels. You understand?" Stuart said, now raising his voice.

"Yes, sir, I understand. But as I said a moment ago, I saved lives by abandoning those tracks," I said quietly.

"Yes. That's true, Lieutenant, but you abandoned them without a fight!" Stuart yelled.

"Sir, it was the thing to do at the time. This isn't World War II or Korea. Stand and fight isn't always the best thing to do. Hell, the VC pick and choose their fights. All I thought I was doing was fighting them the way they fight us. I admit I was juggling a lot of things in my mind at the time. The fact remains that in the end our abandoning the tracks paid off. The gooks thought we had run off. I feel that's why our ambush went so well. All things considered, Habu accomplished its mission. To accomplish that mission, I had to exercise discretion. Isn't that what counterintelligence is about?" I asked.

"Lieutenant, counterintelligence, and I'm not sure that's what you were doing, is about a lot of things. Much has changed in

Vietnam since my first tour in 1965. We had a good counterintelligence program then, Lieutenant. Do you know what it was?''
Stuart said with a smile.

"No sir, I don't. What was it?'' I asked.

"A shotgun and a list of names,'' Stuart said.

October 13, 1968: 1800 hours

Mike Company, Third Battalion, Seventh Marines, found more
than rice in the cache at the base of the ancient wall of An Nhon.
It was clear why the NVA that my Habu team had ambushed
were in such a hurry. Those NVA did not want to risk exposure
in daylight carrying the Strela SA-7 missiles.

Stuart was right. I had been very lucky. Maybe the luck of
old Zero Deuce had been given over to me when the tracks
burned on Hill 36. For I had expected that I would be relieved
once I returned to Da Nang. After all, I had given an order to
abandon five amphibian tracks without a fight. All five had been
lost.

At Division the loss of Schuster and the Cold Steel Crowd
was still being met with shock and disbelief. The circumstances
surrounding the death of Captain Lowy had been an embarrassment. After the burning of the Grand Hotel and the loss of Chad
Holland, some of the brighter senior officers were beginning to
ask probing questions, the outcome of which I was certain would
be an investigation of the methods being employed by Habu.
Most damaging, however, was the suggestion that Habu was in
some way linked to the death of two foreign nationals: a beautiful, but as yet, unidentified woman believed to be of German
origin, and a Frenchman who was a decorated veteran of World
War II.

But again, luck was with me. The find of the missiles seemed
to change everyone's attitude. I returned to Da Nang to find that
I had risen from obscurity. Habu was a topic of discussion at the
highest levels; even the boys from Hoi An wanted to talk to me.

October 13, 1968: 1900 hours

Lukavitch had warned me that the boys were on their way. In the span of twenty-four hours, Lukavitch had been moved from being the S-2 of the Third Battalion, Seventh Marines, to being on the staff of the G-2, First Marine Division. His success story, if you want to call it that, was due, he claimed, to the missiles. In spite of the fact that we had lost the tracks, 3/7 had come out looking good. Yet it appeared that by accident, Habu had made a connection in an area that was of upmost concern to the boys from Hoi An. As Lowy once said, things cohere more by luck than design.

"What are you going to tell them?" Lukavitch asked.

"All that I know. But I definitely want Junge there to fill in any blind spots," I said nonchalantly.

"These people are probing for Division. We'll have to be careful," Lukavitch said.

"Stay loose, Lieutenant," I said, smiling.

"You sound confident," Lukavitch said.

"Hey, we did what we had to do. There it is. I believe in what we did. And I'll be damned if we didn't bring home the bacon. You bet I'm confident. Listen, Lukavitch, I know I don't have all the answers, but I feel real good about this one. It was a long time coming."

Then I reflected a moment. Yes, there was a change about how I felt about myself. I had exercised some autonomy and used discretion to pull off what I felt was to be a major counter-intelligence coup. I disagreed with Stuart. What we had done was indeed counterintelligence. We were just playing by new rules. Moreover, in the process of making Habu happen, I had learned. While I still felt the same about the war, I had seen some of my efforts linked to an outcome of great value, to an event that was to have an impact. Although I didn't know what the extent of that impact might be, I had seen firsthand my efforts and the efforts of others closely associated with Habu lead to something that helped make a difference. More importantly, everyone connected with the effort who had survived had grown. Clearly that growth had overcome some of the doubt that had been eating away at us.

October 14, 1968: 0930 hours

On my way down to Third Tracks to see Major Crandle, I stopped by to see my old friend, Micky Van Der Molen. She was glad to see me, and when I shared with her some of what had transpired in the last few weeks, she seemed amazed. Micky made a point of suggesting we get together later in the evening for a drink. Perhaps we could renew a friendship that I had let slide. I needed Micky's humor and warmth; and I loved her big tits.

October 14, 1968: 1030 hours

"So what did you tell him?" Crandle asked, after hearing that Stuart had called me on the carpet.

"I told him that I made a choice based on the circumstances."

"Good for you. There's no getting away from it. You exercised your judgment. You took personal responsibility. That's all they can ask you to do." Crandle was obviously pleased with my performance.

"I was lucky."

"Luck! Sometimes you make your own luck, Lieutenant! You faced the situation and took the risk. You faced what you didn't know, overcame your fears, and acted. By the way, that's what courage is about—having the grit to act upon what you believe in the face of doubt. It may make you crazy, but it will also make you master of your own fate."

Crazy. Maybe I was already a little crazy. Once one has let go, it's hard to come back. Last night had been sleepless. I kept getting flashbacks. I just figured it was part of the process of coming down from the emotional events of the last few weeks. As for fate, I wasn't sure what that was. I wasn't sure.

"Did you say fate, sir?"

"Fate. By that I mean the final outcome, what each professional marine must be prepared for. But fate is also a power that you can carry with you that can determine the outcome of events," Crandle said.

"I don't follow, sir."

"It's a kind of positive thinking, but it's much more powerful than that. It has to do with what you did on Hill 36. That was knowing what you believed and making the choice,'' Crandle said.

"I think of fate and destiny as the same thing, having to do with the inevitable,'' I said, curious as to where the conversation was going.

"Choices that you make lead you to the inevitable. In our business the final outcome is always right around the corner,'' Crandle said.

"Sounds prophetic,'' I said.

"I'm talking about death, Lieutenant. When you think about what you did relative to that final outcome, you did good. Lieutenant, you did good!'' Crandle said.

October 14, 1968: 1130 hours

Lukavitch, Junge, and I met the boys for lunch at the Naval Support Activity Officers' Club. We sat out on the veranda and ate Chinese, loosening up with a few rounds of Kirin beer. One of the boys was new, according to Junge. The new guy was a SEAL officer who had worked with the Naval Advisory Detachment in Da Nang. He did all the talking. The second officer was a marine major named Chapel who looked nervous and sweated quite a bit. Lowy had worked with this major and there had been some competition between them. Junge called it professional jealousy. I didn't know. The third member of the group from Hoi An was a little Boston Irishman who wore civilian clothes and mentioned that he had gone to Yale. The little Irishman was the youngest person at our table. It had been the Irishman's job to orchestrate the lunch.

"You were aware, were you not, Habu Six, that Captain Lowy was working closely with the major?'' the SEAL officer said, nodding to the marine major, who was looking increasingly nervous.

"No, I wasn't. Lowy played his cards very close to his chest,'' I said.

The SEAL officer looked surprised at this. The little Irishman just smiled and kept taking notes, nodding from time to time.

"How about you, Gunner Junge, you were aware, were you

not, of Captain Lowy's close contact with the boys from Hoi
An, particularly the major here,'' the SEAL officer said.

There was a twinkle in Gunner Junge's eye. Junge smiled and
for a moment said nothing. It was as if he were making a great
inductive leap.

"Oh, yes, sir, on many occasions. I was well aware of the
major's role in the Phoenix program and the special task groups
initiated by Colonel Schuster, before the lieutenant's time on
board,'' Junge said.

The major seemed to relax with that comment. At that point
dessert was served and the conversation momentarily interrupted. Junge kicked me and nodded toward the men's room. I
excused myself to the men's room. Seconds later Junge followed.

"You want to tell me what's going on?'' I said, somewhat
agitated.

"Wise up, Lieutenant. Can't you pick up on what's going
down? These guys want a piece of the action! I know the major's
a jingle-butt. I'll say this, though, he did meet with Lowy and
was Lowy's connection to the Phoenix program. This major is
to Hoi An what Lowy was to Da Nang. Both of them reported
to Colonel Schuster. I suspect that this major is in some kind of
trouble, but I can't quite figure out what it is. I suspect he wants
to hide some things just as we do,'' Junge said.

"Okay, Gunner, but I'm going to let you do the talking,'' I
said, zipping up my fly.

"Get political, Lieutenant,'' Junge said, wiggling his penis
to shake loose several drops of urine.

October 14, 1968: 1347 hours

Junge took over like the silver-tongued devil that he was. The
SEAL officer glowed and the little Irishman took down every
word as Junge gave credit for some of Habu's success to the way
all parties communicated with each other. Lukavitch was in-
credulous, but seemed to know just enough to support what
Junge said when queried by the SEAL officer. At this point I
surmised that the SEAL officer was calling the shots, and that

somehow the well-being of the major depended upon what Junge and I were saying.

"Well, thank you, Gunner. I'm very pleased by what I have heard here today. All of you will be happy to know that the South Vietnamese government has seen fit to recommend Captain Lowy and Colonel Schuster for high decorations for service on the effort we call Habu. Habu Six, you will be gratified, I'm sure, to know that you have been recommended for the Vietnamese Staff Honor Medal, First Class. During my two tours in Vietnam, I know of no other lieutenant who has been nominated for that decoration. You should feel very proud," the SEAL officer said.

"Thank you, sir," I said.

"One last thing before we close. That concerns the matter of Madam Ti. We are certain at this time she is on the private yacht of a French national in Da Nang Harbor. In the interests of our efforts it is very important that no harm come to her," the SEAL officer said with some gravity.

"But, sir—we feel, that is, we suspect that she was closely involved with the death of Captain Lowy," I said, excitedly.

"She was," the little Irishman said.

The SEAL officer gave the little Irishman a dirty look, cleared his throat, and leaned forward.

"Madam Ti will not be harmed under any circumstances," the SEAL officer said.

"It is in our national interests that no harm come to her," the little Irishman added.

The SEAL officer gave the little Irishman another dirty look. The little Irishman just smiled as if he didn't care. I couldn't figure out the relationship among the three from Hoi An. Clearly the SEAL officer was some kind of fact-finder. The Irishman was probably a CIA case officer. The marine major was someone like Junge, Lukavitch, and me who was trying to get through all this with as little pain and suffering as possible.

"I am going to ask for your assistance," the SEAL officer said.

"Assistance?" I repeated.

"Yes. I hope to avoid having to look into the circumstances surrounding how the Grand Hotel came to be burned. I suspect arson, however, I feel that it is not in our national interests to

pursue the matter. You should be aware, however, that a number
of senior marine officers within the First Marine Division dis-
agree with me on this recommendation. I feel confident that my
point of view will prevail, yet I need your support to insure that
Madam Ti remains safe," the SEAL officer said.

"You have it," Junge said without hesitation.

"How about you, Habu Six?" the SEAL officer asked.

"Madam Ti. I suppose I have no choice but to agree."

"Good, now if you'll excuse me, I must be heading back to
Hoi An. I've got some new duties to assume there," the SEAL
officer said with a smile.

The little Irishman got up to leave with him. We all shook
hands and smiled. The marine major had stopped sweating.

October 14, 1968: 1410 hours

After the SEAL officer left with the Irishman, Lukavitch excused himself. Junge and the major and I stayed for quite some
time, drinking Kirin beer while the sun broke through the cloud
cover for the first time in several days.

"Thanks for covering my ass, Gunner," the major said.

"*Semper fi*, Major," Junge said.

"Major, just a couple more things, if I may," I said, half in
the bag.

"Shoot," the major said.

"What about these SA-7s? Is that going to change the way
the NVA are going to do business?" I asked.

"No. Thanks to Habu. Things are in the works at this moment
to put some pressure on the Hill 112 area. I can't tell you all the
details because I don't know them. I have no need to know. Yet,
through several sources I understand that we are working all the
angles. That's all I can tell you other than it was very important
to have those missiles in hand when we began to play our card,
if you know what I mean. Division just doesn't put a value on
what we do," he said.

"What's the deal with Ti?" I asked.

"I suspect that she's playing both sides. Lowy and I had talked
of placing her in a position where she might become a double
agent. You see, we knew she was feeding information to the

Vietcong. How ironic it is that the death of Lowy may have been the lever to place her in such a position,'' the major said.

"Damn, that's crazy," I said.

"Yes. Yes it is. It's crazy and complicated," the major said.

"Do you think that we will win this war, Major?" I asked.

"I don't know. We keep changing our objectives. Our senior officers grow increasingly tentative. Our allies are corrupt. These are three good observations that are a source of concern to me, observations that cast doubt in my mind as to the successful outcome of our efforts in this country,'' the major said.

October 16, 1968: 0300 hours

Habu was abolished as of 1200 hours, October 16, 1968. Weathers and Odum went back to the Sniper Platoon, First Marine Division, whereupon they were assigned out to support the grunts. Ruiz wound up on an interpreter-interrogator team. I tried to get Stuart to let me work with Division to find Odum a slot in the Division rear. Stuart refused. Junge got orders to Thailand. I was sent to Company A, First Motor Transport Company, where I was to spend my last two months in-country as executive officer. In the interests of national security, I was instructed never to discuss the circumstances surrounding Habu.

October 20, 1968: 1515 hours

Octavio Ruiz was working an area called Ap Trung Lap near downtown Da Nang when he spotted Sandman, Madam Ti's old bodyguard, boldly walking down the street, as if the events of the past months meant nothing. Ruiz dropped by First Motor Transport Battalion and passed me the information.

October 27, 1968: 0506 hours

Sandman was walking to his morning toilet, yawning and rubbing his eyes free of last night's sleep. Major Dick Crandle, battalion S-2 of Third Amphibian Tractor Battalion, was stand-

ing in the thick bamboo hedgerow to the immediate rear of
Sandman's new residence. For two mornings in a row Crandle
had waited in the early morning darkness with no success. Now
the opportunity had arrived and Crandle raised his silent rocket
pistol. Major Dick Crandle had been very fond of Captain Lowy.
They had played Quantico football together and had served a
tour together in Vietnam. There was a barely audible whisper as
a thin stream of smoke shot across the open ground and struck
Sandman in the middle of the chest.

"*Semper fi*," Crandle whispered.

October 28, 1968: 1430 hours

Colonel Stuart notified me today that the award papers had gone
through recommending me for a Bronze Star end-of-tour award.
He also said that Gunner Junge was also to be recommended for
the Bronze Star for his part in the Habu effort. Habu was a
success story. The Vietnamese government had already pro-
cessed the Vietnamese Staff Honor Medal First Class he said,
and I should feel proud that I had received such a decoration.
Habu was an example of what organizations can do when they
work together, Stuart said.

October 28, 1968: 1600 hours

I met Major Crandle for a drink at the Naval Support Activity
Officers' Club. He was in great spirits, feeling that he had just
accomplished something that was of great value both personally
and in terms of helping the counterintelligence effort. It's important he said, to see your efforts lead to a meaningful outcome.

Micky Van Der Molen joined us. She was wearing a sundress
and looked great. Soon we were having a few laughs. When
Crandle left, Micky and I stayed, watching the twilight come
on. The flowers on the patio were glorious and the clouds of
little nectar-eating moths fluttered about in the still evening air.

The little Irishman and the marine major from Hoi An sat
across the patio at another table, watching me. There was much

discussion between the two men. At one point I considered inviting them to my table, but decided against it.

"Who are those men who keep looking over here?" Micky asked.

"Those are the boys from Hoi An," I said, smiling.

"So, who are they?" she asked again, feeling my thigh under the table.

"Nobody important. Nobody that's important," I said, reaching out to stroke her long red hair.

WHITE ZEN

November 11, 1968: 1400 hours

I WAS A short-timer. After nineteen months in the Nam it was
almost time for me to go home. Ten days and a wake-up, I
thought to myself. Maybe when I got back to the world, I could
get some sleep.

Things had been up and down for me during the last few
weeks. Even though I had a cushy job as executive officer of a
motor transport company, I couldn't seem to settle down. I kept
getting flashbacks. Whenever I'd hear that rippling, thumping
sound of chopper blades passing directly overhead, I'd get
gooseflesh. At night the flash and pop of pyrotechnics would
have me on the edge of my cot, unable to sleep. The odor of
sweat, river mud, and mildew, the smell of fish in the market-
place, all of these things brought back images in my mind of the
past months in the field. Just looking at the wide panorama of
low hills surrounding Da Nang would bring on a sudden surge
of emotion. Something was wrong.

November 11, 1968: 1430 hours

Lukavitch was on his way home. Together we sat in my office,
drinking one last beer and reflecting on the events of the last
few months. Eventually his attention fell on the spare, Oriental

watercolor that I had hanging on the wall. Two kingfishers were resting on a stalk of bamboo. It had been painted by one of our buddies, a Lieutenant Hardy, who had been blown away some months ago.

Hardy had been an artist back in the world. To keep from going crazy, he sketched whenever he had a free moment. He claimed it was a kind of discipline. He called it White Zen because he began each morning with a clean white sheet of paper and a commitment to sketch something by the end of the day. Hardy found a means of relaxation and contemplation that endured in the form of the sketch. To me that was admirable. By the end of the day most officers would be pounding down cold beers in the Officers' Club.

But it was Hardy's watercolors that were special. He only could do those when he was back in battalion, usually after a major operation. He had said each stroke of the brush was like an action. Each color was an emotion. When the effort was over, what was left was an expression of what was of importance and of value in one's life. More important to Hardy than the painting itself was the process. He felt that painting was a process where one sought balance and proportion in a world governed by extremes. Hardy thought that in all things there was a pattern that connects. White Zen was his way of finding those patterns and making those connections.

When Lukavitch and I reflected back over the last year, we could still see Hardy at the edge of Liberty Road, all around him the dust and din from a convoy of passing trucks and the shouts of marines mounting out. Hardy just sat quietly and sketched the whole scene in a matter of minutes. He had an amazing talent.

"Sam, I'll give you fifty bucks for that picture," Lukavitch said.

"Fifty bucks! If it means that much to you, I'll give it to you as a going-away present. I know where I can get another almost like it," I said, pleased with the look in Lukavitch's eyes.

"Thanks, Sam. Where's the other picture?"

"Your old buddy Cottonhead Atrey's got several of Hardy's paintings. Atrey promised me one. Go ahead and take this one."

Lukavitch accepted the painting. For a moment he just sat in silence and stared at the picture, his eyes watering slightly.

Clearly that watercolor was one of the best things that Hardy had done. The style was simple. There were few colors. Just two kingfishers resting on a stalk of bamboo. I had seen similar birds in the wild. Yet, it seemed that Hardy's watercolor had captured something else, something eternal and unchangeable. It was strange. Somehow it seemed that Hardy was in the picture. I thought for a moment. I wondered if through his process of White Zen, Hardy had found a way to liberate himself from the flashbacks that I was experiencing. I wondered if he had found peace of mind in the madness that was all around us. Peace of mind. Maybe peace of mind was a reality that was possible in the transiency of this war.

November 11, 1968: 1500 hours

Lately Micky Van Der Molen had been my way of reconnecting. White Zen didn't work for me because I didn't have the medium to work in. My emotions were all over the place. The last few months had been a series of one irrational event after the other. It was hard to fit it all together. Maybe I would never fit it all together. One thing was certain, however, and that was the comfort that I found in Micky. Maybe Micky was my medium. She was someone I looked forward to seeing, and she was here and now.

November 11, 1968: 1530 hours

My relationship with Micky Van Der Molen had developed from an impulsive one-night stand to something deeper and more lasting than I ever expected. What had started as something based upon mutual attraction and a simple desire for sexual intimacy had grown into mutual dependence and a sincere desire to please each other. Since my new unit was only two miles away from the Naval Support Activity where she was assigned, we saw each other frequently.

November 11, 1968: 1545 hours

In any relationship one can't help but make comparisons with
past experiences. When I was with Micky Van Der Molen, at
times my mind would track back to the other great love that I
had known, Sky Lady. At other times Dao would creep back
into my thoughts. According to Lukavitch, Dao was now down
in Saigon, singing in a rock and roll band. I daydreamed about
all of them. Maybe those comparisons and daydreams were
helping me move toward some kind of resolution. Maybe they
helped make things fit in a world governed by extremes.

November 11, 1968: 1600 hours

I walked down to the long line of trucks. They were each two
and a half tons of diesel-belching and turbo-whining massive-
ness. Standing next to the convoy, I could feel the drama of
moving out. Senior NCOs walked down the line inspecting this
and that, ducking here and there to inspect each rig. I was impressed.

For the rest of the truck company, the day was winding down.
Vehicles were being washed and checked for fuel and oil levels.
It was called first-echelon maintenance, the equivalent of a ma-
rine grunt cleaning his rifle.

With the day almost over, I began to drift back toward our
little Officers' Club. My plan was to rap with my fellow officers
for a while, down a few cold beers, then see if I could come up
with some excuse to get out of the company area. Clearly, I had
to maintain some semblance of propriety. After all, I was the
company executive officer. I took great care to preserve my
image. My friend Micky was a secret known only to a few, and
for all outward appearances, I was a model marine officer.

I entered the Officers' Club. The discussion was hot and heavy
on the subject of voltage regulators. Apparently the regulators
being shipped in had some flaw and were not doing well in the
humidity. Voltage regulators were what was called a direct exchange item—when one went bad, you took it down to the First
Force Service Regiment to be exchanged for another. In the
meantime your vehicle was deadlined. It seemed that almost

half our jeeps were deadlined due to bad regulators. It also
seemed that First Force Service Regiment was out of regulators.

November 11, 1968: 1615 hours

It was time for me to get back down toward Third Amphibian
Tractor Battalion and the Naval Support Activity. I had two good
reasons. One reason was that we were out of voltage regulators
for our jeeps. Down at Third Tracks, I could cumshaw some
voltage regulators. My new commanding officer had no problem
with that. We swapped parts on a regular basis with folks all
over Division. That was the only way we kept our vehicles off
deadline. The other reason, of course, was Micky. I was always
looking for any chance to get back to NSA to see her. My commanding officer knew about Micky. But he was a laid-back former enlisted man who knew how to motivate people. His only
caution to me was not to get Micky pregnant.

Cum-shaw was the only way to get things done in an expedient
manner. In spite of what all the supply jocks said, our supply
systems always seemed to be going through some kind of shake-
down process. I couldn't get what I needed when I needed it.
In the eyes of the system, I was just some chicken-dick lieutenant. Yet, I could go out on the street and get what I needed in
an hour. And I was good at getting what I needed when I needed
it. I was very effective, and my new commanding officer appre-
ciated the contribution I made. It took a certain kind of person
to cum-shaw and I had that ability. To cum-shaw was to enter a
subculture of corporals and con artists—not everyone could do
that. What it all boiled down to was that there were procedures
to follow using the system, and there was a way to get the job
done. I was rapidly becoming a cumshaw artist.

One of the reasons that I loved to get out and cumshaw was
that I not only did some good for the company, but I maintained
contact with the marines that I had worked with over the last
months. I saw Cottonhead Atrey regularly. Cottonhead had extended again in the Nam. This time he had extended to be with
a Combined Action Platoon down in Nui Kim Son just outside
Third Tracks. He and I swapped both information and material
on a regular basis. I was also able to see Major Crandle and

Lieutenant Kaplan on a day-to-day basis. Both Crandle and Kaplan had a contempt for the Marine Corps supply system. I could
never quite figure out if it was the system or the poor planning
of Crandle and Kaplan.

Kaplan had been both a good friend and a source of needed
parts and material. For some reason, Third Tracks always
seemed to have an abundance of spare parts. Kaplan was probably the Zen master of cumshaw. When it came to getting things
to keep vehicles going and off deadline, Kaplan fit it all together.
Maybe cumshaw was Kaplan's White Zen. Perhaps cumshaw
was a medium that Kaplan found to work in to keep him from
going off the deep end. One thing was for sure, when it came to
cumshaw, Kaplan was connected.

"Sir, I'm heading down to Third Tracks. Going to pick up
some voltage regulators," I said, lighting up a cigarette.

"Go for it. Try to get back tonight. If you can't get back, let
me know, damn it! I don't mind if you stay down at Third Tracks,
just let me know," he said with a wink.

"Yes, sir," I said, stuffing cigarette packs in every available
pocket.

"Lieutenant, anyone ever tell you that you smoke too much?"

My new commanding officer was old enough to be my father,
and at times he seemed to have a fatherly concern for me. I had
been very lucky to work for him. He was a down-to-earth type
who seemed both dependable and predictable. You could trust
him. For the most part he went by the book. He was calm, cool,
and an officer who was quite a contrast to characters I had known
like Captain Lowy and Major Crandle.

Ted Rukavina, short and balding, was from South Bend, In-
diana. He was in his forties and had been lucky in getting his
temporary commission. Ted had resigned himself to the fact that
after the war he would probably be reverted back to master
sergeant. In some ways he reminded me of my gunnery sergeant
back at Third Tracks. He and Junge also had some things in
common when it came to handling technical matters. Each could
be relied upon. Each was an ace, someone that the Marine Corps
depended upon to keep it going.

I was having one of my sanguine moments, feeling really
upbeat and cheerful, confident that I could go out and get
Rukavina his voltage regulators. Just getting two or three

voltage regulators would be quite a success. Those voltage regulators would be my ace for the day. Then it occurred to me that for so much of my tour in Vietnam I had been in pursuit of something tangible, something touched or felt, something definite and objective. What came to mind was that those tangibles were an illusion. Those tangibles were an illusion in that they were misleading. They led one on a chase that somehow distorted what was really important. I thought of Crandle and his rocket pistol, Lowy and his bass sensor, Vilks and his program's computer printouts, myself and the pleasures of the flesh. Now I was chasing voltage regulators.

Maybe what I was really after could not be touched. Perhaps it was something intangible, like the things Junge rambled on about. Then again, maybe that intangible was like the luck of Zero Deuce. The luck of Zero Deuce had proved to be a way of thinking; and that way of thinking appeared to be different things to different people. What mattered was the belief, as Junge would have put it. What mattered more was how the belief elevated the spirit. I thought of Odum and Holstrom, and of how their faith had lifted them up. I would never mock their faith again. I thought of Holland and Lukavitch, and of how their commitment to their program had raised them to what was clearly a higher moral level than their fellow marines. I thought of Hardy and his art, his White Zen. I thought of Mother Africa and his new found identity. I had taken these men for granted. Perhaps, in this time of uncertainty, these men had found an ace they could hold.

"Is four or five packs a day too much?" I said, snapping out of my daze.

"You smoke four or five packs a day!" Rukavina yelled.

"Yes sir, one of my bad habits," I said, now in tune again.

"Shit! You're lucky not to cough up blood! Get the hell out of my office. Be sure to say hello to Micky for me," Rukavina said, dismissing me with a wave of his hand.

"You must be getting pretty short?" Major Crandle said, offering a cold Blue Ribbon beer.

"That's most affirmative, sir. I got about ten days and a wake-up," I said, opening the beer.

"You are that short! Damn! What are you doing running around Division like some chicken-dick?" Crandle said, tossing a cold beer to Lieutenant Kaplan.

"We're lucky, Major. Sam here is our mainline for starters and Kirin beer. I'm going to hate to see him go," Kaplan said, slapping me on the back.

"Well, I'm going to miss you, too. The only person that will still be around from the old crowd is Kaplan, and he's down to something like thirty days. That right, Kaplan?" Crandle said.

"Yes, sir. Then I got sixty days and I'm out of the Green Machine," Kaplan said.

"That's hard to believe. I still got six months active duty when I get back," I said.

"Get an early out for education like I did. Shit, I'm going to law school part-time and they let me out!" Kaplan said with a smile.

"Law school. How about that. And he'll be a good one, too, Sam! Should have seen him handle those Article 15's and those summary court-martials over all that dope. You would have been proud. Old Kaplan showed those chicken-dicks up at Division legal that we got our shit in one bag down here at Third Tracks," Crandle said, opening another beer.

Crandle seemed about half in the bag. It wasn't yet nightfall and Dick Crandle appeared to have been drinking for some time.

"I wondered how that business was going to all come out," I said, concerned.

"Well, old Kaplan came through. He was truly a silver-tongued devil," Crandle said, flopping down in his deck chair.

I looked at Kaplan. Kaplan just rolled his eyes and shook his head. The silence was awkward. Crandle was going down the tubes. It was sad. He had once been a great marine officer.

"Sam, thanks for the starters. I'll see you again before you leave. Take care now," Kaplan said, leaving Crandle and me alone in the quiet of the hooch.

"You still banned from the Officers' Club?" I asked, pulling my chair closer.

"Yeah. But I got no one to blame but myself. I used to say that the Marine Corps betrayed me by taking my ass out of combat, by puttin' me in the rear with the gear. Truth is, I betrayed myself," Crandle said, opening another beer.

I didn't say anything in reply. I didn't know what to say. Here was Turkey Dick Crandle, one of the roughest and toughest, turning into a boozer and wallowing around in what appeared to be self-pity. I didn't know what was happening there. I did know that I wasn't a counselor.

One of the bad things about being at Third Tracks was that there was never enough to do. There was too much free time for men to get caught up in booze, drugs, gambling, or whatever. Idle time had been partially responsible for Kaplan's problems with grass and other drugs down in the motor pool. I was sure that not having enough to do figured into Crandle's drinking.

"So, you like cumshawin' around Division like some chicken-dick?" Crandle said, his eyes bleary.

"Yes, sir, I get away from the humdrum of the company. I get a lot of pleasure out of wheeling and dealing, and I get things done in the process. Yes. I like it very much," I said.

"You're turning into a regular wheeler-dealer, like our old buddy Lowy. Damn! I'm going to miss him. Now there was a con artist," Crandle said, sitting up.

"Con artist?" I said, wondering where the conversation was going.

"He was a trickster. And he tricked us all. He tricked Division. He tricked the gooks. And he slipped up and got himself in a trick. Damn, I'm goin' to miss him," Crandle said, draining his beer and throwing it across the hooch.

I had seen Crandle in these moods before. When he got to drinking in this kind of mood, he was implacable. Crandle was on the verge of exploding, the tension and emotion within building as his drinking became more relentless.

Again I didn't reply. I just didn't know what to say. I looked out over the sand dunes. The monolith known as Chin-Strap mountain rose up from those sand dunes, a great limestone butte. Chin-Strap was also the home of the Linh Ung pagoda, a holy shrine nestled deep within the limestone, shaded by rock out-croppings. I wondered what hid inside that mountain's honey-comb of caves and fissures. I wondered if the enemy were peering back down at me from the fern-covered rocks. There was something inscrutable and enigmatic about the huge gray-green hump. I wondered who or what dwelled within the secret places deep inside. I looked over at Crandle, who was staring in the other direction, at a line of fishing junks strung across the horizon out on the South China Sea. I wondered what forces were churning deep inside Major Crandle.

November 11, 1968: 1800 hours

On the way to see Micky, I stopped in Nui Kim Son to talk with Atrey. I gave him a voltage regulator just in case he needed one. He gave me not one, but two of Lieutenant Hardy's watercolors. Hardy had given several to Atrey, the two men having worked closely together on a number of operations. Suddenly, in the midst of the conversation, I felt a strange sensation. In my mind's eye I could see Hardy's face, ghastly and pale, he and I waist-deep in water, crossing a river, Hardy about to slip from my grasp.

November 11, 1968: 1815 hours

I called Rukavina to let him know that I had got all the gear that we needed and was about to head to NSA. Rukavina said that was fine, but he had a special request from a friend who needed an NVA SKS bolt-action rifle. The SKS was the only weapon that could be brought back to the States legally. The rifle was going to be a present for some colonel. I told Rukavina that I could probably get an SKS from Beau Boden, but I would need at least two pallets of plywood to trade for the rifle. Rukavina assured me that the plywood was on its way first thing tomorrow morning and that I should make the deal and then spend the night at Third Tracks.

November 11, 1968: 1830 hours

"I just don't know, Sam. I'm so drained. I start to get myself together and then find myself breaking into tears," Micky said, looking into her drink.

"You still taking those pills?" I asked.

"Sure, but a person has to watch that. Those things are addictive," she said, giving me a hug.

A smoke haze hung in the still air of the Officers' Club. It hung over the pool table. Because the bar was air-conditioned, the doors to the outside patio were kept closed until the coolness of the evening began to descend as a heavy, opaque fog. It was that time of year.

"This wet weather depresses me," Micky said, lighting a cigarette.

"You're smoking again," I said, smiling.

"You are a bad influence on me, Sam. When I'm with you, I do all kinds of crazy things," Micky said, pinching my side.

"Smoking's okay. Helps you stay loose," I said.

"Smoking's a bad habit. And you smoke too much," Micky said.

"Bullshit. Every morning I have a cigarette and coffee for breakfast. Look how healthy I am, for Christ's sake," I said.

We moved away from the bar. Several chopper pilots came in and began to pound down beers and shots. I waved at the group. I knew them all fairly well, having swapped and cumshawed material with them. Army chopper pilots, especially young warrant officers, were people I depended upon. There wasn't anything that I wouldn't do for them.

These young warrant officers flew a lot of support missions in the area. I had always been impressed by their knowledge of the terrain and how they viewed all of us linking together. They had confidence and seemed to understand how they were supporting the effort. They liked to roll dice for drinks.

"Do you know those pilots?" she asked, sitting down in an out-of-the-way corner.

"Yeah. We have a lot in common," I said.

"I had a chopper pilot die on me once," Micky said, looking off through the window.

"Only one?" I replied.

"What I mean is that he died on me while he was my responsibility," Micky added.

I didn't know what to say so I said nothing. The chopper pilots at the bar were whooping it up.

"Do you believe in ghosts?" Micky asked.

"Ghosts?"

"Sometimes I think that I see this chopper pilot walking around NSA. It's spooky, like that black cat we could never catch, the one who lapped human blood at the NSA morgue," Mona said, lighting another cigarette.

"Fatigue," I said.

"Have you ever seen a ghost? Have you ever dreamed about the dead?" she asked.

"I don't know what a ghost is. And yeah, I've dreamed about the dead. It happens to everyone sooner or later I suppose," I said, trying to downplay the subject.

"Sam, I think that I'm going crazy," Micky said, staring out the window.

"That's okay. Anyone who's been here for any length of time gets a little goofy."

The chopper pilots were leaving. As they left, they yelled and grab-assed around. I waved. Micky looked at me and smiled.

"Micky. This place is full of crazy people, people who are boozers, who are smoking dope, or popping pills. Hell, I think I'm about a half bubble off center myself," I said, smiling.

Micky laughed, putting her hand to my cheek.

"Sam, I don't know what I'm trying to say. I just feel this tremendous pressure, day in and day out," Micky said.

"You're going through a lot right now. Tough things are going down all over I Corps. You are changing, Micky. I can see it. Someone once told me that when things are hitting you, when you are going through changes as a result of those things, it's important to keep things simple," I said, putting my arm around her.

"Sam, maybe that's why I don't want to make love with you anymore. Our being together makes things too complex and adds pressure that I don't need right now," Micky said, looking off through the window.

"Okay," I said, almost in a whisper.

Micky took out another cigarette. I lit it for her.

"Sam, you are like this cigarette. You're no good for me, but you're a bad habit that I crave," Micky said.

I could hear the last of the chopper pilots laughing in the men's room. Their laughter was the laughter of horseplay. It was a loud and roaring laughter of rascals raising hell. There was a crash. The bartender went to investigate. It sounded like the chopper pilots were taking things back to their simplest terms.

November 11, 1968: 1900 hours

Driving over to the Special Forces Camp, I kept thinking about what Micky had said about ghosts. There had been many nights when I had relived experiences in my dreams, but I had never seen a ghost. I would say, though, that I was at times haunted in my sleep by feelings and images from the past. One of my recurring dreams concerns the crossing of a river, crossing onto Go Noi Island. We get ambushed and are forced to abandon a disabled track in the middle of the river. The men in these dreams appear ghastly and pale, and the dream never ends. It always returns on another night and I am crossing another part of the same river.

November 11, 1968: 1930 hours

Major Beau Boden slapped me on the back and handed me the SKS rifle. Boden looked great. Lately he had lost some weight.

"Say hello to Crandle for me, Sam," Boden said.

"Yes, sir, and thanks again for the SKS."

"Have a quick shot of Jack," Boden said, pouring me a drink before I could refuse.

"Here's to lying, cheating, drinking, and stealing. When you lie, lie to save a friend. When you drink, drink with me. When you steal, steal that little Micky's heart. And when you cheat, cheat death!" Major Boden said, raising his glass.

We clinked glasses and drank. I knew the toast. I had heard it many times.

November 11, 1968: 2000 hours

I drove down the beach to Third Tracks. I figured it was quicker that way. I was half in the bag and preoccupied with Micky. I didn't care if the drive was safe or not. I wanted to look at the South China Sea. On the way to Third Tracks one passes a tiny fishing ville. The ville is called Xom Son Tui and there can't be but a half a mile between Third Tracks and C Company, Fifth Special Forces, that point on the beach. Chin-Strap mountain sits just to the west of Xom Son Tui, separating the little fishing ville from the larger village of Nui Kim Son. Either way it's a nice drive, and that night there was no moon. The stars were incredible.

November 11, 1968: 2200 hours

Crandle and the marine major from Hoi An sat in the darkness of Crandle's quarters. I had brought a six-pack with me, but there were no takers. This major from Hoi An, Major Chapel, was the one I had helped look good during the Habu effort. I wondered what brought him up to Third Tracks.

"Hello, Lieutenant. Why don't you sit down? Major Crandle and I have been talking about you and your success with the Habu effort," Chapel said, lighting a cigarette.

"Is that right?" I said, feeling nervous.

There was something in Major Chapel's tone that disturbed me.

"The major here was asking me about Madam Ti's body-guard, Lieutenant. You know who I mean, that big dude they called Sandman," Crandle said, winking.

"What about him?" I said.

"Somebody snuffed him," Chapel said.

"That's the way it goes," I said.

"Sandman was working for us. Knowing how you felt about him, Lieutenant, I was wondering if you had any clue as to how he bought the farm?" Chapel asked.

"No, sir, I don't have any idea," I said, looking out at the South China Sea.

"He was killed by an experimental weapon, by a rocket pistol to be exact. There are only three in Vietnam," Chapel said, blowing smoke into the air.

"Rocket pistol?" I said.

"Like the one Major Crandle here claims was stolen from him. Stolen rather conveniently, I might add. You, Lieutenant, should probably talk to the major about that. When you talk to the major, you should keep in mind that up to now you have been very lucky. Don't stretch that luck. Your success finding those SA-7s didn't give you carte blanche to start running your own counterintelligence operation. Don't start making your own rules. That would be a mistake," Chapel said, rising from his chair.

"I didn't know there were any rules left, sir."

"Good night. Be careful, both of you," Chapel said, walking out the door.

Crandle had snuffed Sandman with his rocket pistol, never thinking anyone would be the wiser. He had used the rocket pistol because it was silent, never thinking that someone would be able to trace the cause of Sandman's death to him. I had assumed the matter of Sandman closed. How wrong I was.

"They got me by the short hairs, Sam. They know it was me," Crandle said.

"Who knows?" I asked.

"Division," Crandle said.

"What about Chapel? What was he doing here?" I asked.

"Chapel's okay. I've known him for years. He was just letting me know that they know. He was risking his ass coming here to tell us," Crandle said.

"Why would he risk his ass for us?" I asked.

"He wouldn't screw me over. We go back a long ways. Anyway, you made him look good. He ain't forgot that either," Crandle said.

"I don't know what to believe," I said.

"What you believe in is your skills and what you have learned. What you believe in is a few good men who you can count on no matter what. Don't worry. Major Chapel is one of those few even though he's caught up with that Hoi An bunch," Crandle said.

"That's not much to put your faith in when it's all said and done, is it?" I said, shaking my head.

"What do you mean, Sam, why that's everything. You put your faith in the people side of things. My big mistake here was putting my faith in that damn rocket pistol. That was an error of judgment on my part," Crandle said, smiling.

"You have no regrets about snuffing Sandman?"

"Hell no! Do you have any regrets about burning down the Grand Hotel?" Crandle asked.

"No, sir. No sir, I don't," I said, opening a beer.

"What you can believe in, Sam, is a few good men. That's where I've chosen to place my faith. That's what I've learned, and I made a lot of mistakes learnin' it, but I don't regret nothing," Crandle said, putting his hand on my shoulder.

My mind drifted back to the Grand Hotel. I thought of Piaf's song "Non, je ne regrette rien." No. I regret nothing. I could see Sky Lady, or was it the ghost of my lover, her smile enigmatic. She was standing by a window, pulling floor-length curtains together, the light on the veranda of the Grand Hotel silhouetting her form against the curtains; and outside the window, in the darkness beyond the veranda, I could once again hear the heavy tops of the thick bamboo tossing in the breeze coming off the South China Sea. No. I regretted nothing about Sky Lady. Nothing at all. Sky Lady and I had taken things back to their simplest terms.

November 12, 1968: 0215 hours

The sound of the Third Track emergency siren had me on my feet. I could hear the dull thunk of mortars clearing a mortar tube somewhere toward Xom Son Tui. From Nui Kim Son to the west and from C Company, Fifth Special Forces, to the north, the snapping crack of AK-47 fire told me the shit was indeed hitting the fan. The volume of fire was steadily growing.

"Major Crandle, Major Crandle! Charlie Company's being hit. Gooks are in the wire!" a marine shouted from outside our hooch.

Crandle and I ran to the Third Track command bunker. Two tracks loaded with marine riflemen churned past us on their way toward Charlie Company, Fifth Special Forces. Overheard illumination rounds were popping, revealing scatterd groups of men moving across the landscape.

November 12, 1968: 0230 hours

The situation at C Company was serious. Two choppers were burning on the helipad. Sappers were inside the wire. It appeared that the C Company command bunker had been blown up. Our only radio contact was with a captain who had reached one of the watchtowers. He had given us what information he could from his position.

Our relief tracks had been ambushed just outside our own wire. A command-detonated mine had blown the road wheels off the first track. The second track had taken two rocket-propelled grenades through its side. Marine riflemen riding on top of the tracks lay scattered about, some wounded, others pulling the wounded under cover and trying to regroup. A squad-light machine gun swept the whole area with grazing fire, pinning down those marines in Nui Kim Son who were trying to reach the ambushed tracks.

Crandle and I grabbed what marines we could and mounted two tracks armed with .50-caliber machine guns. The .50 caliber is an awesome weapon. These two tracks had been held in reserve for just such an occasion as this. Some months before, while serving with Alpha Company, Third Tracks, I had mounted the .50s myself. I had timed the guns, test firing them several times. Chance now had me riding out through our perimeter wire behind one of those guns, short-timer that I was.

November 12, 1968: 0235

Crandle's track led and my track followed to his immediate left, so that we approached our disabled vehicles in an echelon. Crandle's track maneuvered between the enemy fire and a wounded marine who lay trapped in a slight depression in the earth. I opened up with my .50, sweeping the area with bursts of fire. The bamboo hedge that was covering the squad-light machine gun literally disappeared as the big .50 rounds did their job.

In Nui Kim Son our marine patrols had their hands full. The fighting was house to house, with our men moving very slowly if at all. Here and there hooches were burning, the smoke drifting throughout the village to obscure fields of fire, adding to the confusion. The noise of the various firefights made it impossible to hear verbal commands. Under the eerie light of the illumination rounds, I could make out a marine fire team leader gesturing wildly to his men.

November 12, 1968: 0246 hours

We had reached the gate of C Company, Fifth Special Forces. By now it was clear what had happened. With the Mobile Strike Force companies out in the field, the camp had been lightly defended. Sappers had managed to slip in, blow the choppers on the pad, and toss several satchel charges into the command bunker, wiping out all of the officers. I wondered how Beau Boden was doing in his air-conditioned club. Small firefights still were breaking out along the perimeter as sappers tried to make their exit. But for the most part the fight was over. The Green Beret captain in the west watchtower directed our movement into the camp. We entered without resistance.

November 12, 1968: 0615 hours

''You sure that you want to go with us? You got nine days left in-country,'' Crandle said.

''You bet I do,'' I said, loading my shotgun.

Twenty or so sappers were holed up on Chin-Strap mountain. Several were wounded. A marine patrol had prevented their escape into the honeycomb of the mountain caves and tunnels. That patrol was positioned above the sapper group. A Mobile Strike Force company had returned from the field to assist the two platoons of marine riflemen we had in place below the trapped sappers.

Crandle's fingers were shaking. He was chain-smoking cigarette after cigarette. Finally, Captain J.R. Axton, the Green Beret officer in charge of the Mobile Strike Force company, found our position; and it was clear from our first meeting that he had his shit together. Crandle quickly briefed Axton on the situation. Axton suggested that he and Crandle try to work their way closer to the spot where the sappers were trapped.

Crandle, Axton, and five marines started to move up the trail. Chin-Strap mountain is accessed by one of two trails. Both trails are cut into the stone. At various places there are steps cut into stone. The particular trail that Axton and Crandle chose was the one that offered the most cover and clearest fields of fire. In addition, dead sappers were strung out along the trail, killed by the marine patrol who had assaulted up the trail only two hours before, giving the impression that the initial few meters up the trail were secure. That was not the case.

What must have been a large mine exploded in the middle of the group. Axton was thrown back down the trail, his left leg severed at the knee. Through the smoke I could see at least three more bodies. Two marines and I made a rush up the trail just as an AK-47 began to sweep the area. I slammed myself flat against a rock wall as the other two marines dove into a kind of fissure directly across the trail from me. I looked back down the trail to see a navy corpsman and two Green Beret officers pulling Axton to safety. Axton gave me a thumbs-up as they pulled him away.

November 12, 1968: 0620 hours

Fear takes you back to the simplest terms. Maybe the simplest terms are those that have to do with the emotions, especially letting those emotions go. I don't really know how fear is best controlled. I know that I don't deny it, I just kind of let go with it.

"See anything, sir?" a marine sergeant yelled up to me.

"No. Can't see the major. Others are either dead or hurt real bad. They ain't moving," I yelled back.

Long, agonizing minutes passed. Nothing moved. A cicada buzzed off in the distance, and I wiped the sweat from my eyes. Then above us a marine shouted and all hell broke loose.

The marines above us were moving down the stairs. The sappers sprayed the area with AK-47 fire, clearly not intimidated.

We were on their ground and fighting at a disadvantage. From their hidden positions in Chin-Strap's tunnels and fissures, they could snipe at us all day. If we tried to rush them, they would slip deep into the interior of the mountain. All we could do was wait until dark and try to police up our dead.

But what if Crandle was alive? It seemed that the force of the blast had pitched his body upward. My guess was that he was laying just beyond my field of vision. My head began to pound. I pressed myself against the rock wall and waited. Should I move? There was a burst of M-16 fire followed by a series of frag grenade explosions. The marine grunts above me had made the decision for me and were taking the initiative.

Someone popped smoke. A billowing cloud rose up out of the honeycomb. Smoke! What genius had thought of smoke! There were more dull thumps as the marines above us moved down the stairs, fragging every crevice and hole, the smoke offering cover for their movement.

I coughed and my eyes watered. The two marines with me followed as I began to creep up the stairs toward the Lihn Ung pagoda. At a turn in the rock wall I stopped and yelled. Through the smoke a marine appeared. It was Cottonhead Atrey. Behind Atrey two marines were carrying an unconscious but still breathing Dick Crandle.

November 12, 1968: 0700 hours

It was Cottonhead Atrey who had saved Crandle. It was also Atrey who was savvy enough to use smoke to get close to the sappers, most of whom got away by slipping back into their escape tunnels.

I didn't have much to say to Atrey as we brought Crandle down the mountain. All of us were grateful for not having to leave a fellow marine to an uncertain fate.

We loaded Crandle onto the jeep. When I turned to find Atrey, he was already gone, his squad headed back up toward the mountain.

November 12, 1968: 0945 hours

Major Dick Crandle died at 0914 hours of multiple shrapnel wounds and loss of blood. While we were loading him in the jeep, he had briefly regained consciousness enough to recognize me and give me a wink. He was too weak to speak, but his face reflected a kind of resignation, as if he had finally finished wrestling with the forces churning within him.

November 12, 1968: 1030 hours

On the drive back to NSA I found Odum hitchhiking along the road. I picked him up and told him how we had retaken the mountain and about Crandle.

"I'll say a prayer for him and all the other marines that died," Odum said, seemingly very calm.

Odum seemed to have changed somewhat. He was very composed, as if he had come to terms with himself and the events of the past few months.

"Crandle was very quiet at the end. I hope he went out without too much pain," I said.

"Maybe he repented at the end."

"Repented?"

"Maybe he repented, Lieutenant. Remember the parable of the Prodigal, Luke, fifteenth chapter, eleventh verse?"

"No," I replied.

"Well, the Prodigal had a change of mind; and his change of mind effected a change of heart; and his change of heart effected a change of will. No one is ever saved until he wills to be. Repentance is a change of mind, of heart, and of will," Odum said, a distant look in his eye.

"I see," I said.

"I hope he did repent, Lieutenant. Otherwise he may have perished in his own corruption," Odum added.

I thought about Odum's remarks for a long time. Odum didn't say anything further. He was just along for the ride now, and he seemed very much at peace with himself.

I stopped the jeep and let Odum off just in front of NSA. He smiled and thanked me, hoping to see me stateside.

"Just one more thing, Odum," I said.

"What's that, sir?" Odum said.

"Is repentance like a wiping clean?" I asked.

"Yes, Lieutenant, it is. It is a new beginning," Odum said.

"I see. Thanks, Odum. Stay loose," I said, driving through the NSA gate.

Odum seemed much more together. Whatever had happened to Odum, he had found himself in relation to what was going on around him. Clearly, like the Prodigal, Odum had made a change. He had connected through his faith. I thought of Crandle and his faith in a few good men. I thought of Hardy, of his White Zen, and of how he made the connection. Maybe I was going through my own process in order to find that sense of balance and proportion that I was looking for.

November 12, 1968: 1100 hours

NSA had taken seven 122mm rockets during the night. Several sailors had been wounded and several storage buildings had been damaged, but the hospital had escaped.

All kinds of people were running around. The ARVN Rangers had been called in to retake Chin-Strap mountain. It was a purely symbolic gesture because the fighting was over for the time being. That didn't stop the journalists, however. They swarmed over the area like insects feeding on the dead.

I radioed Rukavina to let him know that I was all right. He sounded relieved and told me to get my ass back most ricky-tick. On my way back to my jeep I ran into Major Boden, who was okay. He said that sappers had kicked in an air conditioner and thrown in satchel charges, but that for some reason the charges had failed to go off. Boden then asked me if I wanted to go get a drink. I declined.

I was worried about Micky, but it turned out that she had flown out to the hospital ship *Repose* just before the fighting started. One of the nurses told me that Micky would be out on the *Repose* for at least two weeks. It dawned on me that by the time she got back to NSA, I'd be back in the States. Given the way things were between Micky and me maybe it was all for the better, for clearly she had experienced a change of heart.

I swung around to the NSA motor pool and picked up a starter and another voltage regulator. I showed everyone the SKS rifle. The old navy chief who ran the place offered me a new jeep engine in trade. I told him to talk to Major Boden. Then, on an impulse, I gave him my Swedish K. The old Chief had helped me in the past and I just didn't feel that I needed the Swedish K anymore.

Driving back toward Da Nang, I could still smell the smoke from last night's action on my clothes. My mind was whirling with images. The feelings and thoughts that haunted my sleep for the last few weeks were welling up inside. I gripped the jeep's steering wheel tightly to keep my hands from shaking. In my mind's eye I could see Dick Crandle's face, ghastly and pale. He was wading across the Jordan river. He was just about to reach the other side.

I pulled the jeep over to the side of the road and stopped, letting the engine idle. Fatigue. Perhaps I was seeing ghosts. But I knew that I wasn't crazy. I was just drained. I needed to take a shower and hit the sack. Tomorrow I would wake up and begin the day with a new conviction. For I realized that with the death of Dick Crandle, Chad Holland, Sky Lady, and O. D. Lowy, White Zen had taken on a new meaning relative to living each day as best as one could. It was also clear to me that in the death and sacrifice of some, others are reborn.

EPILOGUE

November 22, 1968: 1730 hours,
Kadena Air Force Base, Okinawa

IT WAS GUNNER Junge who found me on the patio of the Officers' Club. He was on his way back to Thailand and had heard that I was in the club. He sat down and ordered a Kirin beer. I brought him up to date on Crandle and Sandman.

"Lowy and Crandle were quite a pair," I said, sipping my beer.

"They were unique in my experience," Junge said.

"You always had a lot of tact, Gunner," I said, laughing.

"Here's to Lowy and Crandle, they left their mark on what they touched. They were, indeed, artists!" Junge said, raising his glass.

I ordered another round. Junge smiled.

"They were artists all right, Gunner. They were bullshit artists!" I said with a smirk.

"No. They were more than that," Junge said.

"Don't get me wrong, Gunner. I don't mean any disrespect for the dead. I'm just trying to call them as I saw them," I said quickly.

"I understand. But let me point out that both of these men were able to mold their environment. Both were able to give direction in a situation that was otherwise chaos. And both men were able to do what they did in a way that brought new significance to that experience and inspired those who were not so firm in their beliefs,'' Gunner Junge said with a tone of self-righteousness.

I blew a smoke ring into the air. I was down to three packs a day. I felt good about that.

"Are you saying they inspired those like me?" I asked.

"Yes, like you," Junge said without hesitation.

"Well, I guess I agree with that. They were leaders," I said.

"Leaders! You're damn right they were leaders! They were leaders because they had the ability to penetrate to that hidden reality that all true leaders access. They were leaders because they had the character to stand firm relative to what their experience told them. And then they acted upon what they believed! They were in no way tentative and they had no doubts!'' Junge said, almost out of breath.

Several air force officers at the next table turned and stared. Junge had raised his voice enough for them to pick up on the intensity of the conversation.

"You mean like the doubts I had," I asked, somewhat defensively.

"Yes, Lieutenant, like the doubts that you had."

"What's the point of all this, Gunner?" I asked.

"The point is that we shouldn't be so hard on the two men," Junge said.

"I don't think that we should be hard on the dead ever, especially those who served," I said, draining my beer.

"Lieutenant, someday you will understand these men. When you do, I think that you will be able to see that they were masters of their own fate. They were able to strike a balance between freedom and necessity. When their time came, they knew what they were about, and they made a choice," Junge said, again loud enough for the surrounding tables to hear.

"Gunner, this conversation is starting to make my head hurt. I just want to kick back and drink a few beers," I said.

"Lieutenant, I once told you that if you survive Vietnam, someday you would make a fine marine officer. I still believe that! Now, I've got to go. Enough has been said," Junge replied, rising from the table.

"Ah, that's beautiful, Gunner. Thanks. From you that's a compliment," I said, leaning back in my chair.

"No, Lieutenant, that's not beautiful, that's the truth. You still seem to confuse the two notions," Junge said with a smile, raising his voice slightly as he departed.

Junge disappeared through the beaded curtain that divided the bar from the patio. It was as if he moved in slow motion. All around it seemed that people were wreathed in smiles, eating and drinking in good company. I was overcome with a sudden rush of emotion, a great sadness. I doubted if I would ever truly understand Junge and the meaning of all that he had said. For that matter, I doubted if I would ever understand the terrible and unpredictable events that had consumed so many of those that I had held close. But it was clear to me that the vicissitudes of fate had bound all of us together, forever.

ABOUT THE AUTHOR

Dan Guenther was a captain in the Marine Corps. He served in Vietnam from July 1968 to March 1970, participating in Operations Oklahoma Hills, Forsythe Grove, and Pipestone Canyon. As a platoon leader with Alpha Company, Third Amphibian Tractor Battalion, he was stationed at An Hoa, Hill 10, Hill 55, Liberty Bridge, and Da Nang. He holds the Combat Action Ribbon, the Bronze Star with Combat V, and the Vietnamese Staff Honor Medal, First Class.

Guenther is a graduate of Coe College with a Bachelor of Arts in English. He also holds a Master of Fine Arts in English from the University of Iowa. Currently he works for a large corporation as manager for organization development. He is married and has three daughters.